A Question of Consequence

A Question of Consequence

A novel by

Gordon Ryan

Mapletree Publishing Company
Denver, Colorado

Library of Congress Cataloging-in-Publication Data
Ryan, Gordon,
  A question of consequence : a novel / by Gordon Ryan.
    p. cm.
    ISBN 0-9728071-3-6 (pbk. : alk. paper)
  1. Municipal government—Fiction. 2. Political corruption—Fiction.
  3. Political ethics—Fiction. 4. Mormons—Fiction. 5. Utah—Fiction.
  I. Title.
    PS3568.Y32Q47 2003
    813'.54—dc22
                    2003017245

Printed in the United States of America
08 07 06 05 04 5 4 3 2
Printed on acid-free paper

Published by Mapletree Publishing Company
Denver, CO 80130
Telephone 800-537-0414
e-mail: mail@mapletreepublishing.com
www.mapletreepublishing.com

Cover design by George Foster, www.fostercovers.com
The Mapletree logo is a trademark of Mapletree Publishing Company

To all those who have the courage to stand up, regardless the consequence. You know who you are!

Acknowledgments

In the preparation of *A Question of Consequence* several people were instrumental with assistance regarding the technical aspects of molecular genealogy and the microbiological aspects of the story. Specifically, I would like to thank the Department of Microbiology and Molecular Biology at Brigham Young University, and Ugo A. Perego, M.S., Senior Project Administrator for the Molecular Genealogy Research Project. Their assistance in defining how the procurement of DNA material may be achieved (and how it may *not*) was key to particular aspects of the storyline.

I should also note that recently the Molecular Genealogy Program changed affiliation with Brigham Young University and is now associated with the Sorenson Molecular Genealogy Foundation in Salt Lake City.

I would especially like to thank the staff of Mapletree Publishing for their dedicated effort and in seeing that as author, I was afforded all support necessary to achieve our mutual goals. In particular, Dave Hall, Dawn Griesi, Kathy Titze, and Sue Collier all worked unceasingly to ensure a quality publication. I offer them my sincere thanks. Any errors or omissions are the responsibility of the author.

With malicious vapouring dost Man judge his neighbour and how Spartan are the shards of truth whereby he renders sentence. By his judgment are we then shackled to our destiny. Yet we cannot divert from that which we know to be honourable or we are further shackled by the great Deceiver who seeks to enslave us more than those with whom we abide this earthly life. It is only in our God that we are afforded justice and eternal verdict. At such times of despair I feel anxious, nay, compelled, to entice His judgment at its earliest pronouncement.

Journal of Andrew McBride Sterling
April 25, 1782

Chapter One

Whipped by a brisk northerly wind rushing down the river gorge, whitecaps danced on the surface of the Hudson River, lifting a fine spray and misting the morning air on both banks of the great waterway. From where he stood on an east shore promontory, roughly a hundred miles upriver from New York City, Matthew Sterling could just make out the gray cliffs that formed the western edge of the river gorge, nearly a half-mile across the dark, roiling water.

Despite three centuries of increasing human habitation, thick forests still covered the bluffs above both sides of the river. A dense thicket of evergreen and leafless hardwood trees on the western shore was just barely visible in the thin, early morning light.

The previous evening, while standing in the same spot, Matt had listened to the singing of the Benedictine monks, carried on a gentle, westerly wind. The rich, male voices came drifting across the river from within the venerable stone walls of the two-hundred-and-fifty-year-old-monastery atop the speckled granite cliffs. Their traditional Baroque music, so unlike the melodic hymns of the Mormon Tabernacle Choir yet equally soothing, calmed his melancholy, and he found

1

himself wondering if Grandmother Sterling, in her long, lonely years as a widow, had enjoyed the same pleasurable experience. This morning, while waiting for his taxi in front of the open space left by the demolished house, he had walked across River Road for one final view of the magnificent river, knowing, somehow, it would be unlikely he would ever return. His luggage, consisting solely of a small suit bag, evidence of his rapid departure from Salt Lake City, stood mutely beside the colonial-era mailbox, the only remnant of the once proud estate.

He'd asked the hotel shuttle driver to take him to River Road, rather than to the Dutchess County Airport. At first reluctant, she relented when Matt produced a twenty-dollar bill. When she reached the address, she pulled into the driveway and stopped.

"I can't wait, ya know," she said.

"That's okay," Matt replied, exiting the vehicle. "Can you call a taxi for me?"

She nodded, picking up her radio mike. He set his suit bag on the ground and glanced at his watch. "Tell them about nine."

The woman driver nodded again, shrugging her shoulders. She called for a taxi, backed the hotel van out of the drive, and disappeared into the mist.

At twenty-eight, standing just over six feet with black hair, dark blue eyes, and a quick smile, Matthew Andrew Sterling was on an errand not of his choosing. His trip to New York, to settle the estate and to witness the demolition of his widowed grandmother's two-hundred and fifteen-year-old family home had unleashed a flood of nostalgia for the young lawyer. He found the prospect of watching the demolition of a favorite childhood retreat emotionally daunting, but under the probate induced supplication of his beloved grandmother, he had summoned the strength to carry out her final request to her only grandson.

Born in New York City, he had come here often as a boy, traveling from Staten Island with his parents to visit his grandmother, Elizabeth Winchester Sterling. The deep woods surrounding her home had been for him a foreboding yet magical playground. Rather than sit with the adults and listen to their grown-up talk, he preferred to roam the acres of thickly wooded hills surrounding the estate. He was fascinated by the stories told by his older cousins of soldiers, battles, ghosts, and long-forgotten heroes who had tramped these same grounds, and he developed an awe for the land and the river and the history they had witnessed. That the property was, and had been for most of the previous century, bordered by the estates of the Vanderbilt's and Roosevelt's only added to its mystique.

During his youthful, woodland romps with his cousins, he had envisioned the landscape as it had once been: absent the commuter railway carved into the rock between the river and the large, imposing homes; absent the power lines that ran the length of the road; absent the rising condos and commercial developments that were swallowing up the wilderness of his imagination. With the fantasy that only a young boy can muster, he had conjured up a frontier landscape providing concealment for the ghostly Redcoats as they marched through the woods, their bayonets flashing. In his mind he'd watched Jack Tars as they landed from small, black boats, set afloat from the British Man-O-War he mentally positioned in the river. He could see the gun ports drop open as the cannon prepared to enforce the demands of a distant and ever reproachful king—a king increasingly disdainful of the interest of his far-flung, mostly loyal subjects.

In his youthful flights of fantasy and imagination, it had never entered Matt Sterling's mind that there might lay in these romantic settings a *true* tale of intrigue—a tale more complex

3

and compelling than even the fertile mind of a young boy could create. He could not have known that deep within the foundation timbers of Riveroaks lay concealed a profound mystery involving one of his own revered ancestors.

Riveroaks! It was the name his sixth-great-grandfather, Andrew Sterling, had given to his estate—a home to which, in 1790, Sterling had taken his wife, the beautiful and socially prominent Laura Faye Delacorte of the Westchester County Delacorte's, and their young son, Josiah, born the summer after the American victory at Yorktown had ended the war.

The imposing home had captured Matt's imagination when, on his very first visit, at age eight or nine, his grandfather, Jonathan Sterling, had taken him into the basement and pointed out the enormous wooden beams that supported the house. Burned deeply into the center timber, a massive oak beam, was the inscription, "Riveroaks, 1790." Grandfather Sterling had explained to the boy that at the time Andrew Sterling built the home, the United States had been a free nation for only nine years, and its first president, George Washington, had been in office less than a year.

Now, with twenty-first-century property values escalating astronomically, these historic estates had become the targets of developers, eager to gain control of the wooded, scenic landscapes overlooking the Hudson. So long as Matt's ninety-six-year-old Grandmother Sterling was alive, Riveroaks had not been for sale. But with her death, all that changed. Matt was named as executor in Grandmother Sterling's will, charged with settling her affairs, including overseeing the demolition of the ancient house.

Angered by the necessity of witnessing the destruction of the venerable old home, Matt had carefully watched for three days as workers dismantled the structure, floor by floor. Many of the neighbors had dropped by, seeking remnants of the historic home for their bric-a-brac collections. Nearly two hundred rosebushes, dormant in the winter frost, had been uprooted and transferred to the garden of a nearby hospital where Elizabeth Sterling had served on the board of directors. When the workers reached the first floor and basement the previous afternoon, Matt had instructed them to cut a four-foot section out of the central support beam—the section that included the carved inscription. A massive beam it was too, a beam whose internal rings would have confirmed a hundred and sixty-three year life *before* it had fallen to the woodsman's axe in 1789.

After sawing through the great timber and lowering it to the dirt floor of the basement, they discovered a hollowed-out section in what had been the top of the beam—a hand-hewn niche approximately eighteen inches long, twelve inches wide, and eight inches deep. Surprised by the discovery, the workers stopped momentarily and Matt stepped forward. He reached into the crevice and lifted out a leather bundle, loosely bound with strands of rotting twine. Refraining from unwrapping the parcel in the presence of the workers, he placed the bundle in the trunk of his car and continued to observe as the remaining foundation timbers were dismantled.

That evening, in his room on the ninth floor of the Poughkeepsie Grand Hotel, Matt had gingerly opened the decomposing leather pouch. Camphor flakes fell onto a stack of yellowed, dog-eared pages, the top one of which was a brief, quill-penned letter. The letter had immediately intrigued him. Noting its date, the genealogist in Matt quickly realized that before surrendering to the inevitable condominium complex, complete with sailboats and four-man sculls at the new marina, the ghostly inhabitants of Riveroaks had found a way to preserve the secret of why, as a consequence of his role in helping to found a nation, Matt's ancient ancestor had felt compelled to cloak his past in secrecy and change his identity.

In the comfort of his hotel room, Matt read the letter several times, savoring its content and style. Then, with gentle fingers, he lifted from the bundle a twine-bound journal of some length and what appeared to be a manuscript in the same handwriting, entitled *A Light Reign*.

Through the long night, the handwritten pages had fired his imagination, filling his mind with scenes of intrigue, treachery, family honor, courage, sacrifice, and, to his surprise, public shame. Only when gradually encroaching light began to filter through the eastern window of his hotel room did he set aside his reading to get ready to return to the life from which he had so recently and reluctantly departed for this unwanted family responsibility.

This morning, as he stood on the bank of the Hudson, thinking, remembering, waiting patiently to depart, Matt turned his collar up against the rising breeze and the drifting mist. In silent wonder, he contemplated the startling discovery of the previous afternoon. As if to ensure its reality, he opened the slender, leather binder he always carried, to look again at a plastic document holder, a genealogist's foresight, into which he had placed the brittle parchment. Its contents were visibly weathered with age, yet protected from the elements for the first time in nearly two hundred years.

Standing perhaps for the final time amidst the family grounds, mesmerized by the unrelenting flow of Henry Hudson's hoped-for Northwest Passage, he marveled at the circumstance that had put him in touch with a heretofore unknown tale. He read slowly, savoring once again the antique phrasing of the document.

15 August 1821
The Honourable Josiah Sterling, Esq.
New York State Senator
Albany, New York

Dear Senator Sterling,

We have the honour, Sir, of expressing our deepest respect and appreciation for the opportunity you have afforded us to review, with pleasure we might add, the contents of your recent submission, entitled "A Light Reign." Indeed, as you have recounted the events of your father, Major Andrew McBride, and his exploits during the Great War, we have gained a deep measure of admiration for the story and deep respect for the man. Despite the scurrilous public humiliation to which Mr. McBride was ultimately subjected, your father, we are certain, was a man of his times, unjustly pilloried by public ignorance of his true stature. Without such men in service to their country, our fledging democracy would likely have faltered at birth, as so often it was thought to have been imperilled.

Regrettably, Sir, our timing is most inopportune. We are in process of publishing another work of similar content, by a resident of Scarsdale, New York, entitled "The Spy." Notwithstanding his own guarded precautions, which array against the publication of a truly "American" novel and his expressed fears of a lack of readership—fears which we do not share—Mr. James Fennimore Cooper has most graciously acceded to our publishing requirements. In consideration of the comparable intrigue replete within the two stories, we find it would be imprudent to place both before our readers simultaneously.

Given the proper interval, and the hoped-for success of Mr. Cooper's suspenseful tale, we would be pleased to consider a resubmission of your father's rendition of our nation's struggle for independence. We look forward to such an occasion. In that regard, we remain,

Your most obedient servants,
Wiley & Halsted, Publishers
New York City

The sound of tires on the graveled road intruded, and Matt quickly returned the letter to his briefcase. Not noticing that his passenger stood across the road, the taxi driver pulled into the driveway of the now demolished house, barking his horn and shattering the morning silence. He exited the car and lifted the suit bag, tossing it into the trunk of the vehicle.

Matt took a long look around, gazing out over the river, which for more than two centuries had provided commerce and transport for the inhabitants of the middle and upper reaches of New York State. Barely ninety miles down the meandering river lay Wall Street, the twenty-first century's financial capital, despite the physical and mental devastation of September 11 that had so changed the psyche of the nation. But here, on an obscure road in Hyde Park, New York, securely lodged in Matt Sterling's briefcase, lay a tale of ancient intrigue—an untold tale newly come to light.

With one final glance at the hole in the ground that had once been the stately Riveroaks, Matt entered the taxi and was driven away, firmly resisting the urge to look back.

"Dutchess County Airport, please," Matt said.

"Right," the driver responded.

Matt rode in silence during the twenty-minute drive, his thoughts mixed with sorrow at the turn of events the past two months had brought. First, there was the call from her bishop about Grandmother's death, the flight to New York with his parents, Dick and Sally Sterling, and his two older, married sisters, Rachel and Emily, for the funeral. Then, his grandmother's attorney called two weeks ago to advise that Grandmother had directed the estate be settled by her grandson, Matthew A. Sterling of Snowy Ridge, Utah. And then, he made this second trip back to oversee the demolition of the grand old home and to attend to the other details of the will.

Her wits sharp and incisive as always, Grandma Sterling had done well in the sale of the family home. Following the death of her husband, some eighteen years earlier, she had been approached in 1986 by a commercial development company that was buying up Hudson River waterfront property. Intent on acquiring her valuable land, they said that although it had been valued at nine-hundred-thousand dollars, they would give her one million for a quick sale. She agreed to the sale on condition that she would enjoy lifetime occupancy. Since Elizabeth Sterling was eighty years of age, and her husband had died two years earlier, the developers felt they had made a good deal. She set her own terms, and again the company thought they had the old lady under control: half a million down, and one-hundred-thousand dollars annually for the term of her life. Nothing would be due at the time of her death in the event she died before the million had been paid, but she stipulated that should she live longer, all equity would be forfeited by the company should they default in any single subsequent year.

The developer gambled, and lost. The real estate market plummeted, she lived another sixteen years and, by the time she died, Continental Enterprises had paid Elizabeth Sterling just over two million dollars for her home and property. Continental's only victory was having stipulated that the razing and removal of the old house would be the responsibility of the estate and would be accomplished within sixty days of her demise.

Grandma Sterling had lived a long and fruitful life and had died peacefully in her sleep in the home she loved and in which she had instilled in her children and grandchildren a passionate interest in their family history. She had outlived three of her four children and had three living grandchildren, including Matt, from her one surviving son, Dr. Richard Sterling. As Matt met with Grandma Sterling's attorney, he had been astonished to learn the amount of her wealth and of his own inheritance.

When her real estate windfall was added to her husband's considerable holdings, wisely invested since his death, she was able to bequeath just over one million dollars to each of her four survivors as well as designate that five million dollars be given to Brigham Young University, earmarked for use in sustaining the university's molecular genealogy research program. An avid genealogist, Elizabeth Sterling was convinced that the Y's molecular biology project would greatly facilitate the relationship between anthropology and ancient genealogical research.

At the funeral, held some six weeks earlier in an overflowing chapel, Bishop Roland Simpson had eulogized her by describing her extensive charitable contributions, recalling donations she had made to hospitals and a variety of other institutions. He said that what she had not wanted known while she was living was that over the years she had also anonymously funded the missions of some thirty-two missionaries from the stake, including Bishop Simpson's own mission to Australia fifteen years earlier. He had grown emotional when he explained that except for Sister Sterling's generosity, these young men and women would likely have been unable to serve. He concluded his remarks by suggesting that at the time of her arrival, there must have been genuine rejoicing in the corridors of heaven.

All this, plus the unearthing, almost literally, of additional family secrets—secrets probably unknown even to Grandma Sterling—had Matt's mind whirling. What could have brought such shame as described in the few journal excerpts that he'd had time to read? He patted the briefcase absentmindedly as the taxi turned into the circular approach to the Dutchess County Airport.

"JFK shuttle?" the taxi driver inquired.

"Yeah, that's fine," Matt responded, reaching for his wallet. Exiting the cab, he handed his ticket to the curbside porter, declined to check his bag, and proceeded straight through the new security measures, bound for the gate where the flight was already being called. He boarded the American Eagle twenty-nine-seat aircraft and placed his suit bag in the overhead rack, tucking the briefcase under the seat in front of him. Almost immediately, the plane, less than half full, began to back away from the terminal, and the pilot started the port and then the starboard turboprop engines.

Lifting off smoothly, the aircraft banked southeast and leveled out for the thirty-minute flight to JFK Airport, near New York City. After declining the offer of a morning cup of tea or coffee, Matt slipped the briefcase out, laid it on the empty seat next to him, and retrieved one of the plastic document protectors, holding yet another of the single page documents that were originally contained in the leather pouch. He read slowly, once again recalling his surprise, indeed his shock, the evening before as he had first seen this particular document.

Riveroaks
Hyde Park, New York
September 14, 1829

My father was by nature a philosophical man. A single excerpt from his journal, in the earliest days of the struggle, portrays his foresight:

A bold stroke, this new declaration from our brethren assembled in Philadelphia. And now they are irrevocably committed, for there is only one difference between a patriot and a traitor—he who wins is the patriot—for it is the winner who shall write the history, and the traitor who shall hang!

Journal of Andrew McBride
New York, July 1776

He wrote the enclosed account of his activities in the late War for Independence, in the fall of 1815, shortly after cessation of hostilities that had once again erupted between America and the motherland. His journal, of course, is a continuing document from a much earlier time, consolidated, by his own admission, at this later period of his life. Most startling to me, was his personal attestation that he used his true name for the primary character in his narrative—a name heretofore unknown to me, although I was seven when my father changed our name and moved our family from the city to Riveroaks. Therefore, whilst my father was a relatively modest man, not given to excess, a characteristic I now understand to be a necessity of political prudence rather than of nature, I believe these to be the actual recollections of Andrew McBride, late of Kildare, Ireland. His death, some four years later, in 1819, less than one year after my mother's passing, occurred before I had been privileged to read the manuscript and precluded my ability to discuss the origins of the McBride-Sterling name change with either parent. However, many of the stories related in the journal were often recounted around the hearth throughout my youth, but always attributed, in those clandestine verbal accounts, to an "associate" of my father's during the war. I now understand that the "associate" of whom my father spoke, was actually himself and that the events described were his own personal exploits. I cannot, in good conscience, attest to the veracity of my father's claims, specifically those involving his participation at British military headquarters in New York, where ostensibly he served as legal counsel for General William Howe and then General Sir Henry Clinton. No documents confirm his contact with George Washington in his role as Commander of Continental forces, or President Washington's reputed suggestion as to the new family name of Sterling. Nor can I document my father's involvement with the uncloaked Major Frank Talmadge, now known to have commanded Washington's intelligence network. Nor can I affirm his association with Nathan Hale, although I have confirmed that an Andrew McBride did indeed attend and matriculate Yale University at a time concurrent with that of Mr. Hale. Therefore, my father's journal and historical claims must, unfortunately, remain unconfirmed. Yet neither can I dispute them. The truth of the story—of this small portion of our nation's history—we must leave for the reader to discern, and to that great God to whom all men must ultimately appeal.

J. Sterling, Esq.

Below the aircraft, the Hudson River disappeared on the right, and the landscape began to change from open brown fields and verdant forests to green bordered residential neighborhoods. Westchester County, so often described to him by Grandmother Sterling as the original home of Andrew Sterling and the first Sterling wife, Elizabeth Delacorte, passed by below. But perhaps they *weren't* Sterling's? Why Josiah Sterling had referred to *McBride* as a former name was a puzzle that churned inside Matt. Was this new genealogical treasure to change the family history? Would Grandma Sterling have known? *Could* she have known? Did she know about the basement hiding place? The journal? The manuscript? Would the journal or manuscript tell the tale?

At the pilot's announcement of their approach to JFK, Matt returned the document to his briefcase which he once again slipped beneath the seat in front of him. The transfer of terminals at one of the world's busiest airports went smoothly and upon boarding, he found his Delta flight to Salt Lake City also lightly occupied. As the aircraft slowly transited the access runway, waiting its turn to depart, Matt gazed out the window, watching other aircraft land and depart on the parallel runway until the pilot came on the intercom:

"Ladies and gentlemen, we're number two in the queue at present. We'll have you airborne in a few moments, and the flight crew will do everything to make your flight to Salt Lake as pleasant as possible. Weather conditions in Salt Lake are clear, temperature a brisk thirty-three degrees, with unlimited visibility. Looks like good flying weather and we should be right on time. So sit back, relax, and enjoy yourselves, and thank you for flying Delta."

Despite his lack of sleep the previous evening, Matt was too pumped up to doze. As the aircraft lifted clear of the runway, his only thought was to read the manuscript, starting at the beginning. He waited until the seat belt light was turned off, then retrieved his briefcase. Releasing the catches, he raised the cover and gently lifted the bound manuscript, placing it on the lowered food tray in front of him. In fine, antiquated penmanship, *A Light Reign* scrolled across the top of the first page. Andrew McBride had told the tale and the answers *were* here. They had to be!

Ninety minutes later, a light meal and drink having been

served and ignored, Matt looked up from the pages, giving his eyes a rest and going over the story in his mind. He leaned back, resting his head against the seat and closed his eyes. Once again, he was transported back to Dublin, Ireland in September 1772.

Therefore, my father's journal and historical claims must, unfortunately, remain unconfirmed. Yet neither can I dispute them. The truth of the story—of this small portion of our nation's history—I leave to the reader and to our great God, to whom all men must ultimately appeal.

Josiah Sterling, Esq.
Son of Andrew McBride Sterling
September 1829

Chapter Two

It was spring of that year, and nineteen-year-old Andrew McBride, a student of Trinity College, Dublin, and a scion of the Irish Protestant Ascendancy, was able to delude himself into thinking he was in love with the girl of Meagher. Her name was Molly Meagher, to be precise—a servant girl of lower-class origins whose day job was catering to the laundry needs of the students, and during evenings was working at O'Reilly's tavern.

Whether or not Andrew was truly in love is left for the reader to decide, but Andrew surrendered fully to the avid pursuit of his illusion. And in spite of his chaste Irish Protestant upbringing and the differences in their stations in life, he fell completely under the spell of Molly's ample charms.

Molly was under no such delusion. She well knew the difference in their ranks, but it was sport to her. She unabashedly used her looks and charm to catch the attention of several young men during her tenure at the tavern. However, none of Molly's other dalliances had come to Andy's attention, and the smitten youth continued under the false assumption that he was to her, as she was to him, a first love.

That particular evening, Andrew, along with several of his fellow students, had retreated to O'Reilly's, located a short distance from Trinity College and near St. Stephan's Green. As usual, they were enjoying the dark, foaming brew that originated from the newest in a long line of Dublin breweries. Young Andy McBride had perhaps overindulged in Arthur Guinness's potent potion and in process, became rather less restrained than propriety would dictate for one of his elevated station.

A newly commissioned British lieutenant, of approximately McBride's age, had also come to the tavern that night. Attached to His Majesty's 60th Regiment of Foot, the handsome young officer had been seconded to the garrison at Dublin Castle. His appearance created something of a stir in the tavern, for to the knowledge of its occupants, O'Reilly's had not, prior to this night, ever hosted a scarlet-clad British officer of the Foot within its premises. There had been, to be sure, previous visits to the establishment by an occasional British soldier, but always one of the scurrilous blackguards from the ranks, who had merely made an improvident choice of taverns. Unless he was impudent enough to make an indecorous remark about the Irish, such visitation was afforded safe passage—the interloper permitted to imbibe and depart, unmolested, with nothing more defamatory than a derisive spat in his direction.

Lieutenant Applegate was not such a man. It was within his nature and disposition to make his presence known, not so much by vocal pronouncement as by his haughty carriage and a condescending air of superiority. When, in her careless handling of the pint she was delivering, the comely Molly Meagher sloshed driblets of foam on the young officer's tunic, he directed an immediate tirade of angry criticism at the hapless lass. His loud remonstrance immediately cast the pompous Brit, in the eyes of Andy and his Irish fellows, as a prissy sort. They sat in muted silence as Molly responded with a scornful laugh and a playful pinch on the lieutenant's cheek. The tavern keeper, being older and wiser, and not wishing to insult an officer of the Crown, hastened to offer his pretentious visitor a free pint.

Although none of the Irish lads truly knew Applegate, their initial impression of him as being quite infatuated with himself was only enhanced by his exaggerated revulsion over his only slightly besmirched uniform and his otherwise decorous manner. Such discourse continued to be the subject of conversation among those at McBride's table, leading them to speculate as the evening progressed as to whether Applegate's manner was self-imposed or inborn—a result of his "bloody British lineage."

"He's a pretty lad, then," one particularly burly and garrulous student of the law observed.

"Aye, he's nearly as fancy as young Molly, don't 'cha think," another offered, casting a bleary eye toward Andy, whose love sickness was often the focus of his fellow student's good-natured taunting and who, by now, was quite obviously angered by the officer's verbal assault on the lovely, flaxen-haired Molly.

Mocking umbrage at his companion's profane reference to Molly, Andy attempted to stand. His most recent pint, however, added to the evening's prodigious consumption, rendered the attempt naught.

"I say, sir," Andy slurred to his mate through frothy lips, "you'll retract those inapp…uh, inappro…ah, what the devil." He shook his head and downed the remainder of his pint, then wiped his mouth on his sleeve. He looked again at the lieutenant, trying to focus his gaze upon the officer sitting alone at a corner table.

"I beg to differ, sir," Andy said to his assailing table mate, his eye still unfocussed on the lieutenant, "as fair as his highness might appear, Molly has *far* more prodigious…uh, accoutrements."

At that, the entire table of Irish rogues burst into raucous laughter and Andy, eased by humor from the burden of defending poor Molly, fell from his chair, which only served to increase the hilarity of his friends.

Throughout the evening, the lieutenant sat quietly, drinking and silently observing the progressively uproarious behavior of the college students. His mere presence, however, cast something of a pall over the evening's entertainment, mildly subduing the usually boisterous shenanigans. Finally, after several hours, Lieutenant Applegate rose, straightened the front of his tunic and dropped several coins on the table. He smoothed his hair with the palm of his hand and stepped toward the door of the establishment. Andy watched through eyes red with drink as the British officer made his way toward the entrance.

"Be most careful on your departure, sir," Andy called out across the room.

The lieutenant halted momentarily and glanced, seemingly for the first time, toward Andy's table.

"My pardon, sir. Do you address yourself to me?" Lieutenant Applegate said.

"I do, sir," Andy replied, somehow finding the ability to rise, gracelessly as it were, and face the gentleman. "I encouraged you to mind your step as you depart our tavern."

"And why might that be, sir?" the officer replied, standing rigid and braced.

"Well, ye see, me bloody, British dandy," Andy slurred through unresponsive lips, "there's a mirror close at hand, sir, there, by the door," he pointed, "and we wouldn't be wantin' to delay your departure now, would we?"

For a moment, the lieutenant stood silent, questioning the intent of the warning, but as the table of Irish miscreants once again burst into laughter, the officer took the meaning of the insult. His face clouded over, the veins in his neck turned a shade of purple, and he glared at Andy for several long, silent moments. The laughter abruptly ceased and a stillness descended upon the tavern, anxious moments passing in anticipation of the lieutenant's response. The silence grew louder and weighed heavily upon the occupants until the publican rattled a few jars behind the bar and Lieutenant Applegate glanced away, toward the sound. Then, without a word, he turned on his heel and briskly departed the tavern.

It was evident to the occupants of O'Reilly's tavern that the intensity of young Andy McBride's ardor for the saucy Molly Meagher was exceeded only by the love of Lieutenant Applegate for Lieutenant Applegate. Even so, they could not estimate the depth of the offense taken by the British officer at Andy's parting comment, delivered with the reckless abandon that only liquid courage might provide. It was an insult that Lieutenant Applegate would not be able to ignore or be willing to forgive.

The young lads should have known to be more cautious, for each of the collegians from Trinity College was fully aware, as was the publican, that in Ireland, British rule was absolute. British laws were vigorously enforced—every jot and tittle—and to directly affront an officer of the Crown was an established punishable offense.

But these young men, technically members of the Protestant Ascendancy—the artificially insinuated gentry, originally of English or Scottish heritage, which had, over a period of nearly one hundred and fifty years since their insertion by the Crown following Lord Cromwell's invasion in 1649—evolved to be neither Irish nor British. In fact, neither society allowed them the right of acceptance. The younger members of the Ascendancy, some of whom comprised the college students in O'Reilly's tavern with Andrew McBride, had finally taken the bit between their teeth and had presumptively freed themselves of the supposed shackles that restrained their more educated and experienced parents. Those parents, as had their parents before them, continued to court British acceptance, while, for the most part, their sons had forsworn the pursuit and had, without visible success, chosen to be Irish. It should not be surprising then that these young would-be-gentlemen, whom no society fawned to receive, would react negatively to the unexpected visit of a solitary British officer—an officer, who, by his pretentious mannerisms invited—demanded—their disdain.

For Andrew McBride, who intended, under the direction of his successful father, to become a barrister of renown, the events of this evening—or more accurately, of the following morning—would forever alter the course of his life.

And Lieutenant Jonathan Applegate would also have to accommodate changes as a result of the evening's outing. Applegate's response, however, would be vastly different than that of Andy McBride. Though young, the British officer, while living in an unacceptable world not of his own choosing, had developed a social presence unfettered by conscience, one equal to the challenges life had bestowed upon him. For as the son of the unmarried Lady Jane Applegate and His Royal Highness, George, the Prince of Wales (thereafter to become George III, King of England, Ireland, Wales, and the Commonwealth Dominions), Jonathan Applegate's pompous manner stemmed primarily from his knowledge that he, as George's first-born son—albeit a birth of illegitimate derivation—was truly heir to the throne, a throne his royal father was determined he would never see, much less sit upon.

And so the evening's tryst in an ordinary tavern had thrown these three young people together. Andrew McBride's caustic and drunken remark, Lieutenant Applegate's aristocratically inspired arrogance, and Molly's careless handling of a jar of ale set each on a road to their destiny—an excursion that none of them could presently foresee and toward which none of them, except perhaps for Applegate, would have voluntarily traveled.

For Applegate the events that followed would be merely adventurous. For Andrew McBride they would be irrevocable. But for the young and inestimably beautiful Molly Meagher, the elusive fantasy of many a Trinity College young man, they would be fatal.

Chapter Three

As the plane began its descent to the Salt Lake City airport, the altered pitch of the aircraft engines roused Matt from a light sleep. Through the port side window the early evening lights of Brigham Young's "This is the place" were visible, twinkling through the hazy sunset. Stretching to the south were the snow-capped Wasatch Mountains, running south toward Provo and the J. Reuben Clark Law School at Brigham Young University, where Matt had obtained his law degree four years earlier. Beyond Provo, past a string of lighted, smaller communities, he could barely make out the lights of the city of Snowy Ridge, where he lived and worked.

Established in the early days of Utah's development as a way station and overnight rest stop for travelers venturing from Salt Lake to St. George, Snowy Ridge had grown in the seventies and eighties into a Utah County bedroom community of some fifteen to eighteen thousand people. With one of the finest universities in the western United States providing a flow of high-caliber, well-trained college graduates, and easy access to road, rail, and air transportation, over the previous decade it had become home to a number of high-tech manufacturing and computer component facilities. By the turn of the twenty-first century, the once sleepy little community had blossomed into a city of seventy-eight thousand and was still growing. The town fathers knew their community would never return to the old days.

After finishing law school, followed by a mission to England for The Church of Jesus Christ of Latter-day Saints, Matt had accepted a position as deputy city attorney for Snowy Ridge, a job he held for one year until he was promoted to assistant city manager. The promotion was at first only temporary, but accepting the fact that the city was destined to grow and the need for further staff wasn't going to go away, the City Council had eventually made it permanent.

Banking sharply left and entering the final glide path, Delta Airlines flight 81 from New York City crossed the eastern edge of the Great Salt Lake, finally touching down smoothly in a puff of blue smoke as the tires contacted the concrete runway. After exiting the terminal, Matt stepped across the first lane of traffic to the middle island, looking for the familiar blue Chevy Blazer. He spotted it about four cars back, parked on the side, near the Delta curb check-in. He walked toward the car and the driver exited from the vehicle, opening the rear hatch then stepping up onto the sidewalk to greet him.

"Welcome home, Matt. Everything go all right?"

"As well as any unpleasant task, I suppose. I loved Grandma Sterling's old house."

"I can understand that."

"Thanks for meeting me, Mac."

"Thomas McDougal, at your service," the older man smiled. "Taxi driver, street engineer, Public Works director, repository of deadly secrets, faithful husband, golf genius, jack-of-all-trades, and ne'er-do-well, and I've learned all that in just sixty-one years on this earth." He laughed. "And I'm humble, too."

"So I've noticed," Matt said, shaking his head at Mac's incessant humor. He tossed his bag into the rear of the vehicle and both men got into the car. Mac slowly merged with the outgoing traffic, and they headed away from the airport.

"So, your grandmother's finally with her husband, and the house is gone," Mac said as they entered the southbound ramp leading to I-15, the major highway north and south from Salt Lake City.

"She's with her husband?" Matt mimicked, smiling over at Mac.

"Don't start on me!"

"You believe the same things I believe, you old goat. You just throw your golf bag in the car on Sunday instead of—"

"I said, don't start on me. Tell me about your grandmother," Mac said, suppressing a grin.

"She was a finer woman than I understood, Mac," Matt said, "and I already had a pretty high opinion of her."

"How so?"

Matt shook his head. "I don't mean to be rude, Mac, but I can't be specific. She didn't want any of it revealed for public knowledge. But between you and me, she was much more philanthropic than I ever understood. I knew she did charity work and helped people, but my goodness, she was behind the scenes in practically everything—hospitals, young missionaries with no money and poor families, the homeless. You name it, she was in the middle of it."

"A dyed-in-the-wool, Mormon do-gooder, eh, all the way back east in Joseph Smith country?" Mac said, a gentle laugh escaping.

Matt looked over at his work mate and friend and smiled. "Who do you think you're fooling, Mac? Born in the Church, thirty-five years inactive, pooh-poohing everything you can about Mormons every chance you get, yet you're a better man than 'most everyone I know. But I'm on to you, Mr. Public Works Director, Mr. Golf-on-Sunday reprobate. You work for *me* now, and I *know* who you are. Your secret's not safe any longer, Mac ole boy. One of these days I'm gonna publish your behind the scenes help-thy-neighbor activities too, and everyone we know is going to see just what a fraud you really are with this Mr. Humbug nonsense."

"*Me?*" Mac said, keeping a straight face and staring straight ahead.

"Yeah, you. It took me two years to learn about you, Mac, but the analysis is in. So get off my case about my grandmother and Mormon do-gooders."

"All right, all right. I'll acknowledge her sainthood, and you leave me to play golf when I feel like it. How about a burger in Sandy before I take you home?"

"Done, and thanks for picking me up."

"You'll get the bill. I need another eighty thousand for the cemetery reconstruction, and I'll be looking for your help on the mid-year budget revisions."

Matt laughed. "Fine, we'll take it out of your enormous salary account. After twenty-six years, you're practically the highest paid person on the city payroll."

"Yeah, the operative word is *practically*, Mr. Assistant City Manager. You must have forgotten about our queen bee."

"She earns her money."

Mac glanced over at Matt and smiled broadly. "Sure she does—one way or another, huh?"

"Let's not get into that again, Mac."

"Yeah, you think you know *me*, but you haven't taken the time to look at *her*. City manager or not, she...well, she deserves watchin'."

They rode in silence for a time, and then Mac shifted lanes to exit at 90th South, where he pulled into a fast-food restaurant. Mac shut off the engine and sat still for several seconds before exiting.

"I won't belabor the point, Matt, but something's up, and you're really gonna have to wake up and smell the coffee."

"I don't drink coffee. That's for Sunday golfers," Matt smiled.

"I'm serious. The election's just around the corner. Jim Templeton's a shoe-in for mayor, and his brother-in-law's gonna get back on the council. That will assure they retain the majority vote and we'll get right back to business as usual. Shady business at that."

"No chance for Julia Wells?"

Mac shook his head slowly, his tongue clicking a soft tsk-tsk. "A female mayor? Protestant to boot? Only eight years in Snowy Ridge? Are you kidding? She's a laugh."

"Well, how can Templeton and his brother make a difference?"

"They won't, but they'll make sure she keeps a majority vote so she can keep doing whatever she wants. Look, consider this: Where does the city spend the largest part of the budget?"

Matt laughed. "We don't. *You* do, in public works."

"That's right. And why am I never in on the bid openings or contract negotiations? Why are they always handled by the queen bee and several 'select' council members?"

Matt paused for a moment. "To assure open competition. You'll be building most of the projects, dealing with the contractors. It's to protect you from a conflict of interest."

Mac shook his head. "You're twenty-eight-years-old, a lawyer, reasonably smart, been in government—what, two years now?—and still a true believer. Your grandmother wasn't the only do-gooder in the family. If they're not genetic or surgically implanted my dear, Mr. Sterling, I'm gonna knock those blinders off your eyes before I hang it up and play golf full-time."

"I'm open to new information, Mac, but from what I can see—"

"You've been backup quarterback only a short while, my friend. Give it time."

"Well, let's get a bite to eat. The election and the budget will still be there tomorrow. Anyhow, I've got much more exciting news. Guess what I found in New York."

"You found Jimmy Hoffa's body when you demolished the house?"

"Better. I found Andrew McBride."

"Who?"

"Exactly. Who." Matt replied. "That's what I'm going to find out—who Andrew McBride really was." He opened the door, exited the vehicle, and started toward the restaurant.

"This I gotta hear, but you're buying, and I still need the eighty thousand," Mac said as he followed.

* * * * *

The following morning, Matt Sterling sat behind the desk in his City Hall office, quickly scanning through his in-basket, weeding out the chaff from the wheat. He'd arrived shortly before six, intending to catch up a bit of backlog in the relative quiet before the start of the day's business. By quarter to eight, other staff was beginning to arrive, each one popping his or her head in to once again express condolences at the passing of his grandmother. They'd already told him once, some weeks prior, at the time of the funeral, but most knew that he'd gone back to deal with the aftermath of her death. Just after eight, Patricia Harcourt, city manager, appeared in the doorway and smiled at Matt.

"Am I glad to see you. I've shuffled as much paper as I could to your desk," she said.

Matt looked up and grinned in response. "Good morning, Pat. So I see. Did you notice that half of it now lives in this little round receptacle?" he said, glancing down over the edge of his desk.

"Only the important stuff, I hope," she chuckled in return. "Actually, it's really good to have you back. Everything go okay? I mean, did you get it straightened out?"

"I did, Pat. Thanks for asking. I came in early this morning because I wanted to get a head start, but I'm going to need another two days to clear this probate stuff. She left some money to the Y and I have to arrange the transfer."

"Take what time you need, Matt. We're doing fine. I just wanted you to know I'm glad you're back."

"Thanks, Pat. I'll be in town and available on my cell if you need anything."

"Right. You know, come to think of it, why don't you just take the rest of the week and we'll see you on Monday."

"What about the council mid-year budget work session on Friday?"

"I'll handle it with Doug, our illustrious finance director. No problems."

"Fair enough. How's the election shaping up?"

"Right on target. We'll be looking good in about three weeks when we get the right team on the Council," Harcourt replied.

"Great. Well, I'll throw away more of this paper," he said, grinning at her again, "and make a few phone calls. Then I've got to get up to Provo and deliver some good news."

"Your grandmother must have been a fine woman," Pat said.

Matt nodded. "More than I ever knew. Thanks for the welcome home, Pat."

She nodded. "See you later," she said, quickly disappearing from his office.

Matt sifted through several more folders and then rose from his chair, closed the door, and returned to his desk. He picked up the phone and keyed in the numbers. It was answered on the first ring.

"Hello."

"Morning, Dad. How're things in Sacramento?"

"Oh, hi, Matt. Your mother has kept us on the missionary routine ever since we got home. As to Sacramento, you know how it is—sun, sun, and more sun. Typical California golf weather. So, tell me—how did it go back East?"

"It was pretty sad, Dad. I know you'll understand that. That house should have been declared an historic site. It was one of only two original houses left on the river.in that area."

"You're right, son, but it's done now."

"Yeah. Riveroaks is just a memory. But you know that center timber in the basement, the one with the original burned-in inscription?"

"Do I remember? I grew up there," he laughed. 'Riveroaks, 1790.'"

"That's it. I had the workmen cut out a four-foot section, including the inscription, and had it shipped to me here in Utah."

"What for?"

"I'm not sure yet. I just wanted it."

"Good garage stuffer," his dad laughed.

"Maybe," Matt agreed. "It contained a bit of a surprise, Dad. The beam, I mean."

"How's that?"

"It had a secret space carved into it. I found a leather binder with an old journal, a handwritten manuscript, some letters, and a couple of official documents. Old Grandpa Sterling was ordered to be arrested by General Henry Clinton."

"You're kidding. You mean Grandma Sterling had some hidden genealogy?"

"I don't think so. In fact, I don't think she knew about it. It looked as if it hadn't been touched in well over a century or more."

"Whose was it then?"

"Andrew McBride."

"Who?"

"Andrew McBride…Sterling."

"You mean the original owner, Andrew Sterling?"

"It's a long story, Dad. It appears that his name might have originally been McBride but that he changed it after the Revolutionary War. Let me look into it a bit more and I'll keep you up to speed. The documents are quite fragile. I want to talk to Roland over at the Y and see if he knows how to handle them to keep them from disintegrating."

"That sounds smart. So, it was a pretty eventful trip, then?"

"It sure was, and that's not all the news, Dad."

"Oh?"

"Grandma's will was more complex than we thought. Her estate was quite substantial."

"In what way?"

"In the normal way, Dad. It contained a lot of money."

Dick Sterling was silent for several long moments. "What are you saying?"

"Well, she left about half of her money to each of her four surviving relatives; you, me, Rachel, and Emily. The other half went to BYU, to the genealogy program."

"They'll be pleased."

"They'll be *very*-pleased, Dad. She left them five million dollars."

"*What!*"

"That's right, five *million.*"

"But that means…"

"Yep. That means that each of us—you, me, Rachel, and Emily—will receive just over a million dollars from Grandma's estate, after the probate costs."

"My goodness! I never knew. I thought she spent her money on those missionaries and the hospital program. Oh, my goodness. I'm stunned!"

"Pretty amazing, huh? You and Mom are going to have to do a few things you've always postponed. Dad, I gotta run. I've got to call the university and discuss the donation with them. Give my love to Mom and everyone. I still plan on flying out for Thanksgiving weekend."

"You better. Your mom is counting on it. We might even get in a little golf. So long, Matt. Thanks for calling. I still can't believe it."

"Well, believe it, Dad. And go look at one of those Jaguar sedans you always drool over. You might just be able to buy one."

"Hey, what would your mother say?"

"Probably nothing if you take her on that Mediterranean cruise she's always wanted."

"That's my boy, always thinking. Talk to you later, Matt. Take care."

"Right, Dad. I love you."

"Love you, too. Bye."

* * * * *

As Matt replaced the receiver, his desk phone unit beeped to announce a call-waiting request. He pressed the redial button and the caller was identified in a small window on the phone as Doug Bellows, the city finance director. Following his promotion to assistant city manager, Matt had assumed supervision for six of the major department heads, including Finance and Public Works. Matt pressed the recall button and Bellows answered quickly.

"Hey, Matt, welcome back. Any New York news?"

"Hi, Doug. Nothing of importance. Wall Street collapsed, and the DOW is down to three thousand, but otherwise, business as usual. What's up? And be forewarned, if this is a lengthy request, I'm actually not here and you can count me gone."

"Fine by me. Just wanted some quick direction. Besides, if the DOW dropped as you said, this is the time to buy in."

"Yeah, right. Get me some, too."

"Will do," Doug laughed. "Matt, Mac was just in and said you and he discussed adding another eighty thousand to his budget line item for the cemetery."

"We did, but no conclusions."

"How do you want me to handle it then?"

"Do an agenda item for the next Council meeting."

"I could just transfer some funds internally."

"From where?"

"Oh, I'll find them somewhere."

Matt paused for a few moments. "No, I'd rather get the Council to consider the action, make a transfer determination, and get it recorded in the official minutes."

"Fine, I'll get right on it. When are you back, officially that is?"

"Not 'til next Monday."

"Right, see you then."

Matt again replaced the receiver and leaned back in his chair. This wasn't the first time Bellows had suggested moving money from one account into another to "balance the funds," as he had put it. Matt had been uncomfortable the first time Bellows brought it up but not unduly concerned. He shrugged. Bellows clearly knew what he was doing— the city had won several awards for financial programs.

Matt started to shuffle a few more papers around his desk and finally shoved the whole lot back into his in-basket. He smiled to himself, thinking about Mac. The old goat sure didn't let any grass grow under his feet, he thought. Putting in his request for the extra cemetery funds before Bellows could commit all the available funds intended for the mid-year revisions was a smart move. He picked up the receiver again and dialed the main number for BYU information.

"Brigham Young University. How may I direct your call?"

"I'd like the Molecular Genealogy Department, please."

"Certainly, sir. I'll put you through."

Several seconds elapsed and the phone rang through with a slightly different ringing tone.

"Molecular Genealogy, good morning. How can I help you?"

"Good morning. My name is Matt Sterling, and if possible, I'd like to speak to the director of the department. Is he or she available?"

"Yes, sir. Dr. Timothy Amberly is in his office this morning. May I tell him what this is about?"

"Certainly. Please advise him that I'd like to discuss making a donation to the program."

"Matt Sterling, was it, sir?"

"That's right."

"Thank you, sir. I'll put you through."

Another pause ensued, then a deep male voice came on the line. "Mr. Sterling, this is Tim Amberly. How may I be of assistance?"

"Good morning, sir. If your schedule permits, I'd like to meet with you today and discuss a donation to the molecular genealogy program. At your convenience, of course."

A slight pause ensued. "Well, Mr. Sterling, we're certainly grateful for any support that comes our way. What would you say to my arranging a telephone call with the university's donations officer? Perhaps he could handle the issue to your satisfaction."

"I agree, Dr. Amberly. Perhaps he should attend our meeting as well. This particular donation has some, uh, I wouldn't call them *strings*, but some stipulations are involved and they're all to your department's benefit. It would actually be very helpful if you, *and* a representative of the university, could meet together with me and I could explain the bequeath."

"I see. Might I ask how much of a donation we're discussing here, Mr. Sterling?"

"Just over five million dollars, Dr. Amberly," Matt said.

"Oh, gracious me. Well, perhaps we could arrange some sort of initial meeting. Might I call you back after discussing the matter with the university?"

"Certainly, doctor." He recited his cell phone number. "I'm only about thirty minutes away, but whatever advance notice you can provide would be helpful. I have a couple of other chores throughout the day. I'd really like to get this rolling today if possible and contact the appropriate legal officials in New York before the close of their business day."

"I'll be back to you within the hour, Mr. Sterling."

"That'll be fine. Thanks, Dr. Amberly."

Matt hung up the phone, grabbed his briefcase, and quickly left the building by the back stairs before some other staffer could trap him and get him involved in the day's business. Once in the car, he drove toward BYU's campus and the Archeology Department, where a former Sacramento high school classmate was involved in records preservation. If anyone could tell him how to preserve the brittle parchment documents he possessed, it would be his best boyhood friend, Roland Timmerman, now a professor of archeology. Fifteen minutes later, while driving up University Avenue through Provo, his cell rang and he reached forward, activating the hands-free unit.

"Good morning, Matt Sterling."

"Mr. Sterling, it's Tim Amberly again, from the molecular

genealogy program. How would ten o'clock suit you?"

Matt glanced at the clock on his dash. It read 9:20. "That was quick."

"You've gotten our attention, Mr. Sterling, and that's a fact."

"Ten o'clock will be fine, Dr. Amberly. Where are you located?"

"We're in the Eyring Science Center. Are you familiar with the campus?"

"I know right where you are. See you at ten."

"I look forward to it. Mr. Jack Thompson will be with us also. He's the Vice Chancellor."

"Excellent. Thank you for such a quick response, Dr. Amberly. I look forward to meeting you."

"My pleasure, Mr. Sterling. Until ten."

"Goodbye, sir."

Matt disconnected his cell and immediately dialed another number.

"Ancient Records."

"Roland, it's Matt."

"Hey, old boy. What's up? Back from New York already?"

"I am. I was coming to see you but got diverted by a meeting. Can you email me some information on the preservation of old documents, parchment-type stuff? How to keep them from deteriorating?"

"Sure, what have you found?"

"Some revolutionary war records, a personal journal, and an old manuscript."

"You're kidding."

"Dead serious, my friend."

"I want to see them."

"Why am I not surprised? How about pizza and the Jazz game at my place tonight?"

"You're on. See you about six."

"Looking at these records will cost you, my cheapskate friend," Matt laughed, "but it'll be worth it."

"What do you mean?"

"I mean *you* bring the pizza. *I'll* have the drinks and chips."

"Sounds good to me. See you then."

"See ya, R. T."

Second thoughts immediately entered Matt's mind as he got closer to the campus. With Roland coming over, there wouldn't be time to do much reading in what he had begun thinking of as "the McBride Papers." Reading on the plane, drifting off the last hour or so of the flight, and then crashing last night until about four this morning had kept him from further exploring what happened between Andy McBride and the arrogant British officer. Still, there was no hurry, was there? The papers had lain dormant in their wooden repository for nearly two hundred years. The secrets were there and would reveal themselves in time. Everything in its own time, Grandma Sterling had always said. Everything in its own time.

* * * * *

After finding an empty parking space, Matt walked across the campus to the building housing the science complex. He'd been in the Eyring Science Center with Roland on several occasions as the young professor had sought to get some material carbon dated.

As he approached the building, a gorgeous young woman met him at the entrance.

"Are you by any chance Matt Sterling?" she asked, revealing a decidedly British accent.

"That's me. And you must be clairvoyant," he smiled, aware that his pulse was beginning to climb.

"I wish," she smiled. "I didn't recognize you, and since I

know most people who come in here—well, one and one make two."

"A mathematics professor, no doubt," Matt said, trying not to stare at her.

"Hardly," she said, her smile broadening. "I'm a student. Kasia Somerset." She extended her hand and gave him a firm handshake.

"Kasia," Matt said, letting the sound roll off his tongue. "That's an unusual name."

Kasia smiled and nodded. "My mother named me after Cassiopia, the constellation, but put a 'K' in front to make it different. It sounds a bit like the sixties singer Mama Cass, with an 'ia' at the end. Some people read it and think it should rhyme with Asia."

"Well, it's a beautiful name. Do you work in the microbiology program?"

"I'm Dr. Amberly's assistant. I thought if I met you at the entrance, I could save you the trouble of learning the secret path through our labyrinth."

"That tough, huh? Is there a minotaur lurking in there, too?"

Kasia didn't skip a beat. "Oh, by all means. That would be Dr. Amberly, of course," she smiled brightly.

"Lead on, m'lady. I'm indebted for your guidance."

Kasia Somerset entered the building and turned smartly down a hallway, escorting Matt past the laboratory wing toward the administrative offices of the Molecular Genealogy project. As they walked, Matt couldn't help thinking she didn't look like any student he had known when he was in college.

In the few moments they had faced each other outside the building, he'd been intrigued by her eyes. Even without the aid of excessive makeup, they were fascinating. A dark gray in color, they were particularly attractive and sparkled when she smiled.

She had a radiant complexion, stood about five-seven, he guessed, and probably went about eight stone, maybe eight and a half if he remembered his British weights correctly. Walking behind her, he gave her a closer look and nodded to himself. 115 pounds would be about right. Her dark hair was blunt-cut just above the neck with straight bangs in front. Thick, shiny and very wavy—*just right for running my fingers through it*, was the thought that popped into Matt's mind. The terra-cotta colored dress she wore was complemented by a brilliant two-toned green scarf, knotted off one shoulder. The look was a bit flamboyant, especially in light of his memory of British reserve, but on Kasia Somerset it was working—and working well.

"Here we are," she announced as they turned into a small office and an even smaller cubicle for the receptionist.

"Dr. Amberly and Mr. Thompson are waiting in his office," the receptionist said, smiling up at them as they passed.

"We can go right in," Kasia added.

They entered a larger office, where two men were sitting on either end of a dark blue leather couch. They immediately stood.

"Mr. Sterling?"

"Yes, sir. And you must be Dr. Amberly?"

"I am, and this is Jack Thomson, Vice Chancellor of Administration. We're very pleased to meet you, Mr. Sterling."

"My pleasure, doctor. Thank you for such a quick response."

"You're welcome. I presume you've met Ms. Kasia Somerset, my assistant?"

"Yes, indeed," Matt said, smiling again at the young woman. "She and I have had a quick, mythological tour of the facility."

"I see," Amberly said, casting an inquisitive look at Kasia.

"Well, then, let's sit down." He motioned to a small conference table surrounded by four chairs. "I must confess, what you had to say on the telephone was very intriguing. It's not often one receives such a welcome call so early in the morning. Sort of out of the blue, so to speak."

Kasia took a chair directly across from Matt. In the subdued light, her eyes seemed lighter, almost shale gray.

"Perhaps I should start," Matt said.

Amberly acknowledged with a slight wave of his hand. "Please."

"The short of it," Matt smiled, "is that my grandmother, Elizabeth Winchester Sterling, of Hyde Park, New York, recently passed away. She lived to a very active ninety-six and was a graduate of BYU, class of 1929."

"Excellent," Mr. Thompson interjected, "an alumnus donation."

"She and her husband were not what could be called wealthy, certainly not by the standards of some of their neighbors. The Roosevelt and the Vanderbilt family estates are situated close by. But Grandfather Sterling did very well in business, and I was recently surprised to discover how well my grandmother had managed her assets during the eighteen years following his death. She was also an avid genealogist and had followed with interest the work you are doing here, Dr. Amberly.

"In her will, she bequeathed the sum of five million dollars in trust, *specifically*, and I emphasize that, Mr. Thompson, so the university has no misunderstanding about the intent of her gift. She wanted it to be used exclusively to support the molecular genealogy program. Her will stipulates that the interest on the principal—some three to four hundred thousand dollars annually at six or eight percent—is to be used to fund continuing research in what she considered to be an important work.

"Dr. Amberly, I don't know how realistic her expectations were, but my grandmother thought what you're doing here would eventually provide data that might even reveal the identity of some of today's descendants of the twelve tribes."

"I'm speechless," Dr. Amberly said.

"So was I, doctor, so was I," Matt said. "This transfer can take place immediately, according to her attorney in Poughkeepsie. Do you think we can arrange that?"

"Absolutely," Mr. Thompson said. "I feel certain the university would like to arrange a grand public announcement and highlight the program in the process."

Matt shook his head. "I'm sorry, Brother Thompson," he said, using the traditional Mormon form of respectful address, "but my grandmother's will is quite specific. She wants no publicity associated with her gift—at least none that could be attributed to her gift. However, promoting the program would please her very much I think. She just wants the work to continue. If you could ensure her anonymity, I'm sure a public announcement would be fine."

Thompson nodded slowly. "I understand. I'm sure we can take care of that."

"Jack," Dr. Amberly said, "I'm due to leave on Thursday for the Far East. I'm afraid I can't assist in anything if it has to be done quickly. Will that be a problem?"

"I don't think so, Tim. Perhaps Ms. Somerset could look after anything we need from your department, and I'll handle the legalities with Mr. Sterling's attorney."

"Excellent. Does that sound all right to you, Mr. Sterling?"

Matt glanced quickly at Kasia Somerset who was looking directly at him. "That would be just fine, doctor, just fine. Actually, I'm an attorney, too. I work as the assistant city manager in Snowy Ridge. So if I can help in any way, I'll be glad to work with you and your legal department, Mr. Thompson."

"Great. We'll put you together with our donations team

and work out the details." He started to rise. "If that's it, then, I'll get back to my office."

"There is one other thing, Dr. Amberly, if I might," Matt said.

"Certainly."

"A technical question, actually. I've recently come into possession of some rather old documents, part of my grandmother's estate. Documents dating from the Revolutionary War. There are what appear to be bloodstains on one of them. I'm wondering if it's possible to determine DNA from a document stained with blood, say two hundred years old."

"I think it would be, Mr. Sterling. That happens to be one of Ms. Somerset's specialties, but we'd need to see the documents before I could commit."

"The one in question is an arrest order, signed by British General Sir Henry Clinton in New York. I'm not *certain* that it contains blood, but the journal says that's what it is and the paper is heavily stained."

"Fascinating," Dr. Amberly said. "How did you come into possession of the documents? Part of your grandmother's things you say?"

"Yes. If you can spare me another ten minutes, I'll tell you about it."

"Certainly. We've blocked off whatever time you need this morning. Ten minutes in exchange for five million dollars is little enough, I would presume," Amberly said with a smile.

Matt laughed. "I suppose it is," he said, glancing again at Mr. Thompson, who had taken his seat again.

"Well, to begin, until her death my grandmother lived in a house that was built in 1790. Some of my ancestors have lived there ever since, while another branch met the missionaries in New York and moved to Utah in the 1850s. As a part of the sale of the estate, the house had to be demolished. While it was being taken down, I discovered a cache of documents in the basement. I haven't finished reading all the material yet, since I just discovered it the day before yesterday, but what I've learned is that in 1772, one of my ancestors was a young man attending Trinity College in Dublin. He was accused of murder, then kidnapped—shanghaied essentially—and taken aboard a merchant ship. And all this was done by a British army officer." Matt noticed a knowing smile on Kasia's face. He nodded his head. "Another British injustice story, eh?" he said, laughingly.

"Press gangs along the waterfront, both civilian and military, were known to happen in those days," Kasia said in a friendly tone.

"Anyway, I haven't gotten much further, although I've read most of the journal."

"The journal?" Amberly asked.

"Right. I'm sorry," Matt said. "There are two separate sets of documents. One is a personal journal and the other a manuscript, written in story form. Plus there are several letters and even an arrest order, as I mentioned. That's the one with bloodstains on it. But I'm getting ahead of myself. This ancestor, Andrew McBride was his name, was forcibly put on a ship leaving Dublin, and as the story goes..."

Man's darkest hour doth not always precede the dawn.
Truth be known, the seemingly darkest hour may well be
merely the precursor to the total eclipse.
Journal of Andrew McBride
April 22, 1775

Chapter Four

DUBLIN, IRELAND
SEPTEMBER 1772

Sometime after midnight, along with two of his equally inebriated comrades, Andrew McBride left O'Reilly's Tavern. Halfway to his quarters near Trinity College, his two companions veered toward their own accommodations, and Andy continued alone through the darkness. What the hapless lad hadn't foreseen was the ambuscade set for him by Lieutenant Applegate and two dragoons he had seconded to assist him in teaching a young Irish upstart proper respect for the Crown. Oblivious to any danger in his drunken state, he lurched on, his thoughts filled with the winsome Molly, who, acting on the precautionary suggestion of the publican, had departed the tavern earlier in the evening. Walking through the lush vegetation of St. Stephan's Green, his thoughts, jumbled at best, turned to clean sheets and a warm bed.

In the dark, a scarlet-clad man stepped out from behind a tree and blocked Andy's path. Confused in his alcoholic stupor, Andy presented the semblance of a smile, then stumbled on the footpath, dropping to his knees. He turned when he heard a noise behind him, but before he could see his assailant, his world turned black.

"Bind him, Sergeant, and be sure to seal his lips. And you there," the scarlet-clad officer commanded the other man, "get the cart."

"Aye, sir," the dragoon said, as the other strode off.

The officer then knelt and gave closer scrutiny to the unconscious McBride. He turned Andy's slack face toward the dim moonlight.

"It's far too handsome a face for an Irish lout, what say you, Sergeant?" Lieutenant Applegate asked.

"As you say, sir," the sergeant replied.

"I'll have your knife then," he said, holding forth his hand.

Complying, the sergeant watched in awe as his superior slowly and deliberately sliced the earlobes off both ears of the young man who, in his unconscious state, made no response to the assault.

Applegate turned the head slightly, allowing the moon to reflect off the face. "Perhaps a bit of a scar, too," he said, moving his knife with apparent pleasure and drawing it across the left side of his victim's face, following the cheekbone from the ear to the tip of the jaw line.

"That will perhaps curb his insolence," the officer said, leaning forward to admire his handiwork. "At least it will give the young ladies a moment's pause, eh?"

The dragoon stood his ground, slightly in awe, and did not respond to the latest entreaty from the officer to commend his work.

"Will you have your pound of flesh then, Sergeant?" he said, offering the knife back to the dragoon.

"I think not, sir, with your permission of course."

"As you will," Applegate said, standing up. "Perhaps he *has* had enough. We wouldn't want him bleeding to death before he meets the hangman, would we?"

The other dragoon hauled the cart into place, the large, wooden wheels digging into the grass. He stood to attention as Applegate shouldered his way past, lifting a large blood-stained rag from the bed of the cart and wiping the new stains from his tunic. At the passage of the officer, the shorter dragoon stepped closer to the sergeant, observing the unconscious man on the ground, blood streaming from his wounds. The sergeant, now kneeling and tying Andy's hands, glanced over at the officer who remained preoccupied with cleansing himself, and then glanced up at his companion.

"He'd be a cold one, that Applegate," he whispered. "Aristocracy, my eye. And they're supposed to be the nobility. I'd not take lightly to being *his* prisoner, I dare say. Have a look at his handiwork," the sergeant said, rising and nodding toward the bloodied man lying prostrate before them.

The newly arrived dragoon knelt down next to the figure on the ground. Blood continued to ooze from both ears, and Andy's face and neck were streaked by the dark substance. With a shrug of his shoulders, the smaller man looked up at the sergeant who towered over him.

"He do this by hisself, Sergeant?" the man grinned, rolling his eyes toward the officer.

"Aye, but this lad's got off lucky, what with how we did the lass and all. This bleedin' officer will get us stretched on the gallows, if'n we're not careful."

"Mind your tongue, Sergeant," Applegate said firmly, overhearing the comments as he stepped back near the inert body. "It's the bloody Irish drunkard who'll be swinging by his neck if you keep your mouth shut and do as I tell you."

The sergeant and his companion stood quietly for a moment as the officer knelt again beside the still-unconscious body of Andy McBride. Seeking to recover from his unwarranted remark to the officer, the sergeant spoke again. "Shall we kill the Irishman, too, sir?" he asked, using the plural to retract his earlier remark and assume his portion of responsibility, at least for the moment, until they were safely away from the dangerously impetuous officer.

Lieutenant Applegate looked up from his kneeling position and smiled at the sergeant, glanced back once at his victim, and then stood, adjusting the front of his tunic. "It's easy to *kill* a man, Sergeant. It is much more satisfying to disfigure and to disgrace him. Now, get the cart and place the blackguard in it. We'd best be away. We've got to get him in the shed before first light."

"Aye, sir. Here, Alf, get the cart and I'll lift the lad."

"Make haste, Sergeant. You know where to take him. And don't go near the body of that tart again. She'll be found soon enough by her own kind."

"Right, sir. We'll see to it."

Over an hour later and nearly four miles away, in Donnybrook, the sergeant dumped Andy's body on the floor of the wooden shed, eliciting a groan from the yet unconscious, mutilated man. It was not until light came through small cracks in the roof of the decrepit hovel that smelled of animal waste and silage that the young Irishman began to clear his head. As he rubbed his eyes, he grimaced at the pain that shot through his face. Gently feeling his head and face, he discovered the altered shape of his ears and the blood-caked gash on his cheek. Unable to see himself or to know where he was, he sat quietly for some moments, discovering the chains that secured his feet to the wall of the room where he was confined and trying to recall the events of the previous evening.

* * * * *

It was well into the second night of his confinement before Andy heard the sounds of someone approaching the darkened room. He had heard dogs barking and cattle lowing during the previous day, but no human sounds. A chain rattled on the outer door and in several moments a torch flickered through the doorway. Andy struggled to sit up against the wall, but was hindered by his leg irons.

"Well, Sergeant, it seems our guest has returned to the living," a voice spoke, the face silhouetted by the torch being held behind him. "Getting a bit thirsty, are you, Mr. McBride?" he asked.

Andy strained to make out the face, but to no avail.

"Here then, Sergeant, bring that bucket."

A large, muscular man stepped forward. He wore the uniform of a British army sergeant and was carrying a small bucket that he set down in front of Andy, pausing momentarily to take stock of his captive, shaking his head at the sight. "Have a go at that, lad. It's not the cleanest water, but I've drunk worse."

Quickly, Andy leaned forward to scoop the water with his hands to his parched lips, slopping the water around his face and grimacing as the pain returned.

"Ah, yes," the figure silhouetted by the torch spoke again, and Andy could see he was nodding his head, "you've taken note of your new appearance, have you? Perhaps the ladies will not find that face quite so appealing. Shame I didn't bring the mirror from the tavern, so you could have a look. It'll make quite the scar, that," the man continued.

"The lieutenant?" Andy said, hoarsely whispering the words.

"Yes, indeed. Lieutenant Applegate—Jonathan Applegate to be exact. The subject of your ill-mannered disrespect for one of His Majesty's officers."

"And how did I—"

"Bring in the sack, Sergeant, and let's help our friend start his journey to a new life. I have better things to attend to this evening than conversing with bog Irish."

Andy listened to what sounded like a horse and cart being moved outside the shed, and watched as the sergeant, the man who had brought the water, departed the doorway leaving Andy alone with the lieutenant who was now holding the torch.

"Where am I going?" Andy said, his voice stronger after the water had moistened his throat.

"Never you mind, but be grateful you've received a reprieve from the hangman."

"What hangman?"

The young lieutenant laughed and knelt down, holding the torch at such an angle as to permit Andy to view the officer's face. His eyes were closely set, pinpricks of light reflected from the torch, seemingly devoid of soul.

"I had planned for you to meet the hangman, Mr. McBride, for the murder of one Molly Meagher, Donnybrook prostitute, but those plans have, shall we say, been changed. Since your father is a barrister of some repute, he seems to have some unexpected high level influence at Dublin Castle. Actually, that's equally to your disadvantage, McBride. As a result, in my own self-interest of course, I think it best that you take a trip—a long trip."

"But you can't just—"

The man laughed again. "Ah, but I can, and I shall. You're wanted for murder and your absence—your running away—will seal your fate. Within two days your wanted poster will be up all over Dublin, despite your father's protests, and in three weeks you should be rounding the African coast, headed for the slave markets of Zanzibar I should think."

The two other soldiers re-entered the room and proceeded to pull a large, burlap sack over Andy's head and upper torso.

"Pleasant dreams, Mr. McBride. Just remember who it was that arranged your trip abroad, though it's most unlikely we shall ever meet again."

With a sound thump, the sergeant knocked Andy unconscious, and the two men lifted his inert body, dumping it unceremoniously into the cart.

* * * * *

Andy's first conscious sensation as he awoke was the stench of urine, mildew, and saltwater, followed quickly by a jolt of pain that reminded him of his disfigurement and of a head that had been twice cracked in as many nights. His initial movement brought with it an agony of body. As his mental faculties began to function, he discovered that his hands and feet were trussed. When he finally opened his eyes, a young, dark-skinned man of about twenty was bending over him, trying to ladle some water into his mouth. Unable to sit, Andy craned his neck to accept the liquid.

"That be betta," the dark man said. "Yes'day, I think maybe you soon dead."

Andy looked around, trying to ascertain where he was.

"You be at sea," the man smiled, his face kind and gentle, "'board the *Canterbury*."

"At sea?"

"Aye. Two days from Dublin. We come near France now."

"France?"

"That be right. We headed for 'Merica. I been there 'fore."

Andy just looked at the man for a few moments, his mind

racing with the shock of having left Ireland. The ship rolled slightly, and in the shift, the black man lost his balance, falling against Andy. Andy rolled over on his side.

"Can you untie me?" Andy asked.

The man turned nervously toward the ladder, looking through the open hatch to the upper deck and then back at Andy. "Don't know's I can," he replied in a whisper.

"How long have I been here?" Andy asked.

"Like I say, we be at sea two days now. You got a knock on your head, an' you been sleep mos' times. My name be Righteous. That be what Cap'n, he call me. How you called?"

"Andy."

The black man nodded. "We be to sea long time, Andy. Best now you do what Cap'n Amos say. He be hard, but fair, you do the work."

"How long will we be at sea?"

"Oh, Cap'n Amos, he say, four, maybe five weeks. Got's to get the wind. You maybe like 'Merica. I done been there."

"Five weeks," Andy replied, reaching with trussed hands for the water bucket.

"Maybe less," Righteous replied.

Chapter Five

Matt left the Eyring Science Center, his step a little lighter. Crossing the parking lot, he dialed a number on his mobile phone, immediately connecting.

"Good morning, Ancient Records."

"Hi, R. T., it's me again."

"I've been thinking about your records. I want to see them."

"That's what I'm calling about. I can't get together tonight after all. Something's come up."

"Yeah?"

"Or I should say, some *one's* come up. I met a young English woman on campus this morning."

"And that means no pizza and basketball, right?" Roland responded.

Matt laughed. "It certainly does—for you, that is. I'm taking her up to the Delta Center for the live game."

"Dumped for a woman!"

"You've treated me just as shabbily and besides, you need to take Annette out once in awhile instead of hanging out with the boys," Matt laughed. "So, how about I grab us a sandwich and come over to your office this afternoon? We can look over these records, and you can tell me what to do about them."

"Great. See you in about an hour. She worth it, Matt?"

"Got a feeling, Rol. I've just got a feeling."

"Well, you'll get to see the basketball game in any event.

Who's the victim tonight?"

"Houston Rockets. I'll be there in about forty-five minutes. Bye."

* * * * *

Kasia Somerset was ready and out the front door as Matt pulled his car into the driveway next to her small home in Alpine. He had barely gotten out of the car before she came down the front steps, smiling a greeting. His heart skipped a beat at the sight of her.

"You've been in America too long," Matt said as he came around to open her car door.

"How so?" she asked.

"I was planning on actually coming up and knocking on your door," he said. "You know, sort of like a real gentleman and all."

"Oh," she laughed, sliding into the car, "I'd already determined you to be a gentleman, else I wouldn't be here."

Matt walked around to his side of the vehicle, got in, started the engine, and backed out of the drive. "Then you really are clairvoyant."

"No," she said, shaking her head, "perceptive would be more like it. I've always had a keen sense about my friends."

"That sounds like clairvoyance to me, Kasia. In any event, I'm glad you agreed to come on the spur of the moment."

"And miss a Jazz game? Not on your life. Even if my perceptions had warned me, I probably still would have come to see the Jazz play. I'm fascinated by your American game."

"You're putting me on."

"No. I'm quite serious."

"That's a relief. After you accepted my invitation, I started worrying that maybe you'd find it boring."

"Not at all."

Kasia was facing forward, watching the road, and Matt stole a look at her profile.

When she turned to face him, a knowing "gotcha" smile on her face, he quickly looked back at the road.

"Now, how about you fill in all the gaps I haven't figured out," she said.

"I thought the English were reserved, or at least politely non-intrusive. At least the ones I've known."

"That shows how much you know. It's the twenty-first century. Have you been to England?"

"You don't already know—or *perceive*?" he taunted.

Kasia smiled but said nothing as she leaned her head against the back of the seat. Matt drove through the intersection, turned into the on-ramp, and merged with the traffic on I-15, heading up the incline toward Point of the Mountain and into the Salt Lake Valley. After a time, Kasia spoke again.

"Perhaps I'm not perceptive. I'm just guilty."

"Hang her," Matt responded immediately. "Firm British justice, that's what's needed here."

She burst out laughing, turning again to face him as he drove. "I'm entitled to make a defense, m'lord. Or has that tenet of English law not made it across the Atlantic?"

"All right, if we must. Just pretend you're in the Old Bailey on wheels. Let's hear your plea."

"There's a certain BYU professor of law, one Trevor Weatherly, also from England. He's sometimes been known to frequent the Eyring Science Center to have lunch with his wife, Dr. Sarah Weatherly. After your meeting this morning with Dr. Amberly, and your most presumptuous invitation as I was showing you to the door—"

"Objection! A presumptuous invitation that you readily accepted, I might add."

"Objection overruled. As I was saying, I just might have happened to run into Professor Weatherly in the hallway..." She paused, looking down at the seat momentarily, a sheepish grin on her face. "Actually, in the interest of fairness, m'lord, and even though I'm not under oath, I might have met the professor *in* Dr. Weatherly's office, actually...after I called her...actually...and asked her to invite him over...actually. But that's not important. I asked him—purely in the interest of academic research, mind you—if he knew of a particular former law student."

"Of course," Matt chuckled, "'Studs' Weatherly, the piano king of the J. Reuben Clark Law School student's lounge. And did he remember this, uh, *particular* law student?"

"No," she replied, shaking her head.

Matt jerked his head around and looked at her. "*No?*"

"If I recall his words accurately, he said something about his having tried to forget this *particular* student for some time now.'"

"Now *that* sounds more like Professor Weatherly. At least the one I remember. And did you learn anything?"

Kasia held her silence for several moments. "I'm here, aren't I?"

"So you are. And that's the extent of your defense? Guilty as charged. Six months' probation under the frequent supervision of an upstanding American citizen."

"I've committed no crime. I was merely protecting the Molecular Genealogy program from potential danger. Besides, I don't see any upstanding American citizens present," Kasia said, staring directly at Matt and smiling.

"Touché. But I'll tell ya, Kasia, from what I read this afternoon in my great-grandfather's journal, it would more likely be *me* in danger, associating with another Brit. Boy, did Andy McBride get a raw deal."

"Who?"

"Andrew McBride, my ancestor. The character in the manuscript and its author, by all accounts."

"From what you said today, it sounds more like a Robert Louis Stevenson novel. *Kidnapped*, perhaps."

"It certainly does. But before we get too far up the road, do you have any preferences for dinner?"

"I'm in your hands, Mr. Sterling," Kasia said.

"And Professor Weatherly said that was okay?"

"No, of course not. In fact, he recommended strongly against it. But his wife winked at me and punched him on the arm."

"I believe it. I've had dinner at their home several times, and they're a feisty couple. Well, if it's okay with you, I've made reservations at the roof-top restaurant at the Joseph Smith Memorial Building, across from Temple Square."

"Sounds wonderful. But are we dressed all right? I've heard it's pretty posh."

"We're fine. They said in the interest of good foreign relations, I could bring you anyway. That is, providing I supervise you in the proper use of a knife and fork."

"Better I should teach you Yanks. What with McDonald's being America's favorite *dining* establishment, with a Quarter-Pounder as the basic entrée, you've pretty much gotten away from using proper cutlery, haven't you?"

"Ouch!"

Matt exited the freeway and found a parking place on South Temple, between Temple Square and the Delta Center. They walked the two blocks to the restaurant and rode the elevator to the tenth floor. Seated on the west side, at a table overlooking the Main Street Plaza and temple grounds, they both ordered roast rack of lamb and drank sparkling cider while they waited.

After several moments of silence, during which both of them looked out the window at the iridescent sunset over the lake and the view of the six Temple spires from above, the polished granite glowing beneath the floodlights, Matt recalled a particular incident from his L.D.S. mission in England and it reminded him of exactly what was so physically intriguing about Kasia's looks. The British called it a peaches and cream complexion. In one of his missionary ward assignments, an "older" woman of nearly forty had possessed the same attribute and Matt remembered being impressed how someone that age, the mother of several children, could be so beautiful. Kasia had it too. A nearly flawless complexion accompanied by a vibrant hue to the skin that required minimal cosmetic enhancement. He smiled at the memory until Kasia glanced back at him and broke into his thoughts.

"How long have you been at BYU, Kasia?" he asked.

"Almost two years. I've been here several times over the years, with my parents, but my studies at the Y started in early '02. I'm in a doctoral program working on a Ph.D. in genetic biology and felt very fortunate to obtain a paid position as Dr. Amberly's assistant. It's a wonderful program and my work is very exciting."

"Are you planning to stay in America?"

Kasia shrugged her shoulders. "I've no plans at present, but the future's open, I suppose. I'm not tied to any commitments in England, although I do love our home in Surrey. That's south of London."

"No *commitments* you say? Back home, I mean." Matt said.

Kasia smiled across the table. "None of *those* commitments. Now, Mr. Matt Sterling, let's talk about you. I asked earlier if you've ever been to England."

"Two years, from June 2000 to June 2002."

"Ah, the missionary story, is it?"

Matt nodded, smiling. "Is that no longer impressive on campus?"

"Oh, it's obligatory, my dear chap, quite obligatory, Queen's Honours, in fact," she said, a false air of British aristocracy in her voice.

"Phew, I was worried there for a moment."

"Where did you serve?"

"In London."

"How was it? Did you enjoy London?"

"It's fabulous. Except for Hyde Park, where I put in my, uh, obligatory, as you put it, appearance on the soap box, addressing the unwashed multitude and fending off the usual hecklers."

"Did you now?"

"Yes, ma'am."

"Then I am indeed impressed."

"Impressed! Now that's a good start to any relationship."

"Ah, here's our lamb. Just in time," she said, spreading her napkin on her lap.

* * * * *

The Jazz took the Rockets, 102–99, in overtime, and Matt was amazed by Kasia's understanding of the game. She not only knew the names of the players on both teams but spoke knowledgeably about the history of the franchise and even coaching strategy. After the game, they worked their way through the crowd, leaving the Delta Center, found Matt's car, and finally got back on the freeway headed south toward Kasia's place. They rode in silence for a few miles, until the heavy traffic sorted itself out and gradually became lighter. By Murray, it was flowing smoothly. Kasia spoke first.

"You mentioned earlier that you'd had a further look into your grandfather's records. How does the story continue?"

"It's truly amazing how our lives turn on such small things. Especially in those days, I suppose. A geographical move of such magnitude was nearly irreversible. From Ireland to America, I mean."

"So his ship went to America?"

"To Boston, actually."

"In 1772? So he's going into the thick of it, isn't he?" Kasia said.

"Absolutely. I'm finding it hard to believe, Kasia. I mean if this stuff is true...."

"Would there be a chance I could look at some of the material?"

"I'm hoping you'll look at the blood-stained arrest order."

"I'll do that, too, of course, but I meant the actual journal or the manuscript perhaps."

"Of course you can. After I left this morning's meeting with you and Dr. Amberly, I met with my friend Roland Timmerman. He's a professor of archeology. I left the papers with him for some treatment he recommended. But not before he and I read a lot more."

"Tell me a bit more of the story."

"It's become my favorite subject. How about we stop for hot chocolate, and I'll tell you what I know so far."

Kasia glanced at her watch and nodded. "I don't have to be in the lab 'til ten tomorrow, so you're on. I can show you a place in Orem, if you like."

Seated across from each other at a back table, two steaming mugs of hot chocolate and a couple of muffins between them, Matt began.

"After examining the documents, Roland was able to substantiate the authenticity—at least initially—from some records on file, of General Clinton's signature on the arrest order for Andrew McBride. The thing is dated October 8, 1781. That places it within a week of the British surrender at Yorktown, right near the end of the Revolutionary War."

"His signature should make it valuable."

"Probably does. But I'm getting ahead of the story. In Dublin, McBride was taken to the ship, placed aboard, and after several weeks found himself ashore in Boston. While on the ship he made friends with an African slave named Righteous, who had been serving aboard ship for three years. Anyway, Andy and Righteous got off in Boston and Righteous disappeared. The ship apparently sailed without him."

"Jumped ship," Kasia said.

"Apparently. Andy gets a job on the waterfront, makes contact with a lawyer, and has him write to his father in Dublin. His mother had died some years earlier. Three months go by. Then one day Andy gets a visit on the docks from a messenger who says the lawyer wants to see him, so Andy leaves work and goes to his office. The lawyer tells Andy that his father has died, apparently of a heart attack. The letter to Andy's father had been forwarded to the family solicitor in Dublin, who had responded to the Boston lawyer."

"So now he has no reason to go back to Dublin, right?" Kasia said.

"Right. Apparently he had no other family. However, the Boston lawyer advises that Andy's father, never believing the validity of the murder charge, has established Andy's patrimony. Then he—"

"His what?"

"His patrimony. It's a term referenced in the journal. It means the inheritance from his father. Anyway, Andy's patrimony, a considerable sum, has been left in trust for Andrew McBride, son of Sir James McBride, to claim, upon identification and accurate response to a series of questions in the possession of the Dublin solicitor."

"Ah, the intrigue," Kasia smiled. "This is a real mystery."

"It only gets better. Andy provides proper answers to the

questions, the Dublin lawyer transfers the money to the Boston lawyer, and all of a sudden, our shanghaied hero is a substantial Boston citizen."

"What about the murder charge?"

"No further mention of it. Perhaps Andy's father got the charges dropped."

"This is wonderful stuff. Is it from the manuscript or the journal?"

"The manuscript, but so far, each primary event is covered in some detail in the journal as well. I haven't cross-referenced everything yet, but so far it correlates with the manuscript. It almost seems as if Andy McBride, in his later years, used the journal as an outline to write the novel."

"Fascinating."

"So, anyway, McBride enrolls in college again...oh, sorry, Kasia, you may not know about that. He was a student at Trinity College in Dublin when he was kidnapped. Anyway, he goes to Yale and, this'll kill you, for his first year, in 1773, he becomes a fellow student with Nathan Hale and several others who served in the Revolution. Eventually, Yale gets a letter from Trinity College in Dublin, they accept McBride's earlier studies and after two more years, Yale awards him a bachelor's degree in late 1774."

"Nathan Hale. He was the American spy, wasn't he?"

"Right. He was hanged by the British. No appeals in those days. He was convicted without trial by General Howe in New York and hanged the next morning. If I remember my history, he actually confessed to being a spy, so I suppose Howe didn't think a trial was necessary. Haven't seen anything about that in the journal though. Of course, it happens much later. Not until 1776."

"What happens to our hero next? What about his face? Was he terribly scarred?"

Matt smiled, took a bite of his muffin, and sipped his drink. "He hasn't said. If he was, it didn't seem to be much of a handicap."

Kasia smiled and nodded. "Enter the young lady, right?"

"Exactly. Laura Delacorte, of the Westchester County Delacorte's."

"You sure this wasn't the first in a long series of Mills and Boone romance novels?" Kasia laughed. "So Laura was upper class?"

"Totally. Her family was essentially British/American aristocracy. That meant they had money. And they were completely acceptable to the British ruling class of the day. They were colonists, but remained basically British—what other Americans came to call Tories or Royalists. Laura was their only child. Andy and Laura marry and establish a home in Boston. Andy is now a lawyer like his father. Three years have gone by since he was kidnapped and it's early 1775."

"Oh, boy. Andy's world is about to turn upside down again, whichever side he chooses."

"You can say that again."

"How did Andy explain his disfigurement?"

"He told her the truth—that he was framed for a murder by a British officer, shanghaied, and placed on board a ship the officer thought was going to Africa."

"At least he was honest with her. So what happens next?" Kasia asked, leaning even further across the table.

Matt shrugged. "I don't know."

Kasia pulled back. "You don't *know*? What do you mean you don't know? You stopped reading?"

"Yep," he grinned, winking at her across the table. "See how important our date was?"

A smile crept across Kasia's face, and she shook her head. "You're a handful, Mr. Sterling, a truly brash Yank, just like my father warned me about."

"What does *he* know?" Matt smiled back at her across the table.

"Well, to hear him tell it—and to be fair, much of it came from *his* father—the last time the Yanks came our way, they left the paddocks full of tank treads, drank all the beer, all the time complaining it was too warm, produced hundreds, if not *thousands* of half-Yanks, and on their way home, took half the girls out of Surrey back to America."

"Well, from the look of things, the English girls are still coming over this way. And on their own steam. We don't even have to go get them anymore."

"Well, aren't you lucky?" Kasia finished her drink and dipped her napkin into the water glass, dabbing at a small spot of chocolate on her sleeve. "This could turn into *Arabian Nights* in reverse."

"How so?"

"Well, I've been given six months' probation…under American supervision, of course. You know, *A Thousand and One Arabian Nights*—a new story every night."

"I see," Matt nodded. "Are you very, *very* busy with your studies and at the research lab?"

"Absolutely. Very busy."

"Good," Matt smiled.

"Good?"

"That still leaves one '*very*' doesn't it? We can call it the 'story hour.'"

Kasia leaned forward, cupping her chin in her hands, gazing steadily into Matt's eyes. "I suppose we could." There was a slight pause, then they gathered up their things and prepared to leave the restaurant. On the way to the car, Kasia said, "And so what do you think happens to Andy next?"

"Boston is about to go to war. Andy's newly married and his only family connections are decidedly Loyalist."

"Something tells me that isn't going to matter."

"Maybe we can find out together," Matt said.

They left the restaurant parking lot and Matt drove back toward Alpine, along the mountain frontage road.

"Do you want to bring your documents in tomorrow and we can start the testing process?" Kasia asked.

"I do. I'd better check with R. T. first, though, and see if he's finished with what he needed to do about preservation."

"That's fine. Oh, we should get a sample of your blood, too—unless you're afraid of needles," she teased.

"I think I can stand it," Matt replied. "What do you need mine for?"

"We're collecting samplings of blood from all over the world as part of our data bank. And we should also check your blood against the sample. Confirm your lineage, so to speak."

"All right. Unless R. T. has a problem, I'll drop it by your office about eleven. On second thought, why not noon, and I'll take you to lunch?"

"I'd like that."

"Are you supposed to report back to Professor Weatherly?" Matt asked, smiling.

"No," Kasia replied, shaking her head. "Of course not."

"Just as well. He'd have his version all over campus before noon."

"Loose lips, then?" she said.

"That's my memory of the man, and his transparent efforts to 'match up' his students. It was all in good fun, of course. I grew to like him very much during law school. I served my mission a bit later than most missionaries. I actually finished college and then continued on through law school before I put in for my call. I was twenty-four years old in the MTC. When I got home to Sacramento, I called Professor Weatherly about serving as a reference as I began to look for work. He had been contacted by Snowy Ridge about a city attorney position. He referred me, I got the job, and here we are. But he was quick to remind me that I was getting a bit 'long in the tooth,' as he put it. I was far too old to not be married. I've had this job two years now, so he'd probably report me to Church headquarters if he got the chance."

"That's the party line for BYU isn't it," she laughed, "I'm only twenty-five and I get the same cheek from his wife."

"I guess they're peas in a pod. So I'm glad you don't have to report back about this *particular* former law student."

"Not at all. I wouldn't do that," she said, trying to suppress a smile.

"As beautiful as your smile can be, this time I'd say something's up."

"Up?"

"*C'mon.*"

"Well, I'm still not under oath, m'lord, but if I were, I could truthfully say I am not under orders to report back to *Professor* Weatherly about our evening out."

They were silent for several moments while Matt let her statement hang in the air.

"Now *Doctor* Weatherly is something entirely different," Kasia added, "her orders were quite specific."

"Of course, his wife. I should've known."

Matt turned up the hill and parked in front of Kasia's house. This time she remained in the car, allowing him to exit, walk around and open her door. Then he walked her to her front step.

"So, we're twenty-eight and twenty-five. The bachelor and the spinster. Old before our time, according to the resident professor," Matt said.

"It would seem so, although my father would disagree. And my mother...well, you wouldn't want to know. She likes Americans of course, but..."

"But she wouldn't want one in the family?"

Kasia laughed aloud. "Something like that. Actually, that's probably not it at all. She just doesn't like the thought of her daughter being so far away. Getting her to agree to my coming to BYU instead of Dad's alma mater at Oxford took *lots* of persuasion and Dad's help."

"Dinner and a basketball game do not a son-in-law make. Tell her to rest easy."

Kasia stood quietly on her porch step, looking up at Matt as the silence grew into several seconds. Finally she extended her hand. "Thank you for a lovely time. I'll see you tomorrow for lunch. We'll want to draw your blood before we eat."

"Fair enough." He paused. "I had a really good time this evening, Kasia. Thanks."

"It *was* fun, wasn't it? And the Jazz won."

"Right. We'll have to do it again." He was still holding her hand. "Goodnight, Kasia," he said, releasing her hand then turning toward the car. Kasia watched for a moment as he started the engine, waved quickly at him, and entered the apartment.

When he reached home, Matt dumped his jacket on the couch and keyed the voice recorder. The machine whirred for several moments, clicked, and then responded.

"Matt, it's R. T. I've been reading your stuff. Fascinating. You're not gonna believe what your family's been up to. Call me in the morning. Oh, hope you had a miserable time at the game tonight. Annette went to a movie with the girls because I told her I was coming to your place to watch basketball, so I sat home by myself reading *your* family's journal. Bye."

The recorder beeped twice, and a second voice began to speak. "Matt, it's Mac. Call me. Any hour. I mean it, any hour. Call me."

Matt glanced over at the clock on the microwave. It read 12:20. He picked up the phone, dialed Tom McDougal's home number, and waited as the phone rang several times.

"Matt?"

"Yeah, Mac. Sorry to wake you. What's up?"

"I'm not sleeping. Jim Templeton was killed in a car accident this afternoon, down near Nephi."

"*What?* The leading mayoral candidate? You're kidding!"

"Not hardly. This puts a whole new complexion on things at work. The queen bee is gonna blow a gasket. She was counting on him getting elected mayor to keep things secure with the 'good old boy' crowd."

"What do you think will happen?"

"With only ten days 'til the elections, I think we'll have a female, Lutheran mayor, that's what I think. That'll put the cat amongst the pigeons. She's a totally unknown quantity. She could fire every one of us for all I know."

"I'm so sorry to hear about Templeton," Matt said.

"No loss there, trust me. I don't mean to sound callous, but politically he was worthless."

Matt ignored Mac's comment. "Well, thanks for calling me, Mac. I'll talk to you tomorrow."

"Right. Goodnight."

Matt went into the bedroom and began to undress, thoughts spinning of an unknown mayor coming into the city and what changes that would portend for management. Pat Harcourt had not spoken very highly of mayoral candidate Julia Wells on the few occasions they had talked about the upcoming elections and the candidates.

Just as he was drifting off to sleep, his thoughts turned again to Andy McBride—Mr. and Mrs. Andrew McBride, in their new Boston home in 1775, with the first shots at Lexington and Concord not weeks away. Not a promising outlook for a "happy ever after" ending for the new couple. But it made an exciting story and a good read. How strange it was to read a fictional account, a novel essentially, while knowing that the story was true and that one's own ancestors had played the major roles.

Matt knew he had to get the manuscript back from R. T. or he'd never get to read the rest of it himself. Tomorrow. That would be time enough. Everything in its time, Grandma Sterling always said. And perhaps it was time for the intriguing Kasia Somerset to show him another side of the English. A side that had not revealed itself to Grandfather McBride or Sterling, or whatever his name was.

Chapter Six

Two weeks later, on the morning following the elections, Matt arrived at City Hall just after seven-thirty. He took the stairs two at a time and proceeded down the hallway past the empty desks in the front reception area. City Manager Patricia Harcourt called out to Matt as he passed her door on the way to his office. He paused and stood in the doorway.

"Morning, Pat."

Her manner was brusque, and she spoke without looking up from her desk. "We're meeting at eight-thirty, Matt, with all department heads."

"Right. What's the subject?"

Pat stopped what she was doing and stared at him for a few seconds, shaking her head. "What's the *subject?* The *election*, of course. We're going to have to get our act together. Just be there and be ready to formulate a plan."

Matt nodded. "Right, eight-thirty."

He proceeded down to his office and laid his briefcase on his desk. The message light was flashing on his phone, and as he sat down, he picked up the receiver, dialing in his security code. The message was from Mac. "Call me. I'm in the office," was all it said, and Matt pressed the recall button, connecting straight to Mac's desk.

"This is Mac."

"Can't a guy get settled in before business begins?" Matt asked jokingly.

"Can you come over to Public Works?" Mac asked, his tone nearly as brusque as the city manager's.

"Sure. But we've both got to be back here at eight-thirty. Pat's called a staff meeting."

"I know. That's what I want to talk about, but in private."

"All right. I'll be there in about ten minutes."

Matt retrieved a few folders from his briefcase, placed them in their respective slots in his desk filing drawer, and then placed his briefcase down beside the credenza. He retraced his steps downstairs, crossed the parking lot, and entered the automotive bay attached to the Public Works building, located about two hundred yards from City Hall. Half a dozen cars were up on racks with mechanics underneath performing various tasks. Matt saw Mac standing near the parts window and walked slowly past the grease pits, exchanging a word or two with mechanics as he went. Mac spotted him and walked his way.

"Let's go out back."

"It's not summer you know," Matt quipped.

"You can take the cold. You're young. Besides" he said, gesturing with his eyes toward the mechanics, "little pigs have big ears."

They went out a door at the rear of the building and walked across the lot where the snow plowing equipment was parked.

"Well, you were right," Matt said.

"The election?"

"Yeah. Julia Wells, mayor of Snowy Ridge."

"Yep, and she's likely to melt the snow. We might just become known as *Flaming* Ridge."

They stopped next to the metal racks where the large salt-spreaders that fitted into the backs of the snow plows were hanging. "What do you mean?" Matt asked.

"I mean she intends to go right to work, to get her nose stuck into city hall."

"I thought you said you didn't know her, Mac."

"I don't, but Utah is a small place, and Snowy Ridge is even smaller. I know people, who know people, who know *her*. They've told me a bit about her plans and some of them have probably told other people, who told other people, who told the queen bee, too. That's why she's called a staff meeting this morning."

"I know I'm new to government and all, but a new mayor shouldn't change things all that much, should it? I mean the presidency turns over every four years in Washington, at least most of the time, and the federal government doesn't go into a tizzy."

Mac glanced over at Matt and smiled, shaking his head as they continued walking out beyond the Public Works yard and onto the footpath surrounding the baseball field. "Let me put my cards on the table, Matt. No foolin' this time; just listen to me for a few minutes."

Matt walked silently, aware that Mac, at least for the moment, was not displaying his usual easy-going, humorous manner.

"Things don't work here the way they do in most other cities. You know that eighty thousand I wanted for the cemetery? I've got it."

"I told Bellows to prepare an agenda item for the Council. I didn't see anything in the agenda packet."

"Nope. The Friday you were gone, you know, right after you got back from New York, Queenie added it to a long list of rubber stamp items on the work agenda—"

"They can't approve things at a work session."

"They did. Bellows simply called Harcourt the day after he spoke with you and she approved the transfer. Came from...well, I don't know where he got it, and I don't care. With that transfer I can do my job like I'm supposed to."

"Those things require open session Council action."

"Not here. Look, Matt, I've been in the Snowy Ridge Public Works Department for nineteen years, starting as a truck driver. Before that, I worked for the State of Utah. Snowy ran about like other cities in the valley as far as I knew, at least for the first ten years I was here. Then, I was promoted to Section Leader, and I began to see the contracting procedure up close. Like *real* close. As I learned who was who in Snowy Ridge, I came to understand that city hall was essentially being run by three families and their offshoots—sons-in-law, etc. The same names kept reappearing on all our construction contracts. None of the other established contractors from the valley—and we've got dozens if not more, Matt—none of them ever won the contracts. If you've had the chance to notice during the past two years, you'll see that we seldom get more than three or four bids for any public works contract. The other guys just don't bother any more."

"So you're saying it's a closed shop."

"You catch on fast."

"They must have underbid the others," Matt said as he pulled his collar up around his neck against the crisp winter's wind.

Mac smiled again. "I'm sure they did. Do you know what a 'change order' is, with respect to a construction project, I mean?"

"Sure, it's a modification to the original contract, usually dealing with a price adjustment relative to an unexpected circumstance or change in the conditions to the job."

Mac laughed aloud. "Spoken like a true BYU lawyer. Would a 'changed circumstance' include, *Hey, I ain't makin' enough money on this job?*"

"Not legally," Matt laughed, suddenly aware of the legal sounding description he had given."

"Let me put it to you straight, Matt. I've been straight with you so far, haven't I? I mean in the two years we've known each other?"

"Absolutely, Mac. If Mac says it, you can take it to the bank, as you so often remind me."

"Good. Do you remember the Fontana Subdivision project a couple of years ago? Just about the time you got here I think?"

Matt thought for a few moments as they continued walking. "Yeah, I think I signed off on those contracts the first or second week on the job as assistant city attorney."

Mac looked at Matt and paused for a moment. "Okay. That was a project to construct roads and install sewer and water lines and underground electrical connections in the new industrial park up on Crenshaw Heights. It was all in support of the deal with Connectics Industries to build their new manufacturing facility here."

"That's right. It was about a two point four million dollar project as I recall."

Mac chuckled. "It got closer to *four* million by the time they got through playing with it. Do you remember the flap about the contractor having to rush the job because of other commitments?"

"I do, now that you mention it. Something about him having a contract with the federal government, on-time bonuses or some such."

"Right again. A-plus for Mr. Sterling. The contractor also had an eight-million-dollar federal contract on the dam site up beyond Thrusher Canyon. If they finished before a set date they would get a four-hundred-fifty-thousand-dollar bonus from the feds. When they accepted Snowy Ridge's job in Crenshaw Heights, they acted like they didn't really want the job because they were too busy. They wanted the city to guarantee that federal bonus in case our job prevented them from completing the dam project on time."

"I see. I don't recall that, but I understand what you mean. A guarantee clause since we had a claim on their services and the Crenshaw job might delay them."

"Exactly. Now here's where it gets sticky. We *paid* them that bonus. The job contract price of two point four million, *plus* a few hundred thousand in *change orders, plus* the bonus of nearly another half million."

"So they lost the federal on-time bonus?"

Mac came to a halt and stood looking at Matt for several long moments, staring directly into his eyes. "No. They got *both.*"

"Both what?" Matt asked.

Mac just continued to stare at the younger man, nodding as he could see the light dawning in Matt's eyes.

"You're kidding," Matt said. "Why in the world…how could they get *both?*"

"Because we *guaranteed* to pay their federal bonus."

"You mean we guaranteed to pay it *if* they lost it because of work they did for us that put them past the federal due date."

"No. I mean we guaranteed their bonus, and they met the federal deadline, too. They got *both*, Matt, four hundred fifty thousand from the feds and four hundred fifty thousand from the grateful citizens of Snowy Ridge, and that's the dead straight truth."

"Why didn't we guarantee it only if they *lost* the federal bonus because of our time delays? Who approved that deal?"

Mac turned and started walking back toward the public works building. "From what you just said, it might well have been *you.*"

"*Me?*"

"You were the assistant city attorney."

"Yeah, but—"

"No buts allowed. You may not have known a thing about it, and it may have been on your desk before you even were hired and a done deal even before that, but if your memory is correct, *you* signed off on the legal aspects of the contract."

They walked together in silence for a couple of hundred yards. Before they entered the vehicle yard, Mac stopped again and took his young friend by the shoulders. "I didn't tell you that story to worry you, Matt. In fact I had no idea you had signed off on that contract. I assumed it was before your time. But I *did* want you to know the type of inside deal that's been going down in Happy Valley within my recent memory. And that's only one of the shady deals I've watched over the years. Do you recall this particular contractor's name?"

"No."

"Doesn't matter. Harcourt's sister has a married daughter. The daughter's husband is family—and a general contractor. Get the picture?"

Matt nodded as they walked. "I'm beginning to."

"They run a tight ship, Matt, keeping everyone they can't trust out of the loop. And management from outside the family is not generally acceptable, certainly not at the decision-making level. Now we have a mayor who intends to turn on the lights of public scrutiny. It won't be a pretty sight."

"*I'm* an outsider," Matt said.

Mac nodded. "I don't mean to burst your bubble, Matt, but Queenie didn't want you either and nothing crosses your desk they don't want you to see. I'm not saying that every politician in this town is crooked, but the power brokers are well entrenched. Mayor Tomlin, bless his heart, is one of the good guys, but he's a dithering old fool. He did the PR thing—Rotary speeches and all that. He left everything substantial, including the budget issues, for the queen bee to handle. She managed the money and he just signed off on the process.

Now, come January, his term as mayor is over. One good thing he did is that he kind of forced the queen bee to take you on as acting assistant city manager, just temporarily, he told her. It sort of became permanent, didn't it? You were appointed as the acting assistant city manager at first, weren't you?"

"I was," Matt responded, stopping at the entrance to the back door of the building. "I was hired as deputy city attorney, Jim Randolph left a couple of months later for that job in Idaho, and I was appointed city attorney. Then the acting job as ACM.

"So, what are we going to do about this, Mac?"

"*We?*"

Matt grinned. "Oh, I see. I've become a one-man band."

"Now you've got it," Mac laughed.

"And how do you think Harcourt's going to handle it?"

"Bricks and mortar," Mac said.

Matt looked puzzled for a moment.

"She's building the wall right now. We'll hear all about it at staff meeting in…" he looked at his watch, "twenty minutes."

"And how about you, Mac? Since you're not on the *inside*, how did you get appointed Public Works director?"

"I've got friends, too, and *that*, my young friend, is a long story for another day."

* * * * *

By eight twenty-five, the special session of the executive staff was convened and eight people, five men and three women, were seated around the table. City Manager Pat Harcourt had yet to arrive. The mood was somber, absent the banter that generally preceded executive staff meetings.

Doug Bellows, finance director, sat immediately to the left of the head of the table, facing the door. On his left was

Hermann Trenkle, police chief. Next sat Sarah Beckenham, city attorney and the newest member of the staff, personally hired by Pat Harcourt only six months earlier. Tom McDougal, the Public Works director and Matt's closest confidant was next. At the far end sat Linda Holmes, director of human resources and the only executive staff member who came up through the ranks, having worked her way up from payroll clerk. She'd been with the city five years less than Mac.

Working up the near side of the table sat Henry Fielding, director of planning and development, Sally Andersen, city clerk, and then Matt Sterling, assistant city manager. At the head of the table was the city manager's chair, presently empty as the group sat quietly around the table. At eight twenty-eight, Harcourt walked briskly into the room, closed the door behind her, and assumed her seat. Everyone remained quiet.

Patricia Harcourt had been city manager of Snowy Ridge for nine years. An avid mountain biker, at forty-eight she was fit and maintained a trim figure. She used little makeup and normally wore her light brown hair long. Today it was pulled back into a tight bun. The first time he was summoned to a meeting with her and the previous city attorney, Matt had noticed that Harcourt seldom looked directly at the person she was addressing, constantly shifting her eyes, taking in first one person or object, then another. This morning was no different. Without extending her normal friendly greeting to those around the table, she focused on the clock at the far end of the room and began.

"Thank you all for coming," Harcourt said. "This won't take long. You are all aware of the results of the elections yesterday and no doubt will have the same concerns I do. Snowy Ridge has always maintained an excellent working relationship between council and staff and despite the, uh, the confusion that exists in the public's mind at present, I intend to do my best to assure that our cooperative working relationship continues. Sally, have you certified the elections results?" she said to the city clerk.

The young woman jumped perceptibly at the question.

"Well, uh, I have to, uh, the state forms still have to be completed, but yes, the results are official as of …" she paused, glancing at the large clock on the far wall, "uh, they will be by ten o'clock this morning, Pat."

"Right. Then here's what I want done. We have just under eight weeks until the newly elected people take office. We have to make the most of that time. Sarah," she said to the city attorney, "I want a complete review of the City Charter and the legislated duties and responsibilities of the mayor and the city manager's office. Summarize the respective duties of each office and have a report to me by," Harcourt paused, glancing down at her calendar, "the twentieth. Doug, review every budget transfer or financial transaction that requires Council approval and prepare a report on any discrepancies over the past six months—no, make that a year—that might require retroactive Council action prior to the end of their term."

"Right, Pat. I've already started."

"Good. For the rest of you, I want a concerted effort to put our house in order. The Council-Manager form of government demands a strict separation of duties between policy and administration and I don't intend to abdicate my duties to anyone who doesn't fully understand the system. We can't afford to surrender control of our responsibilities or I can assure you, we'll not be of service to our community and we'll be held accountable in the end. Are there any questions?"

Everyone remained silent for several moments and then Matt spoke. "Pat, would you like me to arrange a transition packet of information for the mayor and the two new Council members? Sort of a 'bring them up to speed' assortment of current projects?"

"No. They're not in office until January. And that reminds me. I want no information, and I mean *no* information, to leave City Hall without my stamp of approval. Any request that any of you receive from the press, the Council, and that means the new Council people too, will be forwarded to my office for response. Is that clear to everyone?"

"Pat, all I thought was—"

"I said no, Matt. I'll personally prepare all information for release. If there are no further questions, that's all I have. We'll meet at the regular time on Wednesday at ten. Doug, I'd like to see you in my office."

Pat Harcourt stood immediately and without another word, strode from the room. Matt exchanged a brief look with Mac, who raised his eyebrows and gave the hint of a smile, and then all staff slowly rose, retrieved their folders, Palm Pilots, and cell phones and left the room without much conversation.

"Bricks and mortar, my friend, bricks and mortar," Mac said quietly as he slid past Matt out into the hallway.

* * * * *

As soon as Pat Harcourt closed her office door, Doug Bellows took a seat in front of her desk, steepled his fingers in front of his face and began shaking his head. "I told you six months ago he'd be trouble. He's not a team player."

"He's not *on* the team. I know what I'm doing," Pat Harcourt said.

"I hope so. If he starts digging—"

"Just get those retroactive council actions in order. I'll handle the rest. We've still got four of seven votes on the council."

"And the LGR fund?"

Harcourt paused for a few moments and glanced out of her office window. "The Local Government Retirement fund is running smoothly, Doug. You've said that yourself. It's been running well for nearly five years. If we change it, *that* would be more visible and raise more questions than business as usual."

"I don't like it, Pat," Bellows replied. "Sterling may not be *on* the team, but he's pretty close to the information."

"I said I'd handle Matt Sterling, and I will. You just hold up your end. If Julia Wells or Matt get too close they'll wish they hadn't."

"I hope so, Pat. It's been pretty sweet for a long time. This is not the time to—"

Harcourt leaned forward, her arms stretched out on the desk. "I said I'd handle it. Now get on with it."

* * * * *

Two doors down the hall, Matt sat in his office thinking about Mac's comments and Harcourt's attitude change. Rummaging through his file cabinet, he found the file for the completed construction contracts taking particular care to review the Crenshaw and Fortuna Project files Mac had referred to earlier. He *had* signed the contract, but there was a trail of Post-it notes stuck inside the folder, including one from Harcourt approving the contract terms. He spent the rest of the day reviewing old files, searching for some kind of pattern or support for Mac's increasingly believable accusations. Finally, bleary eyed and tired, Matt placed the entire folder in his briefcase and took it home.

* * * * *

The invitation two days earlier had come as a complete surprise. As Matt parked the car and proceeded up the walkway to the beautiful home overlooking Provo Canyon, he remembered the first time the Weatherlys had invited him to dinner, sometime during his second year of law school. Following his graduation he'd departed almost immediately for his mission and after his return he'd only had one meeting with the professor, and that had been when he'd flown back from Sacramento to interview for the assistant city attorney's position with Snowy Ridge. Atop the steps, he rang the doorbell and was greeted with a chiming sound he recognized as the main theme of *Rule Britannia*. Matt was still smiling and shaking his head when Dr. Sarah Weatherly opened the door.

"It *is* a bit pretentious, isn't it, Matt," she smiled brightly. "But Trevor says he has to maintain his allegiance to the Crown…or some such rot."

Matt stepped inside and the older woman stood on her tiptoes and gave him a quick kiss on the cheek.

"It's so nice of you to come. How long has it been?"

"Too long, Dr. Weatherly."

"Oh, Sarah it is, or there shan't be any pudding. You haven't forgotten your British, I should hope. That would be dessert to you Yanks."

"For one of your puddings, I can go with Sarah," Matt responded.

They walked toward the great room where Professor Weatherly was just adding a couple of sturdy logs to the fireplace."

"Ah, Matt, my lad. How nice to see you. Are you and Kasia engaged yet?"

"That will be quite enough, Trevor," Sarah said, a slight edge to her voice. "Would you be a dear and fetch the drinks for us while I catch up with our long-overdue guest?"

"Yes, m'dear," Weatherly replied, winking at Matt. "If you think *I* was too direct, you're for it now, lad."

"Go about your duties, dear, and see how well the steaks are marinating, that's a good boy...and don't forget about our other guest," Sarah said, gesturing for Matt to take a seat in front of the fire.

"Now then, Matt, tell me all about your life since we last spent time together."

"That's a tall order," Matt laughed. "Where to begin..."

Fifteen minutes later, Matt had reached the end of his abbreviated tale. Professor Weatherly had delivered two raspberry fizzes, departed, and had not yet returned.

"What a wonderful woman your grandmother must have been. We should all be so fortunate as to have such a gracious spirit."

"I must admit, Doc—Sarah, I've always seen her as a role model. Now...well, she seems an *exceptional* role model."

"And your current life?" Sarah asked, her eyes twinkling.

"Ups and downs."

"How true, my dear, how true. I'd like to tell you a little story if I might be so bold. Please stop me if I'm stepping over proper boundaries, Matt, but I hope you'll understand. Kasia Somerset has made an appearance in your life, as I understand it."

"Indeed," Matt smiled. "That's the 'up,' I mentioned."

"I can understand that," Sarah said, returning the smile. "A wonderful girl. But a tad wounded," she added, pursing her lips and nodding slowly.

"Wounded?"

"I'm afraid so. Not so one would notice, mind you. She carries her inherent British reserve behind a façade of Yankee bravado, I should think, but beneath the surface her injuries are quite real, I'm afraid. That's why I asked Trevor to invite you over this evening. Actually, Kasia will be joining us. We told her a slightly later dinner time so you and I would have a few moments to talk. A bit of subterfuge that my darling husband finds so indispensable to his life's journey," she said, chuckling just a bit. "Not meaning to be indecorous, but might I delve into a rather personal matter, Matt? One that you and I have discussed previously. A matter that perhaps has left something of a scar on your own emotions."

"Carole?"

Sarah nodded, a sweet, motherly smile accompanying. "Has it become easier for you over the past few years?"

Matt was silent for several moments. "When I was quite young, my mother explained to me that we are never really alone in our sorrows and I'm not referring specifically to spiritual guidance. She made it clear there are always others with much more difficult problems, life-threatening at times, and we shouldn't dwell on our personal disappointments. Your letters, Sarah, when Carole and I broke it off and I first entered the mission field, were a great strength to me and I've never thanked you properly for that support."

"Rubbish, my dear boy. I just couldn't bear to think of you moping about. You made the right choice. Frankly, Matt, Carole was a fine young woman, but when she refused to wait for you when you opted to serve a mission so late in your youth… well, sacrifices are a part of life, aren't they?"

"To be fair to Carole, Dr. Weatherly, she did wait through my last two years of law school and then when I decided to add two more by serving a mission, well…"

Sarah nodded again. "I understand. It was a lot to ask of a vibrant young woman. But have you recovered, my boy, emotionally I mean?"

"I think so. Kasia is helping, without knowing of course," he smiled. "She's the first woman I've dated more than three times this past two years."

Sarah Weatherly sat looking into the fire while Matt waited patiently. "Matt, I've gone beyond propriety perhaps, and I hope you're not deeply offended, but I've explained your situation with Carole to Kasia."

Matt sat silent, staring at his hostess, trying to mask his distress. "Dr. Weatherly, I'm certain that you have a good reason for your decision, but I'm not certain that my relationship with Kasia—"

"Please, let me explain. I said that the dear girl was wounded and I did not exaggerate. When Kasia first arrived at BYU, just over two years ago, we greeted her and took her into our home as a favor to Trevor's college roommate, Graeme Somerset, who is Kasia's father. They were roommates at Oxford some forty years ago and Graeme has for many years been a successful London barrister, well known in international circles. When Kasia arrived on campus, Trevor was serving as Bishop of the BYU Thirtieth Ward and my darling husband introduced her to Phillip Tremonton."

"BYU's basketball sensation last year?"

"The same. Despite the fact that Kasia was a bit hesitant because he was nearly three years younger than she, they became an instant couple and Kasia was besotted with the chap. Head over heels, as you Americans say."

"I see. That explains why she knows so much about basketball. She hasn't mentioned anything about him."

"That's part of why I felt it imperative to speak with you. She's kept it bottled up. They spoke of marriage as he neared graduation last year and she encouraged him to consider a mission. Then the professional offers began to appear from the NBA. The short version, Matt, is nearly the opposite of yours. Carole refused to wait while you completed a mission…understandable, perhaps, since you were already twenty-four and most returned missionaries were already married with kids…but you went anyway and lost the woman you loved.

"Kasia encouraged Phillip to go on a mission but he was drafted in the first round and opted to sign a professional contract with the Chicago Bulls. Now Kasia didn't blame him or hold that against him. She understood that such opportunities only come along once in a lifetime and there are many ways to serve Heavenly Father. But Phillip immediately moved to Chicago and was quickly caught up in the high life. Within two months he had met…and married…a top fashion model. Kasia heard about it on the evening news and was devastated. Phillip never even called her. She's not spoken to him since and hasn't dated anyone seriously, that is until you came along. And that's why I'm worried."

Matt turned toward the fire and sat silent for long moments, his thoughts rapidly running through the final scene with Carole as she had called him foolish for wanting to serve a mission so late in life. She'd argued that many church leaders had never served a mission and many men went straight into their professions without the need to peddle a bicycle around Europe for two years, and they remained good Church members. He had not been able to get her to understand his need to fulfill this particular experience in a young man's church education.

Finally, Matt turned back to face Sarah Weatherly. "I've seen Kasia five or six times, Dr. Weatherly. She's a remarkable woman, clearly intelligent, and at least to my eyes," he smiled, "exceptionally beautiful. But we've made no commitments."

"A blind man could see, and even *sense*, her beauty, Matt," Dr. Weatherly replied. "Do you care for her?"

"I don't know. I'm a bit confused."

"Precisely," Sarah said, glancing at her watch. "And so is Kasia. Are you ready for someone in your life, Matt? Are you ready for Kasia Somerset?"

"I don't know, Dr. Weatherly. I truly don't. I *want* someone, and Kasia is everything I've always thought a woman should be. It's certainly time for me to find someone...as your husband is always telling me," he smiled. "But I *can* tell you one thing for certain, and you have my word on it."

"Yes?"

"I'll treat her heart as carefully as if it were my own."

Sarah Weatherly leaned back in her chair and nodded, glancing again at her watch. "Thank you, Matt. That's good enough for me."

The sound of a car door closing broke the mood. Almost immediately, the front door opened and Professor Weatherly entered, Kasia directly behind him.

The professor spoke as he came down into the lounge. "Look who I found standing in front of the stadium with a poster board that said, *'Will work for food.'* Do you think we have enough for another destitute person at this dinner party?"

Matt stood and walked over to Kasia, kissing her gently on the cheek and whispering in her ear. "It's good to see you."

"I didn't know about this," she said, removing her coat.

"Neither did I. But I'm very grateful to the Weatherlys, and I'm very pleased to see you again."

Kasia smiled brightly and took Matt's arm, stepping down into the lounge where Sarah was standing in front of the fire. Kasia stepped around the chairs and hugged the older woman. "Is this yours or Trevor's idea?" she whispered as she held her close.

"Occasionally, my dear, the professor and I are in total agreement," the older woman replied, squeezing Kasia tightly.

* * * * *

Professor Weatherly put up only token resistance when Matt offered to drive Kasia home. Dr. Weatherly hugged them both and watched as they walked down the footpath and entered Matt's car, backing slowly out of the drive and disappearing over the crest of the hill into the crisp winter evening.

"Well, my dear," the professor said as he closed the front door, "upon my word, *that* is a young couple who will spend eternity together."

Dr. Sarah Weatherly smiled, reaching up to kiss her husband softly and ruffle his shock of white hair. "Fortunately, my dearest Trevor, that decision is not yours to make. Be content, my darling, that *I* will spend eternity with *you*."

Matt drove slowly up University Avenue with both occupants restraining conversation for several blocks. Passing the stadium, Matt began to chuckle.

"What?" Kasia asked.

"A sign that read 'Work for *food*?'"

Kasia's grin was infectious and they both began to laugh. After several blocks, Kasia regained her composure. "We all work for food in one way or another."

"I guess if you put it that way, we do indeed. So, Ms. Somerset, it's Friday night, and just a little after ten. What else do you want to do?"

"Would you mind terribly if I asked you to take me home?"

Matt glanced at her, a look of concern on his face. "Of course not. Are you feeling okay?"

"No, I'm fine. We could take in a late movie or follow our hot chocolate and Arabian Nights routine," she suggested, "but I'd very much appreciate the opportunity to just sit in front of the fire, hold hands, and talk with you, if that's all right. Sarah's obviously plied her motherly trade this evening, all well-meaning of course, but I'd like to tell you *my* version of things."

Matt nodded. "She means well."

"Of course she does. I understand that and I love her dearly."

Matt changed lanes slowly and pulled to the side of the road, entering the driveway of a Mobile service station, turning around in the entrance and stopping the car. He leaned over toward Kasia, cupping her chin in his hand and, leaning in further, gently kissed her lips. He then leaned back and smiled at her, waiting for her reaction to their first kiss.

"I said *'hold hands,'*" she said, a lovely smile crossing her face.

"And we'll do exactly that. The fire at my place comes on with a flick of the switch and there's a great view of the lights of Snowy Ridge with the moon reflecting off the mountains. Just think of the setting: soft music, hand holding, and…"

"*And?*"

He leaned toward her again. This time Kasia slipped her hand behind his neck and pulled him closer, responding to his kiss, her lips warm and her touch tender. A car horn suddenly blasted three quick times behind them as someone tried to depart the service station. As they parted, in the glow of the fluorescent lighting Matt could see the blush rise past Kasia's neck to her cheeks. His broad smile made her flush all the more brilliant.

She exhaled forcefully. "We're in a petrol station you know, for all the world to see us."

"A display of British reserve?" Matt laughed.

"It has its place," she said, sliding down in her seat so her head was below the head restraint.

"Indeed it does," he said, checking traffic and pulling out into the lane, turning left toward Snowy Ridge.

"Matt," Kasia said several blocks later.

"Yes?"

"I hope Sarah didn't…I mean…she probably said too much—"

Matt glanced over at her and reached for her cheek, stroking it softly. "She didn't. She's a wonderful woman and has come to love you very much I think."

"I know, and she thinks you're a bit of all right, too, Mr. Sterling."

"Well then I guess the rest is up to us, isn't it?"

"Umm."

* * * * *

The moon was absent, hidden behind thick cloud cover and a low fog bank obscured the lights of Snowy Ridge, but the couple didn't notice as Matt tripped the switch and the glass-enclosed fireplace instantly roared to life. He took Kasia's coat, hung it in the hall closet, and stepped into the kitchen. Her first time in Matt's condo, Kasia wandered through the lounge area observing the pictures that covered nearly one whole wall.

"Are these your sisters?" she called out.

"Yeah. Most of those pictures are family. Some are from England with my companions."

Kasia slowly made her way down the gallery, stopping occasionally to take a better look at one or another.

"So it's 'Uncle Matt,' is it?"

"Five times over," he said as he reentered the room with two cups of hot apple cider. "Emily has three girls and Rachel has one of each. Alison is the oldest, just baptized in fact, and little Matt—"

"Matt?"

He nodded, handing her a cup and standing beside her in front of the picture of Rachel's family. "Rachel and I were closest in age as we grew up. I was close to Emily too, but she hasn't had any boys," he laughed. "As the oldest, she always had the joys of watching Rachel and me and we didn't make it easy."

"What younger siblings do?" Kasia said, shaking her head. "And their husbands?"

"Over here," Matt said as he stepped toward the hallway, "is the most recent family shot, taken last Fourth of July. My father, Richard, and my mother, Sally, and the family matriarch, my grandmother, Elizabeth Sterling, at ninety-six years young. She was visiting us from New York."

"She looks about sixty-five or no more than seventy," Kasia exclaimed.

"And acted fifty," he said, pausing and staring quietly at the picture. "She died peacefully about five weeks later in her home in New York. She woke up not feeling well, went to her doctor for a checkup, and he put her in the hospital that very morning. She was gone by seven that evening. All very peaceful. It was not quite three months ago."

Kasia slipped her arm in Matt's. "I'm sorry, Matt. She was a beautiful woman."

"In many ways," he said. "And this tall dude is my brother-in-law, Albert, Emily's husband, and their kids, Alison, Sally, and Jennifer. Albert is a dentist."

"I think every third Mormon male is a dentist," Kasia laughed.

"Yep, and every third Mormon dentist is a stake president or a Bishop, right?"

They both chuckled at the thought for several moments. "Jon is Rachel's husband. Together with his brother, they've built a very successful home construction company in the foothills east of Sacramento. He's holding little Rachel and she's got baby Matt. Two of the kids were born while I was in England, and Matt came along just last February. Ten months old now. And that's the family."

"Except for this lonely guy standing in the back, next to his father."

"Well, you already know him and he's not lonely tonight," he said, putting his arm around her and guiding her toward the leather couch in front of the fireplace. She sat and Matt sat beside her, picking up a small remote unit and turning on the CD player.

"Any preferences?" he asked. Music instantly filled the room from the four corners.

"That's nice," she said, hearing the first strains of Irish folk music.

"Ireland it is then," he said, replacing the remote.

They sat quietly for several minutes, sipping the hot cider. Kasia then placed her cup on the side table, removed her shoes, and tucked her feet up under her on the couch, leaned her head back against the couch and closed her eyes momentarily. The lilting strains of a high, Irish tenor softly surrounded them with the mournful lyrics from yet another poignant story of lost dreams. They listened quietly for some moments as the lyrics told the tale of a young man who had left Ireland for London and become dissatisfied with his lot in life, longing to go home again. *"And for all that I found there I might as well be, / Where the Mountains of Mourne sweep down to the sea."*

"Irish music has always seemed so…so melancholy," Kasia said softly.

Matt nodded his agreement. "I've often heard my dad say that an Irishman is the only person who can be lonely in a crowd," Matt said.

"I've never heard that," Kasia said, smiling. "This song would make you believe it. Do you feel Irish?"

"Only in a genealogical sense. We've been in America a long time. Seven generations and over two hundred and thirty years."

They remained silent again through *The Rose of Tralee* and *My Love is Like a Red, Red Rose*. Matt was softly stroking Kasia's hair and as the heart-rending beauty of *Danny Boy* began to play on their senses, she leaned into him, drawing her feet beneath her, laying her head on his shoulder. When the song finished, Matt broke the silence, his voice soft, almost a whisper.

"I met Carole when I was a first-year law student and she was a junior, majoring in elementary education." He paused and in a moment, Kasia shifted her position, reached her hand behind his neck, and pulled him to her, kissing him gently and then nuzzling her head into his chest.

Without lifting her face, she spoke, also very softly.

"You loved Carole and I…I loved Phillip. They're gone now and I truly hope they're happy. That's all behind us now. I don't think we need to rehash what will someday be ancient history."

Matt lifted her face from his chest and smiled down at her. "Okay, Kasia Somerset, genetic microbiologist, guardian of the molecular labyrinth, and distinguished visitor from the Motherland."

"Thanks for understanding," she said, replacing her head on his chest as *Mother Machree* came from the speakers tucked into the ceiling corners of the room.

Several CDs later, her hair in complete disarray from Matt's finger twirling, the molecular genealogy program fully explained, and the relative merits of cricket and baseball discarded, Kasia finally sat up and ran her own fingers through her hair, trying to restore a semblance of order from the knots Matt had created.

"Maybe I could bring a wig on our dates and you could tie *it* in knots."

"Not a chance," he said. "I love your hair."

Kasia stood up and walked to the hallway, glancing in a hanging mirror. "Oh, my gosh. I don't know if my hair can survive such adoration," she said, quickly grabbing a brush from her purse and tugging at the twisted strands.

Matt came to stand behind her at the mirror, his hands on both shoulders. "Looks fine to me, lady. I can understand why you choose genetics as your field."

"How do you mean?" she said, continuing to brush.

"Well, *your* genes came together quite nicely…including the hair."

"That's all *you* know," she said, brushing quickly and glancing at her wristwatch. "Oh my goodness, it's nearly one o'clock," she said."

"Shall I take you home?"

"Please, it is getting…actually, it's already gotten quite late, and I've got a few Saturday morning chores."

"I'll get your coat, but first I have a favor to ask."

Kasia turned, placed her hands on his chest, and looked up at him. "Yes?"

"I'd like to ask you to consider taking a few days off around the Thanksgiving holidays—in about two weeks—and come out to Sacramento with me for a family gathering. Emily and Rachel will be there with their families and my Mom and Dad."

Kasia looked at him in surprise, her face growing warm with pleasure. "Oh! I—I wasn't expecting—you're sure I wouldn't be intruding?"

"My mom would love it. The whole family would."

"Well, I would love to meet them. I accept. Will we drive or fly?"

"Probably fly, just to have a few more days there. Dad has an extra car we can use."

"Great! I haven't been to California yet."

"Good, then we'll throw in a day in San Francisco as well. It's a beautiful city."

"So I've heard. Sounds awesome."

"I'll get the tickets in the morning and let you know the details at dinner tomorrow."

"Dinner?"

"Dinner," he said, quickly placing a kiss on her cheek."

"All right, Mr. Sterling, but this time on *my* terms. I'm cooking."

"That's a deal."

They left the condo and again entered Matt's car, the brisk cold a stark contrast to the warmth of the room. Kasia snuggled beneath the hood of her parka and wrapped the seat belt around her. On the drive through Snowy Ridge, the car heater returned some warmth to the interior and finally Kasia spoke up.

"We haven't said a word all night about your grandfather's journal. Tell me what's happening to Andy McBride?" she asked.

"Well, he's a character all right. He—"

"Oh, I'm so sorry, Matt, I forgot to tell you earlier. I ran those blood tests. The bloodstains on General Clinton's arrest warrant are positively from one of your paternal ancestors. They match your DNA patterns. You are full-blooded, as they say, and you have an official blood-stained document to prove it."

He laughed. "Well, thank you, but it only proves my family was criminal...from the British perspective. Does this mean I should be a McBride instead of a Sterling?"

"So it would seem. So, what's up with Andy now?"

"As I said, he's an intriguing character. America has gone to war. The shot heard round the world has been fired at Lexington."

By the smallest of circumstance our lives irrevocably change, never again to follow the path of original intent. Surely someone beyond our grasp hath power to pilot the course of life!
Journal of Andrew McBride

Chapter Seven

Righteous scrambled through the coarse undergrowth, trying desperately to avoid further contact with the carnage he had witnessed along the roadside between Lexington and Menotomy. British soldiers lay along the country road in utter confusion and panic as shots rang out from surrounding hillsides, gullies and small clusters of trees, each seemingly alive with hundreds of gathering colonial militia. Even as he ran, the reverberation of musket fire continued to ring in his ears and the smell of gunpowder remained fresh in his nostrils.

Earlier in the morning, his wagon loaded to the brim with casks of sugar, tea, Jamaican rum, and British yard goods, Righteous had made his way north and west from the docks in Boston, headed for his weekly rounds to the smaller communities surrounding the city. He'd seen the British troops marching toward the villages of Lexington and Concord, but hadn't been frightened by the sight. Redcoats had been garrisoned throughout Boston for a long time and unrest was common.

Unloading his goods in Concord and restocking with casks of maple syrup and spring sugar beets for the markets of Boston, he was preparing to leave when a single rider came galloping into the village square shouting that the British were shooting at farmers on the green in Lexington. Panic ensued and soon Righteous was alone in the Concord square as men scattered everywhere to spread the alarm.

He'd mounted the wagon, urged the horses forward, and began the trek back to Lexington, retracing the ground he'd covered earlier that morning, increasingly fearful of what lay ahead. When he spotted the advance British scouts headed toward Concord, he'd pulled the wagon off the road and into the forest, allowing the British to pass. He then resumed his journey to Boston, back through Lexington.

Some two years earlier, following his departure from the *Canterbury*, Righteous had rummaged around the countryside for several months, taking odd jobs and trying to establish a new life for himself. Eventually, the new colonist found steady employment foraging for an ironmonger and assisting in the construction of freight wagons.

A chance meeting on the docks with Andy McBride changed everyone. Recognizing the black man, Andy had approached him, acknowledging the young African's contribution to Andy's ability to remain alive on board the ship. By then in receipt of his inheritance, Andy offered to assist Righteous with employment and the freight business ensued, complete with a fourteen-foot wagon and four sturdy draft animals.

They had been partners for over two years and, while Andy opened a law office, Righteous plied his trade as a freight merchant, the business growing until he obtained, once again with Andy's help, firm contracts with several shipping firms to haul their goods from the docks inland to the communities surrounding Boston.

Entering Lexington, the centre of the town was a bustle of activity. Men remained on the village green and local residents were still proffering aid to those wounded in the earlier skirmish. He drove the horses and wagon slowly through town until someone called to him for assistance.

"What done happen' here?" Righteous asked the man as he dismounted to help.

"Redcoats. Lend a hand here with this man. We'll put him in the back of your wagon and take him to Mrs. Butler's cabin."

Righteous remained in Lexington, helping with the moving of the wounded, gunpowder and supplies until early afternoon when someone rode into the square yelling that the British were returning from Concord and there had been more shooting. One of the militia officers assembled his men and gave terse commands that they were to move to the hills and forest surrounding the road to Menotomy and wait for further orders.

Righteous retrieved his goods from the side of the road where he had quickly unloaded them, reloaded them in the wagon and began to exit the village square. Almost unseen, four British horsemen arrived to block his path, finding the village square empty and no one in sight but the black freighter.

"Where have they gone?" the officer queried of Righteous.

"Dunno, sir. I ain't seen nobody."

The officer stood in his stirrups, surveyed the terrain surrounding the square, and glanced back down the road he had traveled. The first signs of a British column of infantry were beginning to appear from the Concord road, west of Lexington.

The officer settled back in his saddle. "Here there, Sergeant. Have this man unload those goods and take his wagon back toward the troop for the wounded."

"Yes, sir," the dragoon replied, dismounting his horse. "You heard the captain. Unload the wagon!" he said to Righteous.

"I got's to get this load to Boston."

"Do as you're told, darkie, 'fore I have to shoot you too."

In ten minutes, with the help of two other soldiers, the wagon was once again unloaded. The advance party of the British troop had by then reached the green and the officer in charge rode forward on a large, bay gelding. He pulled up beside the captain who saluted and addressed the senior man.

"Sir, I've commandeered this wagon for the wounded. I've seen no further sign of the farmers."

"Good. Take your scouts out again and query the road ahead. We'll follow along directly. This man," he said, pointing to Righteous, "can drive the wagon with our wounded." He turned in his saddle and called out a command to bring the wounded forward. A half-dozen men were loaded into the wagon and the entire troop began to march through the village toward the east end of Lexington. Within a mile of the edge of town, shots rang out from the hillside and the British troops tried to rally to return fire, but as soon as the militia firing commenced, it stopped, and there were no targets to be had.

"Move on," the major commanded. "Corporal, get up on that wagon with the darkie and make haste."

Over the next rise, another volley of shots pelted the troop and several more British soldiers fell by the side of the road. The wounded as well as the dead were loaded into the wagon and the near panic-stricken Redcoats continued their slow march down the increasingly dangerous road. For the next four hours, 'til nearly dusk, it was a series of halts and starts, the wagon piling high with injured British soldiers. Eventually,

Righteous was told to dismount and several injured soldiers climbed into the driver's bench. In twenty minutes, the British contingent had passed and Righteous was left alone on the side of the road, a slight wound in his side from the creasing shot of a militiaman's rifle.

The purple hue of dawn creeping over the harbor found Righteous huddled on the front porch at Andy's home in Boston when Laura McBride rose to light the lamps. Opening the front door and shaking out her floor mat, she spotted him, startled by his ragged appearance.

"Why, Righteous, what in the world—"

Righteous struggled to regain his feet. "Andy be home, missus?" he gasped.

"Yes, yes, he is. Just a moment. I'll get him."

Andy appeared in the doorway, not fully dressed. Righteous just stood there, staring down at the ground and holding his side. He looked up at Andy.

"I think we's gone to war, Andy. And they's took my wagon and horses."

"Come in, Righteous, quick. We heard about it yesterday evening from the gallopers. Come in and have some food and we'll tend to that wound."

Chapter Eight

Some six years earlier, at the relatively young age of fifty-eight, Dr. Richard Sterling had retired as a professor of ophthalmology at the University of California Medical School, Davis, California. He had almost immediately been called as president of the Texas San Antonio Mission of the Church of Jesus Christ of Latter-day Saints. Three years later, he returned to Sacramento, built a new home in the suburb of Roseville near his favorite golf course, and opened a small, private ophthalmic practice.

Both Dick and Sally Sterling were waiting in the Sacramento airport luggage area as Matt and Kasia came down the escalator. Dick's wide grin and his similarities to Matt identified him to Kasia as they approached.

"Welcome to Sacramento, Kasia," Dick said, extending his hand.

Sally was less formal, giving the beautiful young woman a tight hug and moving immediately to hug her son.

"I'll get the bags, Dad. You take Kasia to the car and I'll meet you out front in the pickup zone."

Dick smiled. "Right. You always were more the lawyer than the doctor," he laughed. "Now that I've seen this young lass, I just might take her home and leave you here at the airport to fend for yourself for the holidays. She and I could have a long chat, after which she probably would not want to have anything more to do with you."

"Thanks, Dad. I love you too," Matt said, winking at Kasia.

When Matt retrieved the baggage and exited the terminal, Dick's SUV was waiting in the front slot. Matt threw the bags in the rear hatch, climbed in the back seat next to Kasia, and Dick exited the circular driveway, merging onto I-5 for the forty-minute run up the north side of Sacramento to Roseville.

"Good flight, Kasia?" Sally asked as they drove.

"Oh, yes ma'am. A breeze, actually. I wish I could get home as quickly. Four and a half hours from Salt Lake to New York and another seven to Gatwick, then it's about forty-five minutes to our home in Surrey, south of London."

"That *is* a journey."

"Have you been to England, Mrs. Sterling?"

"We have, Kasia. And please, call me Sally. You can call Dick anything you want considering his impudent comments just now."

"I beg your pardon," Dick said with mock disdain. "I was only trying to shield the girl."

"Yes, dear, and so am I," Sally said, laughing. "Anyway, Kasia, Dick and I traveled to England when Matt was released from his mission about two years ago. Seems a lifetime ago now."

"Did you enjoy the trip?"

"Oh, yes. We certainly did. Much of my family came from various parts of England, but I somehow got stuck with this Irishman."

"Lucky for you, eh, old girl," Dick responded. "On the left out there in that pasture, or paddock to you, Kasia, is our basketball stadium. The Kings have made great strides these past couple of years. This may even be their year."

"Only if they can keep Nichols healthy, and if Kolinsky can up his rebound average," Kasia said.

Dick looked quickly in the rearview mirror and whistled a soft note. "This one might be a keeper, Matt. What do you say?"

"I'd say she knows her basketball, Dad, so watch your stuff. Your usual snow jobs won't work with this girl, that's for sure. And she's a diehard Jazz fan too, so no luck selling the Kings to her."

"What a shame," Dick said, exiting I-5 at the I-80 intersection.

"Dad," Matt said, "I plan to take Kasia down to San Francisco while we're here. We need to fly back on Saturday evening. Kasia's talking in church on Sunday. So what's best? With Thursday being family time, should we go tomorrow or Friday?"

"I've got a round of golf for you, me and the boys on Friday…that is unless Kasia has a scratch handicap and wants to play on my side."

"No such luck, Brother Sterling," Kasia replied. "Dad never got me on the course, although he plays as often as his schedule permits. But you go right ahead, Matt. I can get the real facts from your mom and sisters while you're gone."

"I'll just bet you will. Okay, Wednesday it is for the bay area. And don't call him Brother Sterling or Bishop Sterling or anything else that will inflate his ego. 'Dick' will do," Matt said.

"Spoiled sport," Dick said. "Allow me a few hours of mystery with this lovely young lady. Tell me, Kasia, what's the real difference between schedule," he said, pronouncing it with the hard American "K," "and shedule," he said, giving it the soft English sound.

"Just regional differences, I suppose," Kasia replied helpfully.

"Right. I suppose it all depends on which 'shool' one attends, eh?" Dick said, laughing aloud.

Matt looked over at Kasia in the back seat, just shaking his head. "He's really harmless when you get to know him. I just hope we're not here that long."

"Sally," Dick said, "no dessert for Matt tonight. He's being quite disrespectful to his father, wouldn't you say?"

"It's three to one tonight, my darling, and you lose," Sally replied with a straight face.

* * * * *

Kasia found Alcatraz fascinating and on the boat ride back to the pier, stood on deck, the wind playing with her hair, speculating with Matt about the possible success of the escaped prisoners having made it to shore so many years earlier. By the time the boat reached the pier, dusk was settling over the bay and Matt headed them for the cable car terminus where they boarded for the ride to Chinatown. He'd made reservations at the Empress of China, on the sixth floor overlooking the harbor and just before they arrived, he pulled a tie from his inside jacket pocket and transformed himself into a respectable patron. Three waiters attended to their placement, and in several moments, Kasia found herself seated by a large window with a view of the Golden Gate Bridge, the sun setting to seaward of the double towers.

"What a beautiful city, Matt. This has been a magnificent day altogether."

Matt reached across the table for her hand, nodding his agreement. "I couldn't have planned it any better. Good weather, unusually light traffic and superb company. Now, Ms.. Somerset, you are about to partake of the finest of Chinese cuisine to be had in the San Francisco area."

"I'm in your hands, Mr. Sterling."

Matt placed his other hand over hers and nodded. "At least for tonight. What's your favorite Chinese food?"

"I love it all."

"Good. Then we'll try it all, starting with the imperial shrimp."

"Sounds great."

The train ride back to the Oakland side of the bay where they had parked was full of light banter, but during the two-hour ride back to Sacramento, Kasia actually fell asleep, her head lolling against the small pillow she had found in the back seat. Matt let her sleep, occasionally catching a quick glimpse of her in the passing headlights as they traversed the eighty-odd miles east to California's capital city.

The feelings welling inside him and the solitude of the drive forced him to face the issue he had avoided during the brief six weeks they had known one another. Kasia was taking hold and the memory of Carole was finally drifting further into the past. He knew his mother would find time during their short visit to pull him aside, kiss his cheek, and cast her inquisitive glance up toward his deep blue eyes—her finely tuned glance that, without words, so eloquently asked, "*Well?*"

* * * * *

Tons of Thanksgiving Day food consumed, dishes washed and two obligatory football games finished, the grandchildren were banished to the downstairs playroom, complete with Play Station III and the latest animated DVDs, while the bulk of the Sterling family, including two sons-in-law and their English guest gathered together in the great room.

"Nothing like a good football game on the holidays," Dick Sterling said as he settled into his Lazy Boy recliner.

Matt's mother took her place at the end of the divan, shook her head and smiled. "Kasia, my dear, you should be around this place from Christmas to New Year's. Dawn to dusk football."

"My father is a diehard rugby fan," Kasia responded from her place next to Matt's older sister Emily, the two of them sitting on cushions that covered the combination storage box and bench seat in the bay window.

"Is there much difference?" Dick asked.

"Americans wear body armor," Kasia said with a bright smile.

"This girl's got a way with words."

"I told you, Dad," Matt added, "she knows sports quite well."

"For a *girl* right?" Rachel teased.

"For *anyone*," Matt responded.

"Okay," Sally said, "as the matriarch of the family today, I decree that we are finished talking about sports."

"Hear, hear," Rachel and Emily cheered. "Got that, *President* Sterling?" Emily asked, smiling at her father.

Dick Sterling nodded quietly. "We bow to your superior wisdom, Sister Sterling. Besides there are much more important things to discuss. Matt, I've filled your sisters in a bit on the surprising developments from Grandfather Sterling's journal. I guess I should say McBride's journal. Can you bring them up to date and maybe fill in some of the gaps?"

"First I want to ask how did we become Sterlings instead of McBrides?" Rachel asked.

"Apparently, with a touch of the pen and a presidential suggestion from George Washington," Matt replied. Turning to face his father, he continued. "I've read the whole journal, Dad, and the manuscript, but I still have trouble putting it all together. Andy's partner in the freight business, Righteous, the black slave from the ship, was at the opening action in the war at Lexington and Concord. In fact he had his wagons taken by the arrogant British troops…" Matt paused momentarily and grinned sheepishly at Kasia. "Sorry, but that's what the journal calls them."

"Go on," Kasia said with a smile and a wave of her hand. "You're telling this tale."

"Anyway, Righteous lost his wagons, got wounded, although he didn't participate in the fighting, and found his way to McBride's home in Boston. Apparently from there, Andy tried to help Righteous get compensation from General Gage, but things got out of hand. The minutemen took possession of Breed's and Bunker's Hill, as we know, and the war really took on a new footing. To make a long story short, within a few weeks Andy and his wife Laura decided to move to New York where Andy took a position as a barrister with Laura's father, Jonathan Delacorte. Righteous came too. Andy bought new wagons and they continued their partnership in the freighting business."

"Why New York?" Rachel asked.

"I guess because her father was well established and quite successful. Plus the war was brewing in Boston. Maybe they just wanted to get away."

"Well, it got hot and heavy in New York," Emily's husband Albert said.

"We know that *now*, they didn't then," Emily said, laughing at her husband.

"Anyway," Matt continued, "they settled in New York, and as Albert said, it got pretty hot and heavy. Jonathan Delacorte was a staunch Tory, a loyalist to the core."

"What was Andy?" Sally Sterling asked, now sitting further forward on her seat.

"It doesn't really say, at least at this point, Mom, but certainly he became a patriot, at least from his perspective."

"What do you mean *'from his perspective'?"* Dick asked, also showing a great deal more interest.

"Well, when General Howe took command of British troops and established his headquarters in New York, Andy was introduced to him by his father-in-law and Andy became legal counsel to the British Army in New York."

"He sided with the *British?"* Rachel asked.

"That's what the other Americans thought. And maybe he did at first. I looked up some reference material on the internet. New York was actually a hotbed of loyalist forces. More people supported the Crown than the rebels."

"Matt, you're dragging this story out just to tease us," Emily said. "C'mon, tell us who or what Grandfather Sterling was. Was he a traitor or a patriot?"

"Both," Matt replied, starting to laugh.

"That's not fair," Emily said, getting off her seat and moving to sit on the floor in front of her mother. "We always thought…well, I don't know *what* we thought, but that's not the family history Grandma Sterling told us and she knew it all."

Matt stood up and moved to take Emily's place in the window seat next to Kasia. He smiled at her, took her hand, and turned back to his family. "Well, certainly she thought she did. She always thought we were Sterlings. And now we know we were, or should have been, McBrides. And we're not Irish, we're Scottish."

"Scots," Kasia pointed out.

"What?"

"People from Scotland are 'Scots,' not 'Scottish.'"

"I stand corrected."

"Not Irish?" Dick said, now dropping the leg recliner and leaning forward. "Why?"

"Because Andy's grandfather was part of the great

Protestant immigration to Ireland in the late seventeenth and early eighteenth century, after Cromwell invaded the country. By Andy's generation, sixty or seventy years later, they saw themselves as Irish, but were still of Scot…" he paused again, squeezing Kasia's hand and smiling at her, "as coming from Scotland."

"What a story. So, what did he do in New York?" Dick asked.

"Well, this is the great part of the story. It's where Andy made his choices. He became a patriot but was seen as a traitor."

"Oh, Matt, stop it," Emily demanded.

"It's true. He was there when the British hanged Nathan Hale."

"He was *not,*" Emily protested.

Matt nodded. "He was—at least according to his journal. And from what I can tell, the hanging brought him to a decision point. Andy went to Yale at the same time as Nathan Hale, and then when Hale was hanged as a spy, Andy was serving as legal counsel to the British."

"This is a story I've got to hear," Dick Sterling said, "but let me refill my glass."

"Let's all stop for a moment," Sally said, rising. "Anyone for another piece of pie?"

"Sure," Albert, Rachel's husband said, rising. "More pie and apple cider, then we can come back for the hanging."

"You men are hopeless. If it's not football, it's war stories," Rachel said, stepping to help her mother in the kitchen.

As they walked out onto the balcony overlooking the golf course, the grass dormant in the winter snap, Matt took Kasia's hand again and looked into her eyes. "Well, what do you think?"

"Of the traitor, Nathan Hale?" she said.

"You know what I mean," Matt smiled. "Of my family."

"You're shattering their family image. If you don't spin

this story right, they just might hang *you.*"

"And how do you feel about it?"

"Me? As far as I know, my family had no ancestors who served in the colonies. Besides, how I feel isn't important," she said, a small smile tugging at her lips. "I'm still on probation, remember. Under your custody."

"That you are, my beautiful British subject. A prisoner of war as I see it. Now, let's go back inside and I'll tell everyone the gruesome tale of the hanging."

We are dislocated! With rebellion and armed conflict in the air, we have disassembled all that has been constructed to begin again in New York. Yet as governments become estranged, my internal conflict exceeds that which I see around me daily. I am torn between those whom I love and that which I believe. Shall there be no end to my life's disruption? Shall I be forced to begin anew at each transgression, none of which are of my making? Have I offended our great God yet again?

Journal of Andrew McBride

Chapter Nine

Among New York City's upper class, the rebellion in Boston was the talk of the town, especially among the Delacortes' moneyed social circle, most of whom were staunch loyalists. Laura Delacorte McBride's family had earned their position in society some seventy years earlier through devious means. In 1689, her great-grandfather, Francois Delacorte, had worked his way from Calais to Charleston as a deckhand, marrying a Welsh girl he met in Philadelphia just three weeks after arriving. They had one child, a son. However, lacking the aristocratic lineage necessary to claim a place among Philadelphia's elite, Justin Delacorte, Laura's grandfather, had moved to Baltimore, won a tattered old schooner in a gambling debt, and started a coastal shipping company. For the next twenty years, he made his money through the nefarious acquisition of a bankrupt shipping company that plied the established triangular trade route; England to the West Indies to the colonies. Two decades of successful commerce had seen him into a sizeable fortune. At least that was the public perception. Beneath the façade, fully one third of his ships had traveled a different and much less socially acceptable route—West Africa to Savannah, Georgia.

There was never a mention of how Grandfather Delacorte had made his money, but by the time Jonathan Delacorte, Laura's father, grew to manhood and married into a prominent Baltimore family, the now-retired Delacortes had moved to New York, possessed of a new, more traditional image complete with the financial ability to sustain the requisite lifestyle.

Following his parents to New York, Jonathan became founding partner in what quickly became a successful law firm and, together with his new bride, Martha, they produced one child, their daughter, Laura. Her eventual marriage to Andrew McBride, an educated man of unknown background but ample means—a history not dissimilar to the Delacorte's—was not unacceptable. However, the McBride's decision to live in Boston rather than New York angered Jonathan and drove a wedge between him and his new son-in-law.

Several years later, the McBride's return to New York, following the Boston rebellion, quickly eased the hard feelings, but Andy and Laura's return was not without discord, mostly centered on the growing philosophical chasm between the colonies and the Crown.

The British army had also left Boston, content to winter in Nova Scotia after their troublesome and Pyrrhic victory over the colonial rebels. The feeling among the uninformed rabble of the New England colonies was that John Bull had been sent to the bushes and further conflict would likely be unnecessary. As legal representative for British Crown affairs in New York, Jonathan Delacorte knew better. The upstart Continental general, George Washington, had moved his rag-tag army to Long Island and Jonathan knew that General Sir William Howe, newly appointed British commander following General Gage's resignation, was going to leave Nova Scotia, headed for New York in the spring, with more than thirty thousand British regulars and German mercenaries in attendance.

The Redcoats arrived in June 1776 and headquartered on Staten Island, just across the harbor from Manhattan. In July, Jonathan Delacorte, his partner, Trevor Prescott, and the newly appointed junior partner, Andy McBride, crossed New York harbor to Staten Island for a meeting with General Howe and his key staff. By late that evening when they returned, the law firm of Delacorte and Prescott had been retained as legal counsel to the British Army, based primarily on their experience of nearly a decade of service to the Crown. Andy McBride was appointed lead counsel and, despite the presence of Continental Army troops just across the East River in Long Island, in an attitude of supreme confidence that the British army would prevail, the firm was given the job of locating suitable headquarters in Manhattan for the British high command.

In late August, with Washington's army still ensconced on Long Island, Howe's forces, supplemented by German mercenaries, crossed the harbor, immediately engaging the rebel army and pushing those who were not killed or captured back to Brooklyn, against the East River. After a decided victory, and assuming capitulation, Howe paused his troops just long enough for Washington to arrange an overnight, cross-river escape into Manhattan. British ships then blockaded the Hudson and East rivers, leaving Westchester County, to the north, the only route away from New York City. Washington consolidated his remaining troops and headed north, thereby avoiding inevitable defeat and the rebellion was inadvertently allowed to continue for another couple of months.

General Howe established his Manhattan headquarters in the Berkman Mansion, a large home that Andy had commandeered on British authority. One Saturday morning in September, about four weeks after Washington's escape, a British subaltern came to Andy and Laura McBride's townhouse, requesting an audience with Mr. McBride. Andy met him in the parlor.

"Lieutenant Capston," Andy greeted his visitor, "how may I be of service this morning?"

"The general's compliments, sir. He requests your presence as soon as practical."

"Do you know the matter at hand?"

"I believe we have captured an American spy, sir."

"I see. Please convey my compliments to the general. I will join him directly."

"Very good, sir," the subaltern said, turning sprightly and departing.

Forty minutes later, having walked the necessary distance amid the conflagration that had enveloped New York during the night, Andy stood before General Sir William Howe, several additional staff officers present in the room.

"Bring in the prisoner," General Howe directed.

From the far side of the room, two dragoons entered through a side door, a young, fair-haired man in civilian clothes between them. He was neither shackled nor bound in any manner. He wore his own hair and was dressed casually in fawn-colored leggings, a wide leather strap around the waist, and a rough-hewn, faded cotton shirt. The trio stepped briskly, coming to a halt immediately in front of General Howe's desk. The general remained standing behind his desk. Upon closer view, Andy recognized the civilian immediately, although more than two years had elapsed since they had last seen one another.

Howe spoke first. "I am informed, sir, that you were taken into custody in possession of documents related to British troop disposition, both in Long Island and Manhattan. Is this information correct?" Howe asked.

The prisoner nodded. "Yes, sir, it is."

"And what might your status be?"

"Sir, I have the honor to be a commissioned officer of the 7th Connecticut Regiment of the Continental Army. Captain Nathan Hale."

"And your attire, sir. Why are you not wearing the proper military uniform in British territory?"

"Sir, until several days ago, this was American territory." Hale hesitated, then continued. "General, I have no defense other than that I have been acting on orders from my superiors."

Howe stepped slowly around his desk, stopping several feet in front of Hale. "You understand the gravity of the situation you are in, Captain Hale?"

"I believe so."

"You are in possession of intelligence documents, out of uniform, and captured in British territory, not to mention that half the City of New York has been in flames since the early hours of the morning, likely by the hand of your associates. None of this bodes well for your innocence."

"I understand, sir. I do not plead innocence."

"Then how do you plead, Captain Hale?"

"To what charge?"

Howe stiffened and coughed slightly before replying. "For one in such precarious circumstance, there is much gall in you, sir," Howe replied. "To the charge of spying and conduct treasonous to His Majesty."

"Two months ago, sir, this nation declared its independence from the Crown. I admit to being present behind your lines without proper uniform, but treason is not a valid charge against a citizen of a sovereign government. As to the charge of seeking to obtain information under cloak of disguise, I offer no plea, nor any excuse."

"You admit then, sir, that you were spying for the enemy?"

"General, I was carrying out my instructions to the best of my ability."

Howe considered the response momentarily and then looked toward Andy. "Mr. McBride, as legal counsel do you see any purpose to be gained by continuing this examination? Captain Hale has confessed his transgression."

Andy and Captain Hale exchanged brief eye contact before Hale averted his eyes.

Andy replied. "General, I believe we should proceed with caution and afford Captain Hale every opportunity for defense. Perhaps a court martial would be in order."

"But the man has confessed," Howe replied.

"He was under orders, sir, by his own account."

Howe nodded slowly, looking again toward Hale. "Captain, was this a voluntary assignment? Were you *ordered* to enter British territory in civilian clothes and obtain information?"

Hale shook his head. "General Howe, I volunteered for this assignment. I was under instructions, but not ordered to accomplish the mission."

"I see. Again, Captain, do you recognize the gravity of your circumstance? The nature of appearing under false disguise, as it were? So that there may be no misunderstanding, as I see the situation, Captain Hale, you are guilty of spying and, accordingly, under military custom and law, are subject to penalty of death by hanging. Do you have any thoughts or conditions that would mitigate such a verdict?"

Captain Nathan Hale stood silently for a long moment, before raising his eyes to look directly at General Howe. "General, I volunteered for this assignment and while I might not have fully considered the possible consequences attendant to my capture, I nonetheless am prepared to accept your judgment."

Hale nodded to one of the officers standing to the side of the room. "Major Carrington, escort Captain Hale back to his quarters. I will consider the case and render a verdict this evening."

The two dragoons turned, the prisoner between them again, and, in the company of the British Major, left the room by the same door they had entered.

Once they were gone, Howe turned his attention to Andy. "Mr. McBride, I sense your discomfort with this arrangement."

Andy stepped to the front of the desk. "Sir, Captain Hale likely acted out of youthful exuberance for a cause he believed to be honorable. His death would not further your cause and I believe a summary judgment in this case would prove detrimental to your position and repugnant to you personally."

Howe nodded his agreement. "It is a distasteful business, Mr. McBride, but command is often a cruel mistress. How come you to this opinion?"

"The Americans hold captive several British subjects who have also provided information to your officers on American troop dispositions. Should you execute Captain Hale, they will likely suffer the same fate. In fact, General, most of New York comprises people who are providing information to one side or the other."

"Granted, but most of those individuals are not commissioned army officers."

"Civilians are subject to military justice as well, General, when found in commission of sabotage or acts of insurrection."

"True enough. We are involved in a most uncommon war, Mr. McBride. Were you not awakened half the night by the flames and incendiaries? If I allow this incursion to go unpunished, we can expect more of the same. If the incidents around Boston prove anything, they demonstrate the lack of definition between military and civilian insurrection. We must do what we can to make this war as civil as possible."

Andy shook his head. "I reiterate, sir, it is my recommendation that we convene a court martial, or perhaps offer to trade Captain Hale for British subjects in similar conditions."

Howe stepped behind his desk and resumed his seat, looking up at Andy. "I will consider your advice, Mr. McBride. Thank you for coming so quickly this morning."

* * * * *

Shortly after dawn the following morning, Sunday, September 22, 1776, the young subaltern again called at the McBride home and Andy was roused from his bedchambers by his house servant. He came downstairs clothed in his robe.

"My deepest apologies, Mr. McBride, but the American, Captain Hale, has asked that you attend him this morning if it is convenient."

"What news from General Howe?" Andy asked.

"The general has signed the execution order, sir. Hale will hang this morning."

Andy sighed and nodded. "I feared as much. Please return and inform Captain Hale that I will follow immediately."

"Yes, sir," the man said.

Andy dressed quickly and walked the several blocks to British Headquarters. He was directed to the rear of the mansion, to a small gardener's quarters. Two dragoons stood guard outside the door, two more further along the pathway in the garden.

"May I see the prisoner?" Andy queried.

"Aye, sir, the Major has given his permission for your visit at the prisoner's request."

Andy stepped into the darkened room, only one window available for light. As his eyes adjusted, he heard, rather than saw, Hale rise from his cot.

"Thank you for coming, Andy. It's been a long time."

Andy nodded, stepping forward to take his friend's hand. "It has. I spent most of the night recalling our acquaintance. Two, perhaps nearer three years, I believe, was the last time we saw one another. Shortly after leaving Yale when you obtained your first teaching position."

"A lifetime ago," Hale said, his features now clearer as Andy's eyes adjusted. "You've been told?"

"I have and it appalls me. I counseled the general for an exchange of prisoners or at the very least, for a court martial."

"The verdict would not have changed, I think. I have broken the propriety of British civility, if any form of war could be called civil."

"Is there anything I can do for you, Nate?" Andy asked, using the name by which Hale was commonly known during their years as students at Yale.

"I've prepared two letters, Andy. One for my family and one for Colonel Knowlton. They are unsealed for your inspection, but there is nothing military contained in either letter. Just personal information. I trust you will be able to deliver them for me."

"You have my word, Nate. Anything else?"

Hale stepped toward the window and attempted to view the yard through the dusty panes. "How did you come to work for the British army, Andy?" he said, continuing to look through the window.

Andy lowered his head. "That also caused me considerable consternation during the night. Certainly out of no love for them or their cause, Nate. My father-in-law has been legal counsel to the Crown for some years now and with the military occupation, I suppose it was just a natural extension. He assumed I would accept the assignment, perhaps even be honored."

Nathan Hale, barely twenty-one with light hair and fair blue eyes, turned and stared at Andy for several long moments, his face calm. "You are in a unique position of knowledge, Andy. If you've no love for their cause, then perhaps…"

"Nate, this is no time…you're about to…well, your thoughts should be on your family. Have you requested a minister?"

"I have, Andy." Hale smiled gently, his eyes soft. "He'll be along shortly. Would that it were my brother, Enoch. Perhaps you don't know that he has become an ordained minister."

"I wasn't aware. Is he in New York?"

"Unfortunately, no," Hale said, resignation written on his face. "Give my suggestion some thought. I know you to be a fair and honest person, Andrew McBride. We are engaged in a noble cause and, as God is my witness, we will inevitably triumph. When you deliver my letter to Colonel Knowlton, perhaps…perhaps you will find another cause worthy of your admiration." Hale stepped toward Andy and extended his hand. "Thank you for coming. It has meant a lot."

"The Lord's blessings on you, Nate. May you find His peace in these remaining hours."

Hale turned again toward the window and Andy quietly retreated through the doorway. Immediately outside the cabin, the British Major in charge of the prisoner confronted Andy.

"So, what did the rebel have to say?"

Andy looked back toward the cabin and then turned to face the Major. "We talked about his priest coming, and his family."

"Did he give you any information or letters?"

"Two letters, but he assured me that they contained no information of a military nature."

"I'll have those letters, if you please."

"Major, I gave my word to deliver them to his family."

The Major stood his ground, his hand outstretched, waiting for Andy to hand over the letters. Reluctantly, Andy retrieved the letters from the inside pocket of his surtout. "And what will happen now?"

"The rebel will be transported several miles from here and hanged at noon."

Andy slowly nodded his head and walked away, glancing once again at the cabin that contained his former college friend, barely beginning his young life, now a convicted spy with only a few hours remaining. No matter where he ran, it seemed this war was destined to invade Andy McBride's life.

Chapter Ten

Kasia and Matt flew back from Sacramento on Saturday evening, discussing the trip, Matt's family, and the myriad types of people one could observe in San Francisco. Kasia explained during the flight that she would be returning to England for the holidays and remaining for several weeks following to do some research in England and on the Continent with regard to the Royal houses of Europe and DNA. Kasia casually suggested Matt might like to accompany her to England and spend Christmas with her parents in Surrey. Before the flight landed, Matt had agreed, teasing her once again about the requirement to preach the gospel from a soapbox in Hyde Park.

"Not my cup of tea, Elder Sterling," she had laughed, "but I'm happy to accompany you and watch you make a fool of yourself. Did you actually ever baptize anyone you met at Hyde Park?"

"No, but it made door knocking a lot easier," he replied. "Christmas in England, again. That will make my mother sit up and take notice."

"Why?"

"For the same reasons that you will have to explain to your parents as to why you are bringing home a Yank for Christmas pudding."

Kasia looked out the window of the plane as they approached the Salt Lake City airport. "Touché," she said softly.

After a few seconds silence, the airplane groaning as the wheels were lowered and the flaps changed position, preparing to land, Matt reached for Kasia's hand. "Why *are* you bringing home a Yank?"

Kasia squeezed his fingers in her hand, continued looking out the window, and then turned to look directly at Matt. "For Christmas pudding?" she responded, though her eyes said something altogether different.

"Think that answer will satisfy your mother?"

Kasia shrugged and returned to looking out the window, silent for the remainder of the approach and landing.

* * * * *

On Monday Matt returned to Snowy Ridge City Hall to find a half-dozen voicemail messages, tons of email, and his secretary standing at the head of his desk before he even dropped his briefcase. She remained silent, but smiled conspiratorially at Matt as he took his seat.

Candy Houser was nearing sixty-five and swam several miles each evening. Widowed for seven years, she was reputed to have more than six thousand names in her genealogical files and possessed the proverbial "mind like a computer." She also worked in her off hours as a part-time editor for one of the LDS publishers located in the valley, reviewing "slush pile" manuscripts of wannabe authors. Many a prospective writer had lived or died under the weight of her opinion, yet never knew who she was. Matt's writing skills had sharpened considerably under her tutelage, brought on by a combination of his law school education compared with Candy's high school diploma, her far better command of the rules of grammar, her willingness to "red pencil" his draft documents and a healthy portion of male ego to not be outdone. Candy was second in longevity among the Snowy Ridge employees, having been hired only nine months after Mac McDougal.

"I've seen that look before, Candy."

"I'll bet you have, but I'll save the best news for last. In short order, Pat is gone for the rest of the week. Her younger sister in Phoenix finally gave birth. A little girl. Next, Councilman Nelson is still complaining that he can't have another laptop so he can work weekends, so he said, from his cabin at Park City."

"That's why they call them 'laptops' or portables. So we can transport them. Tell him that one laptop per Councilor is all we budgeted for, but if he wishes to increase the appropriation...in *public* session," Matt replied, a smile forming. "And?"

"And...ta-da!" she trumpeted, "Mayor-Elect Julia Wells has scheduled an appointment with you this afternoon at two."

"*Today?*"

"Today."

"With *me?*" Matt gestured, pointing a finger at his own chest.

"With you!"

"With Pat gone?"

Candy started to laugh. "With Pat gone. I actually think Ms. Wells waited for this particular moment. She's called to try and schedule a meeting with every department head she could since last week. Pat put her off on each occasion, telling her that in our form of government, she needed to deal directly with the city manager."

"And so, why can't she wait?" Matt asked, his smile beginning to match Candy's.

"In case you've forgotten, Mr. Assistant City Manager, you *are* the city manager in Pat's absence."

"Lucky me."

"Better you than me. Shall I call her and confirm?"

"Did Pat leave me any instructions?"

"Nothing more than what she told the department heads at the last staff meeting. *All* information to the Council, including the newly elected members, comes from the city manager's office."

"And…I…am…"

"The city manager," Candy said. "Shall I confirm?"

"Why not? I knew I was going to have to deal with it sooner or later. Sooner it seems. Anything else?"

"The rest is boring. Most of it I can deal with. Want my advice?"

"Do I have a choice?" Matt asked.

Candy ignored the comment. "Don't believe everything you've heard."

"Excuse me?"

"About Julia Wells. Just hear her out. You might be surprised."

"Aha! Do we have a sympathizer in city hall? An in-house spy?"

Candy laughed again and leaned forward, placing her hands on Matt's desk. "I know someone, who knows someone, who knows *her*. They say she can be trusted."

"You sound like Mac. He always 'knows *someone*, who knows *someone*,' and it's never first-hand information."

"But it's always reliable, right?"

Matt hesitated and then nodded his agreement. "Right. On to the paperwork," he said as he lifted the pile from his in-basket. "Oh, and Candy, see if Mac is free for lunch, would you? Can't hurt to see if he has a few more '*someones*' up his sleeve before I meet with Ms. Wells."

"Check your calendar. You'll find Mac penciled in for lunch today. Don't worry, you'll do fine, Matt. Just let her say her piece."

"Yeah, and when Pat comes back and finds that I've met with her, without Pat being present, she'll have a piece of my...well, let's just say I'll probably need stitches."

Candy headed for the door, turning and snickering in a childish voice, *"Is the little boy scared of the big bad wolf-woman?"*

"Which one? I seem to be caught between two such power hungry women."

"Lucky you."

"And who hired *you*, anyway?" Matt laughed. "Aren't you about ready to retire?"

"And miss all the fun this year? Not a chance. This will be the most excitement around here since...since Councilman Houston ran away with the high school principal's secretary."

"Tell you what, Candy. Let's cancel on Mayor Wells and you and I can run away together. *That* should get the tongues wagging."

"No thanks. I could do much better," Candy replied, winking at Matt and stepping through the doorway.

* * * * *

Precisely at two o'clock, Candy stepped into Matt's office and announced that Mayor-Elect Julia Wells was at reception, headed up the stairs. "Shall I show her in?"

"Please. And ask her if she'd like a cup of coffee."

"Coffee?" Candy repeated.

"You heard me. The fact that the great majority of us don't indulge, and that up 'til now all of our Councilors have been LDS, doesn't mean we can't be cordial to those who don't share our view."

"You're giving me a *lecture?*"

"Show the mayor in, please, Candy," Matt said, "and while you're at it, I'll have a cup of hot chocolate."

Candy just stared at him.

"*Please.*"

"That's much better, Mr. City Manager. There's hope for you yet, even though you're such a young fella."

Mayor Elect Julia Wells entered Matt's office and stepped briskly toward his desk, her hand stretched out to grasp his with a firm grip. Her expression was friendly but her green eyes bore into his. She was dressed in royal blue slacks and jacket, a white silk blouse, and a matching cravat. She had vibrant red hair, cut short just above her neck. About thirty-five, Julia Wells appeared relaxed and confident as she quickly surveyed Matt's office.

"Well, I've made it one step further into the inner sanctum," she said.

"Rather entrenched, are we?"

"Bunker mentality, I call it. I think our WASP president would have better luck getting in to see the Pope."

Matt motioned Julia toward a seat on the upholstered divan. He sat across from her, in one of several leather chairs, a small round conference table separating them.

"I've heard a lot about you, mayor."

"Not yet the mayor, as has been pointed out to me on several occasions. I asked for this meeting with you in the hopes that we could develop a better relationship."

"And something tells me you're fully aware of our instructions from Pat Harcourt."

Julia smiled broadly, just as Candy entered the room with a tray containing two cups and a small platter of cookies that she placed on the table between Matt and his visitor.

"Thank you, Candy. Would you please close the door on the way out?" Matt said, turning again to face Julia.

"I was led to believe that you just might not be, uh, *intimidated* by that particular restriction as so many of your fellow managers have seemed to be."

"So you know *someone*, who knows *someone*, who knows *me?*" Matt said.

"Excuse me?"

"Just a bit of office humor. Everything I've heard about you, Mayor Wells, has come from second- and often third-hand sources. That is, other than the corporate position."

"And what is the corporate position, Mr. Sterling? Before you answer that, is it possible that we could assume Julia and Matt for our conversation? It might ease the process."

Matt nodded, then took a sip of his hot chocolate. "Make it a lot more pleasant, wouldn't it? The corporate position, you say? Aptly defined, your office caricature, assuming someone could do it justice, would probably rest somewhere between Dorothy and Toto's 'wicked witch' and 'Freddy Krueger,' coming in to whack off the heads of most of the senior staff. The other version is not much more flattering. It's one of Joan Collins' old characters from Dynasty. You know, sort of a 'witchy' person always in control of everything."

Julia Wells choked down a swallow of coffee, trying hard to suppress her laughter. She replaced her cup on the saucer and sat for a moment, staring at Matt. "How did you pronounce that word?"

"You heard me," Matt laughed.

"And does five minutes with me confirm either of those corporate opinions?"

Matt also replaced his cup on the table and leaned back in his chair, crossing his legs. "Mayor...Julia, I ran track at BYU, played a bit of baseball and was on the golf team. I'm not very good at fencing. What say we just discuss the issues that you've found to be important and I'll do my level best to provide the information you seek."

Julia also leaned back against the cushions on the divan, nodding her head. "A lawyer that can't fence. That's novel. But seriously, providing information could be risky, Matt. For you, I mean."

"Yes, it could. But I've spent several weeks since the election listening to the in-house defense strategy build and I find myself at a loss to understand the reasons behind the, uh...what should I say...the fear and anger I sense from most of the senior staff. I've attributed it to fear of the unknown. No one *really* knows who you are, Mayor Wells. No one is certain what your platform is, why you want to be mayor of a predominately Mormon community, and how you intend to begin your term. What I *do* know is that we've assumed the worst and have essentially been told to filter all requests for information and material through Pat's office. That doesn't equate with the democracy I envision. *Advising* Pat of what information we've provided for your review is just good management practice, so she knows what's happening, but *refusing* to provide information goes against the grain...my grain, that is."

"I repeat," Julia said, "that could be risky for you. I had hoped for cooperation from someone on the management team, but now that I sit here, I have to admit it scares me a bit. Now that we talk, I don't know that I've thought this through. In my quest for, well, for insight into how this city runs, I could jeopardize someone's job."

"You probably will and you should face that possibility right now, much as I have to choose sides, like it or not. Taking sides in such an internal conflict is not an easy decision for most of the staff, but in particular, you and I should understand one another from the start. I will *not* function as a clandestine in-house source of information. Whatever I tell you, I'll advise Pat Harcourt that I've passed along information that was requested. And if Pat orders me to not reveal particular facts about city operations that the Utah statutes say are your right to know, I'll advise Pat of that conflict with statutes and our obligation to comply."

"That will put you at odds with her, at least from what impression I have so far. She fully intends to keep me in the dark as much as possible."

"I have to agree. I hope I can convince her otherwise, but it hasn't looked good so far. It's been ten days or so since I saw Pat, and she won't be here this week, but when she returns, I'll attempt to discuss the issue with her and will immediately inform her that we have had this meeting. That shifts some of the burden to you, Julia," Matt said, leaning forward and holding her eyes. "It means that there will be no behind the scenes investigation, covert spying, or secret meetings. What you know, Pat Harcourt will *know* that you know. At least the information that *I* give you. If you have other sources, that's your business. But understand me clearly, mayor, I won't help you to undermine the city manager or her authority. She has several important and legal points in her favor. The city manager form of government distinctly separates the governance and management roles. Are you aware of the distinction?"

"I understand what you're saying," Julia responded, pursing her lips and running her fingers through her hair. "Some aspects of managing this city belong to Pat Harcourt."

"That's correct, and her prerogatives are protected by the city charter and state laws. Remember, some of these distinctions are there to protect employees from abuse by elected officials who come and go each election and who sometimes seek to push their own agenda."

"That's understandable, but legal information, financial reports, budget expenditures, etc., those are available to the elected officials, are they not?"

"They are indeed. That's the primary aspect of the checks and balances that the system needs to keep us all honest and to assure the public that sufficient transparency exists so they can know what's going on at City Hall."

"And you concur with my right to see those items?"

"Absolutely. And I will respond to each request you present with at least an attempt to provide the information needed. *Attempt* is the key word. From what I can see, Julia, we're rapidly taking sides among the senior staff. Apart from those who are frightened to lean either way, and there are plenty of those and more to take that position, probably, there are still those die-hards who fully support Pat's right to keep a closed shop, so to speak. The we-know-best syndrome, my professor used to call it."

"And who's who in that group?"

Matt shook his head, picking up his cup again. "I'll make no judgments, at least none that I'll share with you or anyone else. You'll find out for yourself soon enough, if you haven't already. But understand, there are many people here, at senior and middle management levels, who just seek to survive. They won't oppose you, but they won't help either if they think it will impede their careers. That's just human nature, the urge to protect oneself, and I'm sure you've encountered it before."

Mayor Julia Wells sat quietly for several moments, apparently considering what Matt had revealed. Finally she nodded and smiled at him. "You're an honest man, Matt. As I was told to expect," she said, smiling even brighter.

"Thank you, Julia. I don't know about that, but increasingly I've become aware that I'm going to have to make some decisions if I'm to carry out what I see to be my responsibilities. Those decisions are clearly going to put me off sides with the majority of my peers at City Hall. I will not be seen as a team player, at least from their perspective."

"Okay, we've set the ground rules. Can I ask some specific questions?"

"The afternoon is clear and I'm at your disposal."

"Procurement. Contracting procedures and good-old-boy

networks. What can you tell me about the objectivity of Snowy Ridge's bid process, double-dipping, and nepotism?"

Matt leaned back again, smiled at Julia and shook his head. "Nothing subtle about your cut-to-the-chase approach, is there?"

"I've only got a few days before you revert to being the *assistant city manager.* And I've got a lot of questions."

"I understand. Any *particular* contract you have in mind, Mayor?" Matt asked, cocking his head.

"I've got some friends who live up in the Fontana Subdivision—you know, where we put the water and sewer system in two years ago."

"What a coincidence!" Matt said, a laugh escaping his lips.

* * * * *

At 5:45, after nearly four hours of discussion, Julia Wells left Matt Sterling's office, a relationship cemented in place and an understanding of the magnitude of the task ahead. Matt sat behind his desk and quickly checked the emails that had arrived during his meeting, responded to three, and opened a new email window, pausing momentarily as his fingers hovered over the keys.

From: Matt Sterling

To: Pat Harcourt

Subject: Meeting with Mayor-Elect Julia Wells

Dear Pat: This afternoon I had an impromptu meeting with Mayor-Elect Julia Wells, wherein we discussed multiple items of concern. In your absence, I felt it necessary, in a display of openness, to grant her request for a meeting. We discussed far-ranging subject matter, but primarily focused on procurement issues, contracting procedures, and financial reporting. There is clearly a disparity between what she has been previously advised (apparently from outside sources) and what are the facts. I tried to dispel her concerns and to alleviate unnecessary trepidation about our standard procedures, however, you should be aware that her interests extend to the establishment of a Council committee to review, and if necessary (in their opinion) revise our practices.

You will be pleased to note that her demeanor, at least from my perspective, is quite pleasant and I found her easy to work with and receptive to candid response. I suggest that we develop an open and receptive attitude that will quickly dispel any distrust on either side. In the end, she is the mayor for the next four years and it is in our best interest to assist her transition as she becomes the titular head of our elected governance body.

Upon your return, I am prepared to review, in detail, the content of our conversation and to assist in any way I can to effect a cooperative bridge between management and the elected members. I fully understand this is your role, but merely mean to suggest that I am ready to assist.

Hope you had a good time in Phoenix as you assume the role of "aunt" to your new niece. Sincere congratulations!

Regards, Matt

PS: If it will not be a problem, I'd like to extend my Christmas vacation from one week to two, as I will be going to England to visit friends. Please advise if that presents a conflict. I'll be gone from the 22nd to the 6th. Thanks.

* * * * *

On Friday, Matt picked up Kasia and they drove along the mountain road to Draper, avoiding the interstate that was beginning to be choked with Jazz fans headed for yet another game at the Delta Center. Turning toward South Mountain, they proceeded to the new block of townhouses, all designed to look like a European village with multiple ethnic styles reflected by the architectural elevations. Roland Timmerman and his wife, Annette, has recently purchased a new three-bedroom unit immediately off the eighth green of the South Mountain Golf Club, which ran parallel along the side of the mountain.

"Nice place," Kasia said as they entered the grounds. "How long has Roland lived here?"

"They bought just before the last term started. Moved in about July. We had a bit of a problem with Annette's piano, I can tell you," Matt said.

"So, the local Elders Quorum helped him to move in traditional Mormon fashion?"

"You could say that. Half a dozen guys from Orem handled the loading, and another half dozen from Draper handled this end."

"And you?"

"As Roland's best friend, I, of course, was privileged to work *both* ends of the journey, piano and all."

"Lucky you. Shall we go in or are they expecting us and coming out?"

"Sure, let's go in," Matt said as he parked the car and turned off the engine. "But first, may I tell you how lovely you look tonight?"

Kasia's eyebrows rose slightly and a bit of color crept up her throat. "Well, thank you...

"You *always* look lovely, of course, but tonight you are radiant."

Kasia reached for her purse. "Well, thank you again, Mr. Sterling. You look pretty swish yourself in your tan slacks, black blazer, and turtleneck."

"Swish! I haven't heard that in a while," Matt said, getting out to come around and open Kasia's door. Some weeks earlier,

Kasia had accepted the fact that Matt was going to continue his chivalry and had decided to wait each time they went somewhere for him to perform his knightly chores.

As Kasia stepped out of the car, Matt stood close to her and gently pressed near her, nudging her back against the car. He leaned down slightly and kissed her lips. "Extraordinarily lovely, I might add."

"You certainly can keep a girl off balance, Mr. Sterling. According to *Cosmopolitan* or some of the other feminist literature, I should assume that either you've done something for which you feel you need to apologize, or you're buttering me up for approval of something yet to come."

Matt laughed and took her hand as they began to walk toward the housing complex. "You don't subscribe to that tripe, do you?"

"It's not all wrong," she retorted. "Statistics bear me out."

"Well, in that case, don't let me confuse you," he said. "You actually look quite common this evening, but good enough to take to dinner. How's that?"

Kasia punched him on the arm and pulled her hand away. "You're a rascal, Mr. Sterling. A true rascal. There's lots of work in store for you if you expect to impress *my* mother."

"And what makes you think I *want* to impress her?" he said as they reached the walkway to Roland's condo."

Kasia took his hand again and smiled up at him as he rang the doorbell. "You do."

"I do?"

"You *don't?*"

Matt retreated. "I do."

Roland immediately opened the door with Annette right behind him. "Let's go, I'm starving," he said, pushing both Matt and Kasia ahead of him back out the walkway.

"And a good evening to you, too, R. T.," Matt said, stepping aside to let Roland bluster down the pathway.

"No need for pleasantries, Matt, old boy, let's just get there before the line fills in and we have an hour's wait."

"We're not going to Country Buffet, Roland. No crowds. Besides, I made a reservation, and," Matt said, glancing at his watch, "we're right on time. Excuse me while I greet your lovely wife," he said as he reached over and kissed Annette on the cheek. "This is probably your first time out in months, isn't it, Annette? With Mr. Tightwad for a husband, always saving for the next largest computer or some other electronic gimmick, he'd be content to eat frozen Chinese dinners every night. Come to think of it, that *was* all he ate in college."

Annette put her arm around Matt and gave him a giant squeeze. "He considers that if I go to women's enrichment night or a church leadership meeting, that I've had my 'night out' for the week."

"*That*, I believe," Matt responded.

Annette released Matt and stepped closer to Kasia, leaning forward and pressing cheeks together. "I'm certain we're going to have a lovely evening, Kasia, despite these two. And how did your day go?"

Kasia hugged Annette briefly and they retraced the pathway to the car, Annette and Kasia chatting, Roland and Matt striding on ahead. "I had a good day, Annette. Getting all my documentation ready for the research I'll do in England and France."

"That sounds *so* exciting. And Roland tells me Matt is going with you."

"Only to England, for Christmas. Then he'll return and I'll carry on with my work. It should be fun."

"Oh, I'm sure it will be. Need a good assistant?" Annette chuckled. "I could leave Roland home with the Chinese dinners."

"It would serve him right," Kasia said as they entered the

car, both women getting in the back seat and letting Matt and Roland take the front.

On the north slope of South Mountain, the South Mountain Golf Club, opened just before the turn of the century, had developed an excellent restaurant facility. Matt was a member of the Riverside Country Club in Provo, the home of BYU's golf team, and had been ever since his time on the college team, but he frequently played South Mountain and enjoyed both the length, at over seven thousand yards, and the strategic importance of side hill shots.

It was only a five-minute drive from Roland's condo, located at the far end of the front nine, to the restaurant. Before the ladies had a chance to complete their comparison of Sean Connery versus Pierce Brosnan as the dashing James Bond in the latest movie release, *To Die For*, they were exiting the car and heading for the restaurant.

Almost simultaneously as they reached the entrance, another couple entered the cross walk and Matt deferred to the second couple as they passed through the door. At the unexpected meeting, recognition took a few moments to dawn and in actuality, it was Julia Wells who offered the first greeting as they stepped into the foyer of the Golf Club.

"Matt! Hello," she said. "May I introduce my husband, Greg Wells. Greg, this is Matt Sterling, assistant city manager at Snowy Ridge."

"Nice to meet you, Matt," Greg said as he extended his hand.

"I'm sorry, Mayor Wells, I didn't recognize, uh, or expect…uh, well, so much for protocol," he laughed to cover his embarrassment. "It's very nice to see you. Let me introduce you to my friends. This is Kasia Somerset, Roland Timmerman, and his wife, Annette Timmerman. Everyone, this is Julia Wells, newly elected mayor of Snowy Ridge, as of January that is," he said, smiling at Julia. "And of course her husband, Greg."

All exchanged quick cordialities, which dissipated briefly as they noticed the receptionist looking back and forth between the people, trying to determine if she had one or two reservation groups. Roland broke the ice, speaking to Julia. "Would you care to join us for dinner? We have reservations, but I'm sure they could add a couple more chairs or get us a larger table."

Julia looked quickly at Greg who nodded. "Sounds good," she said.

"Fine, then it's all settled," Roland said.

They approached the reception counter where Roland continued his leadership role. "We're all together. Six please, under the name of Sterling."

The young woman ran her finger down the list of names. "Six, you say, uh, someone wrote...not a problem. Six it is. Right this way, please."

Roland winked at Matt and the small group followed the receptionist to their table, somewhat removed from the main area and with an excellent view through the plate glass windows of the Salt Lake valley and the lights of the city, some twenty miles north.

"This should be interesting," Kasia whispered to Matt as they wound their way through the restaurant toward their table."

"You've got that right," he replied. "Let's try to keep the conversation off politics."

Kasia nodded her understanding and they were seated, facing the Wellses, with the Timmermans on either end of the oval table. As soon as they were seated, Roland began the conversation.

"So, Mayor Wells, how do you plan to shake up Snowy Ridge? I hear you've got plenty up your sleeve."

Matt's eyes rolled in his head and Kasia surreptitiously took his hand beneath the table, squeezing it and smiling politely across the table at Julia who seemed just as anxious to avoid the topic altogether.

Chapter Eleven

Monday morning as Matt arrived for work, he observed Doug Bellows, finance director, enter Pat Harcourt's office and the door close. He proceeded to his office and began to review the Council agenda for the Thursday evening meeting. Candy entered the office moments later and they exchanged greetings, Matt nodding toward Pat's office, located across and down the hall from his office.

"Don't know," Candy said. "She's been in since about six, according to security. Doug got in only several minutes before you did. She must have called him right in."

"Well, on to business," Matt said. "She'll get around to me when she's ready."

* * * * *

Doug Bellows took a seat directly in front of Pat Harcourt's desk as she banged out a few more keyboard strokes. Then she swiveled her chair around and folded her arms across her chest.

"Did you read Matt's memo I forwarded this morning?"

"I did. I told you he wasn't a team player three weeks ago, right after the elections."

"Knock off the crap, Doug. It doesn't matter who told who, what, or when! We've got to get our strategy together and take command of this or it's gonna get out of hand. Did you know that Matt had dinner with Julia Wells on Friday, with several of his friends there to make nice-nice to her?"

"Where'd you hear that?"

She ignored him. "What do you make of her questions in her meeting with him?"

"Well, Matt doesn't exactly detail her comments, but focusing on procurement issues is just another way of getting a look at how we issue contracts. We're pretty clean in that department. Every contractor we've selected has been the lowest bidder."

Pat snickered. "Yeah, with a little help from us."

"No one else knows that, not even some of the contractors."

"True. And we've got to keep it that way. So, what do you suggest?"

"I did some research myself while you were gone. You remember the Fontana project?"

"Are you kidding? That was where we skirted the closest to being caught in our own web. Matching the federal bonus could have caught a lot more scrutiny if someone had been in close oversight."

"But they weren't. Council members Benton and Overton wanted that project to go through as much as we did."

"How much scrutiny can we stand on this, or, for that matter, other issues?"

"Let me finish telling you about my research."

Pat's eyes narrowed. "Get on with it."

"Guess who approved the Fontana contract?"

Pat Harcourt hesitated for several seconds, her fingers twisting as she kneaded her hands. Suddenly her eyes brightened. "You're kidding."

Doug shook his head. "First contract he approved after assuming the role as deputy city attorney."

"Well, knock me over with a feather. So we're clear on that one?"

"Not fully, but if anyone brings it up, we simply followed our legal counsel."

"And your official role as finance director, regarding financial oversight? Your statutory responsibilities?" Pat asked.

"I think I can cover my tail."

"So the strategy is that we begin to shift responsibility to our legal counsel."

"It's got to go much deeper than that, Pat. Just approving legal issues could show negligence as an attorney, but we need to tie him in to some of the financial transactions. To show that he profited."

"You mean put money into his account?"

"No, but to raise questions about where he got his money. We don't need to prove anything, but we do have to raise doubt. Shift the light. We need to find a number of other areas where he's been negligent or better yet, where we can make people believe he's been *intentionally* misleading the Council. Crandall Russell, over at First Union Bank, told me last week that Matt had paid off his condo and purchased a new Jeep Cherokee, *cash*. Well over a hundred and fifty thousand, according to Crandall."

"Where'd he get that kind of money?"

"That's what *we* need to decide—and demonstrate, if you get my meaning."

"I mean where did he *really* get it?"

"Probably from his grandmother's estate. Rumor has it that she left a bundle to the Y. Matt probably got some too."

"We need to discover some 'improprieties' and get him out of the picture."

"That still leaves us with Julia Wells," Doug pointed out.

"With no Council support, we can probably keep her at bay. But you're right, if she comes on board in a few weeks, she'll start digging around and we'll be on the defensive. Let's let that dog out of the cage ourselves. We start the investigation and point the finger to areas we can cover but will shed doubt on the golden boy. If we can make her understand we only have the best interest of Snowy Ridge at heart, that we are lock-step with her in rooting out impropriety, we can team up with her and take all the credit for dislodging a bad seed. If she asks about the contractors, and why we use the same ones so frequently, we just tell her we're taking these steps, choosing these contractors, because we want the best work done for the city, and it's always the lowest price."

Bellows tilted his head to the side, glancing at Harcourt with a slight grin on his face.

"All right," she said sharply, "we're getting a piece of the action along the way, but the city is in better shape, isn't it? We are actually keeping well within budget and everything is running smoothly."

"True enough. We're going to be on thin ice here, Pat. Once the light is on, there's no guarantee we can control where it shines. How do you want to handle it?"

"Matt's informed me he's going on vacation for a couple of weeks at Christmas. Going to England or somewhere. We can begin the process while he's gone and when he comes back, it will all be downhill. He'll be on the defensive. But first, he needs to think we're in agreement with his premise that we should try to make it work with Wells. No hint of stonewalling. And Wells needs to see a change of heart also. I'll take care of that. Just check with me before you give her any financial information."

"Pat, I'm in this the same as you are. I'll be careful. What about the retirement fund?"

"He hasn't a clue. And it would be very hard for anyone here to make *that* connection, but still, we don't want the light to shine in that direction. It's been running for five years now, or just over, so nothing out of the ordinary has taken place since then. The deposits have all been steady with no suspicions from any front. Even the auditors have missed it, or better yet, seen it as business as usual."

"Thank you very much."

"Don't blow your own horn too much, Doug. You did a fine job, no question about it, but we are skirting the edges of fraud here."

"*Skirting* the edges?" he asked. "You're not facing the issues. We're knee deep, shoulder deep actually, in this whole process. People are in jail for a whole lot less."

"I don't want to hear anymore of that talk, Doug. Just keep the records straight and from this point on, Matt Sterling is out of the loop. But be as friendly as you can. No suspicious attitude. Let's go along with the 'Hail Caesar' routine he suggests we give to Julia Wells."

"I can do that, too."

"Fine, get on with it and on your way out, tell Joan to ask Matt to come to my office."

"Right."

* * * * *

"Matt, c'mon in, please," Pat Harcourt said, rising from behind her desk. "Have a good Thanksgiving with your family?"

"I did, Pat, thanks."

They both took seats in what Pat called her meeting corner, complete with a color-coordinated lounge suite.

"How are your parents?"

"Good, Pat. And your sister? A healthy little baby?"

"Absolutely beautiful. My first niece."

"Congratulations, *Aunt* Pat."

Harcourt smiled and nodded. "Matt, I read your memo about your meeting with Mayor Wells. I know this might come as a surprise, but it made a lot of sense. I couldn't agree more. I've been thinking while I was gone that we need to rethink this whole process of transition of power. As Mayor Tomlin retires and Mayor Wells assumes office, we need to support her all we can."

Matt leaned forward in his chair, nodding agreement. "I'm glad to hear you say that, Pat. She's really not a bad person. She has the best interests of the city at heart. At least that's how I read her."

"That's excellent. I've just had a chat with Doug and told him we needed to give her all the support and material she needs to come up to speed early in her term."

"Anything I can do, just ask."

"That's good, Matt. Now, you're going to England for Christmas. Is that right?"

"If that's okay with you."

"Absolutely, unless you want to stay here and let *me* go," she laughed. "Nope, you put this all out of your mind and have a great holiday. It's been a tough year for you, what with your grandmother dying and all. We understand that and I'm glad you can get away. And the word is you've met someone, uh, someone *new* and exciting," she said, a knowing female look on her face.

Matt grinned and waved his hand. "I've made a *few* friends this past couple of months."

"Right, then," Pat said, standing up. "Get your portion of the Council agenda in order for this Thursday and then we can slide until Christmas. And thank you for meeting with Mayor Wells and for standing in for me. I appreciate it."

"My pleasure, Pat, and thanks for understanding. We'll all come out of this transition in good shape. Snowy Ridge included."

"That's my hope. See you later," she said, stepping behind her desk.

Chapter Twelve

The overnight flight to Gatwick International Airport, south of London, several days before Christmas, was a nostalgic trip for Matt. Despite the hectic pace and multiple events that had occurred in his life through the intervening period, he realized while Kasia was sleeping that it was slightly less than three years since Elder Sterling had been on English soil.

As they cleared Her Majesty's customs, they walked through the glass barrier and Kasia darted ahead as she spotted her parents. Matt followed behind, pushing the overloaded trolley, only one suitcase of which was his. When he had picked her up at her home in Alpine, heading for the Salt Lake City airport, he had teased her about the size of her suitcases.

"I'm staying for over a month," she retorted, "and traveling on the continent, staying in hotels."

"Of course," he'd responded, lifting the bags into the rear hatch of his new Jeep Cherokee.

As he rounded the final corner, dozens of people waiting for arriving family or friends with hugging, crying, and noisy people everywhere, he quickly spotted Kasia enveloped in her mother's arms, a smartly attired gentleman with a thick shock of gray hair standing behind. Matt made eye contact with

Graeme Somerset, the two of them somehow recognizing the other. Graeme smiled, walking toward the queue of people. As they got closer, the older man held out his hand and greeted Matt.

In his early sixties, Graeme Somerset looked exactly like the picture in Kasia's living room. A stately man, erect and just over six feet, he was eye level with Matt. His face was a bit weathered, but not leathery. His dark, piercing eyes spoke of intelligence and perception, perhaps even a hint of compassion. Matt had the instant impression he was being interviewed. But what was most evident, was the warmth in the older man's handshake.

"Welcome back to England, Matt. It was good of you to come. I hope you haven't disappointed your parents this Christmas."

"Not at all, sir. As Kasia probably told you, we visited with my parents last month, for Thanksgiving."

"Oh, yes," Graeme chuckled, "that peculiar American holiday replete with food. I never could figure out whether the colonists were celebrating their survival through the winter or their exodus from England."

"Perhaps a bit of both, sir," Matt laughed in return.

"It's only a short walk to the car. Let me help you with those bags. We might as well leave them on the trolley, wouldn't you say?"

Graeme Somerset's clipped, Oxford-educated British accent was music to Matt's ears. Kasia had a much softer, smoother delivery than her father. Her accent was present— more pronounced when she exaggerated for his benefit. But Graeme spoke much as had Matt's mission president and several of the stake officers while he served as a zone leader, meeting often with various stake presidents.

"Matt, let me introduce you to my wife, that is if I can get her to release Kasia." The two women parted and Kasia slipped her arm into the crook of her Dad's elbow. "Carolyne, this is Matt Sterling, the, umm, ah, young lad Kasia has written about."

"Indeed," Carolyne Somerset said, turning her attention to Matt. Exactly matching Kasia's height, her appearance would not have immediately identified her as Kasia's mother. Her hair was shorter than Kasia, the color of wheat, and her facial features were Grecian, a strong, yet beautifully sculpted nose, high forehead, and a strong cheek line. Only her eyes matched Kasia's, with the same dark gray intensity, brilliant against their matching onyx-colored counterparts on each ear. She looked Matt dead straight in the eyes and said, "Young man, I would like to see a note from your mother that gives you permission to be away from your family at Christmas."

Kasia just rolled her eyes back in her head and Matt stood speechless. The effect lasted about five seconds, but it seemed like two minutes. Then Carolyne stepped closer to Matt and hugged him tightly, stepped back and proffered a broad smile. "But I also intend to write her and tell her that she has a most loving son who was thoughtful enough to bring *my* daughter home for Christmas and I appreciate her motherly sacrifice."

Matt's smile re-appeared and Kasia linked arms with her mother as the entourage began the trek to the car park. Luggage loaded into Graeme's Range Rover and traffic congestion cleared, they departed the airport environs and began the trip home with the two men in the front and the women, the rear.

Before they had traveled far, Kasia spoke up. "Dad, could we take a short detour on the way home?" she asked.

"You didn't notice me turn south instead of west at the intersection?" he asked.

Kasia looked at the passing scenes briefly, got her bearings, and then smiled. "Thank you, Dad. I know I'm surrounded by temples in Utah, but my heart always lives in the London Temple. I just want to drive by."

"I understand," her father replied. "Besides, we need to show Matt the beauty of the Surrey countryside."

"The London Temple?" Matt asked. "I've been there, twice actually. Our mission president took the missionaries each year while I served here. Absolutely beautiful, isn't it?"

"It's just a short detour. Add about twenty minutes to our trip. We live roughly thirty kilometers west of the Temple, in the middle of Surrey. I helped build the temple, actually."

"Graeme was ten years old, Matt," Carolyne said, a humorous note in her voice, "and the members visited the site to do odd jobs, back when the Church used labor missionaries."

"Foundations dug, a stone moved, a dab of paint applied, my dear Carolyne. It all added up to a new temple, and I was Johnny on the spot, I dare say," Graeme said, looking up and smiling at his wife in the rear view mirror.

"That's wonderful, dear."

"It's all beautiful," Matt repeated.

"Have your parents been to England, Matt?" Carolyne asked.

"Yes, ma'am. They came over about three years ago when I was released. We attended the temple too, probably sat in the very room you painted, Brother Somerset."

Carolyne and Kasia burst out laughing in the back seat and Graeme took his eyes off the road long enough to give Matt a stern look, followed by an agreeable nod. "Trevor Weatherly warned me about you, Mr. Sterling. About your rapier wit, that is."

"Sir, no disrespect intended to you or the professor, but with Professor Weatherly, wit was the *only* defense."

"Yes," Graeme nodded, "he was that way at Oxford too. Cheeky chap, isn't he?"

"But with a heart of gold. He helped me over more than one law school crisis and if it wasn't for his recommendation, I'd never have gotten my current job."

"That would be Trevor," Graeme said.

Following a twenty-minute walk around the temple grounds they drove for about forty-five minutes into the Surrey countryside before arriving at the Somerset home. The hedgerow windbreaks surrounding New Marblehead, the name Matt had seen on the small, engraved wood plaque at the gate, reduced some of his ability to see beyond the roads and out into the paddocks. Still, it was obvious that Surrey was as English as any Hollywood presentation and put Matt in mind of his all-time favorite classic about England just prior to the start of World War II, entitled *Mrs. Miniver*, with Greer Garson and Walter Pidgeon.

"New Marblehead?" Matt asked.

"Yes, indeed. Built around 1810. We've added a few improvements since I bought the place about twenty years ago. The original occupants of Marblehead built here in 1670, during the reign of Charles II. The place burned to the ground in 1808 and this was its replacement."

"Lovely home," Matt said.

The 'newer' model of Marblehead was a traditional Tudor style, stucco, brick, and wood construction. It was situated on approximately four acres, at least the portion that surrounded the home, and had two outbuildings that Matt could see, including a stable.

As they unloaded the luggage from the vehicle, two sable and white colored spaniels ran up to the car, leaping up on Graeme.

"Beautiful dogs," Matt said.

"They come with the house. Marblehead and New Marblehead have had Cavalier King Charles Spaniels ever since the original owners. These dogs have actually become a landmark in Surrey. People would ask what happened if we were to lose our Cav's. The bigger male is Jamie and the female is Fleur.

"Then these two must be pretty old, I mean if they came with the original house."

Graeme smiled at Matt's attempt at humor and helped him carry the luggage into the house and up the stairs to Kasia's room. Then Matt took the single remaining suitcase and Graeme showed him to his assigned room, down the hallway on the second landing.

"I hope this room will suffice, Matt. We've modernized it somewhat. There's a private bath over there," he said, gesturing toward the back of the rather spacious room. "And let me say again, in case I haven't, how pleased we are to have you with us through the holidays. Kasia's mother has been looking forward to your visit almost," he smiled, "and I say *almost*, as much as she has to getting Kasia home again. It was very difficult for Carolyne to see Kasia off to BYU."

"I can understand that."

"Perhaps you can," Graeme said, taking a seat in the corner of Matt's room, and motioning for Matt to sit on the bed. "But a parent's love—protective love that is—leaves us bereft of common sense at times. Kasia is intelligent, beautiful, sharp-minded, which, by the way is different than being intelligent, and knows just what she wants in life professionally, her career plans, so to speak. And those," the older man threw back his head and laughed, "are only *some* of her qualities, as expressed by an unbiased father."

"I've noticed a few of those characteristics," Matt replied, agreeing with Graeme.

"Have you, my boy?" Graeme said, suddenly a bit more serious. "How long have you known my daughter?"

Matt thought for several moments, then, on the wall behind Graeme, noticed an oil portrait of a young woman on horseback that to Matt's eye resembled a young Kasia. Finally he looked back at Kasia's father. "I met her in October, sir, about the middle of the month as I recall, at the Molecular Genealogy lab."

"So, you've known her just over two months?"

"Yes, sir."

"And do you think it strange that I would present what could be termed, essentially, an inquisition, only hours after meeting you?"

"No, sir," Matt responded. "I would like to think I understand. You have one daughter, she's known me for two months. She's traveled eight hundred miles to visit *my* parents, brought me five thousand miles to visit *her* parents, and you want to know the story behind the story."

"A very good brief, lad. You are indeed a lawyer. What *is* the story, Mr. Sterling?"

"Well, sir, I've asked myself that question about a half-dozen times in the past several weeks. Ever since Thanksgiving actually, since my mother gave me the same routine you're giving me now. She's about as good at it as you are, sir."

"And what did you tell her?"

"I told her I didn't know the answer."

"Didn't *then*, or don't *now?*"

Matt rose from the bed and stepped to the window, looking out at the vast, well-manicured lawn, and then turned back, facing Graeme Somerset. His eyebrows knitted slightly and his focus seemed more intense.

"'Didn't then' is the correct phrase, Brother Somerset. I know that tradition is more common, or perhaps more expected, here in England. At least that's how Americans see the English. I also believe that proper, umm, procedure is important. Since you've seen fit to, uh, no disrespect intended, sir, but you've decided to *confront* me rather quickly. I'll try to reply as directly as I can. Throughout the flight over—well, for the last several weeks really—I've wrestled with myself about what message Kasia and I were giving each other by our invitations to our respective parent's homes. That's not a step taken lightly by either of us, I'm sure. To be blunt, Brother Somerset, the 'don't know' changed to 'didn't know' about an hour ago, on the temple grounds. Please don't misunderstand. I'm not claiming revelation or a great burst of inspiration. What I *am* saying is that for some reason, I suddenly knew my mind. I knew what was right. For certain, I still don't know the outcome, but I know what I've discovered in my heart. This may seem sudden, but when something is so completely right, it doesn't take a person long to figure that out. With your permission, and Sister Somerset's, I would hope to find favor in Kasia's heart sufficient for us to consider marriage."

Graeme Somerset was quiet for a moment, then he rose from his chair and stood in front of Matt. "Son, if that's not an example of inspiration, I don't know what is, and I've heard a lot of them. Matt, let me tell you a short story. I grew up not far from here, attended local schools and started university at Oxford. Met Trevor Weatherly there. He and I served our missions together in Norway. I re-entered Oxford upon my return, took a degree in economics and then a job with the Foreign Office. Then, I got my first assignment at the British Embassy in Belgrade. I met Carolyne there on the seventeenth of December in 1974. Her father had also been a diplomat, stationed in London for many years. His family was one of the few LDS families in Yugoslavia. With his permission, I married Carolyne on the twelfth of February, 1975, when I was only twenty-eight, not quite seven weeks later, in the London temple just down the road from here. You know, the one that I *built* when I was ten years old," he said, pausing a moment, his lips drawn in a tight smile.

"Two years later we had twin boys. They both died within a week of birth. Three years and a law degree later, Kasia entered our life. She's been my joy ever since. You already have the law degree," he said, placing both of his hands on Matt's shoulders. "I know I'm being brusque, quite likely stepping out of line, but Kasia's mother has been frantic these past two months, the entire year, actually, as she has received correspondence from Kasia. This Phillip chap, the basketball player Kasia met at BYU last year, really threw her a googly. It's not my intention to stand in your way or to prevent the natural course of young love, but I *am* determined to protect my daughter from having her heart trampled yet again and to ease her mother's mind. I hope you understand and are not offended."

"I think we have the same goal, Brother Somerset. And if it will ease your mind, Dr. Weatherly gave me a similar talk several weeks ago."

"Call me Graeme, please. And I'm pleased to know that Trevor and Sarah are looking out for my interests."

"They love Kasia very much."

"Always good to have faithful, caring friends. Now, shall we go downstairs and see if the ladies have had a similar talk?"

"Yes, sir. But I doubt we'll ever find out."

Graeme Somerset put his arm around Matt's shoulders and they exited the room, headed for the stairs. "You seem to know more about women than I did at your age."

"No matter how much you think you know, it's never enough, is it?"

"No, my boy, it never is."

"One more thing, Graeme," Matt said as they reached the top of the stairs.

"Yes?"

"What's a 'googly'?"

"I can see that during your trip I'm going to have to teach you the intricacies of cricket."

* * * * *

Matt and Kasia got settled into her childhood home, had a brunch prepared by Carolyne, then took a stroll around the estate. As Kasia described it, New Marblehead really didn't qualify as an "estate" in the manner so many Surrey properties did, especially the historical country mansions of the aristocracy, but Matt could tell that she was proud of and loved her home and the entrapments of England. The ground was covered in December's winter leaves, dormant rose bushes, and a garden replete with myriad varieties of bushes and scrub, the buds of which awaited the coming of spring. The surrounding trees were bare of cover and the air crisp, a slight scent of wood smoke coming from the east. The gray sky, one endless cloud actually, brought back memories of tracting through the country roads and the sudden afternoon shower that quickly taught missionaries to carry a "brolly" and wear a light topcoat.

In early afternoon jet lag caught up to both of them and Graeme suggested they could benefit from a nap. Matt immediately agreed and without further coaching, went upstairs, took a shower, and crawled into the huge four-poster bed.

The knock on his door seemed only minutes later, and when Matt responded, Graeme opened the door slightly and stepped halfway into the room.

"Carolyne says dinner in about forty-five minutes. We're very informal here, Matt. Please dress casually."

"Thanks, Graeme. I'll be right down. What time is it?"

"Just after six."

"Fine. I'll be right along," Matt said, sliding his legs over the edge of the bed.

To his surprise, dinner was actually a light affair with soup and homemade bread the main course. Cheese, crackers, and hot apple cider completed the meal. Afterwards, they settled into what Graeme referred to as the "great room." Indeed it was enormous. The Christmas tree was at least ten feet tall. In a twenty-first-century setting, Carolyne Somerset had created an eighteenth-century Christmas, complete with what were obviously antique tree ornaments. No electric lights adorned the tree, rather the creative touch of someone who was familiar with tradition and sentimental about family heirlooms. Miniature framed pictures of family ancestors hung from every branch and bough of the tree.

Throughout the oak paneled room, heavy oak beams crossed the ceiling in four places. The only concession to modern convenience Matt could detect was the giant wood burner that had been neatly fitted into what once was a large, open stone fireplace. It had a glassed-in door that provided the ambience of a live fireplace, plus the forced air electric connection offered a much more even flow of hot air than the original occupants had enjoyed during the previous century. Comfortably stretched on a woven rug lay Fleur and Jamie, the two Cavalier King Charles Spaniels Matt had met outside earlier, their position unchanged for the past half hour, but their large brown eyes taking in everything that occurred in the room.

Matt sat on a large, upholstered, four-cushion settee, facing the fire. Kasia sat at the other end, removed her shoes and swung her feet up, placing them on Matt's lap, smiling at him as she did so. As soon as Kasia had assumed her place, Fleur, the female Cavalier, rose from her place by the fireplace, trotted to the couch and jumped up, wedging herself between Kasia's body and the rear of the couch, resting her head on Kasia's hip, her big, brown eyes on Matt. Each time Matt looked down at her tiny body she ever so gently wagged her tail. Carolyne and Graeme sat in opposing chairs, each side of the fireplace. There wasn't a television in sight and the thought crossed Matt's mind that they could very well have been the original owners.

"Matt," Graeme said as they settled into the room, "I'm absolutely fascinated by your ancestor's tale of traveling to America. What little Kasia has told us, mostly through email, is astonishing. How did you come by the story?"

Matt related the account of his trip to New York, the demolition of the house, and the discovery of the journal.

"We heard about the journal," Carolyne added, "but weren't you surprised that your grandmother apparently knew nothing about it?"

"I was," Matt said, "but looking at *this* place," he said, waving his arm in a sweeping gesture around the room, "I wouldn't be surprised if you found memorabilia or other historical treasures should you demolish it. You know, now that I think of it, Riveroaks, Grandmother's Hyde Park home, was built in 1790, twenty years before New Marblehead."

"We came pretty close to demolition twenty years ago. When I bought the place, back in the mid-eighties, we had it completely restored. Gutted everything inside and completely new exterior around the old foundation wood. New plumbing, electric, insulation, the works. We didn't find any gold coins, royal documents, or skeletons." Graeme said, chortling a bit.

"Discovering the journal was astonishing, that's for certain," Matt said. "I wish my grandmother could have known about it."

"And your family name. How surprising to discover your family is not who they thought they were," Carolyne added.

"Actually, Sister Somerset—"

"That ends now!" she said, abruptly and quite firmly. "My husband has convinced you to call him Graeme instead of Elder Somerset, I shall insist on the same courtesy. My name is Carolyne."

"Thank you, Carolyne." Matt looked toward Graeme, hesitating for a moment. "*Elder* Somerset?"

Kasia, who had remained quiet as her parents took up the conversation with Matt, spoke up for the first time since dinner. "Dad is currently serving as Area Authority Seventy for South England."

Matt took hold of one of Kasia's toes and began to squeeze gently. "Another thing you *forgot* to tell me, right?"

"Ouch!" Kasia exclaimed as she bolted upright, retracting her feet from Matt's lap. "It wasn't important." The abrupt move startled Fleur and she jumped down, resuming her place next to Jamie in front of the fire, continuing to eye Matt.

"Oh, of course not. Perhaps to the LDS members in this region, but certainly not to a visitor who should have shown the proper respect," Matt rebutted. "I'm terribly sorry, sir." He noticed Graeme and Carolyne smiling at one another as the exchange took place.

Graeme intervened. "As I said, Matt, we're very informal in this home, and we want our guests to feel comfortable. Besides, Kasia has always seen me as 'Dad.' Actually, I find that particular title most impressive of any it's been my honor to hold."

"I understand, sir. My father served as our stake president some years ago, then, when he retired, as a mission president. I heard him give a speech in Stake Conference when I was about twelve, I think. He said his role as father was more important than any other responsibility the Lord had given him. I believe he feels the same way as you, sir. He's just 'Dad' to me too."

"So there," Kasia retorted. "Now perhaps I'll lay my *head* in your lap. I don't think you'd pinch that. And no hair twirling with your fingers either. You wouldn't believe what he does to my hair, Mum."

"Elder Somerset, has respect for others been a significant part of Kasia's upbringing?" Matt needled.

"Sorry, lad, we've done the best we could. Some of our teachings just didn't take."

"Yes, so I see," he said, sliding several fingers into Kasia's thick, dark hair. "Anyway, Carolyne, you were speaking of the new name for our family. In actuality, according to most American genealogy, it's not unusual at all. Our name changed dramatically, but quite often the European names, especially those from Eastern Europe or the Baltic States changed their name, anglicized it somewhat so they could be more accepted and it could be spelled easier."

"Sterling is a fine name," Carolyne said.

"If the journal is true, then that's exactly how George Washington saw it too."

Graeme rose and opened the doors of the huge wood burner, stirred the remnants around and placed another log in, then closed the doors. Standing in front of the fire, he continued the topic he had started minutes earlier.

"What is most intriguing, from a barrister's perspective, is the arrest document ostensibly signed by General Sir Henry Clinton. Have you authenticated that yet?"

Kasia turned her head to face her father. "The lab's confirmed that the blood on the document was from one of Matt's paternal ancestors." She then resumed her place on Matt's lap.

"We've certified the signature," Matt continued. "Beyond that, there is no real reason to carbon test or try other dating mechanisms to place the document."

"I agree. So for some reason, the war perhaps, this Andy McBride was a criminal."

Matt smiled and Kasia quietly squeezed his hand behind her hips, out of sight of her parents. "From the British perspective, sir. I suppose that's true."

"Can you tell us more about the document? I mean, how did he come to be arrested and more importantly, perhaps, how did he escape or survive an execution?"

"From what I can tell, Graeme, he was probably only arrested for several hours. Certainly no more than a day."

"Had the war ended?"

"No, this happened about a week or so before the surrender at Yorktown."

"Then what happened?"

"Lieutenant Applegate, or I should say, *Major* Applegate happened."

"Applegate? Kasia mentioned that name in one of her emails because she knew that one of my firm's barristers is named Applegate. Wasn't he the British officer who sent McBride from Ireland? The one who—"

Matt nodded. "One and the same. Has Kasia told you about Nathan Hale being hanged as a spy?"

"I know that story," Graeme said.

"Apparently, McBride took to heart Hale's suggestion that he find a worthy cause and contribute. It appears that for the next five years, until late 1781, Andy McBride continued as legal counsel to several British commanding officers, Howe and Clinton among them. He got his information to Colonel Knowlton, then Major Talmadge who headed Washington's spy network, and even to General Washington himself on several occasions. If the account narrated in the journal is true, information he supplied regarding military campaigns, routes, supply trains and Cornwallis' refusal to move north to combine armies, was highly instrumental in helping General Benedict Arnold defeat General Burgoyne's invasion from Canada. That was another turning point in the war and allowed the Americans to continue for another day."

"And how could he get away with that for five years, working daily in British headquarters? How did he get his information out?"

"Righteous."

"What?"

"The former slave who partnered with McBride in the freighting business. He'd take a consignment of goods north into Westchester County, meet with Continental officers, and deliver the information."

"And they never found out?"

"It appears not, but Clinton did order his arrest. But that was for suspicion of murder, not spying."

"Enter Major Applegate," Graeme said, putting the pieces together.

"Enter Major Applegate."

The course of human life is determined not so much by who we are, as it is by what we are, and by the people with whom we associate. By such acquaintance our lives are intertwined with others', never again to resume their intended path.

Journal of Andrew McBride Sterling

Chapter Thirteen

The second week in October 1781, a bulletin from General Cornwallis in Virginia, to the commanding officer, General Sir Henry Clinton in New York, describing the indefensible position of the British disposition on the Yorktown Peninsula, and the inability to evacuate troops due to the French naval blockade, caused immediate consternation within British Army headquarters in New York. But it was not the content of the message that directly affected Andrew McBride. It was the messenger.

Cornwallis' aide, Major Jonathan Applegate, personally delivered the terse statement of intent to surrender and was present in the room when Andy was summoned, along with a half-dozen senior staff officers. Andy thought the man looked familiar but could not place him.

Clinton addressed the assemblage as if he had been prepared for this moment for some time. "Gentlemen, I'm afraid this is the end of the struggle. Generals Washington, Rochambeau, and Lafayette have Cornwallis backed against the sea on the Virginia coast. They are in much the same position General Howe had Washington trapped in Brooklyn, some five years ago." Clinton paused, seeming to reflect. "Would that we could have finished the rebels in that hour." He shook his head and continued. "Our fleet has suffered a defeat at the hands of the French, and we have no way to evacuate our troops. We should prepare for the worst. I want full disposition of official documents, orders directing commands en route to assist Cornwallis cancelled, and my personal escorts packed and prepared for departure on four hours notice. Are there any questions?"

Colonel Anderton, senior staff officer, spoke first. "Sir, had you not already issued a directive for General Cornwallis to dispatch his troops to New York, posthaste, to repel the expected rebel's attack? How came he to the Virginia coast?"

Clinton nodded. "To no avail was that directive issued. Washington clearly understood the impact of Cornwallis' refusal and shifted his intentions to Virginia, superbly it would seem, along with his French allies. We are lost, gentlemen. Carry out my instructions, Colonel."

As Andy left the room, he was aware that the messenger who seemed familiar watched him closely as he departed, but no conversation ensued. In the moment that Andy crossed the threshold of the General's office, one further eye contact occurred between him and the messenger. Andy recognized the particular look in the man's eyes and knew instantly who he was. From the slight upward movement of the officer's head, Andy understood that recognition had also dawned on Applegate. The thought sent a shiver of fear throughout his body; his throat constricted and he felt his heart begin to pound in his chest. Instead of returning to his office, he departed the headquarters building instantly, hastening to the freight office where Righteous had just completed loading his wagon for a trip north. He was strapping down the last cases.

"Andy, you look like you done seen a ghost. What happened?" the black man inquired.

"The war is nearly over, Righteous. We received a message from Cornwallis. He's going to surrender."

"Praise be. That be good news, Andy, but youse don't look good."

"I know the officer who brought the message. He recognized me."

"Know him?"

"From Ireland."

Righteous completed tying the final knot on the ropes and came to stand in front of Andy.

"He be the officer who put you on the *Canterbury*?"

"One and the same."

"What's he doing here now?"

"He's General Cornwallis' aide. He brought the message. And he recognized me."

"You sure?"

Andy nodded.

"What you gonna do?"

"Take Laura and quit New York immediately. Up to the Delacorte place in Westchester. The war's over, Righteous. The British will be scurrying to get out of here. I'll be forgotten in the melee."

"What can I do to help?"

"You're going up country with that load of freight?"

"Yep."

"Good. Come by the house in about two hours. We'll pack a few clothes and be ready. We'll go with you."

"Sure nuff."

Andy departed immediately and headed home, not certain how he was going to explain things to Laura. Arriving at his house, he took the stairs two at a time, catching Laura in the upstairs sunroom.

"You're home early," she said, stepping up give him a quick kiss.

"The war has taken a drastic turn, Laura. It's likely the rebel army will be here shortly. I'm going to take us to Westchester, to your father's place."

"There are more rebels in Westchester than here," she protested.

"True," Andy replied, "but Righteous has a pass and we'll travel with him. Quick, please hurry. He'll be here in a couple of hours."

"Are you certain this is the right thing to do?" she queried.

"Your father's there, isn't he?"

"Yes, but virtually a house prisoner of the rebels, according to his last letter."

"The pass will get us through. Just pack what we need for a few days, and hurry, please."

Andy bolted downstairs, quickly rummaging through his office desk, grabbing private papers and a small bundle of cash, both British Pounds and Continental scrip. Barely ninety minutes had passed and his important personal possessions had been accumulated. Two valises and a large trunk stood in the hall, waiting for Righteous, when Andy heard the front door to his quarters open and the sound of several pairs of boots echoed through the lower hallway. Andy stepped toward the sound.

"Righteous?"

"Mr. McBride, I take it," Jonathan Applegate said, standing in the hallway, a British dragoon at his side. "It has been several years, I believe, since our last acquaintance. And here I was, thinking you'd long since departed this life somewhere in Africa."

"What are you doing here?" Andy demanded.

"The King's business, McBride. Long overdue, I might add."

"And by what authority are you—"

"By authority of the British Commander of the Colonies, General Sir Henry Clinton," he said, waving a piece of parchment that Andy immediately recognized as identical to other arrest warrants he had prepared for the General on many occasions."

"On what charge?"

"What *charge*? Come now, my good fellow. Murder, of course. Of an innocent Irish lass whom you saw fit to dispatch with not so much as a thank you. Did you not think that I would recognize your earlobes? They've become my trademark, my good man. A token to people who cross my path. And the scar on your chin?" he said, reaching toward Andy, who drew back, avoiding the touch. "Could I have missed that? A most distinctive feature, I should say."

"I murdered no one," Andy protested, looking for a moment at the dragoon who stood silently behind Applegate.

"The Crown says differently," Applegate said, his demeanor remaining calm, his apparent composure belied only by the evident pleasure he undertook in carrying out his duties.

At that moment, Laura McBride descended the stairs, stepping between Andy and Major Applegate.

"Andy, who is this officer?"

"My pleasure, madam," Applegate, said, bowing slightly. "I am Major Jonathan Applegate, seconded from His Majesty's 60th Regiment of Foot to General Cornwallis, currently on directed orders to General Clinton. However, at the moment, my present duties, unpleasant as they may appear, involve the arrest of your husband. He *is* your husband, I presume?"

"Arrest? Andy," she said, looking toward her husband, "what is he talking about? What is the meaning of this, Major? My husband is a member of General Clinton's staff."

"I have an arrest warrant, Mrs. McBride, made out for Andrew McBride, for the murder of one Molly Meagher, Irish prostitute, in Dublin, Ireland, some years past."

Laura, her eyes instantly frantic, turned to face her husband. "Andy, is this the officer you told me about?"

"As I told you, Laura, I murdered no one. It was this man who killed Molly."

Applegate shrugged his shoulders and scoffed, turning to the dragoon. "Did you hear that, Sergeant. An officer of His Majesty murdered the poor tart. Now is that preposterous, or what?"

Andy began to discern the hopelessness of his position and took Laura by the shoulders, turning her to face him. "As God is my witness, I've murdered no one, Laura. This is the officer who killed Molly, framed me, and had me sent out of Ireland."

Laura shook her head, tears beginning to form at the corner of her eyes. "I'll go straight to my father. He'll know what to do."

Applegate chuckled. "The last time, Sergeant, it was *his* father who got him off the charge. Now he wants *her* father to do the same thing. Can you believe this blackguard? Shackle this man immediately and we'll transport him to headquarters. The general is waiting."

"No, you can't!" Laura cried, stepping in front of the dragoon.

"Stand aside, ma'am, if you please," the soldier said, moving toward Andy.

Laura jumped toward Applegate, throwing her hands up in his face. She was deflected by Applegate's quick parry and he grabbed both of her wrists, pulling her toward him so her face was mere inches from his.

"A feisty wench you have here, McBride." Applegate hesitated, his gaze steadily upon Laura as she struggled in his grip. "A change of orders, Sergeant," Applegate said more softly. "Shackle the prisoner and *you* take him to headquarters. I will attend to the General shortly. I believe I will remain with Mrs. McBride for a few moments, to uh, gather evidence. It is apparent the poor woman has been misled and is unaware of her husband's previous indiscretions."

"You will not!" Andy cried out, lunging forward toward the officer. The dragoon was quick on his feet and sidestepped Andy's rush to bring his rifle butt crashing down on the back of his head. The last thing Andy saw before being rendered unconscious was Major Applegate pushing Laura back against the desk, her hands flaying and her whimpers rising, the arrest order still clutched in the British officer's hand.

Chapter Fourteen

It was nearly midnight and the fireplace had been re-stoked several times by Graeme Somerset before Matt reached the conclusion of the story.

"That's an amazing tale, Matt," Carolyne said. "The poor woman. You can't leave us there. What happened to Andy?"

"Obviously he survived, my dear," Graeme said, pointing toward Matt.

Carolyne looked at her husband, and back at Matt and smiled. "Of course. But how did he escape?"

"He didn't actually escape. He was taken to General Clinton who asked him what this was all about. Andy tried to explain that he was innocent, that Applegate was lying. They waited some hours for Applegate to return with Andy confined to his office, under guard. Remember, the staff was hectic at this point, preparing for a disastrous defeat. Anyway, Applegate doesn't arrive and eventually Clinton calls for Andy and tells him that there must have been some confusion about the whole incident. On the basis of his five years' service to the Crown, Andy is allowed to go home on his own recognizance until such time as Applegate can shed further light on the issue. The journal indicates that Clinton was very perturbed by Applegate's account, but had been convinced by Applegate that Andy would escape if they didn't arrest him on the instant. In the pressure of the moment, Clinton deferred and signed the arrest order."

"And Laura? Did the British officer assault that poor woman?"

"The journal doesn't say. But she killed him."

"She *what?*" Graeme said, leaning forward in his chair.

"She stabbed him with a pair of scissors. Righteous appeared, saw what had happened, and he put the body in the wagon and took Laura to her father's house upstate, disposing of the body along the way. The next evening, Andy arrived at the Delacorte country home, which was well into American territory north of New York. Nothing was ever said to Laura's father."

"Were they safe in American territory?" Carolyne asked.

Matt shook his head. "Only for a while, but that's another story."

"Whew! And in the hectic pace of the British withdrawal, Applegate's unexplained absence as the primary witness, and Andy's departure," Graeme said, "Clinton ended all inquiry."

"Or it just got overlooked in the confusion of the surrender."

"So what happened to them then?" Carolyne asked.

Kasia stood from her position on the settee where she had been leaning up against Matt and stretched her arms above her head. "The grandfather clock has sounded the midnight hour, Mum."

"What does that mean?"

Kasia looked at Matt and they both chuckled. Kasia explained. "It means that this story has been so compelling Matt and I established a rule several weeks ago; no telling stories after midnight."

Graeme rose from his chair. "That, my sleepy daughter, displays your sheer brilliance once again. It's time for us too, my dear," he said, rising and stepping to help Carolyne stand from her chair. "These folks may have had a nap, but I believe their body clocks are a bit turned around. There's time for more tomorrow."

"Yes, *Elder* Somerset," Carolyne said, reaching on her toes to kiss his lips. She turned toward Matt who had also risen and hugged him once again. "We are so glad you could be with us for this joyous season, Matt. And so very pleased to have you home again, Kasia, my dear," she said, pulling her daughter into her arms. "A good night to all," she said, moving toward the kitchen and a few clean-up chores.

"Anything special tomorrow, Dad?" Kasia asked.

"You kids are free as birds."

"Great. I'm going to give Matt the grand tour." She took Matt's hand and quickly kissed his lips, turning then to hug her father before heading up the stairs. Both men watched her go. When she was out of hearing, Graeme spoke.

"My boy, this shall be one of the most difficult things I have ever done."

"Sir?"

"She has always been my little girl, Matt. That time has now passed."

"Yes, sir," Matt said, catching another quick glimpse of Kasia as she rounded the head of the stairs, heading for her bedroom. "Goodnight, sir."

"Good night, lad, and again, a most sincere welcome to England, to New Marblehead…and to the Somersets'."

* * * * *

The December days passed quickly and then it was early January, only two days before Matt's return to the states. In addition to Kasia's grand tour of "her" England, as she put it, Matt was able to locate several addresses for new members he had taught and arranged visits with two of the families. Kasia accompanied him and they spent the rest of the day in London "touristing."

January 5, the London Temple opened after the holiday closure and Graeme, Carolyne, Kasia, and Matt attended an early morning session, driving to the temple in separate cars. After the session, Kasia's parents returned home, leaving their daughter and Matt to fend for themselves.

They drove to nearby Lingfield, where they had a leisurely lunch, then returned to the temple grounds, parked the car and sat quietly watching the various couples entering and exiting the sacred structure.

Kasia reclined her right side driver's seat slightly, leaning back against the headrest. Although Matt had driven throughout London during his mission, he had deferred to Kasia and she had assumed the role of driver.

After they sat in the car for about five minutes, Kasia suggested they get out and walk.

"That sounds great. We're in no hurry, actually. I've only got *one* suitcase to pack this evening," he said, exiting the car and coming around to open her door.

"Men are all alike," she laughed as she locked the car and they commenced a slow stroll up the walkway.

They walked for nearly five minutes, holding hands and circling the temple building, stopping occasionally to admire the different angles on the building, the spire and the garden features, most of which were not in flower. Finally Matt spoke. "We're not, you know."

"Excuse me?"

"Not all alike."

They continued walking, slowly reaching the spot where they had started and commencing another round.

"How are you not alike?" Kasia asked.

"We're tall and short."

"Yes."

"And fat and thin."

Kasia stopped her forward progress, continuing to hold Matt's hand, turning him around to face her. "And old and young, and smart and stupid, and, and, and. What are you saying, Mr. Sterling who is about to leave England once again?"

"I'm telling you that men are not all alike. I'm telling you, Kasia Somerset, who is about to *stay* in England while Mr. Sterling returns to America, that of the billions of men in the world, I am different than *all* of them."

Kasia tilted her head back, looking into his eyes. "Is that right? And just how are you different, Mr. Sterling?"

Matt also tilted his head upward, looking at the grey, winter sky, the occasional patch of blue breaking the pattern across the horizon. "I could make a list, Kasia, but what I really want to say is that I'm different from all the *other* men in the world because I have two family names," he said, smiling. "And I'm different because, well, because I met *you*. And I'm different because," he hesitated, moving his hands to cup her face in both of his palms, "because I love you, and I'm different because I want to marry you…in this temple…here in England." He allowed a long breath to escape and continued looking into Kasia's eyes.

Kasia closed her eyes for several seconds, breathing slowly and placing both of her hands on Matt's, who was still cupping her cheeks. "I was wrong about *all* men," she finally said, "you *are* different."

Matt removed his hands from her face and they stood there for a minute while two couples walked past on the footpath. "Can we walk?" she said, turning forward. They continued at a slow pace for thirty seconds or so until Kasia stopped, turning again to face Matt. "All women are not alike either, Matt," she said softly. "We have a lot to learn about each other and perhaps it's our differences that are most important, so let me tell you a couple of ways in which I too, am different."

Again they were interrupted by the approach of an older couple who shifted into single file so they could pass Matt and Kasia on the footpath. The man in front smiled at the young couple as he approached. "And how are you today, Sister Somerset?" The older man said.

Kasia turned to see who had recognized her. "Oh, good afternoon, Patriarch Tolbert, Sister Tolbert. How very nice to see you today. May I introduce my friend, Matt Sterling?"

The older man extended his hand, pulling Matt's arm closer and placing his second hand over their grip in a warm greeting. "I've heard a bit about you, Brother Sterling, from Kasia's father. Welcome to England and to Surrey."

"Thank you, Patriarch. It's an honor to meet you, sir."

"And how long will you be with us?"

"I'm afraid I have to travel home tomorrow. It's been far too short a visit."

"I see. You've come to the right place for a final memory of England," he said, releasing Matt's hand. "Sister Somerset, see that you ensure this young man has a memorable visit and he has good reason to return."

Kasia began to blush, the color rising from her throat to her cheeks. "Yes, sir. I'll do my best."

"A good day to you both," he said as they continued down the pathway and Matt and Kasia resumed their walk in the opposite direction.

In several moments, Matt said, "I believe you were about to tell me how you're different from all the other women in the world."

"Was I?"

"You were. And I would hope that you would add the patriarch's instructions to the list."

She turned her head to look at Matt as they continued walking. "Instructions?"

"To make my visit memorable."

"Oh, *those* instructions. You wouldn't know, but Brother Tolbert also gave me my Patriarchal Blessing over ten years ago."

"And have you tried to fulfill your part of the blessing promise?"

"It *is* partially our responsibility, isn't it?" she said.

"That's what my father taught me," Matt replied.

"How am I different?" she mused softly to herself, her steps halting and her hand, clasped in Matt's, once again bringing him to a halt. Continuing to look down at the footpath, Kasia continued. "I'm different because when I was very young, I agreed to follow the Prophet's admonition that we 'dare to be different.' I'm different because...because I confuse myself sometimes." She hesitated and a slight giggle escaped her lips, "but that probably makes me *less* different."

Suddenly Kasia turned and faced Matt again, this time taking his face in her hands. "This is silly. I don't *want* to be different. I want to be exactly what we are encouraged to be by our church leaders. I love you with all my heart, Matt Sterling. I probably have since you took me to that basketball game and put me on probation, under your custody. I felt good. I felt warm. I felt, uh, I felt protected. If I *am* different, it's because I want to be your wife and I want to bear your children and I want us to follow our life together and see what the Lord has in store for us. And I want to get married right here...in this temple...*my* temple...in England. I always have. We're more alike than different, Matt. And I do love you."

"Your father will be pleased."

"Oh?"

"Of course. He *built* this temple just for us, didn't he?"

Chapter Fifteen

In the shuttle bus during the ride from the Salt Lake City airport to Emerald Parking, where Matt had left his Cherokee, he activated his cell phone and instantly was alerted that he had messages. Six messages to be exact. The first was from a name Matt didn't recognize.

"Mr. Sterling, my name is Steve Bracks. I'm a reporter with the *Utah Press*. I'm calling to see if there would be a convenient time to meet with you and go over some of the recent allegations centered around, the uh, the alleged financial improprieties at Snowy Ridge. I've been informed you are out of the country for the holidays. If you could return this call when you come back, I'd appreciate it. My cell phone number is 801-888-3434. Thanks."

Financial improprieties? What was he talking about? The second message was just as confusing, followed by a series of equally perplexing messages.

"Hey, Matt, this is Doug Bellows. Things have gotten kind of hot since you left, old buddy. Pat and I have tried to keep a lid on it, but, well, you know, these things run like wildfire. Give me a call."

"Matt, it's Mac. I think you're supposed to get to town on Saturday, around six. Give me a call as soon as you get this and don't call anyone else. Call me first, I mean it."

"Uh, hello? Mr. Sterling? Mr. Sterling, this is Valley Carpet Cleaning. We're going to be in your area right after the holidays and would like to offer you our special after Christmas carpet cleaning special. If you could give us a call at 766-9897. Thanks."

"Good afternoon, Mr. Sterling. My name is Shelly Porter and I'm an auditor with the State of Utah Fraud Commission. Your secretary has informed us that you would be returning this week. I'd like to schedule an appointment to meet with you if that would be convenient. Please call my office as soon as you return. We're at 334-3849, extension 6820. Thank you."

Instead of clearing messages as he usually did, Matt closed the link to his voicemail service and immediately speed-dialed Mac. The phone was answered after the first ring.
"This is Mac."
"Mac, it's Matt. Just on the ground. What's going on?"
"You got to your car yet?"
"About five more minutes."
"Swing by my place. You can be here in thirty minutes."
"Give me the highlights."
"Can't, Matt. But the game has started, I can tell you that."
"What game?"
"Matt, trust me. Just c'mon over."
"All right. I'll be there in a half hour."

* * * * *

Mac was clearing a bit of snow off the front of his sidewalk when Matt drove up and parked at the end of his driveway. He got out of the car and walked over to the older man. Mac reached to shake his hand.
"Welcome home. Sorry about the James Bond bit, but I

don't trust cell phones for important information. C'mon, let's get in out of the weather. Who left messages for you?" he asked as the walked up the steps and into the house.

"You, some reporter from the *Utah Press*, Doug Bellows, and some woman from the state fraud commission."

"That didn't take long. You got the whole load in sixty seconds. Okay, in a nutshell, the day after Christmas, the lead story in the *Ridge Runner* alleged that finance officers at Snowy Ridge, in performing an end of year internal audit, had discovered that a double payment of nearly a half million dollars had been made the previous fiscal period. It didn't say to who, what company, or how much the payment was. It also said that city hall officials were unavailable for comment due to the holiday schedule."

"What payment was it?"

"I'm not certain, but remember the discussion we had about the Fontana Project? Federal bonus and guaranteed payment from Snowy Ridge. They got *both*. Remember?"

Matt nodded as he slipped off his jacket and dropped into one of Mac's lounge chairs. "What did you mean by 'the game has started'?"

"I mean the queen bee sees the handwriting on the wall, Matt. That Julia Wells is gonna rip their socks off and so they've decided to bat first."

"But they'd only be pointing the finger at themselves."

Mac shook his head. He leaned toward Matt, a steady, serious look on his face. "Matt, you're going to have to get rock steady on this one. To paraphrase the New Testament, these folks are going to put the Mormons with the lions. I think you're the appetizer."

Matt shook his head in disbelief. "I can't believe that. I spoke with Pat just a couple of days before I left. She was fully supportive of Julia Wells. She'd made a complete turnaround from what you called the stonewall speech."

"And why do you think she did that?"

"Because she wants to make the transition easier."

Mac shook his head emphatically and issued a sharp profanity. "Not a chance. She may kiss up to Wells, but there's no way Pat Harcourt is gonna give away the key and open the doors to City Hall. Not voluntarily, no, sir."

"So, just the one newspaper story so far?" Matt asked.

"Several letters to the editor. You know, the same old crowd. 'Who's stealing my taxes, why can't we get honest politicians, etc.' The people who jump on anything to do with government. But if one of your phone calls was from the *Utah Press*, then they probably have a lead on the story and intend to run with it."

"How'd the fraud office get involved?"

"I don't know, but my guess would be that Doug tipped them."

"Doug? Why?"

"You're in their sights, Matt. Mark my words. But I do have a bit of advice. Call the reporter for the News and call the lady at the fraud office. Tomorrow. Show no hesitation."

"Shouldn't I check with Pat?"

"You can if you want, but my advice is look out for number one. There's no help for you *inside* city hall, except maybe Candy. She knows the ropes."

"*You're* inside," Matt said, smiling for the first time since he had arrived.

"Not for long. Pushed or jumped, I'm outta there as soon as I possibly can. But know this, Mr. Assistant City Manager, I'm in this fight with you no matter what. I've seen this crowd in action before and if I can leave a two by four up their, uh, down their throat, then I'm aboard for the duration—as they said to my daddy during the war."

Matt stood and grabbed his jacket, slipping it on and heading for the door. "Nice welcome home, eh? Oh, and for your information, and yours only, I got engaged while I was in England."

"Outstanding! Now marry the girl and get the hell out of Dodge City before the bad guys lynch you."

"And another thing, Mac, about the Mormons and the lions. These folk are Mormon too."

Mac nodded, a sad expression crossing his face. "I know. That's the shame of it. Now perhaps you can understand why I'm inactive."

Matt shook his head slowly and put his hand on his friend's shoulder. "Another day, another time, Mac. But that's not the reason, or the answer, and you know it."

"One battle at a time, Matt. Let's just take this one on and see what happens."

* * * * *

Matt was in his office less than two minutes when Pat Harcourt came through his doorway. She didn't say anything in greeting, just closed the door behind her and took a chair in front of his desk. Her body language reflected compassion, sorrow, and perhaps resignation to their plight.

"You've heard?" she finally said.

"Not much, but I had several phone messages when I got home and I noticed when I booted up that I have several dozen emails. What's going on, Pat?"

"I wish I knew. Doug's controller just brought him a routine issue, something about the bonus we paid to a contractor a couple of years ago. Apparently he'd had a routine inquiry from the feds regarding the project. I can only surmise that they are conducting an internal audit. It usually takes them a couple of years after a project to have a review. One thing apparently led to another and before we knew it, the Utah

Fraud Commission was calling."

"How does that concern *me*? Have they already questioned you, or Doug?"

They've spoken with Doug, Matt, but he could only tell them what happened."

"What *did* happen, Pat?"

Pat shrugged her shoulders. "It's got to be a misunderstanding. I mean it was only a construction contract. It's not like you controlled the bidding or anything or what contractor was selected."

"What are you talking about?"

"The contract. The one that approved the payment of the bonus."

Matt's mind raced as he watched Pat Harcourt shift nervously in her chair, never quite getting to the heart of the matter.

"I don't recall any bonus, Pat. The city doesn't offer early completion or on-time bonuses. The Council is on record as opposing it. We have a delay penalty, but no bonus scheme."

"I know that. That's what makes this so unusual. Anyway, the federal bonus was guaranteed and we paid it. From what Doug said, that's what concerns them."

"Concerns who?"

"The Fraud Commission."

"Pat, this is going around in circles. Can you get to the point?"

Matt noticed that Pat bristled slightly at his directive, casting him a sharp look. Then her face softened. "I've been thinking, Matt. Perhaps you ought to take some time off. Perhaps a couple of weeks or so. Go back to England. Let Doug and me sort this out. I'm sure we can clear it up."

"And not talk to the Commission?"

"Just for a little while. Just 'til we can answer their questions."

Matt hesitated, then shook his head. "Not a good choice. I intended to call Ms. Porter first thing this morning."

"I'd recommend against it, but if you think you should.... You know we'll do all we can to clear this up. We'll take the heat for you if you decide to get out of here for awhile."

"What heat?" Matt was genuinely confused. "This makes no sense. I've done nothing wrong."

"Matt, you approved the contract. The one that approved the bonus. The city had no choice but to pay. Nearly a half-million dollars if I remember correctly. Someone's going to want to know what happened. How that got approved."

"I'm prepared to answer those questions."

"I hope so. We've got a new mayor coming into office and she seems to want to have a close look at our procedures. I'd hate for her to take up her duties amid a scandal."

"Is that what you think this is, Pat?"

"What do you think it is?"

Matt thought for a moment, rocked back in his chair, and exhaled. Without thinking, he repeated Mac's words. "I think the game has started."

"Excuse me?"

He leaned forward again, certain of the truthfulness of Mac's warning, yet uncertain of exactly how to proceed. "Pat, I better give Ms. Porter a call. I don't want her to think I've ignored her request to contact her office."

Pat rose and headed for the doorway, opening the door and turning back to face Matt. "Remember, Matt, Doug and I—in fact the whole Council—are behind you. Just tell me how I can help. We'll be there for you."

"I'll remember that, Pat. Thanks."

* * * * *

Pat stepped through the door and almost immediately, Candy entered, closing the door behind her. "Welcome home, Matt. It's not going to be pleasant for the next couple of weeks."

"What's really happened, Candy?"

"The ship's sinking, Matt. Years of below-decks rot is starting to cause massive leaks. And the rats are scurrying."

"Have you always known, or suspected, something was wrong?"

Candy hesitated for a long moment and Matt could see she was framing her thoughts. "Matt, I really enjoy working with you, but you look at things, and people I might add, the way you think they *ought* to be. You've given credibility to some people who don't deserve it. That's okay. That's youth and inexperience. And it's…well, it's *Christian*. It was not my place to jade your thoughts or your ideals. But now it's time to open your eyes a little wider. Management courses always talk about thinking outside the box. But sometimes more than that is needed. With respect to Snowy Ridge, I use a different term. Instead of looking straight ahead, you need to use peripheral vision. See what's going on 'around you,' not just ahead of you."

"Is this my first real city management lesson?" he asked ruefully.

"It could be, Matt. Your first political lesson for sure. Let's just see that it isn't your last as well. Despite outward appearances, this is a leaky old tub, and remember, when a ship takes on water, not only do the rats jump overboard, quite often a few good sailors go to Davy Jones' locker."

"You're a bundle of cheer."

"I'm old enough to know when to put on the life vest. I'll keep my nose in the wind, but I think those around the queen know I'm not to be trusted."

"What a place," Matt commented, shaking his head. "But, on a bright note—"

"There's a bright note? Please, tell me quick," she said, a smile suddenly appearing.

"There is," Matt smiled. "I asked Kasia to marry me."

"Is that right? Well, from my perspective, the bright note would be if she said yes."

"She did."

"Well then, a hug and a kiss are in order," she said, coming around behind his desk.

Matt rose as she approached and she kissed him on the cheek, hanging on to his hands for a moment. "This could get ugly, Matt. I'll do what I can to help you, but…"

"Thanks, Candy. I understand. But don't give up yet. Beneath this calm exterior beats the heart of a lion."

"Is that right?" she laughed. "Well start roaring, Mr. Sterling. And file your fangs."

"Right. Thanks for your support, Candy. It means a great deal, and I mean that. Both you and Mac are showing what John Wayne called 'true grit.'"

"We're offering to be the range crew, Matt. The true grit needs to come from you."

"I understand. I'm going to call Ms. Porter now. Would you please close the door?"

"Sure thing. Oh, Matt, have you got someone, a good friend, you know, maybe another lawyer knowledgeable about these sort of things? Political in-fighting. Someone you can talk to?"

"I'm going to have to find out, aren't I?"

Matt picked up the phone, checked the note he had made when he had listened to his voice mail the fourth time, and dialed the number.

"Utah Audit Bureau, may I help you?"

"Fraud Commission, please."

* * * * *

Carolyne Somerset carefully wound her way through the increasing traffic patterns as she drove Kasia toward her scheduled departure from Gatwick International Airport. For most of the trip, the two women had talked nonstop about the necessary plans and events that would have to be arranged by June 22, the Wednesday Kasia had set as her wedding day.

"It's only five months, Kasia," Carolyne said, "I don't know if we can get it all done."

Kasia just shook her head, smiling at her mother's motherly approach to the single largest family event a mother can arrange. "We could come back in February, Mum, and keep it to just you and Dad and Matt's parents. Or you and Dad could fly over and meet us at the new Sacramento Temple."

Carolyne risked a quick glance at her daughter and allowed a smile to envelope her face. "I get the point. We'll make it work somehow."

As they approached the entrance to the airport parking area, Kasia reached over and put her hand on her mother's shoulder. "I really do love him, Mum."

"I can see that, Kasia. He's a lovely young man. Your father is quite impressed and you know Dad. That's not easily accomplished."

"Why is that, Mum?"

"Why does your father like Matt?"

"No, why is it difficult for Dad to see the best in people? I've always wondered."

Carolyne was silent as she negotiated the car into a vacant space and turned off the engine. She sat there for a moment, her hands on the steering wheel, then she turned to look at Kasia. "He *does* see the best in people, Kasia. That's his strongest point. But somehow, perhaps the mantle of the Church offices he's held for so long, he also sees their potential—what they *could* be. We haven't spoken about it, although I'm certain we will after you leave," she said, chucking lightly, "but I think he sees much to admire in Matt."

"But Dad only just met him."

"Yes, but he knows *you* very well."

Kasia nodded her head. "I think I understand. He knows me and to some degree is relying on my judgment."

"Something like that."

"I'd like to ask you something else, Mum. Something that I've wondered about. Don't misunderstand me, but why do you think so many LDS couples get engaged on the Temple grounds?"

"I'm not certain I understand the question," Carolyne replied.

"I mean in all the novels, movies, there are many more romantic settings." Kasia hesitated for a moment, her lips drawn tight. "I don't mean to—"

"I see what you mean now," Carolyne said, nodding. "No soft music, flowers, low candlelight."

"Something like that," Kasia laughed softly.

"It's not a worldly place, is it? Inside or outside. It has special meaning to true Latter-day Saints. I've never thought about it actually, but perhaps it's because the Temple is the one place that demonstrates love and spirituality. Each couple wants their partner to possess those qualities. They want to love them romantically, sexually of course, but—and this is the more lasting part— they want them to love who they are as well, what their spirit is like. Does that make any sense?" Carolyne asked.

Kasia leaned over and kissed her Mum on the cheek. "Romantically spiritual. I like it, Mum."

"He's a good-looking guy, Kasia. I think the romantic part is well in hand. And I think your father can see that he is spiritual as well. Perhaps that's why he's taken to Matt so readily."

"I hope so, Mum.

"So, you'll be in Stockholm until the 15th, then Paris, and back on the 27th?"

"Right. But remember, when I return, I'll just use the flat in Kensington since most of my work that week will be in London."

"Your research sounds quite exciting," Carolyne said as they exited the car, retrieved Kasia's two suitcases and began the walk to the international terminal.

"It's a real challenge, Mum. Dr. Amberly was kind to assign me the project. Everybody in the lab wanted to be on the team."

"I'm sure he picked the right person. Remember, I'll pick you up when you get back. I could use a few days in London again. Especially with this hasty wedding I've had thrown at me at the last minute."

Kasia paused in the walkway, leaned over, and wrapped her arms around her mother, pulling her close as dozens of other passengers passed by, oblivious to what was a common scene in airports. "You love it, Mum, and you know it."

They resumed their trek, each pulling a wheeled suitcase. "Will you have a few days to look for a dress when you get back?"

A bright smile lit up Kasia's face. "If I haven't already found one in Paris."

"Oh," Carolyne exclaimed, "the *cheek* of you. You can't do that without your mother."

"If I find one I just can't live without, I'll call and you can fly over for a day or two."

"That will set your father in a mood. His wife and daughter in Paris with the credit cards, shopping for a wedding."

* * * * *

"Thank you for coming, Mr. Sterling. I'm Shelly Porter with the Utah Fraud Commission and this is Hank Andersen, assistant district attorney for Utah County. Our other associate is Claire Aiken with the U.S. Attorney's office. Before we proceed, I want to advise you that although this is a preliminary proceeding, any information obtained as a result of our discussion will become part of the body of evidence in this investigation."

"That sounded almost like a Miranda warning. Am I a suspect in a criminal proceeding?"

Shelly Porter shook her head. "No. At present we're just gathering facts. We requested a meeting with Mrs. Harcourt and Mr. Bellows. They were cooperative, but suggested we talk with you first. Of course, you were out of the country."

Matt gave a questioning look to the man standing on his left. The older man nodded and Matt returned his attention to Ms. Porter.

"This is Trevor Weatherly. From this point forward, Professor Weatherly will represent me as legal counsel."

"Do you think you need legal counsel, Mr. Sterling?" Hank Andersen asked.

"You're the ADA, Mr. Andersen. Are you prepared to advise me that I *don't* need counsel?"

"I'm not here to advise anything. At this point, I don't know if you need counsel, but of course it is your right to be represented. As ADA, it's my job to have a closer look at the situation in Snowy Ridge and to ascertain if there is sufficient cause to impanel a Grand Jury."

"Well," Shelly said, "let's all take seats and see if we can work our way through what appear to be confusing issues. Mr. Weatherly, do you wish to be placed on record as Mr. Sterling's legal counsel?"

"I do. Is this meeting to be treated as a formal deposition?" Weatherly asked.

"No, sir, it is not. All information gathered here will be considered confidential and will not be released to anyone outside the jurisdictions you see represented here today. We will not be recording our conversation, however, unless there are objections, all present are entitled to take notes. Do you have any objections to the procedure?"

Professor Weatherly shook his head and assumed one of the seats on the near side of the table. Matt sat next to him. Shelly Porter, Hank Andersen, and Claire Aiken sat on the opposite side.

"Mr. Sterling, I'll begin if that's all right with you," Ms. Porter said. "How long have you been employed by Snowy Ridge and in what capacities have you served?"

For the next thirty minutes, questions were asked and background information was provided detailing Matt's education, job duties, and overseas travel for the past several years. With the general information covered, Claire Aiken from the U.S. Attorney's office spoke for the first time.

"Mr. Sterling, my office's involvement in this issue is with regard to a federal construction contract awarded some three years ago. It's my understanding that you participated in the approval of a Snowy Ridge construction contract approximately two years ago that entailed a guarantee clause with respect to payment of a federal bonus to the contractor. Snowy Ridge retained the contractor for a project within the city boundaries and guaranteed that bonus in the event the contractor was delayed and was unable to complete the federal job on time. Is that your recollection?

"It is, or I should say it was at the time. But I have since been led to believe that the contract actually called for payment of the bonus *regardless* of the outcome of the federal performance requirement."

"You mean both were to be paid?"

"That's correct."

"Isn't that somewhat unusual?"

"Indeed, it's very unusual, but from my recent review of the contract and case law, perfectly legal," Matt said, glancing at Professor Weatherly. "I know several law professors who would find that reprehensible, to say the very least."

"Can you tell us how that situation came about? Were you aware that both bonus and guarantee were to be paid to the contractor?"

Trevor Weatherly spoke for the first time since the questioning began. "My client can do better than that, actually, but if you seek to obtain his voluntary compliance on these specific issues, federal or state, Mr. Sterling requests that the Utah Fraud Commission or at the very least the Utah County District Attorney's office issue a formal statement indicating that he is not a suspect in these proceedings."

"Are you seeking immunity from prosecution?" Assistant District Attorney Andersen asked.

"Absolutely not," Matt responded.

"Then what are you seeking? Whistle-blower protection? You're well aware the district attorney will neither confirm nor deny that someone is a suspect until such time as the Grand Jury moves to indict. Why are you asking us to publicly clarify your status?"

Weatherly shook his head. "Quite simply, Mr. Andersen, and you should remember this from your first year English Common Law, Mr. Sterling is seeking neither immunity status nor whistle-blower protection, but he *is* seeking the presumption of innocence to which he is entitled under the law. It is our contention that a person or persons within the established structure at Snowy Ridge have sought, or are seeking, to focus responsibility for any misdoings on Mr. Sterling."

Hank Andersen leaned forward in his chair and folded his hands on the table. "From the information we were provided by city officials—"

Shelly Porter interrupted. "Hank, I think we should hear Mr. Sterling out. Professor Weatherly, at present we're not at liberty to discuss the available information. I'm sure you understand."

"No, Ms. Porter, I do *not* understand. If you have information that points in the direction of Mr. Sterling, then we should be advised and we'll respond accordingly. If you're seeking our cooperation, then a show of good faith on your part is necessary."

Hank Andersen leaned toward Shelley Porter and whispered in her ear, after which she nodded and turned her attention to Weatherly. "We have no such information, professor, and certainly nothing that we would be able to consider evidence. Nonetheless, Mr. Sterling, we are asking for your cooperation in your own interest. I can promise you this: If at any time you become the focus of our investigation, I will advise either you or Professor Weatherly before we invite you in for further questioning."

"Does that promise extend to each of the jurisdictions represented here today?" Weatherly asked.

"It does for my office," Porter replied. "Does anyone here disagree or wish to take exception to the request?"

No one responded and Matt whispered something to Professor Weatherly, who nodded his assent.

"Ms. Porter," Matt began, "we're doing a lot of fencing here and frankly, it seems a waste of time—yours *and* mine, not to mention your associates and the professor's. I've been with Snowy Ridge for two years, as I mentioned earlier. But perhaps I've been blind to what someone recently told me to see as 'peripheral operations.' I've had a closer look these past two weeks and I now have reason to believe that activities, shall we say *peripheral* activities such as we have been discussing here today, have been going on for some time at Snowy Ridge. Long before my tenure, I might add. I have no proof at the moment, other than a few documents related to the project Ms. Aiken questioned that demonstrate a chronological chain of authority predating my approval of the contract. But with a bit of time, I think I might be able to glean information more relevant to your inquiry."

"Are you suggesting that there is a conspiracy among the governmental officers at Snowy Ridge?" Andersen asked.

"Like you, Mr. Andersen, I don't know that for a fact and what I *do* know, or suspect, certainly wouldn't qualify as evidence. But from the minute I asked a few questions and offered to help our new mayor in her transition, I've been kept out of the loop. Mayor-Elect Julia Wells has everyone running scared. The moment I spoke with her in private, the inner circle closed ranks, with me on the outside. I think the mayor intends to get into areas that haven't had much oversight during the past few years, and that's making people very nervous. At first I didn't understand why, but as I asked a few questions, some of the long-term employees gave me a very different insight. However, as with most of the senior staff, I serve at the pleasure of the city manager. Her *pleasure* may not last much longer, especially if I persist in sticking my nose where it isn't wanted, but it stands to reason that I can do more good from inside than from outside."

"Do you think you're about to be fired?"

"If I'm publicly seen as a suspect, Pat Harcourt would be able to claim that she has no choice. She'd have to step in, for the public image of the city, I mean, and seek my resignation."

"And what are you asking from us, Mr. Sterling?" Shelly Porter asked.

"A statement that I am not a suspect and a bit more time."

The three people seated across from Trevor Weatherly and Matt Sterling looked at each other for a moment and nodded their agreement. Shelly Porter spoke again. "We can't issue a statement right now, but we're in agreement as regards your request for more time. We will maintain confidentiality on this procedure as long as we have reason to believe you are not directly involved." She paused for a moment and then smiled slightly at Matt. "For background information, Mr. Sterling, this is not the first complaint we've had about Snowy Ridge and contractual procedures. And, as you suggested, most of them pre-date your appointment. Yet we've found nothing definitive to corroborate the accusations."

"I'd like to say that's comforting to know, Ms. Porter, but in truth, it's distressing. I can't believe I've been that blind."

"I understand that. Most of us take other people at face value. This community is worse than most in that regard. The 'presumption of innocence,' as Professor Weatherly called it, takes on a dimension of its own in this LDS enclave. People *want* to believe their neighbors are honest, so they don't look beyond the obvious. So, how shall we proceed?"

Again, Trevor Weatherly spoke. "I propose that I should act as intermediary between yourself and Mr. Sterling, if that is acceptable."

A quick acknowledgment around the table confirmed the offer and Ms. Porter accepted.

Matt continued. "Our new mayor takes office tomorrow evening. At that point, she will likely begin to launch an investigation, or fact-finding mission of her own. That should help since I've promised to assist her in any way I can and the city manager has suddenly seen the wisdom of cooperating...at least on the surface."

"Your new mayor will likely have some issues of her own

to deal with, Mr. Sterling. This, uh, these complaints spread further than the subjects we've discussed."

"I don't understand," Matt replied.

"It's been alleged that her campaign funding was not in accordance with state policy and she may have misrepresented herself in her campaign literature."

"Let me guess. Another anonymous complaint?"

"We have to look into everything that comes our way, Mr. Sterling," Shelly Porter said.

"Fine. Is that all for today?"

"I believe we've about covered it. Do either of you have any further questions?" Porter asked of her associates. Both shook their heads. "I think that will do it for today. Thank you both for coming. You have my number, Mr. Sterling. Either you or Professor Weatherly may call at any time and I'll get back as quickly as I can. One other thing, Mr. Sterling, we can't let this linger on for too long."

"I'll do the best I can, but I'm not flavor of the month at City Hall, if you know what I mean. They would rather I take another vacation and leave the problem to them. They offered to *cover* for me if I chose to go away for awhile."

Porter nodded. "So we understand. For your information, Ms. Harcourt advised us last week that she thought you would be unwilling to testify or to cooperate with us. She indicated she would try to get you to do so, but she felt it was not going to be easy."

"Funny," Matt replied. "She advised *me* to take another vacation, as I said, and let her handle it."

"It's beginning to look like your flavor is not even on the menu at Leatherby's," Andersen said.

Matt stood and picked up his folder and Palm Pilot. "A friend recently warned me that the game had started and I guess he was right. In fact, it seems that it's well underway."

"What do you intend to do?" Hank Andersen asked.

Matt looked at the assistant district attorney for Utah County for a moment, then smiled across the table. "I intend to 'suit up' for the second half."

Chapter Sixteen

SNOWY RIDGE EMPLOYEE UNDER INVESTIGATION FOR FRAUD.

Matt sat at the table in his kitchen, eating a bowl of cereal while reading the headlines that were emblazoned across the Metro section of the *Salt Lake Star*. The story went on to indicate that the *Star* had obtained exclusive information regarding a secret investigation and a meeting held in the offices of the Utah Fraud Commission. According to confidential sources, an unnamed senior management employee of the City of Snowy Ridge was being questioned about suspected financial improprieties at the city. The article described construction contract irregularities, duplicate payments to vendors, purchases unauthorized by the City Council, and large personal cash transactions that were made by the unnamed employee including the all-cash acquisition of a luxury condo and a new sports utility vehicle.

Matt threw the paper on the floor, dumped his bowl in the sink, grabbed his keys, and headed for the door. The ring of the phone caught him just as he was exiting. He paused, considered leaving and then stepped back into the room.

"This is Matt Sterling," he said brusquely.

"I gather you've seen the paper," Julia Wells said.

"I have."

"Good timing on their part. The new Council is to be sworn

in tonight and this leads the news. Did the *Star* call you for comment before they ran the story?"

"Not a word."

"I didn't think so. I know that guy. He's not looking for the truth. He wants headlines. Have you spoken with Steve Bracks from the *Utah Press*?"

"I have an appointment with him later this morning. We spoke on the phone yesterday, after I met with the Fraud Commission people. But if this is the kind of result I can expect, I don't think I'll speak with him."

"That's not a good idea, Matt. Steve is a fair person. I recommend you talk with him."

"Julia, this is getting nasty very quickly."

"I know. My friends have told me to expect as much. How would you feel if we met with Steve together?"

"And tell him *what?* It can only get worse. If you objectively dissect the *Star* article, and that's easier done if you are *not* the subject of the story, there *are* financial irregularities at Snowy Ridge, there *have* been double contractor payments, and a senior management employee of the city *has* purchased a condo and a new SUV. There's nothing false in the article. It's just that it lays a trail to *my* door rather than at the people who are actually involved."

"I know, I know. So let's get Steve on our side. If you compare the *Salt Lake Star* against the *Utah Press*, in my experience, the *Press* is less inclined to be sensational. Steve, in particular. What time are you meeting with him?"

"Ten o'clock in my office."

"Do you mind if I come?"

Matt thought for a moment, not immediately answering. "I don't know, Julia. I'm not sure what he really wants. You say you know him personally?"

"Not personally, professionally. I've run across him in

regard to other stories. Look, Matt, we have to trust one another at some point. If we meet behind closed doors with Steve, the news of our meeting will get around city hall immediately. Isn't it time we put *them* on the defensive?"

"It would be an open declaration of war."

"And today's article in the *Star?* What's that if it isn't a declaration of war from their cowardly position in the bulrushes?"

"I see your point. Okay, I'll see you there at ten. I'm going to swing by the law school and talk to Professor Weatherly first thing this morning, then I'll come in to work."

"Fine, see you later."

"Julia? Thanks for calling. I'm sorry if I was abrupt."

"I think we're going to learn a great deal about each other in this process. How's your girlfriend, what's her name, Kasia? How's she taking it so far?"

"She's in Europe doing research for a few weeks."

"Just as well. Okay, I'll see you later in your office."

* * * * *

Trevor Weatherly's advice to Matt was to cooperate fully with the news media despite their propensity for slanting the news toward sensationalism. It wouldn't do any good, he said, for Matt to call the *Star* editors and complain about the story because no one had been named. Weatherly treated the story casually, as if he had expected as much. To make his point, he told Matt the hypothetical story of a criminal psychologist who was quoted in a newspaper article about a serial killer: *"The perpetrator probably had a difficult childhood, with a domineering and demanding mother who never accepted his achievements."* The next day the murderer called the editor and said, *"I didn't kill anybody and stop talking about my mother.'*

After he got Matt laughing, he explained that if Matt called the paper, they would only ask if he were officially identifying himself as the employee in question. Better to handle it through the other reporter and come clean with the facts of the matter and hope for a bit of journalistic integrity and a more objective slant on the story. It would be too much to wish for a positive slant. Neutral was the best they could anticipate. Matt left with his spirits lifted.

Arriving at the office about nine-thirty, Matt met Pat Harcourt in the hallway, a copy of the Star in her hand, a look of dismay on her face. Matt's spirits immediately spiraled downward again.

"This is not good for the city, Matt," she said, stopping briefly outside Doug Bellow's office.

Matt nodded agreement. "It's not doing *me* much good either, Pat. Do you actually think no one will make the connection?"

"Of course they will. That's what I mean," she continued. "We can't have our public image shattered after so many years of hard work to build a reputation of trust and honesty."

"Is that what you think the city has, Pat, a reputation of trust?"

She drew back, a startled look on her face. "Of course. It's been the hallmark of my administration. I thought you understood that."

"I'm understanding more every day. I'll be meeting with the *Utah Press* this morning and I'll see if the city can't get a fairer shake out of them. Myself included."

"I believe I should know what you're going to say, Matt," she said, glancing over Matt's shoulder toward Doug's office.

"I don't know what the reporter's going to ask. I intend to tell the truth. Do you have any objections or would you like to script that for me too?"

"Matt, I don't think I like your attitude this morning. This is your own doing and all I'm trying to do is protect you, and the city."

"And the anonymous source of the story? Do you have any knowledge of who might have leaked that information?"

"Surely you don't think it was me, or anyone here at city hall?"

"Surely I *do*, Pat. I'm not suggesting it was you specifically, but it couldn't have come from anywhere else. If you can show me I'm wrong, I'm willing to listen."

Pat shook her head in disgust and let out a big sigh. "Look, Matt, I know you're under a great deal of pressure at the moment and we'll do everything we can to salvage your career, but if you become antagonistic, we...*I* won't be able to be of much help. We're going to swear in the new Council members tonight and Mayor Wells. I want that to be as conflict free as possible. I hope you agree with me on that."

"I understand, Pat, and you're right, I *am* beginning to feel the pressure. But unless we come to grips with what's really happening here, conflict is inevitable."

Exasperation evident in her body language, Pat responded, her voice louder, the hallway debate drawing the attention of several office employees who stopped what they were doing to look in their direction. "And what *is* happening here, Matt, in your esteemed opinion, I mean?"

Matt hesitated, looking down the hallway to see Candy standing outside his door, nodding her head toward his office and mimicking holding a phone to her ear. "I don't know yet, Pat, but one way or another, I intend to find out."

"Is that so? Well, while you're finding out, Mr. Sterling, and putting your *vast* two year's experience to work, just remember who's in charge here. *I'm* the city manager. *I* make those decisions and *you* serve at my pleasure. I want to work with you, want to help you out of the mess you brought about by your own negligence, but if you persist in casting wildly about, throwing accusations at honest, long-service employees, I'll have no choice but to protect the interests of the city. Do you understand my meaning?"

"I believe I do, Pat. Now if you'll excuse me, I think Candy is trying to tell me I have a phone call and the *Utah Press* reporter is arriving shortly."

"Fine," she nodded, glimpsing back toward Candy. "And after your interview, I want to speak with you about his questions and I also want to know what transpired in the meeting with the Fraud Commission yesterday."

"I'm afraid I can't do that, Pat. We were put under an obligation of confidentiality. I'm sure you understand. They'll probably do the same when it comes your turn to be interviewed."

"*My* turn? What are you talking about?"

"You *are* the city manager here, Pat. And as you said, you're ultimately responsible for *everything* that happens, right?"

Pat Harcourt bristled at his comments, her lips pulled thin and tight, her eyes narrowed and she squinted at him while the office people continued their silent observation of the unusual scene. Then she turned and, without a word, strode off down the hallway. Matt walked toward his office and met Candy just inside his doorway.

"What's up?" he asked.

"Shelly Porter on line two."

"Thanks. I'll take it at my desk."

Candy closed the door as she left and Matt took his seat behind the desk. He took a moment to compose himself after the run-in with Pat before picking up the handset. "Good morning. Matt Sterling."

"Good morning, Mr. Sterling. I'll keep this brief. I just wanted to assure you that the information in this morning's *Star* did *not* come from my office."

"I didn't think so, Ms. Porter. In fact I think I've just been speaking with the source."

"You know who it is?"

"Circumstantially. But the rats are scurrying on this ship."

"I see," she responded. "Is there anything we can do?"

"I think we've declared internecine war, Ms. Porter. You may simply have to cart away the remains."

"Once information begins to go public, these things usually get very nasty. We'll wait to hear from you or Professor Weatherly. And Matt," she said, using his first name for the first time, "remember the old adage, 'Do what is right, let the consequence follow'?"

The statement caught Matt off guard for several seconds. "LDS proverbs, Ms. Porter?"

"Actually, I'm Catholic, Mr. Sterling, but the sentiment is not exclusive to your Church."

"And do you think it extends beyond the primary years?"

"Do you think it *ends* there? I've been in this investigation business long enough to know that the 'consequences' which the message refers to are not always pleasant. But the real question seems to be, is that why children are taught the principle? Do you think it only applies when people in trouble can be certain that the consequences of doing right will be beneficial to themselves?"

"You surprise me, Ms. Porter."

"And why is that, Mr. Sterling?" she asked, a slight edge to her voice. "Is it not possible for someone *other* that the majority religion to have a committed viewpoint? I saw you as more perceptive than that. Have I read you wrong?"

"No, uh, no, of course not. I'm sorry if it sounded that way. I just meant—"

"You just meant that it surprised you someone other than another LDS person would quote your own beliefs to you.

Look, Mr. Sterling, honesty is not an exclusive province of the Mormon people in this valley. I believe you to be an honest person. I've developed a sixth sense about these things and I'm seldom wrong. I even agreed to give you a bit of extra time to sort this thing out before my office becomes more involved. But knowing how this might pan out for you, I also thought I'd give you the benefit of my experience in this area. *Let the consequence follow* means just what it says. It may be mouthed in a simple song by schoolchildren, but it has real world meaning. And the consequences are not always pleasant even if the action taken was right. Do you understand what I'm saying?"

"Yes, I believe I do. And thanks for calling about the *Star* article. I never thought it came from your office. The rats are on *my* ship, Ms. Porter. And, as you say, they are not *inconsequential.* I'll be in touch. Oh, and by the way, I'm meeting with Steve Bracks of the *Utah Press* in about fifteen minutes. I intend to be as open and honest as possible so you can expect another story this afternoon or tomorrow."

"I've dealt with Mr. Bracks before and for what it's worth, he's never misquoted me or misrepresented the story. He also takes 'for background only' information seriously. My best wishes for you."

"Thank you for reminding me of some important facts. I'm truly sorry for any unintended insult."

"Don't give it another thought, Mr. Sterling. Good day."

Matt replaced the receiver onto the cradle and looked briefly at the clock on his desk, seeing that he had about ten minutes before Steve Bracks and Julia Wells were due to appear. He booted up his computer, opened Microsoft Outlook and received notice of several emails. He didn't recognize the first screen name, *FlyAbout*, and opened the message to quickly scan the contents.

Subject: Disgraceful actions

Sterling: your a disgrace to our city and ought to get out now! I pay my taxs and I want to know why you think you can spend them as you please on cars and trips and whatnot. Your also a disgrace to your church and ought to quit. I hope they excomunicat you. We don't want you!!!!!!!

Matt sat there staring at the message for several moments, the suddenness and the tone of the accusation coursing through his brain. How soon the world turns and how quickly disturbing a slander campaign can be. This wasn't why he'd gone to law school, wasn't what he'd been taught by his parents, wasn't why he'd accepted employment in government. Were these the consequences Shelly Porter had mentioned? What would his parents think if they were to see the message, or the article in the *Star* for that matter? And if this continued, as somehow he knew it would, what would Kasia think when she returned? Could he face her under such circumstances?

He leaned forward and held his head in his hands for several moments, massaging his temples with his fingertips as the impact of the newspaper story and the email competed for space in his head. Deep within, he knew that it was only the beginning. Matt thought for a moment about his ancestor and the troubles Andy McBride had faced. There was some comfort in knowing everyone had his own burdens to bear.

*They came by night. By break of day, when they had gone,
it was darker than when they had come.*

Journal of Andrew McBride
25 April 1782

Chapter Seventeen

There was no warning. The riders came out of the night and descended upon the house with the swiftness of corsairs, emboldened by their victories and the retreat of their enemies. As if it were not sufficient that the Crown had relinquished all claim, they seemed compelled to thrust upon the scrap heap of history those who had deigned loyalty to the Sovereign. And, shackled among their victims, his surfeit of patriotism unrecognized, was yet another who had served under cloak of disguise in the same service they now professed as noble and victorious.

In their nightclothes they were dragged, protests notwithstanding, to the giant Sycamore standing beyond the house and providing shade during the sweltering summer day to those who rested eternally beneath its shady bough. And on this evening, moonless though it were, the torch-borne shadows of ghosts played across the facade of the stately building. Standing mutely in witness, those spectral silhouettes watched as yet another of the endless rampages assailed against those whose only crime had been to serve the Crown, with Andrew among them, yet King and country being furthermost from his mind, thought, and action these past war-ridden years.

The acrid smell remained pungent—fire, tar, fear, and wilful men determined to prevail in their sacrilege. Still, some six weeks hence, the stench provoked the memory. Of his father-in-law, the remaining mercy was the knowledge that his wife of a half-century had not lived to partake. That the poor fellow, sodden by his fear, beset beyond bodily acceptance, whose legs, on knowledge of his captor's intentions, had failed in their necessary and dutiful office, now rests with her beneath the same Sycamore was but scant comfort. And the mindless torment of Laura, dear Laura, now seven months with child, for whom her father's death brought naught but public condemnation and a traitorous ignominy.

That he was broken in mind, body, and most painful of all, in spirit, rested heavily upon the soul. To become such at the hand of compatriots for whom a clandestine service was selfless rested heavily within the heart; for Andy had found the cause of which dear Nate told him, a cause he served with heart and soul, a cause for which he lost the favour of men and of country amidst a service of disguise for which Andy himself, truth be known, could provoke no honour from within. And his sorrow, penned of his own hand in his journal, reflected the desperation of the situation.

I know not the end of this, nor have I true knowledge of the beginning. I know but the enduring pain. They shall leave us now to our own means, bereft of even their contempt I am told by surreptitious courier. That we have ample worldly possessions is little enough comfort. Wealth and property is small surrogate for esteem of peer, or, more regretfully, for that obsequious honour which is perceived dishonourably.

They came by night, but by daybreak, when they had gone, it was darker than when they had come.

Chapter Eighteen

Steve Bracks telephoned about five minutes before his appointed meeting to advise that he was running late and would be there in approximately fifteen minutes. Just as Matt hung up, Mayor-Elect Julia Wells arrived and was shown into his office by Candy. Matt noticed Pat Harcourt pass by his office just as Candy closed the door.

"Steve's going to be a bit late."

Julia laughed softly. "For all his good traits, timely arrival isn't among them. Still, that gives us a few minutes. You look as if the world is on your shoulders."

Matt handed her the printed version of FlyAbout's email. She scanned it briefly and handed it back. "Ignorance knows no bounds."

"I've been sitting here thinking of my great-grandfather, Andrew McBride. My sixth great-grandfather actually. He was an intelligence agent for George Washington and spent the war in New York City working in British military headquarters. After the war, the American militia in Westchester County, north of the city, paid his family a late night visit. Andrew's father-in-law was a true Tory and my grandfather was tarred with the same brush…literally. The old man died as a result of the attack and my grandfather was a broken man thereafter. I know this email doesn't compare, but somehow I have the same feelings he expressed in his journal."

"Tarring and feathering was common in those days. A sort of local punishment outside the law," Julia said. "This isn't much different, Matt. It may not be as visible or painful, but I think I understand what you mean."

"It's only just started, Julia. I don't know if I'm up to it."

"We never know that, do we? Not until the task is in front of us. We know about the few, the Winston Churchill's, the George Washington's, because their travail was so public, but we never even hear about the thousands that made those victories possible, the Jane Does, the Jack What's-His-Names, or the Andrew, what did you say, McBride? Their small victories never make the headlines."

"Are you saying that's us?"

"Isn't it, Matt? Are we doing what's right? Or trying to do so? I'd like to think we are. I don't have a personal agenda. Tonight I assume office as mayor of this city. None of the established structure seems to want me. But someone in this community does. The vote was in my favor. I know the front-runner was killed in an accident and I won by default, but still I was officially elected. I intend to do the job. And you know what? The tougher it gets, the more corruption I...*we*...root out, the more likely I'll not be here next term.

"They don't want to know, Matt. The people don't want to know, especially in a tight-knit community like this. They want to believe everything in the garden is rosy. If we surface corruption or criminal actions, they're not going to thank us for it. They're going to blame us, actually, because everything was hunky-dory before we came."

"Then why do it?" Matt asked, leaning forward in his chair and raising his palms in supplication.

"Because it needs to be done. Because it's right. And because the task has fallen to us."

"That sounds very noble," he said, unable to hide the sarcasm in his voice.

216

"No," she said, shaking her head, "it's not noble. It's just right."

"Let the consequence follow," Matt muttered softly.

"What?"

He smiled and shook his head. "Just a children's song. So, now we fight back with our own form of propaganda, with the *Utah Press* I mean."

"We tell the truth and see what happens."

"Why are you *really* here, Julia? As mayor, I mean."

"You sound just like my husband. He's already taken several phone calls from anonymous citizens with nasty things to say. He's not as, uh, as patient as I am," she said, chuckling. "They get an earful right back when he answers the phone."

"You didn't answer my question."

"I don't *know* why I'm here, Matt. I trust in God every day and pray that He shows me the way and what I should do."

"I guess we'll take this a day at a time, eh?"

"I guess we will. Now, how about a cup of coffee before Steve arrives?"

* * * * *

Steve Bracks was thirty minutes late rather than fifteen. As Candy showed him into the office, Matt stood up and shook his hand. Bracks was about forty, with a ruddy complexion and a full head of blonde hair that hung slightly over his ears. His hazel eyes seemed to take in everything he observed. He stood just under six feet and was slim and athletic-looking. His overall appearance spoke of humility yet there was something more to the man, and Matt couldn't envision a humble reporter. He instantly reminded Matt of a phrase he had read in Andrew McBride's manuscript, describing one of the characters: *...he projected a strength his appearance did not present as belonging to his* *nature*. Bracks greeted Julia Wells and then took a seat across the small table from Matt, who opened the conversation.

"Mr. Bracks, welcome to Snowy Ridge. Do you have any objections to Mayor Wells sitting in on our interview?"

"None whatsoever. All the better. And by the way, congratulations, Mayor. It's been, what, about two years since our last chat?"

"The governor's press conference, I believe," Julia said.

"That's right. The Korean coal dispute. Utah coal for Korea with special pricing as I recall. And now you're in local government."

"For better or for worse."

"It's usually some of each, in my experience." Steve turned his attention toward Matt. "Mr. Sterling, we've not had a chance to meet. I appreciate your taking the time to speak with me."

"I appreciate your asking. It's more than the *Star* did."

"Is that right? No contact from the reporter before he ran the story this morning?"

"I guess he felt he had enough sensational information and didn't want to confuse it with the facts."

Bracks' eyebrows rose slightly. "To be sure *I* get the facts straight, do you mind if I record this conversation?"

"Not at all. I'll do the same," Matt said, producing a small tape recorder and placing it on the table top. "That way we both have a record of what was said."

"That's fair. And you, Mayor, do you mind the recorder?" Bracks asked.

"I think it's the only way to be accurate, Steve. No objections."

"Fine, then let's get started. Before I start the recorder, I'd like to advise you of my personal guidelines. I try very hard not to misquote, including taking a comment out of context. However, I trust that the information you provide will be accurate as far as you understand it. In other words, Mr. Sterling, if you lie to me at some point, and I later determine that the lie was intentional and not an error, or lack of knowledge on your part, then I'll treat all future information with skepticism and we'll lose the credibility I think is necessary to work together. We each have one shot with the other. I will not lie to you in order to obtain information and I don't expect you to lie to me. Is that a guideline you can live with?"

"I understand and agree, but if I'm unable to divulge something you wish to know, I won't lie to you; I just won't tell you." Matt said.

"That'll be fine." Bracks clicked on his recorder and Matt did the same. "I'm Steve Bracks, a reporter with the *Utah Press* and I'm speaking with Matt Sterling and Julia Wells. Today is Thursday, January 20, and we are located in Mr. Sterling's office at the Snowy Ridge City Hall. Mr. Sterling, what is your present position with Snowy Ridge?"

"I serve as the assistant city manager."

"And have you held other positions with the city prior to your current appointment?"

"I have." Matt reiterated his history and they covered his reporting relationship and line of authority for specific departments.

"So you've been with the city overall about two years and four months?"

"That's correct."

"Do you have a police record?"

"Not yet," Matt responded without hesitation.

Bracks nodded and then flipped through several pages of his small notebook. "Are you aware that of the seventeen most recent construction contracts Snowy Ridge has awarded, all seventeen went to the same five construction firms and that each firm has majority shareholders or directors that are related to either the city manager, finance director, or members of the current or past city councils?"

Matt was silent for a moment, looking back and forth between Julia and Steve Bracks. "No, Mr. Bracks, I was not aware of the family relationships. I know that we have dealt with a relatively small number of contractors and we are a small, interrelated community, but I wasn't aware the contractors were *all* related. But in fairness, and I've had to research this point for a contract last summer, there is no conflict of interest if the contractor *declares* the relationship prior to award of the contract and the related council member disqualifies themselves from voting to award the contract."

"That's correct. I've done a bit of homework on that point myself. But doesn't it strike you as odd that so many contract awards continually go to the same people?"

"I had a similar discussion with our Public Works director a couple of weeks ago. He advised that a number of other qualified contractors had simply stopped bidding."

"And did he say why?"

Again, Matt hesitated. "Only speculation. I'm not able to confirm the validity of his opinion although I believe he holds it in good faith."

Bracks made a small entry in his notebook, looked up and rather than ask another question, he waited for Matt to continue. His silence prevailed and Matt added to his answer.

"The short version is that Mr. McDougal thought the contractors felt they were wasting their time and money preparing bids."

"And why was that?"

"Again, speculation."

"Do you have any reason to suspect that inside information has been provided to contractors to assure that they are able to present the lowest bid?"

"You don't mince words, Mr. Bracks. I can understand how it would appear questionable that the same contractors win the award time and again, and that it is doubly suspicious if they're related to either management or Council members. But that fact, in and of itself, without further evidence, is only circumstantial and not demonstrative of collusion."

Steve smiled at Matt, jotted a note and then turned to Mayor Wells. "Is that how you see it, Mayor?"

Julia shook her head. "I am not mayor until nine o'clock tonight. And I am only *attending* this interview, Steve, not participating. But I *will* have a statement after I'm sworn in tonight. At that point, I'll be willing to go on the record with my thoughts."

"Okay," Bracks agreed, albeit somewhat reluctantly. "Let's take another tack. Matt…is it okay if I call you Matt?"

"Of course."

"Matt, what is the amount of the city's budget for the capital improvement plan?"

"Our operational budgets are prepared annually, and construction priorities change each year, but the construction and improvement items are carried out three years forward. We have an extended three-year CIP of approximately $165 million."

"And over the past three years?"

"We probably contracted for roughly $140 million, give or take a couple of million. I wasn't here for all of that, but I've reviewed the expenditures."

"And of that $140 million, do you know what percent was related to change orders that exceeded the original contract amounts?"

"I don't know off hand. I would have to review the financial payments against the original contracts."

"I've done that," Bracks said, flipping again through his notes. "Of the $140 million expended, nearly eighteen percent, or $25 million, resulted from change orders approved *after* the low bids were accepted."

"You're well informed."

"Do you know how many companies participated in those contracts?"

"Not without a closer look. I have access to the records, but from—"

"Nine companies," Bracks interjected, "with fourteen shareholders, or directors, in total. Different companies were occasionally incorporated, for different jobs, but they all had the same recorded directors and shareholders."

"I understand what you're driving at, uh, Steve, but that still doesn't constitute a breech of fiduciary responsibility."

Bracks smiled. "Matt, you're actually an attorney by education, aren't you?"

Matt hesitated and returned the smile. "I am, but I'm not blind, just cautious."

Bracks reached forward and clicked off his recorder, motioning for Matt to do the same. Matt complied. "Let me be straight with you, Matt. I have a lot of sources in this valley. I've been doing this job for nearly eighteen years, almost all of it with local government up and down the valley. After my obligatory year on obits that is," he said, a small laugh escaping. "The expression 'something's rotten in Denmark' applies here in Snowy Ridge as sure as it snows in Utah. You're thinking, and if you don't mind me being critical, you're *acting* like a lawyer. I *know* you're not involved, Mr. Sterling. I *know* you've been swept up in this. And I *know* they're going to feed you to the lions, to quote one of my sources," he said, waiting for Matt to catch the inference.

"You're innocent, Mr. Sterling. *Too* innocent, if you understand what I'm saying. And you're not just cautious, you actually *are* blind to what's going on around you. This discussion has been more of a lecture than an interview. You need to understand the authority and more importantly, the responsibility of the position you hold. Government consists of many levels of checks and balances. We all serve to keep each other straight. Don't let them fool you with the 'team player' crap. Mafioso are 'team players.' They follow one party line: Omerta, no one talks. Perhaps Harcourt and her council lackeys appointed you because they thought, correctly it would seem, that they could end run you. They thought they could work around you and you wouldn't even notice. And it's worked."

Matt fidgeted in his chair, sliding forward and resting his hands on his knees, embarrassment combined with anger beginning to turn his face a darker color.

"I'm sorry if this is hard to swallow. It's helpful for us, including you, Mayor Wells, to know that Matt is innocent, but I can't print any of it. I can't publicly exonerate you. Don't get me wrong. If I even *think* that you've become *part* of the problem rather than a means to an *end* for the problem, I'll roast you every way I can. But until then, you've only got a couple of ways to go if you want to get to the bottom of this. You've got to get in the game, again to quote a source." He turned to look at Julia. "Mayor, are you two saddled up on this? Is Mr. Sterling the first recruit on your posse?" he said, smiling.

Julia looked at Matt, set her coffee cup down on the saucer and looked back at Steve Bracks. "Just be there tonight, Steve. I'll no longer be a private citizen and I'll have a responsibility to answer your questions. Okay? But know this; Snowy Ridge is basically a western town. There are a lot of *saddles* in a western town. And the posses wear black hats *and* white hats."

"Well," Steve said, standing up and picking up his recorder. "I think that's enough for now. Here's my card, Matt, with my cell number as well. I'll either answer or return your call within a short time, night or day. I do sleep, of course, and I have other cities to cover, so I'd appreciate your consideration.

"Thank you for your candor, and thank you, Julia. I'll be there tonight with a photographer as well. Look your best. We'll probably run tomorrow with your picture as well as your, uh, your 'call to arms.'"

"One thing, Steve," Matt asked. "What's the story with the 'Do you have a police record' question?"

"Got your attention, didn't it? I often throw in a startling question just to gauge the response. You didn't blink an eye." Steve paused for a moment, looking down at Matt. "Matt, I should say one more thing to you in all honesty. This will cost you. Perhaps more than you know. Standing up for what's right, I mean. I've seen it dozens of times. You can avoid all that. You don't need to participate or be the 'team player' I mentioned earlier. You can just opt out. Keep your eyes closed, your mouth shut and do your job without rocking the boat. You have a new girlfriend, I understand. A serious girlfriend if my sources are right?"

Matt's face turned quizzical and Steve smiled. "Lots of contacts, Matt, trust me. The point I'm making is that you, and maybe even your young lady, are going to become the source of vile contempt. That story this morning in the *Star* was only the opening shot. You will bleed before this is over, despite what I perceive to be your innocence. And they may bleed your career to death, if you understand what I mean."

"You don't paint a pretty picture."

"No, I don't. But think about what I've said. The choice is yours. You need to think seriously about whether or not you want your neck on the chopping block. See you both tonight," he said, stepping through the doorway.

Matt and Julia sat for several minutes after Steve left, each lost in thought. Matt got up and returned to the chair behind his desk. "I'm afraid to open the rest of these emails. In fact I'm afraid of this whole damn thing."

"I'll bet you are. I've only got one comment for you. Do what you think is best."

"For whom?"

"That's what Steve is telling you to decide. Those you love may well be hurt if you take a stand against these people. But, as you Mormons say, 'Free Agency,'" she said, smiling. "He does a great interview, doesn't he? He usually knows more than he asks. And don't underestimate him. He does indeed have sources everywhere. It's his stock in trade. Well, I better be going."

"Did you know that was going to happen? That he was going to recite my duties to me?"

"Nope. But was he wrong?"

"No, but I feel like a kid."

"Does it matter? A little hurt to your pride is better than an execution. I think he was trying to shock you into either gearing up for battle or getting out while there's still time. Let's just see where the chips fall tonight. I think the game is going into a full court press."

"See you then."

As soon as Julia left his office, Matt picked up the phone and hit a speed-dial button.

"Mac McDougal, Public Works."

"Hey, Mac, you know a guy named Steve Bracks?"

Instantly, Mac replied. "Never heard of him."

"You old goat. See you tonight."

"Suit up, old boy, and be sure to wear your shoulder pads."

* * * * *

The Snowy Ridge City Council chambers were packed as the bi-weekly meeting commenced. Mayor Tomlin presided and the two new council members and Mayor-Elect Julia Wells sat in the audience, waiting their turn to participate in the program. In anticipation of the change of officers, the agenda was light. Routine business items, minutes of previous meetings and the Consent Agenda, containing routine items and monthly expenditures that were able to be approved all at once were read and approved. Finally, the moment for swearing in arrived. Mayor Tomlin moved to the front of the dais, behind a podium set up for the occasion. The two new council members were asked to raise their hands and the oath of office was administered. Then Julia Wells stepped forward to take her turn. Before Mayor Tomlin had a chance to speak, a woman in the back of the audience stood and shouted.

"We don't need your kind of leadership, Wells. Why don't you take that crooked assistant city manager and get out of our town? We done all right 'til now. We don't need you. Get out!"

Mayor Tomlin raised his hands in supplication. "Please, please, let's maintain order in the chambers. This is no way for us to act."

The woman continued, shouting even louder. "She's not one of us, Mayor, and it's been proven that that other guy's a crook. Using all our money for his personal stuff. Says so right here in the paper. I say we have a recall and a firing, right here, tonight."

"Please calm yourself," Tomlin pleaded again.

In the back of the room, two police officers moved toward the back of the chambers, coming up from each side of the woman, one of them speaking softly into her ear. She shrugged his hand off her shoulder and continued shouting as the officers escorted her out the back of the chambers. She could be heard continuing her tirade in the hallway for several moments as they escorted her out of the building.

"Please folks, this is not the way to conduct business in Snowy Ridge. We're an honorable community of honest people. Mayor Wells has been duly elected and we must follow the process of law. Now, Mayor Wells, if you would raise your right hand, please."

Julia Wells acknowledged her responsibilities as mayor of the city of Snowy Ridge, took the oath of office and swore to perform those duties to the best of her ability, and immediately assumed her place at the center seat on the dais. Mayor Tomlin and the two departing council members returned to seats in the chambers with their families. Silence enveloped the hall for several seconds as everyone settled into their new positions. Pat Harcourt, Matt Sterling, Doug Bellows and the city attorney sat quietly in the staff area along the side of the wall at right angles to the Council stand. Harcourt had a stern, angry look on her face and it wasn't certain whether she was upset at the change of mayor or the woman who had disrupted the ceremony. Finally, Julia Wells gave several sharp raps with the gavel that lay before her on the stand.

"That was not a pleasant way to assume office and I'm certain few here would condone such action. Mayor Tomlin, I offer my apologies to you for what part my presence played in that outburst. Council business having been completed this evening, all that remains is for me to say a few words as I assume office. And that is all I intend to say—a few words."

The audience sat absolutely silent as Julia Wells sat in Mayor Tomlin's chair, upright, her gaze steady on the assembled people.

"This past two months I have done considerable research on the form of government as practiced here in Snowy Ridge.

The Council-Manager form of government is an old, established and venerated institution. It has served American communities, indeed communities all over the world exceptionally well for over a century. Inherent in the charter of Council-Manager cities, separate and distinct powers and responsibilities lie within the authority of each the mayor and the city manager. I respect and intend to follow that premise. With that understanding, let me be clear about my perception of my new office.

"The office of mayor is not merely ceremonial. It is not limited in either authority or responsibility. I fully intend to accept and administer both. I will know where every dollar is spent. I will examine, and the Council will approve, each and every deviation from approved budget parameters including interdepartmental budget transfers. And I give notice herewith to all State of Utah registered contractors. Come to Snowy Ridge. Evaluate our contract offers. Place your bids. Build our schools, our churches, our senior citizen community halls, our streets, our sewer and water systems, and help us to make this a city of the future. To our citizens I say, if you want honest government to prevail, come serve on our committees. Bring your talents and experience. Bring your education. Bring your ideals. There is no more 'business as usual' in Snowy Ridge.

"There is going to be, and I make this my final election pledge, from this point on there will be transparent government in Snowy Ridge. I promise that much to each and every citizen of this community. To that end, my office door will be open to anyone, citizen or concerned person, who has an interest with the City of Snowy Ridge. The city staff is here to serve you. The Council and mayor are here to serve you. And if this seems to be political grandstanding, or politics as usual, come and watch it happen. You have my word on it!"

She paused several seconds and looked around the room, quickly making and breaking eye contact with Matt. She then picked up the gavel and stood from her seat. "I declare this meeting adjourned," she concluded, snapping the gavel down again and quickly departing the stand.

* * * * *

Mayor Wells Issues Clarion Call to Snowy Ridge Citizens

In an impassioned speech last night, newly elected Mayor Julia Wells invited citizens of Snowy Ridge to reach for higher levels of involvement in local government. Addressing those who do business with the city, those who seek to improve community services and those who feel disenfranchised, Mayor Wells issued her clarion call amidst the disruptive cacophony of a disgruntled citizen who shouted at the new mayor, "We don't need you. Get out of our town."

Matt read the headlines as he sat in the waiting area of the Sizzler restaurant in Provo. Completing Steve Bracks' article, he set the paper aside and began reviewing several dozen letters that had clogged his email box during the day. Not yet receptive to the idea of being everyone's bone to be chewed, he took pleasure, as he had expressed to Candy, that today the letters included three that essentially said, "Hang in there."

Finally, Mac appeared in the doorway and Matt stood, ready to join the line of people waiting to select their dinner entrée.

"So you don't know Steve Bracks?"

"Who really *knows* anyone, Matt?" Mac evaded.

"I know *you*."

Mac laughed. "Steak and shrimp for me. Did you know *that*, Mr. Assistant City Manager?"

"I know you're paying this time, that's what I know."

"I guess it's my turn. So, what do you think about the new lady boss?"

"Which one?"

"The *new* one."

"I think she's declared war on the establishment."

"That's for certain. Let's get our meal and sit down. I've got something interesting to discuss with you tonight."

"A new scheme or do you need more money for Public Works?"

"Both," Mac smiled.

After thirty minutes and four trips by the waitress with all-you-can-eat-shrimp for Mac, they sat slowly savoring their second dish of ice cream.

"Matt, about five years ago, maybe a bit longer, we had a young female accountant working directly under Doug. She was with us for roughly eighteen months. Sharp little lady, cute and newly married. Then, without much warning and under a cloud of innuendo, she resigned and moved out of state."

"What kind of innuendo?"

"There was some rumor that she wasn't exactly faithful to her husband and it was about to come out."

"Was it true?"

"I don't know. It's none of my business. But before she left, she made a few comments to several of our fellow workers about our new retirement options. You know, the program Snowy Ridge elected to use for their employees who opted out of the Utah State Retirement System."

"I know. We all have that choice. So, what were her allegations?"

"Never found out. The infidelity rumor started quickly after her comments about the retirement system and in a flurry of tears and embarrassment, she resigned."

"So what's that got to do with now?"

"Candy located her."

"And?"

"And she's in Las Vegas."

"Yeah. And?"

"And it's two weeks 'til Kasia gets back, you're all alone, we have a three-day weekend next week, and I thought you and I might run down there and play a round of golf."

"What are you talking about?"

"Think *peripherally*, Matt. Remember Candy's lesson."

Matt finished his ice cream, wiped his mouth and stared across the table at Mac. "Okay, we drive five hundred miles, *interview* an ex-employee, play a round of golf, and drive five hundred miles back home."

"Now you've got it. And we do it in your Cherokee. You game?"

"How soon 'til you retire, Mac?"

"Not soon enough to suit me. But I'm gonna see you though this thing first."

"What's your handicap?" Matt grinned.

"You!"

Chapter Nineteen

The following Thursday, the day before President's Day weekend when Mac and Matt intended to drive to Las Vegas, Candy stepped into Matt's office just before four o'clock and told him Pat Harcourt had asked to see him as soon as he was available, but certainly before the end of the day.

"Not a problem," Matt said, logging off his computer and tidying up his desk. "What better way to start the holiday weekend than a fireside chat with Pat, right?"

"Chief Trenkle and Captain Honeycutt are in there with her," Candy said.

"Is that so?" Matt replied, tilting his head in query. "The chief of police and captain of detectives. Maybe I'm going to jail for a poor attitude."

"Don't underestimate her, Matt. I've told you before—"

"I know. Sorry. I'll put on my serious face when I enter her private domain."

One minute before four, Matt knocked on Pat's open door. She looked up and waved him toward a seat. Captain Honeycutt stood and closed the door behind Matt, then resumed his seat. Rail thin, Honeycutt had sharp features with a hawkish nose, and close-set eyes that locked on Matt as soon as he regained his seat.

Pat spoke first. "Thanks for coming, Matt. We need to discuss a few things that have come to my attention only yesterday. It shouldn't take long." She motioned to Honeycutt.

"Matt, I have a few questions about internal security. Specifically our internal network and internet access. Do you have a personal password that restricts access to your computer when you are away from your desk?"

Matt nodded. "Yep, the screen saver kicks in after about three minutes and a password is required to reactivate."

"And booting up?"

"Same thing. It's all part of the requirements as documented in our MIS procedures manual. Why, what's wrong?"

"Do you suspect that anyone other than yourself has had access to your terminal?"

Matt turned to Pat who was sitting quietly behind her desk. "What's this about, Pat?"

Pat stroked her hair into place and gestured with her hand, as if to indicate uncertainty. "Matt, this is beyond me at the moment, but Captain Honeycutt and the chief are just following up on some concerns expressed by our MIS department. Internet access violations."

"Internet violations? What are you talking about, Honeycutt?"

Honeycutt reached for a folder lying on the table in front of him and retrieved a small stack of papers from within. "Have you ever seen this particular website homepage, Matt?" he said, handing Matt a single page and watching his reaction closely.

Matt looked at the page, entitled *World of Joy*, and shook his head. "I don't recognize this."

"And this?" Honeycutt said, handing Matt another page, this one depicting two men and a woman in nude posture, the woman's hands tied at the wrists."

"What is this garbage?" he said as he threw the paper back at Honeycutt. "What are you talking about?"

"Have you ever seen these pictures or website locations previously?" Honeycutt asked as he laid a series of similar, more graphic pictures across the table."

Matt glanced at the array, looking up at Pat, then at each of the men in turn. "Absolutely not. And I resent the implication."

"Then can you tell us how these images came to be embedded in your computer's history file? On your hard drive, I mean."

"*My* computer?"

"I'm afraid so," Chief Trenkle said, speaking for the first time. "This is not like you, Matt. At least not like the Matt Sterling I thought I knew. There has to be some explanation."

Matt stared for several seconds at Police Chief Hermann Trenkle and then shook his head. "This is garbage, pure and simple. I deny ever visiting this or any other pornographic site on my computer. On *any* computer for that matter. I don't participate in this smut and you know that, Hermann. We've attended the Temple together on many occasions."

Trenkle nodded his head in assent. "We have and that makes this all the harder. Can you provide no explanation for how these images came to be on your computer?"

"I don't know for a fact that they *are* on my computer. How do I know that? I only have Honeycutt's statement."

"You'll have to accept our word for that, I'm afraid," Honeycutt said.

"Honeycutt, I don't have to accept your word for anything. Especially something I know to be false. Are you telling me you have access to my computer, despite my secure password system?"

"Yes, those who have a need to know or to access the system for repairs and maintenance."

"And how many people would that be? Bedsides yourself? I presume as Captain of Detectives you have access. Is that right?" Matt asked, his anger becoming evident.

"Who has access is not at issue here."

"The hell it's not!" Matt shouted. "That's *exactly* what's at issue. By your own admission other people have access to my computer without my knowledge and when you find, or claim to find, pornographic material on my hard drive you assume it's *me*. What gives you that right?"

"That is our assumption, yes. Of course, if you would allow us to access your home computer, and it's clean of this type of material, perhaps we could add some validity to your story that you don't participate in pornography."

"You'll get access to nothing in my home without a warrant, Captain Honeycutt. If you found a way to get this rubbish on my *work* computer, what's to stop you from compounding this...this *evidence*, and putting it on my *home* computer, with my permission no less? This is a travesty and you both know it. And you know it too, Pat. The others were right. They warned me. I've underestimated the depth to which you'll go to protect yourself. So, what now, Pat?"

"Matt, my hands are tied. The city's personnel rules are specific. A first time pornographic offense is an automatic ten-day suspension without pay. I have no choice but to suspend you until, uh" she looked at her calendar, "until the last Monday in February. I'm sorry, but that's the only option I have."

Matt stood and looked down at the two men seated around the table, the disgusting pictures spread before them. "Hermann, I'm not surprised to find Honeycutt involved in this sort of treachery, he's developing quite a reputation for it, even among his own police officers. But I am shattered to find you involved, unwittingly or not. Surely you know me better than this."

"I thought so, Matt, I truly did."

"And I resent your inference," Honeycutt said, rising.

"I don't care what you resent, Honeycutt. You've won this round, and the chips are all in your favor, but the game's not over. Pat," he said, turning to face her desk, "I want that computer out of my office and when I return, I'll provide a personal computer that is *not* tied in to the network. I've lost faith in your ability to be fair. In fact I'm rapidly losing faith in you altogether."

Pat rose from behind her desk and stepped toward the cluster of men. "I've lost a bit of faith myself, Matt. In *you!*"

* * * * *

An hour after everyone else on the top floor had left, Doug Bellows entered Pat Harcourt's office and sat in front of her desk.

"How'd it go?"

"About as expected. A tirade of innocence. He's truly a babe in the woods. But it's not enough, Doug. Have you finished your analysis of financial transactions, contract approval, and anything else we can hang our hat on to discredit him?"

"I've got about a half-dozen significant issues that will put him in a bad light. The Fontana contract is still the primary piece of negligence however. How he missed that guaranteed duplicate payment I'll never know. He's usually smarter than that. There are a couple of other items we could use if necessary, but there's a chance they would reflect on us as well as him."

"Just between you, me, and the lamppost, I approved that contract and directed Matt's boss at the time, our former city attorney, to run it through. But there's no record of that."

Bellows nodded assent. "We have Matt's signature on the contract. That's all we need."

"That's good. Just use those you're sure about. I want you to draft a letter, a *very* distressing letter that's hard for us to write, considering the young man's promise and all, if you know what I mean. Address it to the Utah Bar Association, asking them to consider censure or perhaps disbarment as a result of his actions here. Cap off the charges with the most recent pornographic discoveries, and the obligatory suspension, as if they were the straw that broke the camel's back, forcing us to take action. It should appear as if we are very reluctant to take these steps against a promising young attorney who perhaps only fell into these things through his youth or inexperience."

"You want him disbarred?"

"Why not? That would discredit him completely."

"What makes you think they're going to accept the charges?"

"This is a small state, Doug. Everybody in politics has some connection with someone else. Do you know your Utah history?"

"Some."

"Remember when the Church decided that they would get out of politics and even up the odds. They assigned whole wards to split their members into Democrats and Republicans, just to balance the membership. My family have been Democrats ever since. Three of the Bar Association Board members are friends of my father's. He'll have a chat with them about the 'bad seed' that's putting a disreputable light on local government."

"And *you're* going to sign this letter?"

"Yes, Doug, you will not have to soil your lily-white hands," Pat said, a tone of disgust in her voice.

Doug stood, his hands on his hips. "Pat, you better understand something real quick. We're in this together. Sink or swim *together*. I'm not your lapdog, nor will I respond to your intimidation methods. So cut the crap when dealing with me. We better pull together on this or we won't be *dis*barred, we'll both be 'barred' up at Point of the Mountain, if you get my meaning."

"Don't be so sensitive. Just get on with it."

* * * * *

"Suspended?" Mac repeated as he got into Matt's car at five AM, prepared to drive to Las Vegas.

"For two weeks," Matt confirmed with a calm he didn't feel.

"Unbelievable. We thought they declared war three weeks ago. This is a direct frontal assault. They need to get you out of the picture, Matt, while at the same time taking the spotlight off themselves," Mac said.

"It's working," Matt replied as they cruised down I-15 on Friday morning, en route to Las Vegas. "I want to make the most of this time off but I don't really know what to do, where to go."

"Maybe Jennifer can point us in another direction. She's agreed to see us tonight. I spoke with her a couple of nights ago. She really didn't want to meet. Said it would surface old wounds between herself and her husband."

"You can't blame her," Matt said. "Did she give you any idea what information she has?"

"Wouldn't talk about it on the phone. She used the term 'crooks' when I asked her about Harcourt and Bellows."

"Well, let's hope she's not just out for revenge. If her information isn't solid, it will only look like we're the ones causing trouble."

It took just over eight hours for Matt and Mac to drive to Las Vegas, check in to the hotel, contact Jennifer Simpson, and meet her at the appointed casino. She had refused to meet them at her home and Mac thought she was meeting with them without telling her husband. Mac recognized her as they approached the table in the buffet lounge. She caught his eye and immediately appeared nervous.

"Jennifer, it's nice to see you again," Mac said, his warmest smile in place. "Looks like you've got a nice place to live here in the warm sunshine. Matt and I left about eight inches of snow behind as we dropped down to St. George. Oh, I'm sorry. Jennifer Simpson, this is Matt Sterling. Matt's the assistant city manager. He's been with us for about two years."

"Hi, Jennifer," Matt said as he slid into the booth opposite Jennifer. He slid all the way around to the rear of the circular booth and Mac took the end seat.

"I haven't got very long, Mr. McDougal. I'm sorry, but I've got two kids at home."

"We understand, Jennifer. Not to worry. I'm sure we'll just have a quick chat. How long have you been gone now, about five, six years?"

"Almost six and I wish I'd never gone there."

"I feel the same way sometimes and I've been there twenty-eight years," Mac laughed. "You mentioned on the phone that Bellows was a crook. I didn't really understand what you meant."

"Just that," she said, squirming a bit and glancing around the room. "He's stealing from the city, unless he stopped after I left."

Matt entered the conversation, his tone soft. "We're audited each year, Jennifer, by a national firm. I don't see how he could be stealing, but of course I'm not an accountant."

"I brought proof," she said, reaching beside her for her purse. Matt and Mac exchanged looks. "Here," she said, waving several sheets of paper in her hand. "Here's the resolution. And here are the early deposit sheets."

She handed the papers to Matt and he quickly scanned the first. "This is a City Council Resolution, dated June 1998. It's the establishment of the Local Government Retirement Fund as the official depository for Snowy Ridge employees. Several hundred, if not several thousand, communities across the nation use this municipal retirement fund. It's a very reliable system."

"These other sheets, uh, let's see, look like copies of transfers or confirmation of deposits to the fund. I don't see how—"

"Look at Clause Sixteen of the Resolution, Mr. Sterling. It mandates that the Council shall maintain a six-month reserve of retirement deposits at all times, and that it shall not be mingled with other Snowy Ridge investments, and that it shall not be utilized for speculative investment."

"I see that," Matt replied. "That was most likely a guarantee or protection against the Council or senior management using employee retirement funds for other purposes or investments that were likely to diminish the fund balance. The Council wanted to be certain the employee's retirement money would be available when the time came. Can you be any more specific, Jennifer? I fail to see—"

Jennifer closed her purse and slid a few inches toward the edge of her seat, scanning the room once again, clearly anxious to leave. "He keeps the retirement fund deposits six months ahead. Not with our normal Utah bank, but with the Local Government Retirement Corporation in Denver. Snowy Ridge had nearly four hundred employees and an annual salary payout of about fifteen million when I left, probably more now. With mandatory employee contributions to replace Social Security, mandatory employer match, and various voluntary employee deductions, the deposit was about twenty-two percent of annual salary."

"Those figures sound about right," Matt agreed. "At least the twenty-two or twenty-three percent of contributions. How is that criminal?"

Jennifer shook her head, exasperation evident in the necessity of dragging out the explanation. "Mr. McDougal, what is twenty-two percent of fifteen million?"

It was Mac's turn to shift nervously. "Over three million or thereabouts."

"Three point three million to be exact. The deposits six months ahead means that we always had nearly one point seven million in the fund, accumulating interest and it was *not* in individual employee accounts. It was required to be in a conservative interest fund, safe and guaranteed, by the Resolution requirement. No speculation. Still, even at the minimum of six and a half percent per annum, that much money earns about a hundred and ten thousand dollars a year. And Mr. Bellows always paid the bi-weekly deposits about two or sometimes three paydays *ahead* of the required time frame. He told the Council he was being very careful to protect employee accounts. On the actual payday, each deposit went against the individual employee's account, their retirement fund, but for the four or six weeks of each advance pay period, it all stayed in the holding account, which paid interest into what we called the employee holding account."

Matt and Mac again exchanged looks. "That still doesn't—"

"Mr. Sterling," Jennifer said, her face now firm and resolute, "the two employee holding accounts, which were *not* assigned individual names, were, and probably still are, the same account numbers as the personal retirement accounts of Patricia Harcourt and Douglas Bellows. Every two weeks they receive deposits not only of their own accumulated interest, but the total interest for that two weeks of the one point seven million, the six-month advance fund, and the leading two, maybe three paydays' worth of deposits. Figure the numbers for yourself. It's over five thousand dollars a payday. They are making about a hundred and thirty-five thousand a year between them and have been doing it for the past six years, if it's still going on.

"I'm sorry, but I can't tell you any more and I really have to go now. You can keep the documents. I have copies at home. Please keep me out of this. *Please.* I only want to forget my time at Snowy Ridge. Goodbye," she said, rising and quickly melting into the crowd of tourists at the casino.

Matt looked at the resolution and Mac scanned the numbers on the six year old deposit sheets. They sat quietly, each in their own thoughts for several minutes. Mac finally spoke up. "I'm hungry."

"I'm confused," Matt said. "This makes a lot of sense, but to confirm it, we need to have access to the Retirement Corporation records. Those are considered private and confidential. Doug keeps those under his personal lock and key and if I ask to see them, we'll tip our hand."

"If this is true, I'll bet he does keep them locked up," Mac said. "Matt, if these two are getting any money in return for contract awards to family, we'll never get a look at it. They would certainly keep it pretty close and probably have assets, like houses, etc., kept in someone else's name. But this information," he said, waving his sheets at Matt, "is probably as close to a smoking gun as we're going to get. Now we've got to figure out how can we put it to use."

"You've got that right, but I don't know how we're going to do it. But I'm going to give it lots of thought. Hungry you say?"

"Absolutely."

"Tonight, my good friend, and tomorrow's golf victim I might add, dinner's on me. This trip just might turn out to have been a good idea, Mr. Mac."

* * * * *

When they stopped for fuel in St. George on Sunday, on the drive home, Matt filled the gas tank while Mac grabbed a couple of sodas, two hot dogs, and a copy of the *Salt Lake Star*. Matt exited the service station, entered the on ramp and began the remaining four-hour drive to Snowy Ridge. Five minutes down the road, hot dogs gone, Matt heard Mac exhale sharply and he glanced over at the older man.

"What's up?"

Mac just shook his head. "Pull off up there," he said, motioning to the next exit ramp.

Matt complied and, as the car slowed to a stop, Mac folded the paper in half and handed the section to Matt.

"If we're at war, Matt, then these would be the casualty reports from the front lines."

SNOWY RIDGE EMPLOYEE SUSPENDED FOR PORNOGRAPHY
AND ETHICS VIOLATIONS

UNDER INVESTIGATION BY UTAH BAR ASSOCIATION

Matt read quickly, his heart beginning to pound in his chest and his breathing increasing rapidly. He was oblivious to the car that pulled up behind him at the stop sign and eventually backed up, pulling around and honking in the process.

Matt Sterling, assistant city manager of Snowy Ridge was suspended, without pay, for two weeks following an internal investigation into his alleged pornographic activities on the internet, using the city's computer system. City Manager Patricia Harcourt confirmed late Friday evening that in compliance with city regulations regarding such inappropriate behavior she had reluctantly, but necessarily, moved to protect the interests of the city.

In addition, it was also confirmed by Harcourt that Sterling has been reported to the Utah Bar Association for alleged negligence in the performance of his duties while serving as deputy city attorney some two years ago.

These current infractions follow a series of financial improprieties with which Sterling has been associated over a period of time. The Utah Fraud Commission, which questioned Sterling two weeks ago, refused comment, citing—

Matt threw the paper in the back seat in disgust.

"Keep your head, Matt. They want you to panic."

"Well, I'm close, Mac, damn close. Harcourt's lucky I'm still three hundred miles away."

"Let's just get home and figure this out. You said Kasia's coming in tonight?"

"About ten-thirty."

"Well then, let's get moving. I know this hurts, Matt, but you've got to keep your wits about you."

Matt shifted the Cherokee into gear, checked traffic, crossed the intersection, and drove up the opposite entrance ramp, back onto I-15. "Mac, this is becoming overwhelming. I'm lost as to how to proceed, where to go, whether to quit and run. I just…I just don't know what to do."

"Do you remember me telling you tall tales about my time in the Marines during Vietnam?"

"Yeah. What's that got to do with this?"

"What I did in the Marines has played a part in everything I've done since. It's because of the one fact I really learned as a young know-it-all. I got into Recon, Matt, because they were the toughest, smartest, bravest, etc., etc., etc. And it was true. Not because of their physical strength, but because of their *mental* strength. What I learned was that real strength comes from the mind, not the body. I don't just mean smarts. I mean, as my father used to say, '*tenaciously tough.*' The never-quit attitude. The mind can go much longer than the body but many people give up before the body even quits, never giving their mind a chance to persevere. You've got to find that inner reservoir of strength, Matt. You have it. I know you do. You just haven't learned where to look perhaps because, and I don't mean to be critical, but because you haven't had to look for it. You've had it pretty easy in life, from your own admission."

Matt exhaled, held both hands on the wheel and slowly began to nod his head. "I suppose I have. We don't see it that way, do we, as we grow up? We think everything has come down hard on us. The world has ended because we can't get a car at sixteen, or because Jane likes Joe and not me. Mom used to tell me to be sure I kept an open mind. That other people were usually hurting more than I was. I didn't believe her sometimes, but I understood what she meant."

"So what are you going to do?"

"For the long haul, I don't know, Mac. I can't even comprehend this! But between here and the airport, I am going to pray...very hard." He didn't mention her by name, but Mac knew exactly what he was talking about.

"Kasia's a good kid, Matt. She'll understand."

"She *is* a good kid, Mac. Good enough that she doesn't deserve this. I may just have to let her off the hook...to protect her."

Mac shook his head, reclining his seat back. "Don't be too hasty, Matt. And start your praying while I take a nap."

Chapter Twenty

At 10:40 P.M., Sunday, February 20, American Airlines from New York to Salt Lake City, via St. Louis, changed status on the overhead monitor from "On Time" to "Landed." Matt was actually watching the TV screen as the words flashed and changed. He'd been in the airport for forty-five minutes after dropping Mac at his house, running to his own home briefly to check phone messages and email, and completing the thirty-minute run up the highway to the airport.

In about ten minutes, the first passengers appeared through the portals of Gate 48, some hurrying quickly toward the baggage area, some wrestling with young children thrilled to be freed from the confines of the aircraft, others hugging relatives and friends. Suddenly, without fanfare, there she was, appearing from behind a cluster of three large men who had preceded her down the ramp. For a single instant, Matt locked eyes with Kasia and just as quickly, she averted his gaze. In that instant he knew that she knew.

She approached him and he took her in his arms, immediately uncertain of how to proceed. He kissed her cheek, reached down and took her carry-on bag and they began walking toward the baggage area.

"Tired?" he asked, noticing her red, puffy eyes.

"Oh, yes. Very. The London to New York flight was late getting in and we had to rush to make the connection. I hope my bags made it."

Riding down the escalator to the luggage carousels, Matt began to sense the tension in the air, silently praying it was only his imagination running wild. As they approached the correct carousel, the flight number was already blinking and the warning bell sounded preceding the start of the ramp.

"I'm afraid I have four bags," she said, sheepishly.

"Four? You left with only two."

"I know," she nodded, a slight smile appearing on her face. "But I've been to Paris and Stockholm. Oh, there's one," she said, pointing out the bag. "Thank goodness they made it."

As each bag rose up and dropped off onto the rotating circular belt, Kasia pointed them out and Matt retrieved them, placing them on a luggage cart. Soon, all four bags were stacked and they commenced the walk to the upstairs area of the car park. Matt loaded the bags in the back of his Cherokee, opened her door and walked around to the driver's side, sliding behind the wheel.

"Is everything alright, Kasia?" he asked, softly.

Slowly, Kasia lowered her head and cupped her face in her hands, the soft sound of crying escaping her lips.

"Kasia, I... I don't know how to begin."

She raised her head slightly and looked over at him. "There was a Salt Lake newspaper on the plane, Matt. In my seat pocket," she said, again lowering her eyes to look at her hands folded in her lap.

"Kasia, please, give me a chance to explain. I just—"

"I need time to think, Matt. It's been a long, hard flight. I'm just bewildered. I don't know what to think."

"It's not true. I swear it."

"I know. I understand and I want to believe you. I just need some time."

"I can explain. Truly."

She looked at him again, the sadness in her eyes piercing deep inside Matt's soul. "Can we just go home, please? I'm scared, Matt. I'm really scared. I just need time to think, to understand all this."

"But I wanted to tell you—"

"*Please*, Matt. Take me home, please."

"Okay," he said, starting the engine. "But promise me you'll give me the chance to explain what's happened. I deserve that much."

"I will, Matt. I just need to go home, take a hot bath, and go to bed. I'm exhausted."

The drive south was very quiet, both lost in their thoughts. Kasia laid her head against the headrest, closed her eyes, and appeared to Matt to be asleep for the entire thirty minutes, opening her eyes only when the engine stopped outside her house. Matt exited the car, came around to open her door, and began to unload the luggage. Kasia carried the lighter suitcase and Matt made two additional trips to place each of the bags inside the front door. On his last trip, Kasia was standing at the front door as he placed the bag at her feet.

"Matt, please don't be angry with me. I've cried all the way from New York, unable to understand what happened. I know the newspapers exaggerate and sensationalize, but I—"

"Take your bath, Kasia, and get a good night's sleep," Matt said softly. "Perhaps we can talk tomorrow or the following day if you need a bit more time. I know this has hurt you. It's hurt me too. The last thing I want to do is cause you pain. But please, give it some time and don't make any hasty decisions."

"I promise, Matt," she said, reaching up to kiss his cheek. "Thank you for understanding."

"Can I call you tomorrow?"

Kasia hesitated, averting her eyes. "Give me a couple of days, Matt. Please understand."

"I do. When you're ready, call me, okay?"

"You have my promise."

As Matt entered the car and prepared to drive away, the porch light went out and immediately the front room light darkened also. He drove south through Provo, his thoughts jumbled and his worst fears realized. By the time he arrived home, his spirits were as low as they had ever been and he was certain that his world had turned upside down. He went immediately into the bedroom, undressed and slipped between the sheets, not even turning on the CNN news broadcast. The last conscious thought as he slipped off to sleep was of Andy McBride's journal entry. *They came by night, and when they left at dawn, it was darker than when they'd come.*

* * * * *

Kasia left her suitcases where they were, entered the bathroom and began to draw a bath. She returned to the bedroom, quickly undressed and slipped into her robe, then turned on her computer. The email box flashed a warning and she noted that she had thirty-two unread messages. She quickly scrolled through the list, opening two from personal friends, and ignored the rest. Then she clicked on "New Message" and the form opened up and she began typing.

To: SomersetGA@Somersetlaw.co.uk

From: DNAGirl@aol.com

Subject: Home Safely

Dad: I have sent a separate email home so that you and Mum know I arrived safely. But I wanted to write to you at work, without worrying Mum, to ask your advice. I arrived home and Matt met me, but I am absolutely shocked and saddened by a newspaper article I read on the plane from New York. I don't want to believe it, but I just don't know. I know you will be at work in about an hour. Please pull up the website for the newspaper, read the article, and if you have a moment about 3 or so your time this afternoon, give me a call at home so we can discuss it. The website is: www.utahstar.com.

Thanks, Dad. I love you.
Kasia

* * * * *

At 8:15 the following morning, President's Day, Kasia's phone rang. She was still in her robe, settled into her favorite lounge chair, had her feet tucked up under her and had been sitting silently in the room for over an hour. She leaned over and picked up the receiver.

"This is Kasia."

"Hi, Sweetheart."

"Hello, Dad. Thanks for calling." Immediately the tears began to form in her eyes.

"You've come home to a dilemma, it would seem," Graeme said.

"Dad, I'm so confused. This is just not the person I thought I knew. How could this be true?"

"What makes you think it is?"

"What do you mean?"

"Just because it's plastered on the front page of the newspaper doesn't make it true."

"They must have *some* evidence."

"They probably do, Sweetheart, but that still doesn't make it true."

"Oh, Dad, I wish with all my heart that it's not true."

"What does Matt say?"

Kasia hesitated several seconds.

"You haven't let him tell you his side, have you?"

"No, Dad. And I woke up about four this morning and was ashamed of myself for that. I just told him to go home and not to call me."

"Kasia, that's not like you. This is the man you said you loved. The man you said you'd marry."

"I know," she sobbed, the words breaking up as she spoke. "I just haven't been able to comprehend what's happened. I read the story fifty times on the flight from New York. I couldn't believe my eyes."

"Yet he was waiting for you at the airport. Is that the sign of a guilty man?"

"I hadn't thought of that. He probably didn't know that I knew."

"That's probably right, Kasia, but still it took courage to meet you and try to tell you what had happened."

"What do you think happened, Dad?"

"I'm going to tell you a story, Sweetheart, but first let me say that I woke your Uncle Trevor early this morning and had a chat with him. He's been in the political scene there for many years through the law school. To put it bluntly, which, as you know, is Uncle Trevor's forte, he said the whole thing was bullshit."

"Dad!"

"I know, Kasia," Graeme chuckled, "your mother would chastise me for days if I let that word out in her presence, but Uncle Trevor is adamant that it's a put up job."

"Has he spoken with Matt?"

"No. And that bothers him, but he feels that Matt needs to contact him first. He feels that Matt is probably reeling with the thought of how all his friends will see him. How they will believe it."

"Why is Uncle Trevor so certain Matt's innocent?"

"He said it was Belgrade all over."

Kasia hesitated again. "I don't understand."

"I know. I'm going to tell you a story, Kasia, and I want you to listen carefully. I've never told this to you, or to hardly anyone else either for that matter. I'd rather leave it in my past, but I think it will help you with this situation."

"Does Mother know this story?"

"She does, although why she believed me and stuck by me I'll never know. You know that I was a Foreign Service officer with the British Embassy in Belgrade, Yugoslavia when I met your mother."

"You've told me that story."

"Not *this* story. I was a junior officer when two British intelligence officers came to Belgrade and had me seconded to their operation. I didn't want to get involved, since I had some knowledge of the overall operation and what would be required, but my refusal would have meant the end of my career with the Foreign Office. To put it short, Kasia, I balked at several of the things we were going to be required to do and I was branded a coward and sent home in disgrace. Then, I was asked to quietly leave the service. At twenty-five, my public service career was over."

"What did they want you to do, Dad?"

"I'm sorry, Kasia, I'm still not at liberty to reveal the details because of the Official Secrets Act, even forty years later, but suffice it to say that when I met your Uncle Trevor in law school, he told me it wasn't the first time the system had ground someone up and thrown them out. But I was disgraced and couldn't face your mother. Remember, her father was a senior diplomat with the Yugoslavian Foreign Service."

"And Uncle Trevor said this reminded him of that time?"

"Only in the sense that it was completely fabricated to destroy someone who got in the way."

"Oh, Dad, if I could believe that, I would be overjoyed."

"Now it's time for you to take the next step."

"What's that?"

"You know what it is, Kasia. You've got to find the truth for yourself the way we always taught you to look for the truth."

Kasia was silent again, fidgeting in her chair and shifting the phone to the other ear. "I know what you mean, Dad. I'm actually going away for several days. It will give me the opportunity to be alone, to think, and . . . to pray."

"But you just got home."

"I know, but in my email was a note from Dr. Amberly, advising that we had a small team going to Florida and Georgia to collect blood samples. He said Marilyn was supposed to lead the team, but that her son had come down sick. He asked if I could go for just three days. I emailed him back and agreed. I wanted to run away, Dad. I'm sorry."

"I understand, Kasia. Perhaps it's just as well. When do you leave?"

"Tomorrow morning."

"Will you see Matt first?"

"I think not. Now I'm the one who's embarrassed. I'll email him and let him know where I'm going and that we can talk when I come home."

"Kasia, if you can feel in your heart to do so, let him know you're going away, and why, and give him some hope."

"I love him, Dad. I just need this time to sort out my feelings and come to grips with how to deal with this. I'm sure it has devastated Matt too."

"You can count on it. Call me if you need anything or just to talk. I love you, Sweetheart."

"Thank you, Dad. I love you too. You won't tell Mum, will you?"

"We'll keep this between us until you feel comfortable telling her yourself."

"Thanks, Dad. Bye.

"Have a safe trip."

* * * * *

Matt slept until nearly nine on President's Day, undisturbed by the sunlight filtering through his window. After a fitful night, rising twice, each time sitting briefly in the living room watching CNN news headlines on the hour, the last view Matt could recall of his bedside digital clock, it had read 4:33.

As he finished the last spoonful of cereal while standing on the balcony, the chill air brisk against his robe, the phone rang and he walked to the kitchen, placed the dish in the sink, and picked up the receiver.

"Hello."

"I'll pick you up at 10:30," Mac said abruptly.

"For what?"

"We have a tee time at 11:30 at Hobble Creek."

Matt shook his head. "Mac, I don't feel like—"

"That's a good reason for getting out on the golf course. It'll clear your head. I'll be there at 10:30," he repeated and hung up. Matt looked at the telephone in his hand as if he could convey his displeasure to Mac, shook his head, replaced the phone on the cradle and headed for the shower. At 10:25, he was standing in front of the condo complex as Mac drove up in his Ford pickup.

"That's more like it," the older man said as Matt placed his clubs in the back of the truck and slipped into the passenger side. "It's already 48 degrees and headed for 55. Ideal golfing weather for a Utah winter."

"What would I do without you, Mac?" Matt said, a small smile crossing his tired face.

"You don't need to. I'm here. Let's play," he said as he drove out of the parking lot. "Kasia get in alright?"

Matt nodded silently.

"You told her?"

"She knew."

"They always do, don't they?"

"You've got more experience with that than I do. But it shocked her to the core."

"Of course it did," Mac replied, pulling onto the interstate for the twenty minute drive to the golf course. "She's young, Matt, just like you are, but she's not stupid. She can see through the garbage."

Matt shook his head and clicked his lips. "I don't know, Mac. There are many who will believe it."

"True. And that's the shame of it. Throw some mud and some of it will stick."

They drove in silence for the next ten minutes, exiting the freeway and winding east up the canyon to the golf course that was tucked between two ridges in the foothills. The Starter matched them with another twosome, an older couple out for a holiday round of golf, and the two carts drove toward the first tee, parking behind two other foursomes who were ahead of them. Mac put his feet up on the front of the cart and leaned back into the seat. "Not a bad way to spend the first day of your suspension, Mr. Sterling."

Matt laughed softly, nodding. "I'd almost forgotten about the suspension. If the weather holds, maybe I can knock a few strokes off my handicap."

"Nah. Not much chance of that," Mac chided. They kept silent as the first foursome teed off, driving down the fairway after their shots. The next foursome took the tee and began to limber up with practice swings.

"Mac," Matt said, turning to face his partner, "I'm about ready to surrender."

It was Mac's turn to nod. "I thought as much. That's why I asked you out here this morning. It's too much, isn't it?"

"Of course it is. I've been suspended, branded a pornographic pervert, had my law license challenged and now the woman I love doesn't know whether to believe me or not. It's just too much, Mac. The price is too high. What would you do?"

"I'd like to tell you to hold your ground, but this whole episode has caused me to rethink my own position. I've closed my eyes to what's going on for over ten years. I've got no right to tell you how to react."

"Did you ever challenge them?"

"Can't say as I did, Matt. And that's my shame. Have you thought that you might be in too deep to get out? That Pat will only use your surrender against you and fire you anyway, labeling you a thief, or incompetent in the process."

Matt let the words sink in and again they held their silence as the next group teed off.

"And what about Mayor Wells?" Mac continued. "Do you think she'll let up?"

Matt shook his head. "No. She's bound and determined to rid the city of what she calls an incestuous conspiracy."

"That's as apt a description as I've heard. From what I can see, Matt, you did fine until you thought, or started thinking, that you might lose the lady you love. The rest of it you were handling pretty well."

"Well, you can't blame me."

"No, I can't," Mac replied, shaking his head. "Do you want me to talk to her?"

"I think I need to leave her alone until she's ready to talk about it. It must have been a shock. I know it was for me yesterday in St. George when I read the paper. I can't imagine how it hit her on the flight home. Here she's coming home to the man who loves her, who she's going to marry, and she reads that he's—"

"A pervert, immoral, and soon to be a disbarred lawyer, the dirtiest scum on the face of the earth and not worthy to be the father of her children," Mac finished.

Matt jerked his head around to look at Mac. The older man just stared back at him, a soft smile forming on his face.

Matt grinned for a moment, his sense of humor overtaking his self pity. "Yep, that's me."

"Have you talked to your parents?"

Matt shook his head. "I was hoping I could find a solution and call them after it was all worked out."

"It's a small world, Matt, the Mormons I mean. Everybody knows somebody who knows somebody you know. Your parents might already have heard and be concerned about you."

"You're right, I'll have to call them."

The last group in front of them drove off the first tee, chasing down the fairway after their tee shots. Mac drove the golf cart up next to the back tees and stepped out, pulling his driver out of the bag.

"I swear that thing gets longer every time I play with you. What's the standard length for a driver anyway?" Matt asked.

"Used to be forty-three inches. Now most drivers are about forty-five."

"And yours?"

"Forty-eight."

"It looks like a light-weight aluminum telephone pole."

"Care to put your money on long drive, Mr. Sterling?"

Matt pulled his golf glove on his hand, selected his driver, and began to stretch with the club behind his neck. "No, thanks. I've seen you use that thing. However stupid it looks, it works."

"And don't you ever forget it."

* * * * *

After their golf match, which Mac won 4 and 3, and outdrove Matt six times, they stopped in Provo and had a bite of dinner, then proceeded to Snowy Ridge and the home of Mayor

Julia Wells to discuss the information they had discovered in Las Vegas. Julia focused on the new information like a drowning person grabs for the life ring. She paced her kitchen floor, reading the financial documents about the retirement corporation, while Matt and Mac sat at her kitchen table.

For more than an hour, they had been reviewing the known facts and the speculation regarding other issues that seemed to be out of place in Snowy Ridge. Matt had made a brief apology for Kasia's absence, but he knew that Julia could sense something was wrong.

"If this woman's information is correct, you've *got* to go to Denver, Mayor. If we just contact the retirement company from here, they might phone Pat or Doug for verification and they'd tell them to show us nothing," Matt said.

"What authority do we have to demand to see the records?"

"I think we can get a little help."

"From where?" Mac asked.

"From Shelly Porter. Utah Fraud Commission. Surely they have the authority to require the Retirement Corporation to open their books for a look at the records of a Utah city."

"I like it," Julia said. "When do we go?"

"I'll think you should go alone. I'll contact Shelly Porter tomorrow morning. If she agrees, you can fly over one day this week, review the records, gather what evidence you can, and fly back the same day."

Julia looked at Mac, cocking her head slightly in question. "*I* should go? I thought we might go together."

"He's having second thoughts, Mayor," Mac added. "And quite justified I might add."

Julia looked back at Matt. "What does he mean, Matt?"

Matt fumbled with the pencil he been using to doodle on a scratch pad and finally laid it down on the table. "He means I'm thinking about throwing in the towel. That I've had enough."

"It's the newspaper article, isn't it?"

"Of course it is, Julia. Kasia saw the article on the plane last night before I had a chance to speak with her. I haven't told my parents anything, and for all I know, the Utah Bar Association is drawing up the disbarment papers right now."

Julia sat down across the kitchen table from Matt. "I understand all that. And I can't tell you what to do, but from what I can see, we've got them on the run. Their attack on you is pretty desperate."

"And it's working. Most of this community thinks I'm a pervert."

"Are you?" Julia smiled at him across the table.

"What the hell do you mean by that?" Matt shouted.

"I mean, 'are you?'" Julia replied, softly.

Matt paused, just starring at the woman across the table. "No, I'm not."

"Well then, what good would tucking your tail between your legs do for you? Would it disprove their allegations? Would it restore your credibility in the eyes of the community? Would it make you proud the rest of your life?" She leaned forward, reaching across the table and taking his hand in hers. "Would it show Kasia that she was right about you the first time? That you're a worthy husband and future father?"

Matt's head drooped and he stared at the floor for several long seconds before responding. Finally, he looked up at Julia. "I don't know. I honestly don't know."

"That's as honest an answer as you can give, Matt. And neither do I. But I do know this: if you let them brand you and you walk away quietly, it will be with you for the rest of your life. It pains me to know that you're likely to be sacrificed in this dispute, this war, but the choice of how you go to the gallows is still yours. You can die a lion or die a lamb."

Matt looked over at Mac who was stone-faced, his expression

revealing nothing. Then he looked back at Julia. "I'd rather not die at all, Madam Mayor, if you don't mind."

"Good," she said, rising and stepping to the sink. "I'm telling you we have them on the run. We've got to nail them before they destroy your career and destroy any chance we have of proving their conspiracy. They're shifting their campaign to discredit both of us into high gear. Let's fight back. Let's get in touch with Shelly Porter and see what assistance she can offer."

"I'll call her tomorrow. But I'm not making any promises. I will likely talk with my Dad and get some advice. And I still may determine in the interests of all, to call it quits, resign and walk away."

"And Kasia?" Julia asked.

"What do you mean?"

"Are you going to walk away from her too?"

"I may not have a choice. Three weeks ago we got engaged to be married. Yesterday I was her fiancee. Today, she asked me not to call her while she thinks this through."

"Do you think she'll give up on you that easily?"

Matt pondered the question for several moments. "No, I don't."

"Well, then, why are *you*?"

"Why am I what?"

"Giving up on yourself."

Matt sighed deeply, rose from his chair and put his jacket on. "It's time for me to go home, Julia. Thanks for the advice," Matt said, stepping toward the door, Mac right behind him. He paused at the front door and turned back to face Mayor Wells. "My father once told me that trouble usually affects those around us more than it does us. In high school, I didn't understand that piece of advice. It's becoming a lot clearer. I'll call Shelly tomorrow and see what she can do. Goodnight, Julia."

"Goodnight, Matt, Mac. You know where to find me if you need me."

* * * * *

Tuesday morning, Matt woke early and called Shelly Porter's office.

"I'm very sorry, Mr. Sterling. Ms. Porter is gone this week on personal business. She'll be back in the office on Monday, the 28th. Can I leave a message for her?"

"No, thank you. I'll leave one on her cell phone and perhaps she'll check in before she returns. Thanks."

"I'm certain she will. Have a nice day."

Matt dialed another number, reaching Julia Wells' answering machine at her home.

"Julia, it's Matt. I tried to call Shelly. She's gone to Colorado for a few days. I left a message to call me when she returns. I guess all we can do is wait. I'll let you know when I hear from her. Meanwhile you can reach me on my cell phone if you need to talk. Have a good day."

Completing the call, Matt booted up his computer and waited for the email to download. He scrolled immediately to the one from DNAGirl.

To: Par4Matt@aol.com

From: DNAGirl@aol.com

Subject: A short trip

Dear Matt:

I acted appallingly Sunday night and I hope you will forgive me. I was very confused. Still am, actually. I have been asked by Dr. Amberly to fill in for Marilyn as Team Leader on a short blood draw trip to Florida. We leave this morning and should be back Friday evening or Saturday. Perhaps this time will give us both some time to consider our positions and find the answers we both seek. I do love you, Matt. Please don't think that has changed. But I need to understand how to deal with this and how I might be of help, rather than a hindrance. Right now I'm distraught and useless to anyone. I imagine you are too. I could take you in my arms and say, 'it will be alright.' But life isn't like that, is it, Matt? I will call you as soon as we return.

All my love, Kasia

Matt ignored the remainder of the email messages, shut down the computer and sat at the terminal for several minutes, starring into space. Then he rose, went into the bedroom and lifted down a small overnight bag, stuffed some underwear, an extra pair of pants, his toiletries kit, and stopped briefly in the kitchen. He picked up the phone and dialed a number.

"This is Mac."

"Mac, it's Matt. Just wanted to let you know I'm going to drive out to Sacramento for a couple of days."

"Going to see your Dad?"

"Yeah. Should be back Friday or Saturday. You can reach me on the cell phone if anything breaks."

"Drive carefully and drop a few quarters for me in Reno."

"I'm gonna fly right by it, Mac. See ya."

"Have a good trip, Matt."

* * * * *

Three days later Matt drove steadily through eastern Nevada, having spent two days in Reno with his father, playing two rounds of golf in the process. Matt had called his father on the drive out to Sacramento, explained that he needed to talk to him, but that he didn't want to worry his mother. He'd asked to meet privately with his father. Dick Sterling suggested they meet in Reno.

By Friday morning, when they parted in opposite directions, Matt had a much better feeling about the situation and his father's ability to understand what had happened. The subterfuge to exclude his mother had been handled well by his father, who had explained that a medical associate in Reno had asked him to come up and consult on a particularly difficult case. Dick had suggested that Sally Sterling fly up to Portland and visit her sister for a couple of days. She readily agreed.

"There's only one piece left then, Matt," Dick Sterling said in the parking lot of the Golden Phoenix Hotel.

"It's the most important one, Dad."

"Do you love this girl?"

"With all my heart. I've got to convince her that I'm innocent. I'm just afraid that even if she comes to believe in my innocence, she won't want to be involved in the scandal that's bound to come."

"Give the girl some credit, Matt. From what you say, she comes from good stock."

Matt stepped close to his father and wrapped his arms around him. "So do I, Dad. So do I."

"Drive safely and keep me informed."

"I will, Dad. Thanks for coming."

"Two days of golf, a loving son coming to confide in the old man. What more could a father ask for?"

"I'll call you tomorrow," Matt said, getting in his car and departing the hotel parking lot.

Clearing the salt flats about ten o'clock, approaching the Toole exit, Matt's cell phone beeped to signal a message. Fifty miles or more of the barren area over the salt flats was a dead cell zone. Matt picked up the phone and speed dialed the answering service.

"Matt, it's Kasia. I've just gotten home. It's Friday night and I was hoping we could talk. Please call me when you get this message."

Forty-five minutes later, Matt pulled up in front of Kasia's house, switched off the engine and walked up to the darkened house. He knocked lightly on the door. In a moment, a light went on in the back of the house and soon the porch light came on and the curtains parted. Kasia opened the door, dressed in her robe and slippers.

"I'd just gone to bed and was reading."

"I could come back tomorrow," Matt said.

She reached out, grabbed his elbow and pulled him through the doorway. Once inside, Kasia closed the door and turned to face the man she loved. She took one step closer and threw her arms around his neck, pulling his head down and kissing him ardently. Several long seconds later, she released her grip.

"Wow. I could go away for another three days if I could get a kiss like that when I returned."

"Sit right down in that chair, Mr. Matthew Sterling. I'm going to make some hot chocolate and we're going to spend whatever time it takes to talk this through. But know this if you know nothing else. I love you. I love you with all my heart. And as sure as I am that the Lord lives, I know that you did not do these things you are accused of. I believe you, Matt. I believe you completely."

* * * * *

It was nearly three AM and several dozen kisses later before Kasia got to the part of the story where she became convinced of Matt's innocence.

"It was the Elders, Matt. They told me you were innocent."

"How—"

"Not the Elders personally, but what they were doing. They were having a scripture study in the Sarasota chapel where we were drawing blood samples. I sat with them for awhile. Like

I've already told you, I'd been praying for several days for the Lord to somehow show me the way. He did. Through the scriptures."

"How did that—"

"Please, let me finish, Matt. I know you'll understand. The scriptures that Elder Ryan was studying in Sarasota gave me my answer. Two specific scriptures, actually. Dad has explained to me so many times that our answers sometimes come as we go about our day, but I never felt it the same way I did this time. The Lord loved me and He told me what I needed to know. It doesn't matter what the newspaper story said, Matt. I know I need to understand why it happened and what's happened to you while I've been gone so we can work through it together. I assume it has to do with the new mayor, problems at City Hall, but I want you to know this: I love you, I know you're innocent, and we can get through this together. I'm home now, Matt, and I'll be with you through all of this. Whatever it takes. You don't need to do it alone."

Tears were running down Matt's cheeks and his head was slumped forward as Kasia completed her story. After he composed himself, he asked, "What scriptures, Kasia?"

"That's the best part. What day did I come home from England, Matt?"

"Sunday, the 22nd of February."

"And our wedding date?"

"The 22nd of June."

"That's right, and don't you ever forget it," she said, emitting a small laugh through her own tears. "Even fifty years from now I don't expect you to forget it. But listen to this scripture. I memorized it along with the missionaries. It's John 4:35. *Say not ye, There are yet four months, and then cometh the harvest? Behold I say unto you, Lift up your eyes, and look on the fields; for they are white, already to harvest.*

"Four months, Matt. To the day. Our wedding is our harvest. And the Lord told me not to worry, that the field is white and the harvest is ready. You're the field, Matt. And *we* are the harvest. He loves us, Matt. And we must never forget that."

"You said two scriptures."

"I did. The other one was icing on the cake. But I already knew my answer. I hadn't misjudged you. And the Lord knew. The other scripture was almost exactly what you had been telling me in our email exchanges. Remember you said that Mayor Wells said that most people didn't want to know about the problems. Even those who had nothing to do with the corruption, but especially those who were guilty?"

"That's what she said."

"The Lord feels the same way. With these two scriptures, which I will never forget, the Lord answered my prayers."

"Did you memorize the second one too?"

"I did. It's 1st Nephi 16:2: *And it came to pass that I said unto them that I knew that I had spoken hard things against the wicked, according to the truth; and the righteous have I justified, and testified that they should be lifted up at the last day; wherefore, the guilty taketh the truth to be hard, for it cutteth them to the very center.*

"Do you know that I love you, Matt?"

"I don't know why, Kasia, but I'm certain that you do. Even more certain that the Lord loves us both. Do you know how scared I was when you came back from England? I had no idea how I was going to tell you. I was terrified of losing you, all the while knowing none of this was true. And then when you already knew, I could see it in your eyes. I thought I had lost you forever."

"You'll never lose me again," she said, once more kissing him and wrapping her arms tightly around his neck. "Now we need to get on with our lives, face this challenge and plan for our wedding. How did your parents take the news?"

Matt immediately developed a blank look on his face. Kasia knew instantly what it meant. "Oh, Matt, don't tell me…" she said, cupping her hands over her mouth.

"Kasia, I've been at war since the minute I got off the plane," he protested. "Voice messages, emails—you aren't going to believe the emails I've received from supposedly good church members. I just…just never could face the thought of calling Mom and Dad. I've just returned from seeing Dad, but I met with him alone. I didn't know how to tell Mom about this disaster and if I couldn't tell her that, I couldn't tell her about the wedding."

"Matt Sterling! Did you not believe that your parents would have the same faith in you that I did? That the Lord did? Tomorrow morning, first thing, we're calling. Your mother is going to *kill* you."

Matt looked at his watch. "It is tomorrow morning, Kasia," he laughed. "I better run home, get a shower and some clean clothes. Can I come back for breakfast? I have some business downtown tomorrow…today, actually."

"It's 3:30. Come back at 8:00. I'll have breakfast ready."

"I love you, Kasia Somerset. And I'm so grateful for your courage. This isn't over yet. In fact I've considered giving up and just getting out of here."

"You'll do no such thing. We're going to fight this. We're going to bring out the truth."

"It's not that easy, Kasia."

"Life never is, but now you have a partner to share it with."

"I don't deserve you, you know."

"I'll help you to work on that part," she said, smiling and rising off the couch. "Now, go home and come back freshly shaved with clean clothes."

* * * * *

At 8:45, after breakfast, Matt tried to call Shelly Porter from Kasia's kitchen while she rinsed the dishes and put them in the dishwasher.

"Did you reach her?" Kasia asked.

"She's still not back, but I'll try her cell phone a little later. Are you off to the lab?"

"I am," she said, drying her hands on a towel. "With a little practice, I could get used to seeing you in the morning," she said, putting her arms around his neck.

"You sure brighten my day, Ms. Somerset. I think I'll call Steve Bracks this morning too, just to see what he thinks. He said he has lots of contacts. Maybe he can help."

"Who's that?"

"Steve Bracks. He's a reporter with the *Utah Press.*"

"Oh, that's risky, isn't it?"

"He's been a very fair person, Kasia. If you read all the past stories, *Star* and *Press,* you'll see how he tells the truth. You read the *Star* on the plane. That was as bad as it could get. I mean Steve hasn't made me look like a saint, but he doesn't sensationalize it like the *Star.*"

"Oh, I didn't tell you last night," she laughed, "Mom and Dad are coming to Salt Lake for April Conference. They told me to ask you if perhaps your parents could come also and they could meet."

"That sounds excellent. We can all be here together for my hanging," he said, only half kidding.

"Oh, Matt, stop it," she laughed. "Things are looking up, aren't they? I mean with what you told me last night, about the Las Vegas paper trail, you have the proverbial smoking gun, right?"

"It's politics, Kasia. Smoking guns disappear or, from what I'm told, those that don't want to know about it just ignore them."

"Well, let's get our parents together. The timing is great. I'll finish the requirements for my Ph.D. in early April, maybe by the end of March, if I can complete the statistics I need to put into the thesis. Then I'm free to go home and plan to meet some young guy who might just happen to show up at the London Temple."

"Just *any* guy, huh," he said, squeezing her tighter.

"Probably. Maybe an American this time."

"*This* time?"

"I'll try it *once*. Now I have to get to work, really. My FedEx shipments probably arrived several days ago and I need to run some DNA tests, compare families, and see how royal the European houses really are, or were."

"Did you find what you needed in Europe?"

"Did I ever! Remnants of hair, some other documents like yours with blood stains. Lots of stuff. Now I just need to correlate it all and run the statistical profiles."

"Right. Well, *you* determine the validity of the world's royalty, and *I'll* try to catch a crook. Dinner tonight?"

"I have no other plans," she said, smiling, "for *life*."

Matt kissed her on the forehead and then turned her face up to meet his, followed by a proper kiss. "See you tonight."

"Before dinner, Mr. Sterling, we are going to call your parents."

"Tonight?"

"Tonight. *Before* dinner."

* * * * *

Once he got in the car and headed for Salt Lake, Matt retrieved Steve Bracks' card from his wallet and dialed the cell number listed. On the third ring, he answered.

"This is Steve."

"Steve, it's Matt Sterling. Snowy Ridge."

"Good morning. You're up and about early on your involuntary vacation."

"Thanks for the reminder. *Unpaid* vacation, I remind you. Are you free this morning, or sometime today?"

"I'm in the car on the way to Sandy City Hall. Should be through by, uh, say eleven. Want to meet for lunch?"

"Great. Where?"

"Schlotzky's at State and 103rd."

"Fine. See you there at eleven-thirty."

Matt was already seated when Steve came through the door, stopping at the order desk and placing his lunch order. He took his number and came toward Matt. "No tan?"

"It's February, in case you hadn't noticed."

"Sure, but with two weeks off during winter, I would have spent it in Hawaii."

"So would I, but I have work to do."

"Clearing one's name can be a full-time profession."

"So I'm told. It's time to test your 'for background only' confidentiality agreement."

"What've you got?" Steve asked.

"Some financial records that need to get to the Fraud Commission."

"Right. So as of this moment, we are officially 'off the record.' If it gets beyond what I can promise, I'll stop you and we can discuss whether to go further or not."

"Fair enough. I tried to reach Shelly Porter this morning. Utah Fraud Commission."

Steve nodded. "I know Shelly."

"Why am I not surprised? She's out of town 'til Monday."

"Yep, Snowy Ridge is not the only place that needs a close eye. Have you got something she can sink her teeth into?" Steve asked. "Oh, wait. Hold on a minute." His number had come up on the sandwich board. He picked up his sandwich, sat back down, and motioned Matt to carry on.

"Let me cut right to the chase. Steve, we have reason to believe that Harcourt and Bellows have been robbing the Local Government Retirement Corporation. Snowy Ridge's employee contributions and the interest they earn."

"Doesn't that go into each employee's account? Wouldn't someone have gotten suspicious if their account didn't rise by the basic deposit each pay date?"

"Yep, they would. Most of them, anyway. Some never look at all. This is a holding account. A six-year-old Council Resolution required that six months of contributions be maintained in the account to assure that employees were always protected. Plus I'm told that Doug Bellows stays another two or three paydays ahead with his contributions. He tells the Council that he is ensuring the employees are protected. The interest earned, from the six-month's holding account and several advance paydays, goes into his account and Harcourt's. To the tune of about a hundred and thirty-five thousand each year. For the past six years. In their personal accounts, it continues to earn interest. I'd love to know their balances compared to other employees who have been with the city the same length of time."

Steve put his sandwich down, wiped his mouth, and took a drink of his soda. Matt could see he was thinking hard. "How sure are you?"

"I've got the original Resolution, which is public information anyway, and several deposit forms from the earliest deposits. That's six years ago. A former employee, an accountant, who by the way desires to remain anonymous and I assured the person they would, knows they carried it on for at least a year before my informant left Snowy Ridge. Now we need to find out if it's still in place."

"And Shelly can provide the authority to have a look," Steve added.

"Right. And she's gone for a week. Of course I could go to Hank Andersen in the DA's office."

Immediately Steve shook his head. "Stick with Shelly."

"Why? We'll lose a week."

"Nope. Stick with Shelly or you'll lose more than a week."

"Are you telling me he's not reliable?"

"I'm not telling you anything other than stick with Shelly."

"All right, I understand. Any other thoughts?"

"Plenty, but I want to think on it for a bit."

"Should we take this higher than Shelly?"

"Probably, but she should be the one to bring it up the ladder. She's been straight with you so far, right? Given you the time you need to find some of this stuff?"

"Yes."

"Then keep her in the picture. She's put her neck on the block for you. Let her be the one to uncover this stuff. Coming from you, Matt, it's going to look like revenge or sour grapes."

"I see your point. So, we sit back and wait?"

"Not quite. What we do next depends on how much you trust me."

Matt watched Steve for a moment, and the two men took that time to appraise each other. Matt spoke first. "Look, I just want to do the right thing here. I need to know, or at least have a general idea, of how you intend to use this information and copies of this material. I presume that's what you're asking."

"I am," Steve said. "I can get a lot done behind the scenes before Shelly comes back. I can't be more specific, but I can tell you that Shelly and I have worked together before. You have my word that I will not reveal this information to anyone other than my editor, who needs to know what I'm doing. He won't know, in fact he won't even ask, which city, what persons, or anything detailed. All he needs to know is that I'm working on uncovering a financial fraud at the local government level."

"And you get the exclusive."

Steve smiled quickly, his teeth white and even. "That *is* the business I'm in, Mr. Sterling. Scooping the other paper is the name of the game. And I just might be able to save your, uh, your *reputation* at least."

"You can save any part of me that needs to be saved, Steve," Matt said, trying to laugh through the hopelessness he was feeling.

"In truth, Matt, when these things happen, no matter how right you are, or which side you take, neither side ever fully recovers. When fraud hits the front pages, no one involved is ever totally exonerated. It's sort of like the old adage, 'blood is thicker than water.' Even some members of the public who have nothing to do with it refuse to believe what's right before their eyes, especially if they wanted it to go the other way or in favor of the other person."

Steve went silent for a moment, looking closely at Matt. "I need you to hear this, Matt, and consider it seriously. Even if we break this ring of corruption, prove to a district attorney who was responsible, you would most likely never get another job with local government in Utah, or perhaps in the Rocky Mountain west for that matter."

"You're kidding, right?" Matt stared at the reporter in disbelief.

Steve shook his head, not the hint of a smile on his face. "Matt, every city has some degree of, well, for lack of a better description, some degree of maneuvering. They shift their financial records, rob Peter to pay Paul. You understand I don't mean they steal, and certainly not to the extent we see in Snowy Ridge. But once you're on record as having brought this to light, be seen as a goody-goody boy, maybe even a whistle-blower, those who applaud you publicly will be afraid of you privately. They will not want to hire you onto their management team. They'll be afraid you might discover something wrong in their place and it's been proven you can't, or won't, keep your mouth shut. The team player concept I mentioned earlier."

"So I'm out no matter what?" Matt asked incredulously.

"Most likely. It's not fair, Matt, but there it is."

"What happened to 'Truth, Justice, and the American way'?"

"It went west with the Lone Ranger."

"Right here in Happy Valley. Can you believe it? And everyone thinks our community is full of decent, honest people."

"It is, Matt," Steve responded. "There are very few bad eggs, but it only takes a few to make everyone suspicious."

"But these are public officials. They're at the forefront of what *should* be the group with the highest integrity."

"There's more truth to that than you know. I was shocked when I first was assigned to local government, but I wouldn't work anywhere else now. The great majority of people are fair and honest and try to do right. Some, the strong ones, even step forward to keep things honest or try to. But the great majority of people are those who try to live the law themselves, but will take no notice or part in ferreting out someone else's dishonesty. I used to be one of those people. The 'live and let live' bunch. But the newspaper game wipes away any illusion of fair play. You have to take sides."

"You don't paint a pretty picture."

"Perhaps not, but every once in a while, a Matt Sterling comes along. I'm not trying to make you a hero, but you *could* have turned a blind eye. Many do."

"Not seventy-two hours ago that's exactly what I intended to do. Throw in the towel and call it quits."

"I've seen it happen before. What changed your mind?"

"I don't know that it was a single thing. But those whom I love, and love me, are ready to stick by me. I can't understand why exactly. It has been, and from what you say, will continue to be, very public and disgraceful."

"I'll try to write it as I see it, Matt. I can't just exonerate you in the press, but I can tell the truth as I see it."

"That's better than what I've been getting."

"You're still through in this career, Matt. That won't change."

Matt was at a loss for words and stunned by the thought that no matter how this worked out, he would likely lose his career. "I guess I'm pretty naïve. But I'm committed, no matter what. I've got copies of the documents in the car."

"So, you *planned* to give them to me?"

"I'm taking a crash course in reading people, Steve. Trust was my hallmark. I'm nowhere as advanced as you are in the human perception game, but I am beginning to exercise it selectively."

Steve finished his soda, stood up, and nodded his head toward the door. "With that lesson firmly imbedded in your thinking process, you just might survive in this world longer than I once thought you would, Matt Sterling."

Chapter Twenty-One

Matt telephoned Professor Weatherly's office and set up an appointment for the next morning. He then spent the rest of the afternoon in downtown Salt Lake City, performing a task he had intended to accomplish before Kasia returned from England, but which had taken a back seat to the events that had filled his life since he'd stepped off the plane.

Tonight he and Kasia would call his parents and put a finishing touch on what his mother had been waiting for ever since he returned from his mission. Mrs. Richard Sterling would learn the identity—as if she didn't already know, Matt chuckled to himself—of the next Mrs. Sterling. Mrs. *Matthew* Sterling.

And also tonight, Kasia Somerset—who Matt had learned this past several weeks was more important to him than any of the current events, and who had surprised him beyond words with her spiritual insight as she had sought to discover the truth of a situation that would have scared most people from ever having further contact with the culprit—tonight, this light of his life would receive the proper certification herself, after dinner, in the form of a two-carat, emerald-cut diamond engagement ring.

When Matt arrived home, included with the usual junk mail was a letter from the Utah Bar Association. He opened the letter and found a single paragraph, advising him of a Standards and Practices hearing scheduled for ten days on issues of ethics and negligence. He was advised that he was entitled to have an attorney present to represent his interests. He sat re-reading the single paragraph for five minutes, unable to actually comprehend the magnitude of how this simple issue was beginning to affect his life. He stood up, walked through the sliding glass doorway onto the balcony, and leaned against the railing, looking out over the mountains and the growing community to the south. Slowly, he lowered his head and closed his eyes, grasping the railing tighter. "Father, I know I've decided to continue on this path, but I can't get through this without you. If I ever needed strength, I need it now. Please, stay with me."

Matt opened his eyes, allowing them to follow the snow line where so many times he had led a group of young Boy Scouts when he had served as assistant scout master the previous year. He stood there for a long ten minutes, silently contemplating his lot in life. Then, with a deep breath, he turned and stepped back into his apartment, walked to the desk, penned a few comments on the notice from the Bar Association, and faxed it to Trevor Weatherly.

Stepping into the kitchen, he saw the flashing light on his telephone recorder. There were several voice messages, the first of which was from Brother Smart, executive secretary to Matt's stake president, Richard Topham. The message advised that if possible, President Topham would like to meet with Matt the following evening at seven, in the president's office. If Brother Smart didn't hear back from Matt, he would assume the meeting time was acceptable.

The second voice message was from Shelly Porter. She gave a contact number and asked Matt to call her when he got the message. The following two messages were routine issues and Matt erased the tape, immediately picking up the phone and calling Ms. Porter's number.

"Shelly Porter," she answered.

"Hello, it's Matt Sterling."

"Hi, Matt. Sorry it took a couple of days to get back to you but I'm in Colorado with my fiancé and I promised to put the office behind me for a few days. We're doing a bit of skiing. How can I help you?"

"You told me to call you if I found something of interest. Let me give you the highlights."

Matt summarized the story of the Retirement Corporation contributions and suggested that he and Mayor Wells could fly over to Denver and meet her, and they could visit the RC offices.

"Not a good idea, Matt. I would like to come back to the office, next week, and go over this material and make some preliminary inquiries, discreetly, of course. I want to discuss it with the chief of my department. If you're correct in your assumptions, then we don't want to jump the gun on this. I want to have it sealed up tighter than a diver's watch. Have you told this to anyone else?"

"Tom McDougal from Snowy Ridge, our Public Works director, went to Las Vegas with me to get the information. I told Mayor Wells, and my girlfriend—well, actually as of a couple of weeks ago, she's my fiancée. Oh, and this morning I told Steve Bracks. I know that was risky—"

"Not at all. We've worked together before. If he gave his word to keep it quiet, he will. That's probably why he's also called me and left a message this afternoon. Look, Matt, just lay low on this 'til I get back. You might have just found the evidence you need to clear yourself."

"How long will all this take? To confirm it, I mean?"

"Truthfully, I don't know. I'll get right on it when I come home."

"I had a letter today from the Utah Bar Association. I have a hearing on ethics and negligence charges in ten days. I could face disbarment!" he said, trying to keep the sound of desperation out of his voice.

"They don't play fair, do they," she commented ruefully. "I'll see what I can do. You just might have to defend yourself with what information is already public and I'll see if I can help behind the scenes. But in case they also have inside contacts, I don't want to tip our hand. I don't think we'll have this locked down in ten days."

"Okay, Shelly," he agreed reluctantly, knowing he had no choice but to wait. "I'm in your hands, so to speak. Call me if I can do anything on this end. Otherwise, I'll talk to you next week when you formulate a plan of action."

"Fine, Matt. Thanks for calling me. I know I'm on vacation for this week, but this has been playing on my mind."

"I've been thinking about it a bit myself," Matt said.

Shelly laughed over the phone. "I'll bet you have," she said sympathetically. "Hang in there, Matt. Bye."

"Bye."

Next, Matt called Julia Wells to inform her of the day's events and to tell her to hold tight until they heard from Shelly Porter.

"It's not going to be a slam dunk, is it, Matt?"

"Probably not, Mayor. I'm kind of getting used to being the outcast. My closest friends haven't discarded me yet, so it's tolerable…barely. Being on suspension, I don't even have to wade through my office emails, all of which are unsigned of course. Brave people that they are."

"Matt, people are often cowardly, especially when they see someone on the ropes. I'm going to hang around my office at city hall for the rest of the week and see if I can pick up the flavor of things. I'll try to meet with Harcourt and test her new found cooperation. Maybe she'll even try to get me to side with her against the young upstart that likes pornography."

"That's not too funny, Mayor."

"I know," she admitted. "Just trying to put levity into the situation. You know I don't mean it."

"Yes, I do. So, I'll talk with you later in the week if anything comes up. Other than that, I'll just carry on this week and get done what I can."

"Right. Thanks for calling about Porter."

Stripping his coat and tie, Matt sat at the kitchen table and made two further calls, one to book a table at the rooftop restaurant at the Joseph Smith Memorial Building, where he had taken Kasia on their first date, and a second to the Molecular Biology Lab, where he left a message with the receptionist for Kasia, telling her what time he would pick her up. Then he went into the bathroom where he took a long, hot shower, shaved a second time, and laid down on the bed to rest for a few minutes, turning on the overhead fan to circulate the warm air in the room. He immediately fell asleep. When he awoke, it was only twenty minutes before he was supposed to pick up Kasia, so he raced through the process of dressing in his favorite suit, selected a matching tie, made certain to slip the ring box in his pocket, and ran out the door.

* * * * *

"*After* dinner."

"Nope, we agreed. *Before* dinner."

"Let me make my case. First, it will be a long phone call, I can assure you. Second, it's an hour earlier in California. And third...well, I can think of a third, but I can't tell you yet. So let's go eat where we had our first meal together, properly dressed this time, and come home early and call the Sterling family in Sacramento. We'll tell Mom to add another stocking to the fireplace next Christmas."

Kasia picked up her wrap, tucked her scarf around her neck, and handed her coat to Matt who helped her into it, and then she stood in front of the door. "I can see I'll need to develop a strategy of my own if I'm to be married to a lawyer."

"The truth always works," he said.

"Is that right?" she said. "Did you learn that from Patricia Harcourt?"

"Touché. Let's go eat."

* * * * *

All the way home from the restaurant, Kasia spent the entire time with the passenger seat overhead light on, twisting and watching the light reflect off her new engagement ring. By the time they reached her house, Matt had used all the clichés he could think of but none had fazed Kasia and she hadn't reacted to his teasing. She'd not even argued when he told her that his third reason for going to dinner first was so she could tell his mother about the ring. As he came around to open her door, he gave it one more shot.

"I almost forgot to tell you. The jeweler said that this particular type of ring is of the highest quality diamond, but only comes with a ten-thousand 'look' warranty. From your effort tonight, I think I should go back tomorrow and see if they have one with a fifty-thousand look warranty."

Kasia exited the car, stepped up on the curb and stood face to face with Matt, looking up at him. "I *know* you don't think I'm taking this off! This ring is coming off my finger only once, and that will be to allow me to slip its companion on the inside next June. And I don't care if they have a ring with a five-*million* look warranty—this is the one. Understood?"

Matt nodded. "Understood."

"Now, are you ready to take your punishment?"

"Punishment?"

"The call to your parents."

"That'll be easy. Mom will be thrilled."

"Everything hasn't gone exactly as you've planned this past two months, has it?"

"Not hardly."

"Neither will this, I can assure you," she said as they started up the walkway.

"I'm not sure I like your confident tone. You know something I don't?"

Nodding and beginning to laugh as she inserted the key into her door, she said, "I know *lots* you don't know, Matthew Sterling. And you're about to find out just one of those things."

Inside, they both removed their coats, and Kasia slipped off her shoes, placing a pair of soft, woolen slippers on her feet to keep them warm on the wooden floors of the old house. She then suggested they go into the kitchen to use the speaker phone. "I don't want to miss a single word of this call."

"Kasia—"

"Just make the call."

"Hello, Matt," Dick Sterling said as he answered the call, "hold on, I'll get your mother and we'll get on the speaker phone together."

"Matthew, what a surprise," his mother said, the chiding motherly tone with which he was so familiar evident in her voice.

"I have some good news for you both," Matt said, trying to lighten the tone.

"Do you now?" Sally Sterling replied. "And what could that possibly be? Perhaps it's that you've been accepted for the astronaut program? Or called on another mission? No, let me see, perhaps you've been incommunicado on a secret mission for the CIA. Is that it?"

"Mom—what are you talking about?"

Kasia sat on a stool in her kitchen, trying her hardest not to laugh aloud. Matt watched her in confusion as his mother continued her jibbing until finally the penny dropped.

"Who told you, Mom?"

"Matthew Andrew Sterling, I am probably the only mother in the history of the *world* who was called by her son's prospective *mother-in-law* and invited to stay at her home when her daughter married my son. Do you understand how embarrassed I was?"

"I'm beginning to think I understand very little, Mom. Sister Somerset called you? When?"

"When she felt that her prospective son-in-law had had ample time to call his parents and tell them he was planning to marry her daughter. *That's* when. I'm certain she felt seven weeks was ample time."

Matt grimaced. "Sorry, Mom. But on the bright side, it was only tonight that we got officially engaged, I mean with a ring and all."

"Well, it's certainly nice that you took time out of your busy schedule to do that much for the poor girl. It's a wonder she still remembers your name. Or wants to, for that matter."

"C'mon, Mom. Give me a break here. Kasia is rolling on the floor laughing right this minute and you're wasting the most precious moment of a mother-son relationship. The one you've been waiting to hear for a long time."

"Yes, dear, the one *another* mother brought to my attention."

"Sally," Dick Sterling said, his voice firm and confident over the speaker phone, "I think you've had your pound of flesh from our only son. Now let's congratulate him, welcome this lovely young woman into our family, and tell the kids we are coming to Utah for Conference and the whole family is going to England for the wedding. Can you bring yourself to do that, dear?"

"Kasia, my dear, can you hear me?" Sally Sterling asked.

"Yes, ma'am. I'm right here, doubling over with laughter as Matt said."

"I'm glad you have a good sense of humor, my dear, because heaven knows, you're going to need it." Sally's tone softened. "From the bottom of my heart, Kasia, we couldn't be more pleased. We are looking forward to meeting your parents in April. I've had two lovely chats with your mother and she is a wonderful woman. I can't wait to meet her. I suppose we'll have to include Matt in these meetings, but right now he'd be lucky to get a sandwich if he showed up on my doorstep."

"Sister Sterling, I wish you could see my ring. It's gorgeous."

"I think Matt has a digital camera."

"Oh, wonderful! I'll get a picture off to you as soon as we can take one. Perhaps this isn't the time, Brother and Sister Sterling, but I want you to know how much I love your son."

Matt could hear the tears in his mother's voice as she replied. "And we love you, dear, dear, Kasia. I am so pleased for you both. And don't worry. I've grown used to Matt's male characteristics. I'm sure I'll take him in my arms and hold him tightly the next time we meet. Right after I spank him."

"I'll bring the switch," Kasia offered helpfully as she grinned playfully at Matt. "One other thing, Sister Sterling—"

"Kasia, I would love it if you could find it in your heart to call me Mom, or perhaps Sally."

"Thank you, Mom. I would love that. If possible, I'd like to take a three-day weekend sometime before Conference and come out with my dress so you, Emily, Rachel, and I can do some coordinating. I'm hoping that both of your daughters would be willing to serve as brides- maids. I have two other close friends in England who will also serve. Mum's planning a reception at our stake center after the Temple ceremony."

"I'm certain they would love that. I'll speak to them both and we'll set a weekend. Conference is only about five or six weeks away, so we better move fast. And Matt?"

"Yes, Mom?"

"You can come home too if you'd like."

"Thanks, Mom. That's always good to know. Actually, I have several issues to discuss with Dad that are better done in private."

Dick Sterling spoke again. "You're not looking for another 'birds and bees' talk are you, son?"

"Thanks for the offer, Dad, but you gave me that little talk when I turned twelve if you remember."

"Whew! Didn't want to have to go through *that* again."

"You're off the hook, Dad. We'll see you guys. Probably in about two weeks or so. Love you both."

"And we love you both too," Sally said. "Bye."

* * * * *

Wednesday evening at seven, Matt was dressed in suit and tie and sitting in the foyer outside the stake president's office. Two people had gone in before him and the first had already come out. Brother Smart, executive secretary, worked on paperwork in the stake clerk's office by himself, occasionally smiling out at Matt as he patiently waited his turn.

The door to the president's office opened, and President Topham came out, his arm around elderly Sister Wordsmith. She was wiping her eyes with a small, pink handkerchief and thanking the president. Topham saw her to the outer door, reassured her once again, and then turned to greet Matt. Matt rose and shook the president's hand.

Richard Topham was about sixty, slightly balding, and stood about six feet two inches. He had a pleasant, comforting look about him and presented an instantly open and caring approach to those over whom the Lord had given him responsibilities. Matt had met with the president on several occasions over the two years he had been in the Snowy Ridge North Stake.

"How nice to see you again, Brother Sterling. Please, come in."

They stepped into the office and Matt took a seat in front of the president's desk and President Topham sat next to him in one of the visitor's chairs.

"Thank you for coming on such short notice. It's been a busy few weeks for you, hasn't it?"

"Yes, sir. That's an understatement."

"I understand. How are you feeling, Matt? Are you coping with the vagaries of life these days?"

"President, it's not the script I would have written to say the least, but I've learned that I have some very good friends and my family has also been great."

"That's wonderful. And your young lady?"

Matt smiled and looked away for a moment. "Not much escapes you, does it, President?"

The older man smiled in return. "We live in a small community and it seems everyone knows someone who knows someone else, if you understand."

"I think so, President."

"Do you know why I asked you in this evening?"

Matt hesitated, shifted in his seat and then looked directly at President Topham. "I haven't presented the best image of a good Latter-day Saint these past few weeks, President. I presume you have called me in to determine what needs to be done about it."

Topham acknowledged with a nod of his head. "To some degree, that's true. But mostly I just wanted to have a chat with you and see how you were coping."

"People who are in a position to know much more than I do, President, have told me it's most likely my city management career is over, at least in Utah, no matter what I do or how this turns out."

"Do you believe that?"

"I'm beginning to see that it's possible."

"And is it justified?"

"That's the question, isn't it, President? Did I do what I'm publicly accused of doing?"

Topham shook his head. "No, Matt. That's not what I asked. Is it justified, what's happening to you?"

"No, President Topham, it's not. But that doesn't seem to be the most important issue."

"How so?"

"My innocence doesn't seem to hold much weight. Certain segments of my management team, at City Hall I mean, are determined to put me in a bad light. To make sure I don't have the credibility I need to work with our new mayor to review and evaluate what appear to be improper procedures."

Topham smiled again, nodding his understanding. "I'm not that sensitive, Matt. You can tell it straight. What you're trying to tell me is that the rats are scurrying around on the ship. Is that right? And you're in danger of going down with all hands on board."

Matt looked startled for a moment, Candy's familiar theme ringing in his ears.

"Yes, Matt, we have some mutual friends and they care for you very much. But that's only part of the issue. They, like you, understand that not much can be done once a slander campaign begins. The mud sticks, Matt. I think you know that. That's probably what your friends mean when they say this will affect your career no matter the result.

"I'll share with you a few thoughts, if I might. Over the past week or so, three of my High Councilmen have come to me, separately, and suggested that it might be appropriate to convene a Church court and invite you to explain these allegations. Each indicated they had spoken to someone who knew the inside story and that you needed to be confronted."

Matt knew that he was unable to conceal the startled look on his face and the fear he suddenly felt in the pit of his stomach. "President, I—"

"Let me finish, Matt. Do you believe in the Gospel as we know it in the Church?"

"I do, President," Matt responded, subdued in his tone.

"And you believe the Lord speaks to the Prophet in these latter days?"

"Absolutely."

"And what lessons have you learned from the recent events that have tossed your life upside down?"

"President, I'm just struggling to keep my head above water at the moment. I haven't had much time for reflection. I've been suspended at work, publicly branded as someone who participates in pornography, I'm in danger of losing my job—even my career since next week I'll likely be disbarred—and now I'm scared to death that my most valuable possession, my church membership, may also be in jeopardy."

The emotions of the past weeks he had tried to keep bottled up came out in a rush. "And not one word of what has been spoken about me is true. If there are lessons to be learned from that, President Topham, and I know there must be, it will surely take some time for me to figure them out."

"Do you believe that your innocence is important?"

"Not to those who are seeking to discredit me, but it is to me and to my family. I hope it's important to you, President."

"Matt," Topham said, reaching forth to put his hand on the younger man's knee, leaning forward to close the gap between them. "I know your father was a Bishop and a Stake

President. I know that you understand how the Lord works through his mortal servants. We seek to keep in tune with the spirit so we can discern the truth. Besides speaking to several people about this issue, including those who I mentioned earlier who wanted to bring you into a Church court, I've also taken your situation to our Father in heaven. I trust my judgment, Matt. More to the point, I trust *His* judgment. Your innocence of these allegations was not in question when you entered my office tonight. I didn't call you in to determine your innocence. I called you in to see how you were coping and to help you understand the lessons that need to be learned from such an experience. Let's use your profession for a moment. Consider some of the legal principles. For instance, case law or precedent is an important aspect of proving one's legal point, is it not?"

Calmer now, Matt nodded agreement. "It is, President."

"Have you ever had an assignment, in law school perhaps, that required you to research case law where innocent men were accused, perhaps even convicted, of a crime they didn't commit?"

Matt thought for moment and then shook his head. "I don't recall such an assignment."

"Do you think there are any people in the prison up at Point of the Mountain who are not deserving of their fate?"

Matt smiled briefly. "All of them, if you ask each one individually."

President Topham also laughed. "Probably right. But do you think some of them are telling the truth?"

"Yes, sir, some probably are."

"Can you think of anyone you know who was convicted unjustly?"

Matt thought for several seconds, slowly beginning to understand President Topham's meaning. "But, President, wasn't that the plan? I mean wasn't the conviction part of the eternal plan?"

"Yes, it was, Matt. Our Savior knew what was in store and how He would be called upon to sacrifice for us. Do you see any correlation between the Savior's mission and yours?"

"No, sir. My trouble in no way matches the impact of the Savior's persecution and certainly not His atonement," he responded humbly.

"No, Matt," Topham said, patting the younger man's knee, "it doesn't. But it *will* be important to many people within your circle of life. Those who love you, those who observe you at work, and those who know the truth will also understand the unfairness of what has been happening to you. I know this is hard to accept, but even those who have caused these charges to be laid against you understand the unfairness of it all. To make themselves feel better, and perhaps to show the rest of us that their charges are correct, they would like nothing more than for you to discard your testimony, to blame God for your troubles and to go inactive. That is the ultimate sin in this community and it would prove their point that you're not a good person."

"President, that's not going to happen, but if they *do* understand this is unfair, they don't appear to be showing any remorse. In fact it's getting worse. And worst of all, these people are all Church members in good standing. They hold important leadership callings as well. I don't understand."

"I know. That's very hard to accept, isn't it? Let me tell you a quick, illustrative story. I'm not a native Utah Mormon. I lived most of my life in the far reaches of the Church, even in several foreign countries where the Church was in its infancy. To be an active Mormon in those places one needed to have a strong testimony because it was often looked upon negatively by the general public. If someone lived in those places and said they were Mormon, it was because they truly believed and had developed a strong testimony. If someone didn't *really* believe, they never admitted to having anything to do with the Church.

"Then, about fifteen years ago, my family and I moved to Utah. I've met some of the finest people I have ever known in these valleys. Fine, upstanding LDS people—and non-LDS people as well. But I've also learned that for some in Utah, being a member of the LDS Church, specifically in the greater Salt Lake City area, is just good business. It has nothing to do with testimony. They profess belief and attend meetings to demonstrate their faith, but it's a charade. But the Lord is not fooled, Matt. Know that, if you know nothing else. The Lord knows their hearts. They can fool some of the Lord's servants, like me, because we're human and fallible. The Lord's leaders are entitled to inspiration, but these are cunning people, Matt. And willing to lie. I'm sure you've learned that."

"Indeed I have, sir. It's not been a pleasant lesson."

"I imagine not. And do you understand *why* you've learned this lesson? Why you've been placed in this situation?"

"President, I know that I've always loved the Savior ever since my father explained to me the magnitude of His sacrifice. As a child, I hated the men who did that to Him. I saw His death as so unfair, unjust. But as I look at unfair accusations in the light of my *personal* situation, I feel highly indignant that I could be made to suffer public humiliation for something I didn't do. It's *personal*. It hurts. I've been close to tears a few nights as I've gone home and wondered how it would all work out. Yet somehow, I still know the Savior loves me. I know it even more this past two weeks as I've seen how those who love me have come to stand by me. Perhaps the lesson to be learned is that whatever happens to us, guilty or innocent, we all can rely on the Savior's love. And the judgment of men, however painful and humiliating, is not really important. It's the love of the Savior that we should focus on and trust in Him to provide righteous judgment."

"And can you do that, Matt? Can you accept what comes with a steadfast heart? Not let it destroy your testimony?"

"I believe I can, President Topham. My testimony is firm, and so is the testimony of those I most love. They have been my earthly rock. But that doesn't mean I won't fight as much as I can to recover my good name. President, it's a long story and not for tonight, but one of my ancestors lost his good name as a result of his honorable service to our country. He was misread by his contemporaries and branded a traitor. He suffered for it the remainder of his life. I'm not ready to accept that as my fate."

"Good for you, Matt. I can see your parents did a good job of providing you with the tools you need in life. I want to thank you for coming to see me tonight. You've justified my faith in you and buoyed my spirits. I have little ability to affect the professional outcome of your trouble, Brother Sterling, but be comforted by the fact that the Lord loves you and understands what is happening. For what reason you have been subjected to these issues, we don't know. But your Church membership is *not* in question. And Brother Sterling, I want to meet this remarkable young woman who has so quickly taken your heart and who has stood by you in this time of trouble."

"Thank you, President. I'm grateful for your understanding. One thing, President. The sinking ship and the rats, uh…I…"

"Sister Candy Houser is a remarkable woman, is she not?" Topham smiled as he rose from his chair. "I was a personal friend and counselor to her husband when he was bishop."

Matt stood as well, understanding what had transpired. "She's a fine work colleague, too."

"Indeed. Remember, I want to meet your young woman."

"I'll see to it, President. Might I ask one further favor before I go?"

"Certainly. How can I help?"

"I believe I have the fortitude to ride this out, but, perhaps...a blessing to help me have the strength to persevere."

"It would be my pleasure, Matt. My pleasure indeed."

* * * * *

The Utah Bar Association Ethics Committee met for nearly two hours in early March, with Matthew Sterling represented by Professor Trevor Weatherly of the J. Reuben Clark Law School. Nearly ninety minutes of that time had been taken up by representatives of the City of Snowy Ridge Police Department as they presented their voluminous file of pornographic material, most of which the members of the committee declined to view beyond the first few pictures. Nonetheless, the stack of images, reputed to have been removed from Matt's work computer, sat in full view of the committee members and amply demonstrated that Captain Honeycutt had made his case.

Snowy Ridge finance director, Doug Bellows, and city attorney Sarah Beckenham were given time to present their case for negligence, specifically with regard to a construction contact that had been signed by Deputy City Attorney Matthew Sterling. Their contention, that the contract demonstrated insufficient protection had been afforded to the city in defense of duplicate expenditures, was the cornerstone of the negligence charge. Noticeably absent from the hearings was City Manager Patricia Harcourt.

Matt's presentation of documents signed by Patricia Harcourt approving the contract, a fact that momentarily stunned Sarah Beckenham who was unaware of their existence, only served to stall the verdict but not to deter the committee from assessing Matt's degree of culpability. Ms. Harcourt's approval, the committee said, did not negate Mr. Sterling's responsibility, as deputy city attorney, to exercise due diligence in protecting the city's interests even at the risk of overriding Ms. Harcourt's recommendation to approve.

Within two hours it was over, and the committee asked if there were any further comments to be made before they adjourned to consider a verdict, which would be delivered to the accused within ten days.

Professor Weatherly indicated his desire to make a statement. The committee Chair agreed.

Weatherly stood, remaining behind the table at which he and Matt Sterling had been sitting. "Mr. Chairman and members of the Ethics Committee. It has been my great displeasure to attend this hearing today, hastily convened in contravention of standard practice, and in abrogation of my client's right to review evidence or prepare sufficient defense. I listened carefully to the demagoguery of the prosecution, and that's what they were, ladies and gentlemen of the committee, little demagogues peeking out from behind stacked piles of manufactured trash. As they sought to prosecute one of their own who had dared to question their rejection of a duly elected public official, I had one thought consistently running through my mind. Not since the original inhabitants of this valley ran west to escape the persecution of their neighbors has such a public flogging taken place.

"If you extend credence to their disgusting and totally unwarranted presentation, then, to use an oft-quoted phrase among undergraduates, you should return your parchment to your respective law schools and get your money back. A parchment, I might add, that was extended to you on the premise that you would render honorable application of that credential in defense of justice.

"I have been a lawyer for over forty years and a member of the Utah Bar for twenty-two, ever since my appointment as

Professor of Law at the J. Reuben Clark Law School at Brigham Young University. In that entire time, *never* have I seen such a rush to judgment and seldom have I seen a more circumstantial case presented. These police officers and city officials have presented a wealth of disinformation that would make any reasonable body of legal professionals cringe. An astute district attorney would not even consider prosecuting such a case or impaneling a Grand Jury. Yet you have accepted, without sufficient opportunity for refutation, their version of events without question. Were the decisions of this body subject to appeal to a higher tribunal, there is no doubt in my mind that your verdict—not yet delivered, but certainly predictable from your pusillanimous actions today—would be swiftly reversed.

"It is with a heavy heart that I wish to make known to this august body that if, in its wisdom, and absent proper procedure or adequate knowledge of factual data, the committee sees fit to permanently remove this young man from the practice of law within the State of Utah, I will immediately resign my membership from the Utah Bar Association and have my name struck off the register of certified Utah attorneys."

Matt's head jerked up at the pronouncement from Professor Weatherly and he tugged at the older man's sleeve. Weatherly leaned down and Matt whispered in his ear.

"I can't allow you to do that, Professor. This is just costing too much. I can't—"

Weatherly shook his head. "That's right, Matt. You *can't*. I know what I'm doing. Just stay silent for a few moments longer."

Weatherly stood erect and resumed his presentation to the Committee members. "My apologies for the interruption, Mr. Chairman. As I was saying, I will not have my name or, more importantly, my professional reputation, associated with politically motivated actions such as this committee has been asked to render. That is all I have to say to the committee, Mr. Chairman."

A flurry of head bobbing, whispered conversation and discussion ensued on the raised dais as the committee considered Professor Weatherly's remarks. Finally the chair addressed those in attendance.

"Professor Weatherly, this committee wishes to acknowledge the value of your membership within the Utah Bar Association and the esteem in which you are held by this organization. We also desire to commend you on your fervid presentation on behalf of your client. However, we also wish to remind you that should you see fit to voluntarily relinquish your status as a member of the Utah Bar, there would be some question as to your eligibility to continue in your position as professor of law at BYU. Are you aware of that circumstance?"

"Indeed I am, Mr. Chairman. It is with full understanding of the gravity of my intended actions, actions that would be subject to widespread opinion and, ultimately, public review of this body's actions, that I submit my intentions. May I remind the chair, that if we, as officers of the court, are not able to separate ourselves from the political nature of scurrilous and unwarranted charges such as those we have witnessed today, then we serve no purpose in our pursuit of teaching the law and its honorable application. If that were the message to be delivered by this committee today, to those who seek to enter what has always been seen as the highest profession of integrity, what lesson would be learned? To continue as a member of a professional association of attorneys that would allow this travesty to take place would only serve to demean my understanding of my responsibility as a professor of law. Yes, Mr. Chairman, I understand the implications of my statement and wish to go on record as standing by my submission."

"Thank you, Professor. We will now adjourn and deliberate our verdict. As previously announced, it will be transmitted to your client within ten days."

"Mr. Chairman, I beg the committee's indulgence for a moment longer. If indeed it is your intention to deliberate and reach a verdict today, a hasty process that is certainly in keeping with the entire rapidity of today's proceedings, then I respectfully request that you reconvene following your deliberations and announce your verdict forthwith. I see no reason for further deliberation or extension of verdict. If it is your intention to destroy this young man's career on the basis of the horrendous and cowardly presentation we have seen this day, surely the committee has the fortitude to do so in his presence."

"That would be highly unusual, Professor Weatherly."

"Agreed. As have been these entire proceedings. I reiterate my request for a decision today, a decision I might add, that will enable public dissemination of the verdict and the method whereby it was rendered, in this evening's newspapers, so that those of interest may speedily be aware of the new dispensation of prejudicial law this committee has seen fit to initiate."

Again, a flurry of whispering, discussion and head movement amongst the five committee members ensued. Then the Chairman rapped his gavel once more.

"Professor Weatherly, Mr. Sterling, the committee has determined to agree with your request and will reconvene as quickly as we can reach a unanimous verdict in this unfortunate episode."

"Thank you, Mr. Chairman and members of the committee. We will await your return."

The Utah Bar Association Ethics Committee deliberated for less than fifteen minutes, whereupon they returned and reopened the hearing. Professor Weatherly, Matthew Sterling, and the staff members from Snowy Ridge were also present as they reconvened. "If I may have your attention," the Chairman announced. "After full consideration of the evidence presented, and in light of the abbreviated tenure of Mr. Sterling's membership, the committee has determined to exercise its prerogative to be lenient in its judgment. It is our decision that Mr. Sterling be afforded a temporary six-month suspension of his right to practice law in the State of Utah. Without further incident, this suspension will automatically be removed from the records of the Association at the end of the six-month period. A formal letter will transmit this finding to Mr. Sterling within ten days. This verdict is not subject to appeal.

"Professor Weatherly, it is the sincere desire of this committee, in representation of the entire Bar Association, that you find this temporary suspension insufficient cause for removal of your membership from our Association.

"We thank all who have participated in this hearing today. This hearing is adjourned."

Chapter Twenty-Two

The second Thursday following Matt's return to work and two days after the Utah Bar Association Ethics Committee hearing, the Snowy Ridge bi-weekly Council meeting was held. Following preliminary routine, reading of minutes and apologies by those who could not attend, the Public Comment section of the meeting commenced. In light of the packed house, Mayor Julia Wells opened the session by reading the Public Comment rules and regulations from the City Council's procedural manual.

...and speakers will be limited to three minutes each, followed by questioning from the Council if desired. The Council reserves the right to curtail a speaker's time if the comments are determined to be repetitive of previous speakers or if the language or decorum does not meet publicly acceptable standards.

"Now, we have a lengthy list of persons who desire to speak and they will be afforded ample time in the order they signed the request sheet. First person is Tamara Hawkins. Ms. Hawkins?"

A woman of about thirty rose and made her way down the aisle, slowly walking toward the podium set up for audience comment. Five police officers were stationed around the room, a precaution that Pat Harcourt had effected upon observation of the size of the crowd.

Ms. Hawkins got to the stand and coughed a few times, glancing nervously back toward her friends who nodded their heads in support.

"Mayor, Council. This is the first time I've spoken at a public hearing. I usually just stay home and keep my nose out of politics. It's not that I'm not interested, but, well, I've got a busy life. My friend called me today," she said, glancing and nodding toward the audience, "and asked if I would come and say my piece. We think that it's a shame what's happening to our community. We didn't have such problems, Mayor, until you got elected. I'm sorry if that offends you, but that's the way it is. We think, my friends and me, that if you just stepped down and let Mayor Tomlin resume his office, things would get right again. That's all I have to say."

Mayor Wells spoke. "Are there any Council questions?" There was no response. "Thank you for your contribution, Ms. Hawkins. The next speaker is Jeff Hornsby. Mr. Hornsby?"

A large man, over sixty years of age, stood and made his way to the front. Dressed in jeans and a blue denim work shirt, he smiled and nodded to friends among the crowd. Reaching the podium, he clamped both hands on the wooden sides and stared at Mayor Wells.

"Ma'am, my mother taught me to be polite to females, but I'm going to make this an exception. You got no business here. We don't need your meddling in our community. I'm gonna say this but once, but I'm gonna say it. Get out! We don't want you and we don't need you." With that remark, he slapped his broad hands on the polished surface of the wood and turned back toward the crowd. A large round of applause filled the room with very few people not participating.

"Any questions?" Wells asked. "None, then we'll proceed. Ms. Jean Patterson."

A young twenty-something woman stood and quickly strode to the front of the room. She wore hip huggers and a short top, approximately three inches of flat, bare stomach exposed between the two. "I think the young people of our town ought to have a say too, like we really know what we want and we should be listened to." She giggled briefly, glancing back toward a young man who sat next to where she had been sitting. "I was in Young Women at church and Sister Harcourt was my teacher. She was great and if it weren't for her, I might not be coming to church. Not as much as I do anyway." Again she laughed, a high-pitched sound. "Anyways, you got no business telling her how to run our city, Mayor Wells. She's been doing it for years and doing it good." She turned abruptly and stepped lightly back to her seat where her boyfriend put his arm around her and the people around her patted her on the back.

Wells looked around the Council for any questions and seeing no indication of interest other than nods of agreement with the speakers, rapped her gavel. "There seems to be a standard line tonight, so in the interest of time, does anyone have a different perspective, or wish to add a new dimension to the opinions already presented?"

Several hands shot up in the audience. Julia Wells pointed to a man toward the rear of the room. "Sir, your name?"

"Greg Johnson," he replied, standing.

"And you wish to speak?"

"Yes."

"Please, come up."

He slipped quickly down the row and moved to the podium. "Mayor, members of the Council, ladies and gentlemen of the audience. I have no particular position for or against either faction here tonight. I do, however, have an abiding faith in our democratic system. Those of us who have been in this community for many generations know first hand the injustice of persecution. Mayor Wells has been in office for less than a month. I say we give her time to adjust to the office. There's nothing wrong with having a fresh look at how we do things. What do we have to hide? Let's have a good look and confirm that the way we are doing business is the best we can do. Thank you, Mayor," he said, returning immediately to his seat.

"Thank you, sir," Julia replied. "Are there any comments from members of the Council this evening?"

Third-term Councilman Pressley Shanks nodded and raised his hand briefly.

"Councilman Shanks?" Julia acknowledged.

"Mayor, this has not been easy for you, but it is necessary that you see how public opinion has formed around the recent spate of public condemnation this Council has undergone. I think we cannot afford to tolerate either elected members or hired staff whose conduct does not measure up to the high standards expected by our city manager, Pat Harcourt. In this regard, I ask for a vote this evening to include an Executive Session at the conclusion of regular business to discuss personnel matters."

"I second the request," Councilwoman Conners added.

"It is your right to add an item to the agenda if sufficient support can be obtained. Are there any objections to the councilman's request?" Julia asked of the Council. Hearing none, she rapped her gavel. "So be it. Are there any other members of the audience who wish to speak with a *new* item or perspective to our discussion tonight?"

One additional hand went up in the front section of the room.

"Yes, ma'am. Please come forward and state your name," Julia said.

The woman rose and took only two steps to stand behind the podium. "My name is Helen Creighton. Like the lady before me, I have never spoken in public Council session but I felt this was important. We've heaped a lot of abuse on our new mayor tonight. Maybe it's due, maybe it's not. Don't know. But we're missing one important point. You Council people," she said, pointing toward the staff table, "need to set the example for our youth. Mr. Sterling, I've got nothing against you personally, and I don't know if them charges laid at your door are right or not, but a bunch of your fellow lawyers said they was and they took away your right to practice law. Now we cannot tolerate pornography in this town, and certainly not from our Council people. I think you need to resign and to do so quickly. If you have any honor left, that's what you should do. That's all I have to say, Mayor."

Another round of applause from well over half the audience filled the room for several long moments until the mayor rapped her gavel again. "Thank you for those comments, Ms. Creighton. That will conclude our public...yes, sir," Julia said to a man who stood in the middle of the room. Without further comment, he moved forward and stood behind the stand.

"I'm Frank Mobley. Been here all my life. Now I don't know Mr. Sterling nor the mayor, for that matter. But I do know that this evening my fellow citizens have shamed me. We've seen or heard nothing from the public media since the election but what a small crowd of determined people want us to know. As to Mr. Sterling, well, you have to make your own decisions about these things. I think you can see that if you are participating in the activities you've been charged with, this community won't stand idly by. If you are not, then there is clearly a campaign to smear you and it wouldn't be the first time in the history of politics." A spate of nervous laughter broke out throughout the room for several seconds. "As for me, I think we've been acting like a bunch of hypocrites. The Savior taught us that we should not throw the first stone. Who among us can claim total knowledge of these supposed charges, against either Mr. Sterling or Mayor Wells? Who can stand here and justify saying 'get out,' simply because it seems to have become the popular opinion of this small group of people determined to have things their own way?

"That's not what our Church teaches us. I would think that if Mr. Sterling was guilty of such behavior, his Church officials would call him on the carpet. Isn't that the way we work things here in Utah? Are *we* going to assume that responsibility?" he said, sweeping his arm to encompass the entire audience. "Are *we* going to cast the first stone because we're all so innocent ourselves? Mayor, do the best you can. If we don't like what you do, we'll vote you out next time. That's the American way. And," he said, turning again toward the audience, "it ought to be the Mormon way. Haven't we had enough of lynch mobs in the history of our church?"

* * * * *

The following morning as Matt entered city hall, Pat Harcourt was waiting for him outside his office, speaking with Candy Houser. Mayor Wells also appeared almost simultaneously. Pat ignored Julia Wells.

"Matt, I need to speak with you this morning."

"All right. I'll put my briefcase in my office and I'll be right in."

Julia spoke up. "I'd like to attend that meeting. I was at the Executive Session last night and I believe I have an opinion to contribute."

"In this instance, Mayor Wells, you have *no* opinion to contribute," Pat stated bluntly. "In fact, you have no function at all. *I* work for the majority of the Council. The *employees* work for me. They do not answer to the Council. You have *no* say in how I deal with employees of Snowy Ridge."

"I disagree with you, Pat," Julia said with a polite smile. "Matt, do you object to my participation?"

Matt looked between the two and glanced at Candy, shaking his head. "I'm sorry, Mayor. I don't believe I have a choice in the matter. Pat is right about the line of authority. If it were a disciplinary hearing, I would be entitled to representation. I'm not sure what Pat's request is about, so I don't wish to cause you any trouble that will only be added to the list of your so-called indiscretions." He turned back to face Pat. "I'll be right in, Pat. I have a phone call to make first."

"See that you make it quickly and come into my office," she said, giving Julia another withering look and striding off down the hallway toward her office.

"Matt, you don't need to do this alone," Julia said. "The Council called for your head last night. Pat put up a false defense, saying you needed to be disciplined, but that she would deal with the issue."

"It's okay, Julia. I'm going to call my attorney, but just to advise him what's happening. I think we've entered the fourth quarter of this game. I'm ready for whatever comes."

"Let me know, will you?" Julia said kindly, patting him on the shoulder and walking toward her office in the opposite direction.

Candy followed Matt into his office. "They want your blood, Matt. This is indeed the end game. Pat had Sarah in there first thing this morning."

"A meeting with the city attorney just before mine, eh? Sounds ominous. I'll be fine, Candy," he assured her with more confidence than he felt. "Just give me a few minutes alone and I'll enter the lion's den."

Within five minutes Matt came out of his office and walked down the hall to the city manager's office. Knocking lightly on the doorjamb, he entered, closed the door, and sat in front of

Pat's desk. She remained seated behind her desk.

"Matt, this has gotten out of hand. You saw last night the feeling of the public."

"I don't think the public was represented last night."

Pat slammed her hand down on her desk and leaned forward, snarling at Matt. "Are you *crazy?* The public was nearly unanimous in wanting both of you out of here."

Matt remained calm, nodding. "That wasn't the public, Pat. That was a vocal group of supporters who someone, *you* perhaps, put together to shame Mayor Wells publicly. They got their shot at me too, I admit."

"And well they should. If all you got was a public whipping, you'd get off easy. Pornography will not be tolerated in this government. Do you understand that?"

"Actually, I do, Pat. How about deception, lying, shameful actions, closed groups of cronies awarding contracts, and even theft of public funds? Are *those* allowed in your hallowed halls?"

"I've had about enough of you, Matt. You and our illustrious mayor are some team," she said righteously, shaking her head. "*You're* straight out of college, green behind the ears. *She's* basically a high school dropout. Don't you understand that without proper leadership, and by that I mean people who *know* how to run a government, the mob would take over? I have an MBA, Matt; Wells has a GED after quitting high school. I've checked her out. I've managed local government for nearly twenty years, you've been around for barely two. It's *my* field. I know it. Without such people to reign, to govern properly, anarchy would happen everywhere. *We* run this city, Matt. *I* run this city. Without us it would fall apart and the streets wouldn't get paved, the water wouldn't flow or be clean, the sewers would back up. That's our job. And I do it damn well. *I* run this city, Matthew Sterling, and that's something you're never going to forget."

"I think you're right there, Pat," Matt said, maintaining his reserve.

Pat relaxed a bit and leaned back in her chair. "I tried to help you, Matt. I gave you the benefit of the doubt on several issues. But the disbarment? That was too much. The Council demanded last night in Executive Session that I dismiss you. I told them that was *my* call, not theirs. But I have to say, with your non-repentant attitude this morning, I agree with them. To save us both further disruption, I want your resignation on my desk this morning."

"That's not going to happen, Pat."

"*What?*"

"I said, no."

"You serve at *my* pleasure."

"Yes, I do. But I resign at *my* pleasure. I do not please to do so."

Pat sat quiet for several moments as both parties alternately looked at each other and other places in the room, a temporary stalemate in effect. Finally Pat spoke again.

"As of today, Matt, you are on indefinite suspension, with pay of course, until I determine how I'll handle this issue. Pornography was your first infraction. The disbarment was a second issue that brought great disrepute to the city. Your insubordination today is a third disciplinary issue. I think there are sufficient grounds to terminate your employment."

Matt stood. "That's your choice, Pat. I'll clean out my office and head home if you have nothing further to say." Matt headed for the door, but before he opened it, he turned around again and faced her desk. "You know, Pat, in some respects, giving a loose interpretation to the word 'reign,' I agree with you. Government officials *are* supposed to reign. But in our democratic form of government, as one of my ancestors was told by George Washington, it should at best be a *light* reign.

We should always have the interests of the general public at heart. When that doesn't happen, it's time for a change. You may be able to continue to humiliate Julia Wells and disrupt her function as mayor, but rest assured, your day is coming."

"And what do you mean by that?" Pat said, standing up behind her desk.

Matt smiled slightly, nodding his head in her direction. "I mean that someone is bound to get enough information on you to, pardon the pun, *rein* you in. Enjoy it while you can, Pat."

Matt walked to his office and Candy immediately followed him in. In less than two minutes, Julia Wells was right behind.

"Indefinite suspension. She'll terminate me when she finds enough courage and doesn't think she'll be in the spotlight over it. It will be 'reluctantly,' of course."

"She can't do that," Julia said.

"Yes, she can, Mayor. You have to define the separate aspects of your duties. Only by knowing exactly what you can and can't do, will you be able to be effective as mayor. Candy will be without a boss as of today. Perhaps she can double as your assistant. I'd listen to her."

"What are you going to do, Matt?" Candy asked.

Matt sat behind his desk, pulled open a drawer and pulled his Palm Pilot out, flipping it open. "Well, ladies, in two weeks I'm going to introduce my parents to Kasia's parents. Then I'm going to get ready to get married. Other than that, I haven't a clue."

"Oh, Matt," Julia said, "I'm so sorry."

"This does not lie at your door, Julia. And you have a tough fight on your hands and four years to accomplish it. Anything I can do, just ask. But as you can see, my input will be limited."

Candy walked behind Matt's desk and stood looking down at him. "Stand up, Matt."

Matt stood.

"These were hard lessons, Matt. And the result was not what I would have hoped for. But I'm proud of you." The older woman wrapped her arms around Matt and hugged him for several long seconds, stepping back with a glisten in her eye. "I'll help Mayor Wells all I can, Matt, but I think my time has come too. I don't want to be associated with what's happening here. Besides, I think I have a wedding to attend and I've never even been to England."

"Consider yourself invited, Sister Houser. And I know a place you can stay and the house is less than two hundred years old," he said, laughing.

"You rascal," she said, taking a tissue from the credenza behind his desk and wiping her eyes.

"My best wishes, Julia. You've got a tough, but honorable task ahead of you."

"I was afraid this would happen, Matt. I feel so terrible."

"This is not your doing, Julia. Don't ever think that."

"Let the consequence follow?" Julia said, smiling through her own tears. "Is that what you're telling me?"

Matt smiled brightly, all anger gone from his face. "Yes. I've heard that before. *Do what is right. Let the consequence follow,*" he said softly. "It's a good principle. I don't know that I've understood how important it really is before now." Indeed, he thought, it is a good principle that has stood the test of time.

President Washington paused for several long seconds and then a soft smile appeared, his eyes suddenly brilliant as if a beam of light were escaping his deep inner thoughts. "If there is to be a reign, my dear Andrew...Sterling...I pray God it be a light reign, for I firmly believe that our gracious God would have us rule over ourselves, if we can but gather the moral strength."

Journal of Andrew McBride Sterling
March 28, 1789

Chapter Twenty-Three

McBride saw General Washington but once thereafter, in early 1789, in New York, shortly after his inauguration. The new president seemed devoid of the anger and frustration that had characterized his demeanor during the years between Yorktown and the presidency. When Andy queried as to his health, he replied, "There are but few years remaining. I pray that I may use them to a higher purpose.

Hesitant to burden him with a personal request, Andy was bold enough at last to say: "I've found it difficult, General, to endure the condemnation I have suffered at the hands of my fellow citizens, considering the things I contributed to the cause of liberty."

Washington looked deeply troubled, nodding his understanding and initiating a brief conversation.

"I have oft thought how the merit of one's actions can truly be judged only by God, while the earthly consequence is unfairly determined by man. Perhaps many of us were ill-used, all the while engaged in a noble cause, friend McBride. What would you have me do?"

"I thought perchance…my name, General…some restoration of honor."

"Aye," the president said, shaking his head slowly and clicking his tongue sadly, "would that were possible. Perhaps you can take comfort in the knowledge that you are not the only patriot who has sacrificed that which his father honorably bestowed upon him."

"Sir, I think not of myself—it is too late for that. I am publicly condemned as a traitor. But my children, sir. What consolation will devolve upon my children?"

Obviously saddened, the president did not reply, turning instead to the window, where he fixed his gaze on the Hudson and a copse of green willows just emerging from the fetters of winter's frost.

Set upon his course, Andy continued his plea. "Surely, sir, now that you are president—now that you reign—surely you may right the wrong of it?"

President Washington turned again to face his old comrade in arms, an even sadder countenance reflecting the weight of his burden. "Our recent struggle was to free ourselves from the tyranny of a malevolent king, who dispensed reward—or punishment—by capricious whim. For all its strengths, our new government, I fear, shall have its limitations. The service you and others rendered during those long years under Major Talmadge's hand was invaluable and selfless. It required that you cloak private honor beneath public shame. Yet it was a patriotic service, Andrew, indeed a sterling service."

He paused for several long seconds and then a soft smile appeared, his eyes suddenly brilliant as if a beam of light were escaping his deep inner thoughts.

"If there is to be a reign, my dear Andrew…Sterling…I pray God it be a light reign, for I firmly believe that our gracious God would have us rule over ourselves, if we can but gather the moral strength."

His shoulders stooped beyond what Andy remembered from their first meeting, many years earlier, Washington turned one final time to face the window, the new nation's future somewhere out beyond the willows and the water and the winter.

Andrew McBride, the former legal counsel to the British High Command, and clandestine source of intelligence for the Continental Army withdrew slowly from the room, determined that the person who had come to see his president and former commander, would be no more—that Andrew McBride would remain a fleeting, discarded remnant of history, and that the new Andrew Sterling would begin anew. And, true to his word, some years later, in reflection, he penned his recollection of the tumult that his family endured as they took upon themselves a new life.

"My dearest Laura, ever possessed of the Delacorte pride despite the ravages of our history, was not quite so accepting of the idea. But slowly, with comfort afforded, the punctilios of her feminine fears assuaged, she came to accept the loss of our former identity and the prospect of a new home. For Josiah and the little ones, it came as an adventure. And for me, it came as relief, a freedom from the weight of intolerance.

And so, farther afield our great waterway,

Riveroaks was born, the home in which I would spend the remainder of my days. That Alice, Matthew and little Laura knew no other home, nor memory, was joy embodied. That Josiah, his memory of things but fleeting, grew to manhood among the woods, hills and the great river, was of inestimable pleasure to me and, praise God, to him. His departure for my Yale brought tears of sorrow to his mother and tears of joy to me. For in those waning days my reluctant memory recalled dearest Nate and the days we spent in contemplation of Cato, Socrates, and Plato—those who had left us their wisdom – wisdom we had so soon discarded in the maelstrom of life. Yet wisdom that Nate has left in the hearts of men to be remembered to this day despite the confiscation of his letters on that fateful morning.

And what pray tell had I left for Josiah? Not my name, for he no longer recalled our former registry. A Sterling he was, and destined, as fathers are wont to believe, for further sterling service such as would be deserving of the honours of men. And if it is God's will that, in consequence of our rightful actions such be the case, then my sacrifice on the altar of freedom and that of Nate will have paid the price.

And we gave it willingly. In God's name, Amen!

Chapter Twenty-Four

Conference weekend in early April came quickly. The weather had cleared and it looked as if Temple Square would be bathed in flowers and sunshine.

Nine days after his suspension, Matt had received a registered letter from Snowy Ridge, signed by both the city attorney and city manager. It delivered the determination that due to his inappropriate actions and disbarment, which lessened the credentials he needed to adequately perform his duties, he was officially terminated as assistant city manager of Snowy Ridge.

Several days later, Dick and Sally Sterling drove to Salt Lake City, arriving on the Thursday afternoon before Conference. They accompanied Kasia and Matt to the airport late Thursday evening as they went to meet Graeme and Carolyne Somerset. Thursday evening was spent at Kasia's as they got to know one another and learn more of the details of Matt's new unemployed status. Matt took it in good stride, explaining to his parents in particular that he felt good, despite all that had happened. Later that evening, in the privacy of his condo, his parents got a bit more personal.

"What are you going to do, Matt? Disbarment is terrible," his mother said.

"I know, Mom. And I apologize for the humiliation it must cause you at home. I'm truly sorry."

"Oh, rubbish. Don't even think such things. I'm worried about you. How will you and Kasia live?"

"I'm thinking about it, Mom. Don't worry, at least not yet. We'll find something."

Dick Sterling stood and walked to the kitchen counter, pouring himself another cup of cider and turning to face his son, leaning up against the counter top. "I'm not embarrassed by your actions, Matt. I'm actually quite proud of you. I don't know how I would have handled a similar situation had I been faced with one."

"It was your teachings, yours and Mom's, that probably finally took hold. I'm not proud. This is truly, as Mom said, a difficult time. But I don't see any other outcome, Dad. I came face to face with a situation I would never have chosen. But, that's how it happened. Let's just have a good Conference weekend and see how many sessions we can get seats for."

"Sounds good to me. Now, I'm ready for bed. How about you, Sister Sterling?"

"I think I'll sit on Matt's deck for awhile, unless it's too cool out there. I just want to think."

"Don't be long, sweetheart," Dick said.

"Goodnight, Dad," came a voice from the other direction.

"Goodnight, son."

* * * * *

Sunday evening, after the closing Conference session, all six gathered at Matt's condo for a final get-together. The Sterlings were driving back to California the following morning and the Somerset's were flying back to England on Wednesday, after Elder Somerset had met with Church authorities at LDS Headquarters. After dinner, Kasia assembled the group in the living room.

"For the past several months, Matt has told each of us the growing story of Andrew and Laura McBride and the tragedy that befell their lives. In some ways," she said, standing behind Matt and putting her hands on his shoulders, "the story of this particular ancestor has probably given him the strength to withstand the events of his life these past three or four months. On the Wednesday before we met with you guys, I had a long talk with Matt and discussed some of the findings from my research while I was in Europe and London. I think what I'm about to tell you will be a surprise, but once you have a few days to think about it, it will not really change anything in your lives in the same way that learning about the name change from McBride to Sterling didn't really change who you were today." She paused a moment and Matt reached his hand up to cover hers, looking up at her, over his shoulder.

"You're doing great, Kasia."

"Goodness," Sally Sterling said, "this is like a mystery story."

"You're right, Mom," Kasia said. "A true mystery. So, here goes. Dad Sterling, this affects you and Matt directly, everyone else by association only. When I came back from England, I rushed to complete the statistical analysis of my research to complete the requirements for my Ph.D. By the way," she smiled happily, "in late April, I will be *Doctor* Kasia Somerset Sterling. I've got the university to agree to put my soon-to-be married name on my diploma. Of course I still have some research to complete for Dr. Amberly and I'll need until the middle of May to complete the work, but I should be home following that, Mum, and we'll have a month where I can help with the wedding plans."

Carolyne Somerset reached over on the couch and held her husband's hand, smiling at her daughter.

"In the process of that research, I noticed some similarities to other work I had previously done." She let out a deep breath and continued. "I explained all this to Matt last week and we agreed to keep it to ourselves until we were all together. The short version of the story is that Dick and Matt are neither Sterling *nor* McBride. You all know that I took a sample of Matt's blood some months ago and it matched the blood on the arrest warrant. The catch is that the blood on the arrest order for Andrew McBride, the blood that is definitely from one of Matthew's ancestors, isn't Andy McBride's. It came from Major Applegate."

"*What?*" Graeme said, leaning forward and shaking his head. "That means—"

"That means, Dad, that Dick and Matt are direct descendents of King George III and his illegitimate son, Jonathan Applegate. It seems clear that Major Applegate did indeed assault Laura McBride the day Andy was arrested before she killed him with the scissors. We'll never know if Andy ever found out or not, but his first born son, Josiah, was Applegate's son, born the following summer, shortly after Andy and his father-in-law were tarred and feathered."

"That is incredible," Graeme said, still astonished by this revelation.

"The man was despicable!" Sally Sterling said. "Dick, I don't care if he was royalty. You don't want to be related to him."

Dick laughed softly. "We don't get to pick our ancestors, my dear. Besides, you know what Grandma Sterling always said," he paused, glancing over at Graeme Somerset, "and I don't mean any disrespect to your Sovereign, Graeme, but Grandma always said that royalty was much more than bloodlines."

Graeme nodded. "President Harold B. Lee said the same thing some years ago. There is a 'royal' within all of us. We are all members of Heavenly Father's royal household."

Sally Sterling stood and walked across the room, standing beside her husband. "Does this mean you'll expect me to call you 'Your Highness'?"

"That would be nice," he said affably.

"Don't count on it, Your Majesty. You still have to mow the lawn," Sally teased.

"What do you think about all this, Matt?" Carolyne asked.

Matt reached up over his head, gently pulled Kasia's head down and gave her an upside down kiss. "I think, *Mum*," he said, using the English pronunciation for the first time, "that I love your daughter because she loved me *before* she knew I had a small inheritance and *before* she knew I was royalty. *English* royalty."

All six broke into laughter at that and everyone began talking at once. Finally, Kasia asked for their attention again. "This news is quite spectacular, but it really is of no more import to the Sterling line, *my* children's line," she said, giggling a bit, "than it was to Major Applegate. In fact, despite how his circumstances probably made him the angry young man he was, knowing that his connection to the king would never be acknowledged, he still had the choice to *act* as if he were a royal. So do we all, I guess, from what President Lee told us. I suppose it's up to each of us to decide whether we tell our children or not, and of course to Emily and Rachel and their children. Matt and I will make that determination when the time comes."

"Soon, we hope," Carolyne Somerset added. "I want grandchildren, royal or common."

"We'll see, Mum," Kasia smiled at her mother. "In the meantime, we will all, except Mum and Dad, remain Sterlings. And from my point of view, I can't wait."

* * * * *

Tuesday afternoon, Matt met Graeme Somerset in downtown Salt Lake and they walked to the Inn on Temple

Square where Graeme had made lunch reservations. Directly across the street from Temple Square, it was a quick walk from Church headquarters where Graeme was meeting with other area authorities before he returned to England.

"You getting your career action plan worked up, Matt?" he asked as they took their seats.

"Still a bit confused about that, Graeme."

"Good. I have a proposition. You know me to be a man of few words, don't you?"

Matt opened his napkin and nodded his head.

"Then I won't mince words this time," Graeme continued, "I'd very much like you to come to work for me in London."

Matt stared at the older man in surprise. "Sir, I—"

"Hear me out, please. This is not charity. Your undergraduate degree is International Relations, is it not?"

"Yes, sir."

"And your law degree had at least a smattering of international law?"

"Yes, sir, but—"

"No buts, just yet. Let me tell you about my firm. I am managing director—senior partner that would be in the States—of my firm, created in 1977. I have two other senior partners, both older than myself, and five general partners. We have thirty-six associate barristers, about twenty paralegals, and a clerical staff of about forty. Just over a hundred employees. I have one particular branch specializing in international law and, within that division, one director of the American interest section. I actually have U.S. corporate or government clients in seven European countries, American Embassies among them, who utilize my firm for their in-country legal issues. The young woman who currently holds that position, an American by the way, is marrying a doctor from France. She's leaving in August. So there is a *real* position, not just a created one."

"Sir, if I could interrupt. I've been disbarred."

"Rubbish. That will be over in several months and never appear again. I've spoken with Trevor."

"But the knowledge is public. I would not be able to bring a reputation worthy of your firm."

"Ah! I knew that would come up. Let me tell you another story. Do you remember me telling you that I was a foreign service officer in Yugoslavia with the British government?"

"Yes, sir."

"Why do you think I left the service? It's not all that usual once you come aboard."

"I don't know, sir."

"Well, I won't go into details, but suffice it for you to know that my circumstances and yours are not that dissimilar. I was faced with a situation that I could not tolerate. International government is not that much different from your local experience. At least in the caliber of people it forces into difficult positions. Do you understand what I'm telling you?"

"I think I do, Graeme. So you started your own firm."

"Indeed. With the blessings, mind you, of another woman with the grit of Kasia. Her mother, Carolyne. She believed in me, she trusted me, and that was all I needed to start afresh. You're not yet thirty, Matt. You can have a wonderful career. People who have a very high ethical standard often don't do well working for others with lower, shall we say, value expectations."

"Have you spoken to Kasia about this?"

"Absolutely not, but I can tell you it will please her and her mother will be absolutely thrilled."

"May I think on it, sir?"

Graeme smiled and flipped open his napkin, placing it across his lap. "And pray about it, son. You'll come to the right answer."

"May I ask a question?"

"Certainly."

"How were you so certain that I was innocent of these charges, this disbarment issue?"

"I knew. Plus we had a few new Area Authorities called this conference, didn't we?"

"Yes, sir."

"Well, I've been fortunate to sit next to one in our training sessions. Elder Richard Topham. You've heard of him, I expect."

"I certainly have."

"Well, you have a supporter there, Matt. I can tell you that much. So, do we have a deal?"

"I'd still like to give it some thought…and prayer."

"But you're in agreement in principle?"

"Yes, sir. I'm actually quite excited about the prospect."

"Good. Then I can buy you lunch as my prospective employee and not only as my son-in-law."

"Will you tell Kasia, sir?"

"I'll leave that to you, Matt. She's going to be your wife. She should hear such career plans from you. But I'll tell you this much. The minute the plane leaves the ground, I'll tell Carolyne. If I spoke a word on the ground, she'd be all over Kasia, planning everything. This way, I'll have about twelve hours to convince her not to contact Kasia until she is certain that you have already spoken with her."

"Yes, sir. I've already pulled that stunt. Not telling my parents quickly enough, I mean."

"So I hear. Now, what's good on the menu here?"

Chapter Twenty-Five

In early July, Matthew and Kasia Sterling were met at the Heathrow Airport by Graeme and Carolyne Somerset. Mother and daughter hugged as was required and highly desired, and they began the drive to New Marblehead.

In May, some three weeks after Conference weekend, Kasia had gone to Sacramento as planned and worked with Sally, Emily, and Rachel in planning their outfits for the reception. Matt had told Kasia he had a bit of work yet to accomplish with his grandmother's estate in New York and was going to help a law school friend in upstate New York with some legal issues. He told Kasia he would be gone for about two weeks. It was the first and only time Matt would ever lie to his bride-to-be, but he had other plans in mind.

The Temple sealing and wedding reception in June had been attended by the entire Sacramento branch of the Sterling family, all grandchildren included. Candy Houser was the hit of the reception as she told people she had added more than four hundred names to her genealogy files during her first ever visit to Ireland and England. Those in attendance were astonished to find that the new names brought Sister Houser's total genealogy to more than seven thousand names.

The trip to England was Dick Sterling's treat to his family, after which he and his wife continued on for a Mediterranean cruise. Sally finally got to visit the Holy Land, Athens, and several of the biblical Greek islands where Paul had preached to the early saints.

After the wedding, the newly married couple had flown to the Virgin Islands and spent two glorious weeks lying on the beach, shopping in the native markets, and in general, acting like newlyweds. The return to England, to which both were looking forward, came about much earlier than either had anticipated.

"So, Mrs. Sterling," Carolyne said from her seat in the front of the vehicle as they left the Heathrow area, "you have quite a tan for an English girl."

"And I'm bringing home a Yank for dinner, Dad. What do you think of that?"

"We'll work on him, Kasia, you can count on it. He may not know what a googly is, but give me a couple of years and he'll be rooting for England in the World Cup."

"Mum, we'd like your help in thinking about an area to live. It needs to be close enough for Matt to commute to his office. What about the flat in Kensington?"

"What do you think, Graeme?" Carolyne said.

"Well, we don't use it too much anymore, and if the kids stayed there, you probably would have fewer excuses to go into town for shopping sprees at Harrods's. On second thought, you would probably have *more* reason to go. Nope, not a good idea, Kasia. Sorry."

"Well, we need to start looking for a place to live soon, right Matt?"

"First thing tomorrow, sweetheart. First thing."

Graeme caught Matt's eye in the rear view mirror and winked at his new son-in-law.

"I'm sorry, Kasia, but from this direction, we better go home rather than drive by the Temple first. Is that okay?"

"That's fine, Dad. I think I'll see much more of it now than I have the past couple of years."

"Oh, Kasia, a letter came for you from Oxford the other day. I have it at home," Carolyne said.

"Great. I wrote and asked about the possibilities of working in their lab."

"Did you now?" Graeme said. "And what do you think?"

"I hope they're asking me to come in for an interview."

"Well, you'll know in an hour or so. You tired?"

"Very, Mum."

"Well, we have your old room ready for you again."

"Thanks, Mum, but I think I might sleep down the hall with the Yank, if that's all right with you, Dad."

* * * * *

The next morning, Kasia and Matt got up early, had a bite of breakfast with her parents, and got ready for their opening survey of the real estate market.

"Where should we look first, Dad?"

"I'm not sure. There are a few new subdivisions just north of us, about twenty kilometers, but they're small I'm told. And the closer to London, the more expensive."

"That's true. What do you think, Matt? Did you see any areas when you were here last time, or on your mission that you really liked?"

"I did. Why don't we just drive around today and have a good look. Maybe we'll spot something."

"Fine. Dad, can we borrow the car again?"

"Actually, I've got a new Range Rover around behind the stables, Kasia. Why don't you and Matt use that. Help me break it in."

"That's great, Dad. Thanks."

While Kasia climbed in the passenger side, Graeme walked around with Matt to the driver's door, the two of them speaking softly.

"See you two when you get back," Carolyne called out. "Good luck house hunting."

"Thanks, Mum. See you tonight," Kasia replied as Matt drove out the driveway.

They drove for a half-hour, observing the countryside, not pressuring themselves toward any specific direction.

"What type of house should we look for—new or old?"

"I love both. But there's something *English* about the old English homes, isn't there?" she said.

"Sure is. But expensive to maintain sometimes if they're *too* old."

"That's true. Let's just drive through a few communities and let you get a feel for things. I love all these communities and have friends in most of them. Do you think maybe we should stop and see a real estate agent?"

"Maybe after we spend a day or so looking for specific areas we like. What's out this way?"

"Several small communities between here and the Temple. We're headed northeast from Mum and Dad's. Up the road a bit is Benton. The Young Women held several youth conferences there when I was younger. They have a large Church camp there and it has a beautiful lake, several streams running through the area. I used to feed the ducks there."

"Well, let's head over that way first, what say?"

"You're driving, Mr. Sterling," she said, reaching over and kissing his cheek.

Twenty minutes further up the road, they entered and drove through the other side of the township of Benton, spotting and turning down a small country lane.

"I don't think I've been down here before. The stake center is not far from here. It's not our old stake, but a new one recently formed," Kasia said.

Several large country homes were on either side of the road as they continued down the smaller blacktop lane. Then the homes grew a bit smaller and newer it seemed, but built in the replica of some of the older English Tudor style houses similar to New Marblehead.

"Oh, Matt. These houses are beautiful."

"Yeah, they are, aren't they. Let's see if we can get a closer look at one."

"Oh, that wouldn't be proper. We should check with a real estate agent first."

"We can just look, can't we?"

"As long as we don't trespass or bother the residents, I guess it would be all right."

They drove slowly down the road for another five minutes, pausing in front of several houses and admiring the gardens and foliage. "There's a nice-looking house, Kasia. I don't see any cars. In fact it looks empty."

"There's no For Sale sign anywhere. It must be occupied. But it is beautiful, isn't it? It looks just like a miniature of New Marblehead. Not the same, of course, but similar."

"Old or new?" Matt asked.

"It's an old style," she replied as he pulled the car to a halt on the road in front of the arched gate. "But it looks as if it's recently been built. Maybe they refurbished or just built it new in this old style."

"Let's go have a look."

"Are you sure?" she said, looking around behind them on the road. "Shouldn't we talk with someone first?"

"Let's risk it. We won't bother anything."

They walked up the small drive path, the house taking on a whole new dimension as they got closer and could observe the newly flowered garden and the side view of the home."

"It's beautiful, Matt. And look, there's a small stream out back, there near the tree line. I can barely see the next home, just there through the trees. It must have several acres."

"Two and a half," he said. "Do you want to see inside?"

Kasia looked at him, uncertain of his meaning. "We can't do that, Matt. But we could call a real estate agent, like I said, and maybe she could show us something in this neighborhood or one like it. And how do you know it has two and a half acres?"

"Do you want to see inside?" he said again, his face beaming. "The real estate agent wouldn't mind at all. In fact she would see your name, right alongside of mine, on the title."

Kasia looked at the home, back at Matt, and at the home again, her lips beginning to quiver. "Matt, you're not serious."

"Kasia Somerset Sterling, the woman of my heart, this is number 5, Birdsong Lane, soon to be known as 'Consequence Cottage,' the home of Mr. and Mrs. Matthew Sterling. I hope you grow to love it. If you'd permit me I'd love to carry you over the threshold."

Kasia was fully crying now and holding her face in her hands. She stepped toward Matt and laid her head against his chest. "Matt, oh, Matt. It's so beautiful."

"Welcome home, my darling. I trust this home will be a happy place for many years to come and all the little royal Applegates, McBrides, Somersets, and Sterlings will enjoy their country estate. I have very little of my inheritance left, but we have a new home, a new Range Rover, and tomorrow we'll look for a car for you. And your parents will be here in about an hour, bringing our lunch and sharing it with us in our new home."

"How did you do all this?" she said, wiping her tears with the back of her hand.

"You went to Sacramento and worked with *my* Mom. I went to New York, *briefly*, and then England and worked with *your* Mum. I worked longer than you did, and the house isn't quite as beautiful as you were in your wedding dress, but this is the result of my effort. Are you happy?"

"Oh, Matt. Let's go inside. I want to see my new home."

"And there's one more thing."

Kasia stopped and looked again at Matt, her face showing that she was not certain she could stand another surprise.

"Your father said to tell you that Fleur is going to have puppies. I think Consequence Cottage will have a little Cavalier King Charles Spaniel come winter."

Matt reached down, swept Kasia up in his arms and proceeded up the walkway toward the front of the cottage. She clung to his neck, tears of happiness streaming down her face as he carried her throughout Consequence Cottage.

Epilogue

Mr. & Mrs. Matthew A. Sterling
Consequence Cottage
5 Birdsong Lane, Benton
Surrey, England

5 October 2005
Elder Richard Topham
Area Authority Seventy—Utah South
The Church of Jesus Christ of Latter-day Saints
2335 South 1733 East
Snowy Ridge, Utah 84000

Dear Elder Topham:

It is with profound appreciation that I take the time to write this long overdue letter. You will be well aware of the happenings in my life over the past six months. More correctly, the past year. I thought that it would be appropriate that I extend to you the gratitude which I feel in my heart for your patience, Christ-like love, and gentle guidance you provided during a time of extreme difficulty in my life.

In retrospect, I have realized that it was the evening I came to see you that my heart began to heal. Even amidst the turmoil that had not yet reached conclusion, I knew later that evening as I spoke with my Heavenly Father that the burden would not be more than I could bear. Your gentle explanation that retention of my testimony, my capacity to understand the meaning of all that was happening, and my ability to refrain from blaming those around me, including the Lord, was paramount to my salvation, was absolutely correct.

This past week I received an email from Steve Bracks, a reporter at the *Utah Press*. He included his article about the district attorney issuing indictments against Patricia Harcourt and Doug Bellows for financial fraud against the City of Snowy Ridge and their prosecution by the Utah Fraud Commission. This news brought no joy to my heart, no feeling of vindication. Indeed, I felt sorry for their families and the burden they would carry for the rest of their lives. Beyond that, I knew that the Lord would fairly judge their hearts. What more can we ask?

In living among so many of our LDS brethren in Utah I came to understand one very important truth. My testimony is strong. I expected to find a perfect body of people, with the highest degree of ethical conduct. That I did with such acquaintance as yourself was inspirational. Where I did not, perhaps I learned even more from that experience. For we all have the right of agency, as the Prophet Joseph told us. We can choose what to become, how to act, and how to put those lessons to work for others. I pray that my learning will not stop with that initial experience. I am sure you will also understand, and perhaps laugh with me when I admit that I would not prefer a repeat performance either.

Kasia is now an Associate Professor of Microbiology at Oxford University and I am director of American Affairs for the London law firm of Somerset, Prescott and Wolsley. In June, I will have the greatest blessing our Lord can provide: I will become a father. Truly life has provided for me consequences beyond what I deserve.

As we continue our lives here in England, it is our sincere hope that you and Sister Topham will find it possible to join us, perhaps on Church assignment or, if possible, as a bit of pleasure travel. I owe so much to you for your spiritual guidance. I know you would smile, pat my knee, and tell me that the Lord is behind all good things that happen to us.

Until it is our great pleasure to host you and your wife at some future date, please know that I carry your wisdom in my heart and I am a better person for it.

Sincere regards,
Matt Sterling

* * * * *

Mr. & Mrs. Matthew A. Sterling
Consequence Cottage
5 Birdsong Lane, Benton
Surrey, England

5 October 2005
Thomas McDougal
13434 South 1845 West
Snowy Ridge, Utah 84000

Dear Mac:

The news of your retirement was no surprise. In fact it brought joy to my heart to know that you finally achieved that which so long eluded you and that now, with winters in Mexico and summers on the Utah golf courses, your life was complete.

You know from previous communication of my happiness with Kasia and my new job. May I now tell you of the pride that fills my heart as I prepare to become a father? I have often thought of the pride you exhibited in your children and their accomplishments. If I can become such a father it will be a great joy.

Mac, I know you are not a man for receipt of praise, but know this: I could not have accomplished what little I did without your steadfast support. The courage you placed in my heart made all the difference.

I recall at one point when we were discussing certain people who were creating our problems that you felt their membership in the LDS Church was hypocritical. I also remember telling you that a discussion of Church and activity was another story, for another time. Perhaps it is time for me to express my feelings to you.

Utah provided several lessons for me, Mac. The primary lesson was that despite all the entrapments of Church programs, support as a majority religion and understanding of beliefs even by those from other denominations, there were LDS members who did not present a level of ethical behavior that an LDS person should seek to achieve.

That isn't the Church, Mac. That isn't the Gospel. That's the person.

As long as I have known you, your actions and behavior have been toward the betterment of those you loved, those you worked with, and those in need. That IS the Gospel! In action. Whatever historical memory remains to keep you from shedding that last impediment to a return to your core beliefs, I pray God you find your way home.

Know that I love you, owe you, and will teach my children what kind of person you are. You took off my blinders, Mac. And you were God's servant in the process.

Sincere regards,

Matt

Other books by Gordon Ryan:

State of Rebellion

Daniel Rawlings is a bright, honest Stanford Law School graduate. His position as county administrator in Yolo County, California, and his commission as a National Guard JAG officer provide a fulfilling professional life.

The State of California wants to secede from the Union—or so it appears—and people want him to take a stand. Dan is a loyal fifth-generation Californian, but also a loyal American, and is torn by the conflict. California Governor Walter Dewhirst doesn't believe in secession, but he is obligated to carry out the mandate from the special referendum, assuming the referendum results aren't fraudulent. He puts Dan in charge of drafting the constitution of the new Republic of California. In the process, Dan stumbles on information that threatens to expose the entire secessionist movement.

The stakes are high. Federal troops are already gathering in Sacramento, while those who dare oppose the secessionists are dropping like flies. $25.95, hardcover.

Threads of Honor

The process Bill Tolbert was required to go through in his attempt to obtain flight clearance for Troop 514's flag would have deterred a lesser man. But the responsibility he felt for those young men, now numbering fourteen scouts, and the image of their eager faces at each meeting, kept him going. Their excitement over the possibility that their flag might actually go into space and return inspired him to persist. He enlisted the help of all his resources to get the flag included in the official flight kit. Finally, beaming with satisfaction, he stood one night before the troop and announced that their request had been approved. Troop 514's flag would be on the next shuttle mission, due to launch in eight weeks.

This is a true story of courage and sacrifice, of Boy Scouts learning about perseverance, of the great men and women of the American space program, and the unquenchable spirit of a most remarkable American flag. $11.95, softcover.

Easy Order From
CHECK YOUR LEADING BOOKSTORE
OR ORDER HERE

Item	Quantity	Price

Please include $1 shipping for each order.
Colorado residents add 7% sales tax.

____ My check or money order for $_____ is enclosed.
____ Please charge my credit card.

Name _____

Organization_____

Address_____

City/State/Zip_____

Phone_____ E-mail_____

____ MasterCard ____ Visa ____ Discover

Card #_____

Exp. Date_____

Signature_____

Please make your check payable and return to:
Mapletree Publishing Company
6233 Harvard Lane
Highlands Ranch, CO 80130

Call your credit card order to: 800-537-0414
Fax: 303-791-9028
Secure online ordering: www.mapletreepublishing.com